To June and Ron, Best Wishes Enid

Beyond Pendowry Water

Enid Michael

km
Kempton
MARKS

www.kemptonmarks.com

A Kempton Marks Book

An Authors OnLine Ltd Company

ISBN 0 7552 0502 2

Kempton Marks
40 Castle Street
Hertford SG14 1HR
England

This book is also available in e-book format, details of which are available at
www.authorsonline.co.uk

ABOUT THE AUTHOR

Enid Michael has worked in journalism in London, Manchester and Plymouth, but writing novels is her first love. She is a tireless researcher, using real locations to bring her stories to life.

Home is in a moorland village in West Yorkshire, but she usually spends spring and autumn in Cornwall, where her roots are.

Writing Beyond Pendowry Water she spent more than two years in Cornwall, sailing and exploring watermills to bring the story to life.

Her first book 'The Runaway National' published by Corgi was later considered for a Disney film in Hollywood.

To Andrew, who always showed me the way.

CONTENTS

CORNWALL. May 1953

CHAPTER ONE

She cried when she saw the river, saw the grey mudflats shining, flecked white with feeding gulls, saw the broad reaches, the wooded banks darkening, only the water holding the light; saw it joyfully through mists of quelled tears, her face pressed against the carriage window.

Somewhere out there, beyond the bend of the estuary, hidden beneath the trees, was a muddy inlet, silted up and inaccessible except to shag, red shank, heron and gull, or to those who knew how to pole the narrow channel creeping surreptitiously to the head of the creek.

It lay, mirrored in her mind, the brown shallows, the peace; crumbling steps climbing to a green slimed jetty, rusted mooring rings and the dinghies hanging from the weed-draped frapes, tilted like dead things in the mud. She saw herself in the boat again, the man at the oars facing her; his blue jersey stretched over broad shoulders, broad from years of pulling boats. She saw his face, weathered, creased with wrinkles, brave blue eyes resting on her with fatherly pride, felt his hand rough and firm helping her ashore.

"Mind you make her fast, maid, the tide's falling." His voice, softly Cornish, came to her, clear as yesterday.

She remembered how she had watched him board the *Restless*, watched him fend off and make her ready; heard the chug-chug of the old Kelvin, the noise filling the creek, soaking up the silence. She saw him sitting up on the transom, one arm round the tiller, the other raised behind in farewell, the little craft pitching as the channel met the tide.

It had been just a routine call for the local river pilot, just a carefree wave from his eight-year-old daughter... the tears brimmed now, misting it all; man and boat, bows pointing seawards towards the Trefoy river, where the American landing craft had waited, rocking on their moorings, that day in May, just before D-Day in 1944.

It was the last Charlotte Ives was ever to see of the *Restless* – or of her father. And, but for the few months that followed, it was the last she was to see of Cornwall – until this moment. And to think the joy of homecoming might easily have been denied her, but for her school friend, Jenny.

It was Jenny who listened, who understood. An orphan of the London blitz, she too had been hit by life's injustices. She had seen her home laid to dust, those dear to her buried beneath the bomb-flattened Anderson shelter. Left, broken, slotted conveniently away into foster care, Jenny knew the ache of wanting and could appreciate her friend's frustration as Charlotte talked openly about Rachel, the stepmother she despised.

Rachel had taken her from Cornwall when her father died, from all that was sweet and familiar, to the internment of the stuffy flat over the dress salon in Fulham, the sky shut out by tall houses and streets that went on forever.

The times Charlotte had lost herself in those streets trying to run away, only to discover how far Cornwall was from London, too far to walk, only to dream of the creekside cottage in the tiny port where she was born, of the Pendowry estate where her great Uncle Silas had lived and promised that one day it would be hers. But Rachel stubbornly refused to allow her to go back –not even to his funeral. She told Charlotte that the family fortunes had dwindled. What was left of the properties would have to be sold up to meet death duties. There was nothing left, no future for her in that run down Cornish backwater.

"Wait," Jenny had told her, "wait until we've finished school, then our chance will come. I'll get a job abroad and you can escape to Cornwall."

"How can I? Rachel will never let me go back. She's afraid I might discover her dark secrets – why for some reason, she herself won't return or allow me to do so."

"But not when you're older. She can't stop you then."

"She'll always find a way – she'll work out some devious plan, you'll see."

And so Rachel had. An aunt in Wiltshire, over from Australia, who wanted a travelling companion on the cruise back to Sydney, had offered the ideal opportunity. Charlotte remembered the long telephone calls, plans being put into motion, her protests waved aside, filling her with despair.

She remembered complaining to Jenny. "She's told this aunt that I'd jump at the chance, that I love the sea, love sailing, and that she couldn't have a better companion. Now I've been given the job and she wants Rachel to take me for a passport."

"Without even *seeing* you?"

"Says there's no need. I'm family – that's enough- and Rachel can put me on the train to meet her in Wiltshire the day before her ship leaves for Sydney. But I *won't* go, I won't."

"Then don't," said Jenny thoughtfully. "Suppose we are *both* on that train, and I get off to meet your Aunt – and you stay on for Cornwall."

"We'd *never* get away with it. My photograph would be on the passport."

"Remember that school play" said Jenny, "when we were chosen to play the twins and nobody could tell us apart?"

"That was because of the wigs."

"Identical hairstyles and awful passport pictures. We could get away with it," Jenny insisted, "and it *is* the answer to my dream, too, a job abroad."

It was, Charlotte remembered thinking. This would be a chance for them both. They were roughly the same height, blue eyes, and almost the same honey blonde hair...it might work...

"But," Jenny had pointed out, "you'll have to change your attitude, show Rachel you really mean to go or she might want to travel to Wiltshire with you."

Charlotte agreed. "I'll slowly come round to the idea, start getting excited about seeing the sea again. Convince her I'm really looking forward to meeting this aunt. She'll believe me because she knows I hate London and that I only want to get back on the water again."

Charlotte recalled how her change of heart had lifted Rachel's hopes and filled her with fresh enthusiasm. The relief was obvious in her sudden readiness to please; to give in to Charlotte's every whim. Of course, she must go on her own to get her passport pictures done, and have her hair styled as she wished. Rachel even trusted her to see the local JP about a character reference. One uncomfortable moment was when she produced her passport photographs with their close resemblance to Jenny. Rachel had squinted at them disdainfully. "Not a bit like you," she said, "But then passport pictures never are." And the tired clerk at the passport office hardly gave the photograph a second glance as he hammered the stamp across the corner.

As the days drew on the thought of seeing Cornwall again had trembled within her; the blue dusted hills beyond the Tamar Bridge, southwards the wide reaches of the Trefoy estuary. She pictured the still creek at Pendowry, Granny Bunt clipping the honeysuckle round her cottage door, the neighbourly soul she would go to for help.

Now her mind went back through the long day to Paddington Station, Rachel seeing her off. The Plymouth train half-empty – always was on weekdays, according to the porter, who hoisted her suitcase up onto the rack. The window down, Rachel on the platform, looking in, chic in her black suit as she had handed to Charlotte the thick envelope addressed to Mrs Millicent Potter. It contained the passport and the letter of authorisation Rachel had written, giving her aunt permission take her stepdaughter back with her to Sydney. The letter also acknowledged that her aunt had kindly agreed to pay the return fare on Charlotte's passage home.

Rachel's voice had been raised, shrill against the escaping steam. "Now take care, dear, and look out for Mrs Potter when you leave the train at Westbury. She's rather stout, and she's going to be wearing a fox cape and a peacock blue hat. I've told her to look for your mimosa yellow coat. Be nice to her, darling. She's awfully rich, and you could meet some nice young man on her yacht in Sydney...."

Charlotte was hardly listening, she was stealing glances down the platform. Jenny was late. The guard with the green flag was glancing at the clock. Then she spotted a girl in corduroy trousers coming through the barrier, a bulky haversack swinging over her shoulder as she leapt aboard. She'd made it.

It had been easy then to return her stepmother's smile. The whistle blew, drowning that glorious "Goodbye Rachel. Goodbye!"

A jolt and the station gloom, her stepmother's painted face framed within it slid by, replaced by the windows of another train across the platform. Suddenly, morning light flooded the compartment; the tweed seating, linen over the headrests and faded pictures of Bognor Regis looking out from under the luggage racks. Then, in no time at all, looking in from the corridor, Jenny, making her excuses about the bus being full and having to walk all the way to the tube.

The journey had been exciting, changing clothes, swapping luggage from Charlotte's suitcase to the rucksack she had asked Jenny to bring for her, and, of course, the envelope containing the passport. But it had also been sad, having to say goodbye as they neared Westbury. But the moment she would always remember was of Jenny, walking down the platform in that mimosa yellow coat to be greeted by the large bosomed Mrs Millicent Potter, smiling, open-armed, in furs and pearls and the enormous peacock blue hat.

It had been evening when the Plymouth train steamed into Lostwithiel. Across the platform was her last connection, a tall-funnelled locomotive waiting to shunt its two dumpy carriages down the riverside line to the sea, all the way evoking memories, sad, beautiful, with every bend of the river.

Now tired from the long journey, she watched from the carriage window, the mist drifting thinly over the broadening estuary and moored craft marking the approach to the halfway halt. Two passengers rose, a brown, freckled Cornishwoman, balancing herself along the gangway with a basket of eggs, a gaunt old man in threadbare tweeds stooping after her.

They jogged on, Charlotte peering through the steamy glass, and seeing little evidence of the war but for a dilapidated air-sea rescue boat on the moorings at Wiseman's pool. There were cargo ships berthed at the Number Eight jetties, dusted white with china clay – the lifeblood of Cornwall, her father always said. Then, with a brief glimpse of the town quays and the white houses of Trefoy, the train slid into the shadowed station.

She rose, slinging on her haversack, her mind on a Cornish supper at Granny Bunt's cottage; the pasty warm from the oven, the sooty kettle spluttering on the hob. She pictured the old lady in her copious skirt and flowered pinafore. How surprised she would be to see her! What raptures of compassion would flow! The old neighbour had never had much time for Rachel. She had been angry to hear that she was taking Charlotte away. "You're always welcome to come and stay m'dear," she'd whispered to her on their day of departure.

It had been raining and the narrow streets were washed clean. She hurried, making for the car ferry, her most direct way to the creek, but the night boat was already on the frape.

An old salt sitting on the sea wall nodded to her. "He's gone home early, m'dear. Not many visitors about, and not much doing this hour o' night. You might get the last ferry from Whitehouses though – if you're quick, mind."

Thanking him, she sprinted off towards the town, but as she reached the harbour, she could see the passenger ferry was already halfway across the estuary, heading for St Ruan. For a while she waited, hoping it would return, but only to see it being moored for the night near the opposite shore.

"'Must be someone to take me across," she sighed, hanging over the harbour wall, but all the dinghies were on the moorings and the quayside deserted. "Perhaps, when the pubs come out," she thought, looking up at the lighted windows of the white-washed inn across the square, where a large painted sign of a pirate hung, rattling in the wind.

She waited, exhilarated by the smell of the salt wind and the gulp and splash of the wash against the jetty. Across the water, St Ruan was still lit with the last of the reflected light, the colours smudged and shadowy. It had always looked like that, the other side of the river, where once Cornish industry thrived and coals boats docked. Through the thirties nobody ever had enough money to give the place its holiday lick of whitewash. So it remained, stubbornly untouched, through poverty and war. Charlotte looked at it fondly; it was where she had climbed the hill to school, dug in the muddy sand on the boatyard beach, toddled after her dad down the coastguard paths to watch the pilchard fleet come out of Mevagissey on autumn evenings, a convoy of fairy flares along the horizon.

But the river had changed since the war years. No landing craft, no Americans, no mines across the harbour. The river was at peace now, as it must have been before the war came, the war that had taken her father.

Beyond the headlands a yacht slanted on the grey horizon, a schooner. She watched it coming in, watched it dipping over the bar. Then, the big red sails crumpled around a man on deck. The yacht glided inshore, a rakish looking vessel, with chipped cream paint, and she saw there was a dog standing in the bows – like a figurehead. The man, busy stowing the sail, wore the white-topped cap of a skipper.

CHAPTER TWO

The long terrace of tall white houses backing the Trefoy Esplanade commanded unrivalled views of the river, their verandas and sun lounges almost over-hanging the cliff edge. Many had steps down to private landings, where small moored craft took the first slap of the incoming tide. As desirable properties they were much sought after, usually bringing the highest prices, and Richard Ellis knew that when the time came, he had some fairly hefty assets to draw from a house he had never quite regarded as his own.

It had been bought merely as an investment. In his position as partner to the late owner, he had been able, with little opposition, to make the purchase at a ridiculously low price, complete with Victorian furnishings, bric-a-brac and all the paraphernalia hoarded by the elderly lawyer. Ellis had hardly waited for the funeral flowers to wither before he had stripped the walls bare of the faded photographs, cramming with them into the dustbin personal papers and other sentimental rubbish cherished by the old man. Wilfred Penrose had died alone, without a living relative and no friends close enough to treasure his belongings, least of all Richard Ellis. His interest had been in the house itself, together with the table silver, the good china, and some nice pieces of eighteenth century furniture, all of which he saw as necessary trappings to match his present status.

Unlike most newcomers to the little port in South Cornwall, Ellis had never fallen under its spell. The twisted streets, the landlocked harbour, the river, wooded to the waters edge, left him unmoved. To Ellis it was no more than a convenient retreat, a place where no one knew his background, to bide his time, until he was able to harvest one particular resource he had coolly watched over for nine patient years.

Now, sitting out on the patio, his eyes rested on the terraced town of St Ruan across the water. '*Like an old watercolour*' said the fools who painted it. '*Enchanting*' raved the visitors...until they boated across to discover that the dingy alleyways stank of fish, lamp oil and cats, and that the harbour was a slum, with yelling children climbing barefoot up the iron ladders. It reminded Ellis of his own miserable childhood, the squalor of the dockside neighbourhood before they moved to Whitechapel. The wharf where he used to play had the same tarry smell. He wanted no reminders of those days; his father in Wormwood Scrubs, his mother picking coal from the railway and pushing it through the back streets in a battered pram, himself holding on to her apron so as not to be left behind. Dole queues, pawn shops, bundles of washing on the doorstep; thankfully those days were behind him, the memory dulled...except in certain lights when that faded watercolour raised the ghosts.

That place was due for a clean up. And it would come. Already the wide-boys from London were moving into Cornwall, full of plans for gift shops and cream tea parlours. A crinkle of clean pound notes and the properties would soon change hands. There was no stopping tourism. Not that the Cornish would ever do it themselves, they preferred to doze out in a boat in the bay, trailing mackerel lines for their supper.

But Ellis' interest was not so much in property investment, but a certain property inheritance which, through his foresight and patience, he believed would soon be in his possession. Luck, his father would have called it, but to Ellis luck was fragile, not to be trusted. It wasn't just luck you needed in life, it was the ability to foresee the opportunities, to manipulate people, manoeuvre yourself into the desired position.

Not that luck hadn't ever been a factor in Ellis' life, it had. He had been lucky to win a grammar school scholarship back in the thirties when there were few to be had. He had been lucky to have parents prepared to make sacrifices to keep him there, not that the money had always been honestly obtained, a failing his father paid for with more than one prison sentence; but luckily for Ellis, his mother had toiled at her sewing machine to see him go to law school. But perhaps, luckiest of all, he'd been able to find an opening with a firm of Jewish solicitors, all of them in their twenties.

In those days he was still Mark Abrahams – changing his name to Richard Ellis had come later – with another piece of good fortune. But growing up in the East End in times of the blackshirt marches, of bricks through the window, early rumours of Hitler's persecution of the Jews, had left their marks on him, a bitterness bottled up inside. Ambition had been the outlet, an executive position the goal, and he headed for it without scruples.

The outbreak of the war could have been a serious threat to his career but a permanent limp, caused by a fall in childhood, gave him exemption from military service. Not so his colleagues. One by one he saw them claimed by the call-up board, leaving him in the seat of authority, and later obliged to take on a junior partner to ease the office workload. As a solicitor in wartime London, he had made a very comfortable living. But the insight it offered into the way his clients did business brought even richer rewards, particularly in the black market, while the knowledge to hand gave him easy access to buyers and suppliers. Without even moving from his desk, he was able to broker deals in every kind of commodity from Scotch whisky to forged clothing coupons, and as the man in the middle, he took a high percentage of the profit. Sometimes he even operated as a fixer for clients in prison, stashing away substantial cash payments from his commission.

It had taken considerable nerve to operate so freely on both sides of the law, but he had always believed that he had the intelligence and the cunning to steer clear of trouble. He had been wrong, of course, and by the time he realised how deeply involved he had become, it was too late. He was under certain obligations. When he had chosen to turn down a deal with the Raby family, the warning, when it came was nearly fatal.

It happened when he was walking to the underground station in the blackout, taking his usual short cut. The car had come roaring up the alley behind him. He'd had thrown himself into a doorway as it screamed past. Next time, he knew he might not be so lucky.

Even so, he had made up his mind. He had no desire to finish up like his father – doing time. But going in fear of his life had been a strain. Everywhere he went he believed he was being followed.

Then came that terrifying day in 1943. That was how it had seemed at the time. In fact, it had turned out to be the luckiest day in his life, and even now after nine years, the memory was still startlingly clear.

The junior partner's name was Richard Ellis. He had been invalided out of the army after Dunkirk, and now free to return to Civvy Street and practice again as a solicitor. He had been glad to join Mark Abrahams at his chambers in Neil Street, and it must have been fate that he had been in the office at the time.

That particular day, Ellis recalled, it had been necessary to make a large withdrawal of cash from the bank, and he had arranged to collect it at three that afternoon. The money was destined for an American serviceman he was meeting at the Savoy that evening; it represented the accumulated pay-offs on a series of very profitable black market deals.

It had been raining most of the morning, and his coat still wet from lunchtime, a fact his partner pointed out when he saw him putting it on. "Why don't you take mine? It's been airing on the radiator" he'd suggested, nodding to the secretary to reach it down.

He remembered walking down the stairs, fastening the belt of the other man's raincoat. It had been better than his own, almost new. He remembered the white haired commissionaire opening the door for him, the old dear shivering with her papers on the corner. The day had been dull, dark November, wet streets shining, fog rolling in from the river.

He had been coming out of the bank when he spotted a familiar black Wolseley parked beside Aldgate East tube station, the engine idling, the windscreen wipers obscuring the occupants. Even to this day he could not be sure which of the Raby boys might have been in that car, but he was taking no chances. He turned off down a side street and, clutching his brief case, he ran for it. Hearing a car turning the corner, he plunged off across a bombsite, his mouth dry, his heart hammering. Blundering on, his breath coming painfully, he could hear footfalls behind, but the sirens were wailing and everybody was running! Distantly, he could hear the heavy, uneven drone of enemy bombers, a rumble of anti-aircraft guns, followed by the sudden, unmistakable whistle of falling bombs. The earth shuddered. Blimey, that was close!

He had sat through the raid with his head in his hands, oblivious to the hubbub of brave cheerfulness all around him. It wasn't the Jerries he was worried about; it was the long arm of the Raby family.

It was almost five o'clock when he left the shelter, the all clear just sounding. The air had been acrid with smoke, a glow of fire flickering behind the buildings in the direction of the Commercial Road. Yet, what an amazing night of good fortune it had turned out to be, and after such an inauspicious afternoon!

He remembered fighting his way back through the chaos, the shock of seeing the great gap where Portland Chambers had been. There was nothing left of his side of the street but the hanging remains of the building on the corner, the floors sliced through down to the auctioneer's showroom. He had stood staring at the mountain of smoking rubble, rescue workers dragging bodies out from under the twisted girders, blackened faces under white helmets, lit from the glow of the burning warehouse across the way.

Voices came back to him. "Second floor? There are three floors on top of that, Guv. Work here, do you? Blimey, you were lucky! All happened so quickly. No time to get to the cellars."

He remembered leaning against the ambulance, trying to take in what had happened; his rooms gone, nothing left, his staff buried under the debris. The man in the helmet had been running his finger down the list in his hand. "Solicitors you said, Guv? Then which would you be? Mr M. Abrahams or Mr R. Ellis?"

In that long moment before he had given his answer his brain had been racing. They didn't know who he was! Nobody did, everyone was dead, the staff, the commissionaire, even the old paper seller on the corner. Suppose he admitted to being Richard Ellis? Who was there to doubt him? This was just the escape he had been looking for, here in the identity of another man. *Hadn't* he picked up a package from the bank that afternoon in *his* name? Wasn't he wearing that man's *raincoat*?

He remembered muttering his partner's name and the warden circling the name of M. Abrahams on his list.

How many others in the office? They had wanted names, addresses. He had done his best to supply the details.

He walked away from Neil Street that night in a daze, knowing he would never be able to return home to his flat. Neighbours would be told he had been killed in a raid, it would reach the ears of the Raby family, and they would no longer be looking for him. To have to leave behind all his personal belongings, even his bank account, was a sickening prospect, but he did have £15,000 in cash in his briefcase, enough to take him far from London, and to eventually re-establish himself in a town where he was not known.

He had hurried, choosing the darkest streets for fear of being recognised, heading westwards towards the city, to lose himself in the rush hour stream. In a crowded Cheapside pub, over a couple of stiff brandies, he began to work out what to do.

Most important was to parry any questions which might be asked about Richard Ellis. The man's landlady would be sure to contact the police when he didn't return to his lodgings. He remembered thumbing urgently through the telephone directory, looking for the number, and having to shout against the honky piano hammering out *Roll out the Barrel* behind the booth.

"Mrs Biggs, isn't it? Ah! My name is Davies, Doctor Charles Davies. I'm an old friend of your lodger, Richard Ellis..." He would never forget the calm authority he put into that impression of a doctor he once knew. "I'm ringing to let you know that Mr Ellis won't be returning tonight – nor for sometime. I'm afraid he's had a very bad shock. There's been another nuisance raid in the East End. His office building got a direct hit. Everybody killed, as he would have been if he hadn't popped out to the bank. Yes, isn't it? Absolutely terrible! Dunkirk! Now this! Naturally you will appreciate the shock he's in. Yes, yes, indeed. That's why I think it advisable he should get away from London completely, so this evening I'm taking him by train to some friends of mine in the country...

"Unfortunately, time does not allow me to come over to Finsbury to collect his stuff, so I would appreciate it enormously if you would put his things into his suitcase, together with his ration books, and I'll send a cab for them. The driver will have an envelope for you – a little recompense for your trouble and to cover any rent in lieu of notice. Could you have the case ready – say in an hour?"

The woman had been only too ready to oblige.

Fate had taken him by the hand that night and led him to his destiny. He remembered the bus queue, the clippie arming him aboard. 'One only-Paddington!' The taxi rank, waiting in the rain for the cab driver to return with the suitcase, the booking hall crowded with uniforms, a porter yelling 'Bath! First four coaches!' The West Country, he thought, just the place to lie low for a few months.

Once during the journey he had thought about the unfortunate American waiting for him at the Savoy, expecting to be paid for all those consignments of Chesterfields. The poor sucker needed the money. Well, too bad, so did he.

It had been March 1944 when he saw the advertisement. He was staying at a pub in Bridgewater. Some sailors from Plymouth, calling on their way home on leave had left behind a newspaper, The Western Morning News. Glancing through he had seen the advertisement.

Junior partner required by elderly solicitor.
Old established practice in small Cornish port.
Write for appointment to Wilfred Penrose, Solicitors,
61, Fore Street, Trefoy, South Cornwall.

Ellis recalled how his hand trembled as he'd copied down the address, the mixed feelings of hope and faint-heartiness when he posted the letter; the bolt of surprise when he received the answer four days later, inviting him for an interview.

He didn't know then that he had been the only applicant, and that the ailing Wilfred Penrose had been trying for months to find a partner to share the firm's modest workload of litigation and property transfer. But most men with acceptable qualifications were in uniform and Penrose, relieved to find somebody even interested, had been an easy man to impress.

But Ellis had given his best; inventing a story of losing his office in the blitz, his family, illness he had suffered as a result and how eager he was to start a-fresh in his own profession which, until now, he had been unable to face. He needn't have gone into any of it. Penrose had already made up his mind before Ellis stepped into that musty little office with the faded wallpaper and the yellowing brown paint.

Penrose was a heavy man with a sagging face and tired drooping eyes behind gold rimmed spectacles. Ellis could see him now reclining in his chair behind the littered desk, his black pinstriped waistcoat dusted with grey ash from his pipe.

Funny how every word of their conversation came back. He could hear it now, the deep crusty voice, the thick cough lifting through the tobacco smoke.

"Edward should have joined me. First class honours-Cambridge. But for the war he'd have been here now. Met somebody out in Singapore. Settled there. My younger son got it at Dunkirk. The wife never got over it. When I lost her two years ago there wasn't much left, but the firm. Pushed myself too hard, I s'pose. Doesn't do. Now that old quack down Church Walk says my ticker's on the blink. Have to ease up. Wonderful opportunity for a man like you, though. A good practice, easy time to settle in, my hand to guide you. Quiet times, I dare say, but divorce is on the up, due to this influx of Americans we have stationed here. Marshalling ground the Second Front, y'know. We are to become a restricted area from April the 1st. But when the war is over, property will boom again. Not that we don't handle a tidy quota now. What with the affairs of the local gentry, all the Pendowry estate..."

That was the gem, Ellis recalled, but then he could only see opportunity in the location of the place; sleepy Cornish port, restricted area, and not only an ideal hiding place, but what potential! An established family firm of solicitors, the old man already puffing his last. A couple of years and Ellis had seen himself having it all.

He'd had a silent celebration that evening in the bar at the Ship Inn. It had been crowded with Americans, a swaying throng appropriately singing *You'll Never Know*. And nobody would, he'd thought to himself.

That was the first time he'd seen Rachel. He remembered how she'd given him her Rita Hayworth smile over the rim of her gin and lime, bought by the Yank at her elbow. He had sensed then that she was one of his kind.

Rachel, whose aspirations to work in the fashion world had been disrupted by the war, had fled from London to avoid conscription. Her bedridden aunt in Cornwall made a useful dependant. When the aunt had been moved into hospital, Rachel took up with Bill Ives, the river pilot. He was a widower with a small child and she had married him obviously to obtain exemption from essential work. Ellis liked her style, but later when Ives was killed during the D-Day operations, there was something he liked even better – her connection with the Pendowry inheritance. In her he saw a unique opportunity to convert it to his own.

He smiled to himself now. The late Silas Trevelyan would rattle his coffin lid if he knew how his wishes were being abused, but Ellis had no scruples about putting one over on the miserly old recluse, who had sat on the Pendowry fortunes for eighty odd years and never been known to give a penny away. In Trevelyan history Ellis had been well briefed. The times he had been forced to hear out the Wilfred Penrose account of it, the illustrious sea-faring saga, coughed and spluttered through the pipe smoke, until Ellis knew it by heart.

There had been a Trevelyan at Pendowry since Captain Jenkin Trevelyan launched his first sailing ship in 1775; a four masted barque called The Constantine. Earlier that year he had married Victoria Killigrew of Falmouth, part of her dowry being the old manor house standing above the river creek. All his sons had gone to sea except the youngest, Jonathan. He had been the one to develop the estate and the tenancies down by the river. But his own boys were to follow their grandfather's sea faring tradition, and went into fair trading which was having its heyday in the eighteenth century. Brig Trevelyan, the most notorious of them all, became an outlaw.

It was his brother Thomas who inherited Pendowry and built up the small fleet of sailing ships in the Trefoy harbour, trading with the West Indies and South American ports in china clay. Serving with him was his youngest son, Silas, and three elder brothers, but tragedy struck the family when their schooner was driven on the rocks in a storm and foundered not two miles from their home port. Silas was the only one to survive, but he was left crippled by a falling spar and never went to sea again.

Robbed of the adventure in his blood, Silas became a cantankerous invalid, venting his bitterness on anyone who came within a yard of his chair. They couldn't keep a servant after that – except Hiram Bunt, the gardener, who wouldn't be parted from his flowerbeds.

Silas became a recluse, visited only by his sister Sarah, who lived in the boat house cottage at the head of the creek. She had married Bill Ives' father, Dan, a ship's master in the merchant navy, but Silas was to out-live them all.

For years, Penrose had been badgering Silas to make a will, but the old man seemed to resent the idea of parting with his property, even after his death. Then quite suddenly in April 1944, a message arrived summoning Wilfred Penrose to the manor house. But the old solicitor was unwell. It was one of his 'off' days, breath coming short, a blueness in his lips.

"You go," he told Ellis. "Get one of the boatmen to ferry you over there."

It was the first time Ellis had been to Pendowry. The place left him in awe, the grandeur there had once been; the oak panelled passages, the staircases hung with family portraits, veiled now with cobwebs. The rooms were full of shadows, so grimed were the windows. Occasionally the sun found a broken pane and slanted down, catching a swarm of dust specks sailing through. He had seen the heavy furniture, magnificently carved and inlaid, the old silver tarnished, tapestries faded, books blackened with centuries of dust. Looking up at the beautifully moulded ceiling, he had seen a chandelier hanging with hardened tears of tallow encrusted still over the candleholders, while underfoot the colours of the Persian carpets were dulled with age.

Silas Trevelyan's study was at the back of the house, its tiled veranda overlooking a walled garden. The old man had barked at him to come through. He was sitting out in his wicker chair; a rug round his bony knees and a tattered straw hat pulled down over a furrowed brow. He had the face of a hawk, pin sharp eyes, astonishingly blue and a beaked nose like a pirate. He sat forward, grim with intent, a morocco leather writing case open before him, at his side a sturdy stick which he would bring down heavily to emphasise his demands.

Ellis found himself bowing to please without meaning to do so. It was not his usual style, but the power of the old man's personality seemed to have that effect on him.

"Everything goes to Charlotte. That child shall inherit it all. Not a penny of my money will go to that hussy Rachel, not a penny," the old man told him.

He didn't know then, of course, as he drafted out his proposals, how justified his foresight had been, nor did he doubt the integrity of his solicitors, who he was also making the executors of the will. He had no need while Wilfred Penrose was alive. But when the old solicitor died later that year the position was to change as Ellis, in full control, saw his chance.

A trip to London found his old friend, still printing illicit clothing coupons in his East End basement, and two days later Ellis was able to return to Cornwall with a perfect replica of Silas Trevelyan's will, but made out in favour of his daughter-in-law, Rachel Ives. All he needed then was to wait for Silas to die, and, at a discreet moment, put his proposition to Rachel. He had been seeing her even before the war claimed her husband, but now, until Pendowry became hers, marriage was out of the question, due to his own involvement as executor.

When he told her of his scheme she'd laughed, first in disbelief, then at the irony of it. To think the old man's bitter deed against her was to be reversed! But she did have her doubts about their pulling it off.

"But what about the witnesses?" she'd cried.

"Dead. Both of them," he'd told her. "As for the will, it's a perfect forgery. There should be no problems. It will go to probate and be accepted without question. And you, my dear, could become a very rich woman."

"Provided I marry you, darling, that's the catch, isn't it?"

"Then what do you say?"

He recalled the twinkle in her eyes that came as she answered.

"I didn't really plan to marry again – unless I found a man to make me rich."

"Looks as if you've found one."

Later he decided it would be unwise to flaunt their relationship openly; better for her to go away, back to London, take up her career in dress design. He would put up the money for a workroom, a shop, and with the child to bring up she need have no worries about being directed into essential work. They could meet secretly for occasional weekends. With old Silas already in his eighties it might only be for a couple of years. Better, too, for the child to be brought up away from Cornwall, away from her Uncle Silas and the village gossip. She must know nothing of her rightful inheritance. Once he and Rachel were married and the estate sold up, they could all settle abroad somewhere, and the girl would be none the wiser. But he'd had to wait nine years for Silas Trevelyan to die, and by then Rachel was having more doubts.

"Charlotte is never going to believe Uncle Silas left Pendowry to me," she complained.

"Then tell her the properties have fallen derelict, the family fortunes have dwindled and the land sold off to pay debts and death duties. Your newly acquired wealth will have come from a friend, who suddenly wants to marry you."

"You forget. She's not a child anymore. She's nearly seventeen and already set on going back to Cornwall. Once she leaves school and starts earning there will be no holding her – or the tongues of the local gossips when she gets there."

"Are you sure you haven't a sister in Timbuktu to take her off your hands?" It had only been meant as a joke, but her eyes had narrowed thoughtfully.

"No, but I do have some friends in Wiltshire, who are entertaining an aunt over from Australia, who, I believe, is looking for a companion to take back with her. A sea voyage! Now that would suit Charlotte. Suppose you let me work on it."

He had, and an hour ago he had received a call from her in London. Charlotte had arrived safely in Westbury and the Australian aunt was delighted with her. They were sailing tomorrow from Southampton.

Ellis finished his brandy and laid down the glass, his gaze resting on the river, on a yacht coming in. It was the rakish looking schooner, with weather-faded red sails. Ellis watched it jealously. He fancied a big yacht. But his would be a luxury job, one to make his boat down on the moorings look like a dinghy. It would have to be a powerful, twin-screw motor cruiser, with sun decks and staterooms and a permanent berth at Nice, with every ugly reminder of his past left behind in the shadows of that faded watercolour across the harbour.

CHAPTER THREE

The skipper was coming ashore in a motor dinghy, the dog with him, up in the bows again. It was a long haired, tawny dog, patched with white, with well pricked ears and a laughing face, head up, tongue hanging with pleasure. Nearing the jetty the man bent to cut the engine and arm round the tiller, guided the dinghy cleanly alongside the jetty slip. The dog leapt ashore and sped off for a series of leg-stretching laps round the quay, while his master made fast the boat.

Charlotte watched him coming up the steps. He was tall, boyish looking, with sunburnt good looks. The peak of his white-topped cap was tipped up from a quiff of blond hair, and printed across the front of his dark blue jersey was the name of his yacht, the *Cape Columbo.* He whistled and the dog came bounding out from behind a heap of fish boxes, carrying a stick, which he instantly despatched at the skipper's feet.

The man bent to pick it up and the dog stood back, paws apart, ready, his laughing face lit with pleasure. The stick went flying seawards, the dog after it into the water for a hard swim against the tide to retrieve it. Then back he came, nose and stick above the surface, moving like a weasel. He came out, dripping and shaking with spray, to drop it for another throw.

"Now come on, Matelot, No more games to-night."

He threw the stick, this time into the boat. The dog started after it, but changed his mind when he saw where it had landed. Instead, he spread out his paws, shook himself dry and followed the man across the square.

Charlotte gazed after them, tempted to beg a lift across the water to Pendowry Creek, but she had hesitated too long and he was already half way up the steps to the inn. Darkness was falling. Tiny lights now replaced the smudged landmarks above St Ruan harbour. Up river she could just see the dark belt of trees at the end of the creek. It was not so far away by water. The skipper would have taken her over if she had explained about missing the ferry. Too late now. He had probably gone to his lodging at the inn and wouldn't be back until morning.

The night wind felt cold against her cheek, weariness and apprehension beginning to dull her optimism. The chances of other boatmen turning up at this hour seemed unlikely, but if she didn't reach Granny Bunt's cottage soon the old lady would have gone to bed.

She leaned against the rail, looking down longingly at the skipper's boat. It was a clinker built, varnished job, with an inboard motor, just like the one her father used to have for getting about the river, the one he had had taught her to handle soon after she started school. She wandered down the steps for a closer inspection and saw it was called the *Dipper*. Inside were some mackerel boxes, ropes, and a shallow bowl for bailing.

Her heartbeat quickened. Suppose she borrowed it? She could easily have it back for him before daybreak, with the Bunt dinghy in tow for the return trip. It was the sort of thing her father would have done. Neighbours always shared their boats in emergencies, and although the skipper was a stranger to her, he sounded like a Cornishman, and that would be enough to justify the act. She glanced furtively at the inn, the lighted windows throwing square reflections on the cobblestones, song lifting above the murmur of voices from within.

She inched her way down the jetty steps. The little craft was lifting with the swell of dark water. She bent, taking the painter, sandy wet in her hand. One tug and the bowline would be free. She pulled, watching the knot fall apart and the craft drift outwards from her hand. There was nothing to do then but leap aboard. Her hands groped excitedly for the ignition. It started first try, the noise enough to bring everybody out of the inn, but the rousing chorus of *Blow the Man Down* did not falter as she pushed out from the jetty. Swinging round the tiller, she stooped to let out the throttle to full ahead, and sent the bow weaving in and out between the moored craft to the open river.

The wind came damp against her cheek, iced with spray; and she felt a sudden wave of exultation, to be back, to be afloat again. Ahead she could see the shoulder of the creek headlands, wooded dark against the night sky, rising on either side as she headed the boat into the narrow inlet. The tide was full and coming, but she hung close to the north bank where she remembered how the channel crept between hidden mudbanks. Soon they were out of the wind, the darkness closing in, full of earthy scents of moss and mud, and steeped in silence, but for the occasional squawk of a night bird.

She throttled down, keeping her eye on the bankside, judging the distance from the gnarled roots of the trees, her way lit only by the starlight and the dim reflection of the water. She used to do it with her father at low tide, so at high water it should be easy, she told herself, with chattering teeth. Once she thought of Jenny and wondered how she was making out, but without envying her.

The creek was still; the full tide shining in pale sheets as the moon came out from behind a cloud, the ripples barely touched by the soft wind, the only sound now the steady chug of the two-stroke motor. Round the bend of woodland she peered for the lights of Granny Bunt's cottage, but all lay dark and still. Must be the hedgerows where the honeysuckle climbed, hiding the lighted window, must be.. but then came a great barrier of darkness rising up at the head of the creek, where the pines grew tall into the clough and the hills rose behind.

Still no lights from the cottage. It must be late; Granny had already gone to bed, Charlotte decided, trying to console herself with the thought that the creek was not as still and as deserted as it seemed. But her fears were washed aside with sudden emotion to see on the opposite side of the river the grey outline of her old home taking shape; the slip, the boathouse where she used to play, the river pilot's cottage above, so long loved and longed for, so familiar, even under the shroud of nightfall, and the happy years came crowding back. Then gritting her teeth, she headed towards the other bank where the stone jetty below Granny Bunt's cottage loomed up out of the darkness. Cutting the engine she took the Dipper in slowly, sliding cleanly beside the iron ladder. Making the painter fast, she climbed ashore. The silence came down heavily all around her, but she wasn't afraid. She was home, home at last.

For a moment she glanced back at her old home across the water; the boathouse, the iron gate, the narrow stone steps leading up to the garden, the moonlight reflecting on the dusty windows. Then with a sigh, she began to feel her way along the stony track from the jetty to the old neighbour's cottage, but long before she reached it she knew that there was no one there. Even in the darkness she could see the broken windows, the door half open, weeds growing up behind the garden gate. Granny Bunt's old home was derelict. She stood for a long time taking it in, the emptiness, the loss, the utter hopelessness of her plight, creeping over her like a bad dream.

Eventually she wandered back to the head of the creek and crossed the bridge to pilot's house. She had no inclination to return immediately with the boat to the town quay. Tiredness and disillusionment had drained her of all purpose. Instead she decided to try the barred doors and shuttered windows for a way into her old home, hoping for some place of comfort behind the dark walls, but all was bolted, forbidden.

Down at the boathouse, on the stone slipway, she found wooden bars loose on the window. Almost angrily, she pulled them away, the timber creeking free until there was room for her to squeeze through. Inside it was black dark, but it smelt of home, smelt of tar and sailcloth, diesel and fish bait. She could feel rope and canvas under her feet. She stumbled over them, groping for the cupboard on the sidewall. Below it there used to be some drawers; in the top one there should be a Woodbine tin, where the matches were kept for the lamp. She felt for the knob and pulled it open and the tin was still there, rattling with matches. She struck one against the rusty surface and it glimmered over a litter of dust-shrouded gear, buoys and boat hooks, the dresser before her, the lamp.

It took two matches to light it, and then after a splutter the flame settled to a steady glow that reached into the shadows of the store. Not quite the comfort Granny Bunt would have provided, but it was warm and dry, out of the wind, and she still had some of Jenny's sandwiches left.

Supper over, she kicked off her shoes and curled up, using an old kapok life jacket, that must have been her father's, for a pillow. She wept a little over it, but not for long and sleep soon brought relief.

****

The Pirate Inn was crowded, scrumpy glasses raised in song. Nick Bonet shouldered his way through the crush of dockers, sailors and Trefoy locals. His dog took the floor level route, nosing between the trouser legs and clay dusted boots, to surface onto the bar stool beside him, a fiendish eye on the fresh baked pasties. The young barmaid, setting down a pint for a singing seaman, gave the dog a sour glance.

Nick nudged him down. "He'd rather have that ham bone you have for him in the back," he said, giving her a wink.

"And you'll be wanting your pint of brown ale and a green cheese sandwich, I suppose."

"That's right, m'dear, and from the prettiest barmaid in town,"

She gave him a wry glance. "The sauce you have, Nick Bonet!" she said, pulling his pint.

The dog was up on the stool again, lapping the froth off it as Nick pocketed his change. But Hannah, on her way to the kitchen, didn't notice and when she returned with the sandwich, the ham bone was on the plate beside it.

"Hannah," said Nick, "You'll be Matelot's friend for life."

"Now away with 'ee," she cried, as the dog disappeared towards the taproom with his supper.

Nick, ready to follow, turned to her. "If Jed arrives, tell him where I am, will you? He's been up Plymouth. Dunno what time the train gets in, but I've a boat down the jetty to give him a lift over to St Ruan."

"Right you are, my handsome," she said, reaching for a glass to serve another customer.

Nick found the taproom crowded with the locals, most of them seated in tight rows before the wooden tables under a haze of tobacco smoke. Matelot had vanished, but bone-crunching sounds coming from under the window seating, betrayed his lair.

Nick found standing room against the lofty fireplace, where driftwood and bents glowed red, and a group of Trefoy men were warming their backs. A fisherman with a lobster red face and flint blue eyes, nodded to Nick.

"Seen you bringing in the *Cape Columbo*, boy. Nice job you landed yourself on her."

"Handsome," said Nick, biting hungrily into his sandwich. "Just had her down the coast to see my old mother."

"She'm a big yacht for one man. Bet she took a bit of holding off the Dodman."

"She's a beauty!" said Nick, "Sails herself. Didn't I bring her single handed all the way from Marseilles?"

"You tells we you did. You tells we about an owner, too, but we'm seen nothing of him. So where's he be to, then?"

"On his way," Nick assured him. "Any day now."

"So you said last time you was in here," said the fisherman, with a wink at his mates, and a titter ran through the group.

Nick downed his ale He had been half expecting the conversation to work round to the subject of his boss, whose non-appearance in port was becoming something of an embarrassment. He knew comparatively little about the quiet American, who had bought him too many brandies in the waterfront bar in Cassis, near Marseilles, then offered him the skipper's job aboard his yacht.

Nick had gone to France in search of the opportunities he failed to find in post-war Cornwall. His two years in the navy had left him restless and unfulfilled when the war ended, without him seeing any action. With no wish to return home to Newlyn, he had gone to live with his married sister, Joanna, in St Ruan. The apprenticeship in his brother-in-law's boatyard was not particularly lucrative, and although he was able to appreciate its usefulness as a trade, he had found it hard to settle to a shore job.

Tales told in the riverside pubs by foreign seamen had lured him abroad; tales of the tobacco runners' fleet of MTBs in the Mediterranean and the fortunes they made in contraband. He had hung about the French ports for months trying to make contact with them, but had found nothing more adventurous than casual labour aboard laid up-yachts. He longed to return to Cornwall, but shrank from the thought of arriving home broke, with nothing to show for the experience.

Meeting the owner of the *Cape Columbo* had seemed a lucky break. The job offered him responsibility, a chance to use his seamanship, and the passage home in command of a big schooner from the South of France, gave power to his ego.

The American had told Nick he was contemplating spending the summer on the Cornish Riviera, but he first had to fly to London on business. Nick was to await his arrival in Trefoy. Now, after three weeks in port and no word, Nick was suffering jibes from the clannish Trefoy locals, who were always ready to pay scorn to those not born on their side of the river. So it was time to divert the conversation onto another topic of local gossip.

"Seeing you're all in the mood for prying into other people's business," he said, "What's this about the Pendowry estate being sold, and the creek being turned into a boating marina?"

This, as he expected, sparked off an indignant exchange across the room.

"Tez how t'will end up if they people from up country gets their hands on it."

An old man, thin as wire, with a woollen cap pulled down to his white eyebrows, leaned out of the shadows, blue eyes bright with intrigue. "T'was a couple o' they buggers staying at The Ship and Mester Ellis buying 'em brandies to hasten the sale."

A woman sitting behind a glass of cider looked down her nose at him. "You'm talking as though Pendowry was Mester Ellis' property to sell," she said haughtily. "Silas Trevelyan left everything to Pilot Bill's maid."

"But she'm gone. Dead. Buried up country- so tes said."

"That chile dead!" cried her companion. "Ah! The dear li'l soul! That's Rachel taking her away."

The woman sniffed disapprovingly, "Looks as though t'will be that 'uzzy Rachel to get Pendowry then."

"Or Mester Ellis," suggested the old man, his eyes glinting. "Wasn't 'ee her ole fancy man?"

"Years back!"

"That's where you'm wrong, Megan Crump. Cos I see'd her down here!" cried the old man.

"You see'd un?" When was this, m'dear?"

"Easter. Getting out of Tom Willie's taxi, all toffed up like a ladybird, she was, and she swishes past me straight up the stairs into Mester Ellis' office."

Nick, enjoying his ale, was pleased with the result of his little ploy. The mention of Pendowry never failed to spark off a noisy debate. It had been the focus of town gossip since the day Silas Trevelyan died, rumours of property developers moving in. A pity, rightly so, Nick believed. It was a pretty creek, nowhere better for courting, for digging worm or losing visitors, whose hired craft became trapped in the mud. But he doubted it ever becoming much use as a boating marina, the dredging it would need as Jed always said ... sudden thought of Jed prompted him to take a peep in the bar to see if his brother-in-law had arrived.

He had, and half way through a pint of scrumpy, was looking slightly out of place in his city clothes. Ten years older than Nick, Jed Marney's well-developed paunch was more used to the comfortable give of a woollen jersey than the de-mob suit his wife had insisted on him wearing for Plymouth.

Nick greeted him with a grin and hailed Hannah to fill up his glass.

"How'd your day go?" he asked, dropping some small change for her across the counter.

"Aw, nothing tearin', boy. I picked up a couple of cheap outboards but the price they wants for timber these days, tez ludicrous!"

Jed had always been on good terms with his wife's younger brother. He admired the gutsy independence which had taken the boy farther than the occupational limits of the Trefoy waterside. Naturally, Jed had been disappointed to see him quit the yard to seek his fortune' out foreign', but had no desire to stand in his way. Now here he was home again, a man richer for the experience, and at only twenty-three years old, the skipper of a tall schooner, weather-bashed and sea stained from the Biscay passage.

"Don't mention prices," said Nick, "Maintenance on the yacht is just crippling. To be hoped the boss pays up."

"Or shows up?" said Jed ruefully.

Nick shrugged. "He will. Haven't I got his yacht and wages in advance".

"How'd you come to meet up with him?"

"In a bar. He was reading the back of my newspaper; a copy of the South

Cornwall Gazette Joanna had sent me. Finished up giving it to him. Seemed he'd been stationed here during the war, and seeing the paper got him yarning about the place. Suddenly he wanted to see it again."

"Young, is he?" Jed asked.

"Middle thirties, I'd say. Ex-US Navy. He was a Lieutenant in landing craft. There are plenty of Americans over there, left over from the war."

Hannah was calling last orders and Jed drained his glass. "You having another."

Nick heaved a sigh. "We'd better not. Joanna 'll have the pasties warming."

"You got the *Dipper?*"

"Down at the jetty steps."

"Proper job."

Nick whistled the dog and Matelot slooped out of the taproom with the remains of the ham bone protruding from his jaws, and he followed them out, down the steps to the quay. The gas lamp cast a sallow hue over the wharf, the greenish light gleaming on the wet breakwater, and, but for the suck and gulp of the swell, it was very quiet.

Reaching the jetty, Jed pulled up short. "Thought you said you'd brought the *Dipper.*"

Nick looked blank. "I did. She was tied up at the steps."

"You couldn't have made her fast."

"I did too!" he retorted.

"Well, she'm gone now and we're stranded!"

Nick scanned the dark basin. "There's a craft on the frape over there. I reckon we'd better pull her in."

"Not that old pulling boat of Jake Vardo's," Jed groaned. "She's always half full of water." He was thinking of his best suit that Joanna had pressed only that morning. But Nick was already hauling in the dinghy. Jed went to help him and together they heaved on the heavy frape-rope.

A local man, leaving the Institute stopped at the jetty rail. "You looking for your boat then? T'was a maid who had her – not long after you tied up. Never seen her before. Trousers, rucksack, one o' they ramblers."

"Where'd she take it?" Nick cried angrily.

"Up river. Could be up at Lerryn Creek by now."

"She won't get that far," said Nick, "I was low on fuel."

"Then she'll be beached somewhere," Jed said.

"The bleddy cheek!" Nick raged.

The pulling boat scraped against the jettyside. He climbed down the ladder and started baling as soon as he was aboard.

With a heavy sigh Jed carefully rolled up his trousers and followed, but with the gigantic splash the dog made as he jumped in after them, he needn't have bothered.

CHAPTER FOUR

Charlotte awoke blinking into chinks of sunlight coming down through the wooden bars, dusty beams throwing a striped pattern over the heap of sailcloth where she lay. For a while she remained listening to the birdsong, the echo of it, coming from the depths of the creek with the acoustics of a cathedral. Raising herself, she saw the mudflats beyond the gaping square of window and the gloom of last night's findings came flooding back.

Climbing out, she wandered down the slipway and stood, taking it all in. Although the sun was up, it was early; mist faintly dusting the trees, and the creek dried out to a narrow channel winding through the mudbanks, where a few oyster-catchers were preening themselves and a stalky heron beaked the mud.

Sadly she rested her gaze on the ivy-covered cottage on the opposite bank, honeysuckle creepers trailing the hedge and the wicket gate pushed open against last summer's weeds. The garden used to be full of flowers, with a vegetable patch at the back and pigeons coming for crumbs at the wooden cote.

Whatever must have happened to Granny Bunt? Had she died, too, like Uncle Silas? Surely not! But for her arthritis she was a lively old soul. It was more likely that she had moved up to St Ruan to be nearer the shops. Charlotte hoped so. She had been depending on Granny Bunt as a confidante. She could think of no one closer to the family problems than the old neighbour. No doubt, there were other villagers in St Ruan who would remember the pilot's daughter, but how could she be sure some might feel it their duty to let Rachel know where she was?

Her gaze ventured to the steps leading up to the house, but with no inclination to look beyond the boarding over the windows, the padlocks on the gates. She knew the house would be empty, the rooms stripped of all that had once made it home. Instead she glanced towards the bridge over the river, where a trackway beckoned, a trackway that twisted away from the creekside, and up through the woods to the manor house.

Below, in the jetty basin, the *Dipper* lay tilted where the tide had left her, hooked up from the mud by her painter. There would be no tide for an hour or more yet to get her back to the town quay. She hoped the skipper had slept late.

She walked on, past Granny Bunt's cottage and up the track. The tall hedgerows were full of spring flowers; masses of gorse and blackthorn, stitchwort and campion, with banks of late primroses and bluebells growing out of last years dead bracken. It smelt dank, with the stench of deadnettle and high with wild garlic, and as the path climbed between the tree trunks, there were glimpses of the creek and sunlight fluttering mottled patterns between the trees.

Ahead was an iron gate marked 'PRIVATE,' the gate to the old house, always forbidden in her childhood, except when she was taken to see Uncle Silas. She remembered how he always crouched over his stick, croaking out orders to the ever patient Granny Bunt, who came in to see to his needs. The gate was always kept locked, the ferns behind it so tall they almost buried one, and it was wise to watch the pathway carefully for adders. There was no lock on the gate now. It swung sideways on broken hinges, the notice peeling and faded, and the undergrowth trampled into a muddy path. Charlotte followed it hesitatingly, with a sense of trespass.

She came upon the house quite suddenly, its tottering portico of stone greened by lichen, with mossy steps reaching to where the ivy took over, climbing the walls and the bark of the trees around it; and yet more lichen, flourishing over the roof slates, and in the walled courtyard, mosses and plantains thickly carpeting the cobblestones. It was almost as though the woodlands, the plant life had embraced the old house and now they were one, part of the green copse of undergrowth that had once been a garden, the creepers and brambles smothering it all, as though nature had staked her claim.

But the place had not been without visitors. The trampled path led round through the garden and into the yard. Looking down over a stone balustrade, she saw imprints of mud on the steps leading down to the cellars, but when she tried the door at the bottom, it was locked. Walking back slowly, she paused to look up at the house, the turrets crumbling under the ivy, the cracked windows, blue with dust, the creepers trailing over the doorways. Beyond, tall pines towered skywards from the wooded clough, where the Pendowry river found its way down to the creek from the hills, sweeping around the parkland like a moat.

There the house slept with its secrets, claimed by the forest, the birds, the wildlife, guarded now as Uncle Silas had guarded it, possessively. Perhaps, she thought, he was still there, sitting somewhere in the depths of it, hunched over his stick, ready to vent his wrath on anybody who dared to trespass on his territory.

Charlotte shuddered, gooseflesh pricking her skin, even though the early sun through the branches of the trees was warm. She turned away to hurry down the path, without heeding the mud or the adders, to the less disturbing sanctuary of the creek.

The tide was coming now, stealing over the mudflats, the channel broadening as the early flood crept in to meet the rippling river water; it filled the shady hollow below the slip, carrying a little froth, a skin of dust, dead leaves and flower petals. For a while she sat on the warm bankside, chewing a grass stalk and watching a mallard teaching her brood to forage. The water looked inviting. On impulse she pulled off her shoes, rolled back her trousers and paddled back to the slipway, the seaweed tickling her toes, the water warm round her ankles. Then she climbed up on the boathouse window ledge and sat dangling her legs to dry in the sun.

The mallard swam by with her chicks in close formation, telling them, no doubt, about their enemies, the herons and the swans. Charlotte sighed as she watched them, half-wishing she'd been born a mallard, free to live from the river – or even better, to still be living here in the creek, a child again.

She closed her eyes, erasing the ugly years with Rachel in London, and let time roll back. Today was yesterday again, it felt exactly as it did then; the same birdsong filling the creek, the same sun-warmed smell of weed and mud, and in her fancy she was not alone any more; Granny Bunt was sitting in the doorway of her cottage, shelling freshly gathered peas, shining in the bowl on her knee. A gate rattled somewhere, the postman with the mail, all so real in her imagination that she even thought she heard the whine of his dog. Listen hard enough and it will all come back, she told herself.

Perhaps it had never really happened, perhaps it had only been a dream, and she really was here, a child again, waiting for her dad to come home. Could she hear the soft dip of an oar, the scrape of a rowlock? Perhaps if she opened her eyes just a peep she would glimpse the bow of his boat and see the tall blue-clad figure standing, legs slightly apart for balance as he sculled up the channel.

Through the veil of her lashes, came the sun dancing on blue water, and there was a boat...a man! Her heart lurched, eyes wide open now, a hand up to her mouth because he really was coming up the creek, sculling a green dinghy, his back to her....but there was a dog in the bows. It was the skipper coming to look for his boat.

Her fantasy faded into cold reality.

****

Nothing calms anger like curiosity and all the rage and blasphemy Nick Bonet had ready for the boat thief he was hunting down melted when he saw the girl's frightened stare. She was only a slip of a thing, a face as white as the clay up river, dressed like a hiker, but she was too lost-looking to be one. Besides, there was no Primus stove hissing and the usual camping litter scattered about.

Even so, she was the culprit. He could see the *Dipper* hanging from the jetty ladder. But what really startled him was how she had managed to reach the head of the creek, when only a local or a boatman would have found the channel through the silt? She must have somebody with her, some varmit from over Trefoy out for an evening's courting, and lurking back there in the boathouse.

He fumed afresh, thinking of the toil he'd had coming up here with the tide, having to pole each time the dinghy scraped the mud, having to wait for the little eddies to lift her afloat, then another pole, another wait. Matelot had been whining his impatience to be ashore, but was instinctively aware that those grey mudflats were too soft to hold his weight. Now with the tidal flow carrying the *Dipper* into the slipway pool, he was able to splash through the shallows for the woods, to leave his scent on the tree trunks.

Nick eyed the girl coldly as he came ashore, lines of displeasure creasing his sunburn. "You make a habit of stealing people's boats?" he asked tartly.

He saw her mouth drop open and two pink spots begin to deepen into her pale cheeks. "I didn't steal her," she protested.

"Then what's she doing tied up at the jetty over there?"

"I only borrowed her," she said, "I didn't think you'd have minded. I was going to bring her back, but the tide..."

"Minded!" he roared. "I minded alright, especially last night, getting my brother-in-law home to St Ruan in a leaky old boat. You should have seen the state of his suit, and heard what his missus had to say about it. You could be 'ad up for borrowing people's boats! You know that? Only down here they call it thieving."

"But local people always borrow their neighbours boats when they can't get home across the water."

"And you're a local, I suppose," he said, casting a glance at her white bare legs hanging prettily over the window ledge. "And home across the harbour! Whose home? Certainly not yours." His gaze travelled past her to the broken window spars. "So who's the varmit you're hiding back there in the boathouse? Come on, let's have a look."

She slid down from the ledge, standing back to watch him shoulder against the remaining spars, splitting the wood apart for easy entry.

"Come on, out you come!" he cried, swinging himself in through the gap.

Then he pulled up short, taking in the heap of sail cloth, hollowed in the centre where she had slept, the lamp with the glass cleaned and the Woodbine tin with two spent matches on top. His gaze travelled along the bench to a crumple of sandwich paper, to the haversack hanging over the cupboard door, to the dinghy, draped with cobwebs, tilted on its side, dry as the dust it had collected. He could see nowhere for anyone to hide. She must have spent the night here alone, but what baffled him was how she had managed to navigate the channel. It was uncanny.

He turned round and saw her looking at him, piercing blue eyes, full of resentment as if he were the intruder, and she was the one who had the grudge. He climbed back into the sunshine and, facing her, demanded. "Just what are you doing here?"

"I've come home," she answered, a sadness clouding her expression. "To Granny Bunt – but she's not here any more."

"Granny who?"

"The old lady, who used to live over there."

He followed her glance to the old cottage across the water. "That place has been derelict for years," he said, the eerie feeling returning. "These tenancies belong to the Pendowry estate, part of the old manor house, up there through the trees."

"I know, "she said. "I used to live here. My father was the river pilot."

Nick's eyes widened. The pilot's daughter! Little Charlotte Ives, who died up country! Christ! They said this creek was haunted! But she'd be making it up. She'd read it somewhere, been talking to someone.

"Now don't lie," he said, "I know that's not true because she's dead. 'Been dead years up country. I heard so only last night in the Pirate Inn."

Charlotte stared at him aghast, her blood running cold as it suddenly occurred to her that perhaps the yesterday of her fantasy was really today, her today and not his...if Charlotte Ives was dead... The notion sent the strength draining from her knees, and she saw the trees and the water blurring into one.

Slowly it all came back, and she was sitting against him on the bankside, his handkerchief wet with river water dabbing at her forehead.

"Better?"

His voice seemed hollow, unreal, but the strength was returning, the faintness leaving her.

"I expect I'm hungry," she murmured, "I haven't eaten since yesterday."

She rested her face against his jersey, feeling great comfort from the smell of the rough warm wool, the protective shelter of his encircling arm bringing back her confidence, dissolving her silly confusion with past and present.

"I'm not dead," she told him, "I'm still here."

"Course you are," he said gently.

Poor little thing, no ghost, warm flesh and blood, she was, and full of some great trouble which he, in his blundering way, had made no easier. He should have questioned her more closely before he judged, listened to her story as he was doing now, blurted out to him, between tears and nose blows into his handkerchief.

She told him of hating London, homesick for Cornwall, and how her stepmother's one object was to prevent her ever coming back. By arranging for her to go to Australia she might have succeeded, had Charlotte not swapped places with a friend. At first Nick had found this hard to believe and was beginning to suspect the Pendowry fortune was the real reason behind her homecoming. But it was soon obvious she knew nothing of her inheritance. All she wanted was to settle in the port where she was born.

Not once did she mention her stepmother's acquaintance with the lawyer, apparently knowing nothing about that either. This made him wonder if there wasn't some truth in the Trefoy rumours of a conspiracy. That would account for them packing her off to Australia. They could have tricked the old man into changing his will, and didn't want her to find out about it. It could have been Ellis who told Jake Vardo she was dead. He saw to the lawyer's boats, did jobs for him, fuelling up his cabin cruiser and baling out the dinghy. If Ellis wanted to put a rumour round who better to tell than that old busybody.

Nick had never had any particular liking for the up-country lawyer. He had watched him in the local bars, sipping brandy with his clients; the servile stoop, the thin smile, the narrowed eyes, shifty, mean, as he counted his change. It was said he was a clever man. And so he would have to be to outwit the miserly Silas Trevelyan. But at this stage it was all supposition, there was no real proof. No proof either that the girl was the late river pilot's daughter, even though it would make sense of her getting the *Dipper* down the creek, but that he would only believe when he had seen it for himself and sounded her out on some local knowledge.

He was pondering over a question to ask when Matelot came scampering back with a stick in his mouth, and flinging it down at their feet, lifted his laughing tongue in command. The girl picked it up and threw it for him into the slipway pool. Splash, retrieve and he was back, his shaggy fur dripping, and the stick at her feet for another throw.

"He'll have you at that all day."

"I don't mind. He likes to play in the river."

"You know what it's called – this river coming down into the creek?"

"Pendowry Water," she answered promptly, and picked up the stick for the dog again. "It flows all the way down from Lanreath, through the valleys and the woodlands. At one time it used to turn thirteen watermills on its way."

"Thirteen?" He frowned, trying to remember how many there were dotted down the valleys.

"There's a legend about them," she told him.

"Oh, yes," he said, encouraging her to go on.

Matelot, tired of waiting for her to throw the stick again, rested his wet nose on her knee and she stroked his silky head as she continued.

"My Uncle Silas used to tell me the story when I was young, how his great-uncle, Jonathan Trevelyan, built the watermills, then quarrelled with his son Brig, who thought a thirteenth mill would be unlucky – which it was when you look at the family history. Brig, who was hanged as an outlaw, had always blamed his misfortunes on that thirteenth watermill, and before he died he put a curse on the family, swearing that one day Pendowry Water would swell into a great torrent and surge down the valley, taking with it, all the watermills, the manor house, the tenancies – everything in its path and many Trefoy townsfolk would be drowned."

Nick smiled. He had heard about the curse on the family, but the yarn she weaved around it sounded like something from the Brothers Grimm.

"You read that in a book."

She shook her head. "It's not in any book. It's a legend Uncle Silas used to tell," she insisted. "He really believed it. My father said it was as though he was looking forward to it happening. It was how he wanted to die, to drown like his brothers who had all been lost at sea. But he was a cripple. He only had his dreams."

Nick's smile faded. The girl fascinated him. She was hard to doubt. Obviously she knew more about the Trevelyan family history than he did.

"I think I had better take you back to the yacht with me," he said. "Give you some breakfast. I've some fresh caught mackerel aboard, and only the dog to share 'em with. Later we can find out where your neighbour Granny Bunt is now living. My sister Joanne will know."

She lifted her eyes to him, tempted at the thought of white fish, buttered crisp and eaten afloat. "That's very kind of you, mister..."

"Nick – Nick Bonet. Skipper of the *Cape Columbo*," he told her, "You're welcome. So while I knock back these boards over the window, you'd better fetch the *Dipper*. Take the dinghy."

He stood watching her pull free the painter, wade with it and swing herself aboard. Then he smiled, noticing how she stood astride to scull away with one paddle like the locals did, and how, when she reached the *Dipper*, made the dinghy fast astern before casting off. He waited for her to start the engine – always a cuss first thing, watching as she cranked it without response. But not for long. She soon had the lid off and was flooding a little petrol into the carburettor. Good girl! Then the engine was away, blue smoke hazing up behind the transom.

"Proper job!" he complimented her, as she brought the *Dipper*, with the dinghy bobbing behind, into the slip. He whistled the dog. Matelot bounded aboard and Nick seated himself up in the bow beside him, leaving Charlotte at the tiller. "Now let's see how you shape getting her back to the yacht," he said.

Hotly aware of his scrutiny, she reached for the gear lever and the engine roared as they went astern, then, throttling low she swung the bow round to head back, praying her knowledge of the channel would return to her. He still didn't believe she had brought the Dipper up the creek on her own. He wanted to see her do it for himself, but he couldn't have chosen a more tricky time to test her skill – half tide, when the mudflats were only just covered.

The creek was languid. Hardly a breath of breeze to stir the ripples. On either shore the giant trees stood motionless, their great branches overhanging and dipping into the shallows, lazy sunlight filtering through, dappling a pattern on the brown water. Charlotte peered ahead, looking for movement of current, of colour changes, of the tell–tale grey silt near the surface, and all the time keeping a calculating eye on the distance from the bank. The skill she had learned from her father was coming to her now, almost as though he was there beside her, his hand over hers on the tiller.

Occasionally, she felt the bow pad the mud, warning her of shallows and misjudgement, but her response was sharp, her action prompt. Soon they were rounding the last bend into rippling water, a puff of breeze in their faces as the creek headlands broadened out into the wide Trefoy estuary, with dancing craft and beyond, the white houses, climbing to the trees on the skyline.

Now, with a swell of pride she bent to the throttle to pick up speed, and the *Dipper* lifted to it, with a crisp bow wave and a mist of spray.

"Not bad for a river pilot's daughter!" Nick shouted above the engine roar.

She looked up and saw he was smiling, the peak of his white topped cap, tilted up from the sun blond quiff of hair. Not at all like her father really, but handsome she decided, returning his smile. "Good job I remembered the channel."

"If you hadn't – I'd have murdered 'ee!" he cried. "Now head for the big schooner just astern of that blue cabin cruiser – see her? Careful you don't miss the tide."

"I won't," she answered, watching the great round hull of the *Cape Columbo* looming ahead. Her red sails had been stowed and her rigging climbed in tall spires against the blue sky.

Nick stood ready with the boat hook, leaving the girl to bring the *Dipper* alongside, unable to credit her seamanship. He watched how she steered astern, judging the tide to bring them in just right for the portside ladder, leaving him now in no doubt that her story was true.

On board Charlotte found herself standing under an archway of shrouds, a white scrubbed deck beneath her feet. It smelt of tar, hemp rope and sun warmed combing. She looked out for a moment on the river front; the moored craft, the tugs and dredgers, the yards and jetties ashore, St Ruan harbour, the white terraces of Trefoy, and she suddenly remembered Rachel seeing her off at Paddington. The thought brought a bubble of triumph as she hurried after Nick down the companionway to the galley.

****

Across the water in his office in Trefoy, Richard Ellis was making a telephone call to a certain Dave Weller in London.

"Listen Dave," he said. "There's something I would like you to get done for me. This evening the *Orion* leaves Southampton for Australia. There's a woman travelling to Sydney with a young girl companion. She's a Mrs. Millicent Potter, lousy with money, but it's the girl I'm interested in – Charlotte Ives ... No, I don't want them tailing, I just want you to check that they are on the passenger list at Southampton and still on board when the ship leaves both Lisbon and Gibraltar ... If they're not I shall want to know what's happened to them... You can send one of your agents out there. Put a good man on it – I don't care a damn what it costs ... Good! I shall look forward to your report."

The conversation over, Ellis replaced the receiver.

CHAPTER FIVE

"Rachel was back here – in Trefoy?" She was staring at him, eyes round in disbelief.

"Seen at Easter," Nick told her.

They were sitting in the saloon, elbows on the table, plates cleaned up, but for the mackerel bones, a faint haze from the sizzling butter still drifting in from the galley.

"She couldn't have. At Easter she went to Bristol – to see Richard."

Nick raised his brows "Richard?" he asked curiously.

"One of her men friends. I don't know his second name. I only heard her talking to him on the telephone." She paused, then said bluntly. "They go away together for dirty weekends."

He didn't look surprised. "She told you it was Bristol, but she was down here – with a man named Richard."

"But she'd never come back She hated the place. I used to plead with her to bring me, but she never would."

"Perhaps because she didn't want you to meet her fancy man,

" Nick suggested.

Charlotte didn't answer. She was thinking bitterly of the times she had helped Rachel to pack a suitcase for one of her weekends. And to think all the time she had been coming back down here. How could she have been so cruel? Leaving her behind in London, knowing how she longed to see Cornwall again.

She looked sharply at Nick. "Who is this Richard?"

"Richard Ellis is the Trevelyan family solicitor and the executor of Silas Trevelyan's will."

Charlotte's eyes blazed. "Rachel said Uncle Silas didn't leave a will! She said he'd died in debt and what was left had to be sold to pay the death duties."

Nick gave her a quizzical look. "Died in debt! Silas Trevelyan? He must have been one of the richest men in Cornwall; all the land he owned, the scattered properties, investments and trusts stashed away. It was all in the papers when he died. Now everybody is waiting to see what he was really worth when the will is published."

Charlotte was shaking her head. "And Rachel told me it was all gone, the estate sold up," she said bitterly.

"Not yet, it isn't. There's been people coming down here to view it, property developers from London, who, so the word goes, want to turn the creek into a boating marina."

She looked at him in horror. "Oh, they can't do that! Not our lovely creek..."

"They will if Richard Ellis has his way. As executor of the will, it's his job to dispose of the assets."

"On whose authority?"

"Your stepmother's, so t'is said, given on the day of the funeral, when the will was read."

Charlotte frowned. "But she didn't go to the funeral. I wanted her to take me, but she wouldn't. Said she'd already made arrangements for that week with...with Richard in Bristol." Her voice trailed off, the thought bringing a flush to her cheeks. "You can't be suggesting Uncle Silas left all his money to her!"

Nick shrugged. "That's what they say."

She stared at him in disbelief. "He'd never leave it to Rachel! He despised her. He wouldn't have her in his house. I was only a kid at the time, but I remember the rows there used to be."

"Of course," Nick said quietly. "There are those who say that you should have been the rightful heir."

She looked at him then without speaking; not daring even to voice her hopes as the old man's promise came back to her. She could see him now, his yellowed face carved with tiny wrinkles, his blue eyes, flint bright, resting on her as he told her that one day she would reign queen of Pendowry. "I know he once meant me to inherit the estate. But I can't believe he would leave it all to Rachel."

"But he did," Nick assured her. "The will was read after the funeral. It said so in the paper."

"Then it's a forgery!" she cried. "A trick! That's why she's been coming down here secretly and going to bed with the family lawyer – to get the will changed in her favour. She's always known she'd never get a penny from Uncle Silas, but she couldn't bear the thought of it coming to me. Don't you see? That's why she why she wanted me out of the way. She must have been afraid of me finding out. She'd know I'd dispute it. especially since she's selling the creek for a boating marina-" She broke off, tears smarting her eyes. "They-they must have put it around I was dead to shut the locals up, squash the rumours."

Nick felt suddenly annoyed with himself. It had not been his intention to upset her, only to discover the truth, first out of curiosity, now from concern. It was obvious there was a plot to deprive the girl of her inheritance, unthinkable conduct for a man who practised law, but what worried Nick was the lengths such a man might stoop, once he knew the girl was here and ready to expose him. Nick decided she was going to need both support and guidance if she was to contest her rights.

"Don't you worry," he told her, "They're not going to get away with it – not now you're here. You'll have to get proper legal advice."

"That costs money. All I have are the spends Rachel gave me at the station and the few pounds I've saved to live on until I get a job."

"Perhaps your old neighbour, Granny Bunt, would help you."

Charlotte nodded. "I'm sure she would," she said, her eyes resting on the river front and the blue sky gliding past the portholes as the schooner swung round on the tide.

Nick leaned sideways to glance at the galley clock. "My sister 'll know where to find her. If you don't mind staying aboard while I do a job on the engine, I'll take you up for supper with me and we'll see if the family can help."

Charlotte looked at him gratefully, "I wouldn't be any trouble?"

"Course not, but t'would do no harm to give me a few minutes with them first to explain – while you give Matelot a run along the cliff path. He'd like that."

Matelot, lying full length along the cabin seating, lifted a whiskered ear at the sound of his name.

"And I'd like that, too," she said, watching the slow wag of the shaggy tail. Then she got up and began collecting the plates and dishes. "You go along and work on your engine and I'll wash up in the galley."

"Proper job!" he grinned.

Nick spent the afternoon sprawled in the cockpit, bent over the auxiliary engine, Charlotte watching his oily hands take apart the faulty carburettor. All around them came the chatter of the tide against moored craft, gull cries and river sounds. The south-westerly breeze was bringing a slight swell into the harbour, and when she wandered to the foredeck with the dog, she could feel the lift of the bow, as though they were at sea. The blue waters glittered, diamond sharp, the wooded banksides a cool eye-rest from the glare, calming after the disturbing revelations the past hour had brought.

Just before five they went ashore, tying up the pram dinghy at the St Ruan jetty by a greasy petrol pump. Nick filled the cans and passed them down the ladder for Charlotte to stow away under the pram seat. The quayside was crowded; the ferry was in, packed with grey faced claymen in faded dungarees, visitors with sun hats and box cameras, waiting on the steps for the return trip to Trefoy.

Charlotte waited while Nick paid for his fuel at the chandler's store, then joined him as Matelot led the way up the flight of stone steps beside the Lugger Inn. At the top they turned and came into Fore Street, a lumpy strip of macadam, stained with gulls droppings, twisting up the hill. The pokey shops and tall, yellowed houses were built so close they appeared to be pushing against each other like a tumbling stack of cards.

It was all there, just as it was the day Charlotte left it behind; the smell of fresh splits coming from the bakery, next door greengrocery set out under a faded awning, dumpy women gossiping outside the Post Office, turning from its window full of small ads to nod to them.

She followed Nick into a labyrinth of passages. The alleyways rang with their footfalls, with singsong Cornish voices and the cries of gulls that swooped low from the strips of blue sky. Chimneys smoked over garden walls, cats slept on roof tiles, and over the open cottage doorways, hung seaboots and lobsterpots. The noise from someone's radio boomed into the sunshine, washing billowed above and below, the clean laundered smell catching on the wind as they walked by. Matelot padded ahead, the tip of his white shaggy tail swinging to the rhythm of his stride.

"He's a fine dog," Charlotte remarked.

"He's a villain," Nick answered. "Causes me no end of trouble. What with his passion for chasing sticks and his thievin'. You have to watch he don't pinch the pasty off your plate."

Charlotte laughed. "He's a real character!"

"And a pest!" said Nick, "I should have let him drown like he was meant to."

"Drown?"

"That's how I came by him. Fished him out of the sea off Newlyn harbour two years back. I'd noticed him about the jetties most of that summer. He belonged to some French crabbers who berthed there. They didn't want him when they went back to France, so they chucked him overboard."

"Oh, no!"

"You should have seen him swim after them. Kept up for nearly a mile. I'd been fishing in the *Dipper*, so I followed – just to see how far he'd get. He was too young to die, so I went up alongside him, gave him a whistle and wasn't he glad I pulled him aboard?"

"Poor old dog! How could they?"

"Trouble was, he didn't understand a word of English, but I remembered they used to call him Matelot. I was down the Med. all winter, so I had him with my ole mum in Newlyn. Since my dad was a Breton fisherman, I reckoned she'd get along with a Breton dog, but Matelot's such a thief she was glad for me to have him back. Now my sister is having to suffer him at meal times. There's where she lives..."

He nodded to the house at the end of the alleyway. It was double fronted, approached by steps up to an iron-railed veranda that looked out over the harbour. Below was a passage under a stone archway, the way down, Nick explained, to his brother-in-law's boatyard.

Matelot was already scampering towards the turnoff for the cliffs. "I won't be long," Charlotte called back as she followed him.

"About half an hour," Nick reminded her, turning into the house to face the family.

****

Joanna Marney's kitchen, by St Ruan standards, was remarkably well equipped. Jed had fitted a second hand Aga so large it heated the whole house. The floor had been set with tiles, dropped from a truck going too fast down the steep hill to the village. The shelves and cupboards Jed had built from off cuts he brought up from the boatyard, and tea coupons had provided enough willow pattern to fill the whole dresser.

Joanna was six years older than her brother Nick, with the same half-blonde hair and pearled teeth, looks that came more from their Flemish ancestry than from their Breton father. Her slim figure deserved pretty clothes, but she usually made do with washed out jeans and sloppy sweaters her hair rolled up in curling-pins – just in case Jed should decide to take her for a cider or to the pictures in Trefoy. It was not often he did. He was always out fishing in the evenings or making up the choir during scrumpy sessions at the Lugger Inn. Life, it seemed to Joanna, was all cleaning up the kitchen, to mess it up again in time for the six'o clock meal.

This particular evening Jed had come home early, bringing his fisherman friend, Luke, with him. Drawn by the warm smell of baking they had already taken their places at the kitchen table, and Joanna, her damp dish cloth skirting their jerseyed elbows, found she was not only cleaning up flour, but hot ash from their pipes as, oblivious to her, they droned on about the mackerel shoals moving down the coast. The family meal seemed to be gathering more places at every sitting, what with her kid brother just back from France with the appetite of a mating bull, to say nothing of his thieving dog ever ready to lap the food off the kids plates. Now here he was with news of yet another mouth to feed, some maid he'd found in the creek, who said she was the late river pilot's daughter.

"You won't be bringing her to dinner because she's dead," she told him. "Everybody in St Ruan knows that."

"T'is her right enough," Nick insisted, helping himself to a warm saffron bun before Joanna swept the tray from his reach.

Jed was giving him a puzzled, sideways glance. "You said you found her up by Pendowry Water?"

"Up by the old boathouse. sitting dangling her toes in the pool," Nick answered, with his mouth full.

Fisherman Luke puffed thoughtfully at his pipe, humour glinting in his close set eyes.

"Australia. Didn't want her to find out about the will did they?"

Jed looked puzzled. "They?"

"Rachel Ives and the Trefoy lawyer. All the talk in the pub last night. Just before you came in."

Joanna swung round from the stove. "Course' If that girl isn't dead, she will be the rightful heir."

Nick dried his hands on the towel behind the kitchen door. "Wait until you hear the whole of it," he said, and proceeded to give them the full account of Charlotte's story and the rumours circulating among the Trefoy locals. As he expected the family response was of indignation and their full support for the girl.

"I never trusted that Trefoy lawyer," said Jed, "Something evil about him. She will have to watch who she gets to advise her? These bally solicitors are all in league with each other."

"First," said Nick, "We have to find this old neighbour, who'll help her. I was hoping you'd know where she lived. She might shed some light on it all."

"Someone will know," said Joanna, "Meanwhile the maid needs a place to stay, quiet, away from wagging tongues."

Jed nodded in agreement. "The last thing is for the lawyer to find out she's down here. He's a bad bugger. You never know what he'd do."

"That's just why I'm going to offer her the bosses bunk aboard the *Cape Columbo*," said Nick. "That cabin's going spare until I get word he's on his way down here. Suppose we put it round she's his daughter over from the Med. That would account for her borrowing my boat last night."

"He's right," said Jed, "No place better."

Joanna didn't look too sure. "Suppose somebody should recognise her?"

"What – in nine years?" said Nick, "She's not a kid any more. Quite the young lady, just like any of the summer yachting folk visiting the port."

"Then you mind you behave yourself, boy," she warned.

"Me!" Nick exclaimed innocently, spreading his hands.

She turned back to the stove as the others joined in to taunt him. Tomorrow she would see the vicar – he might know where old Mrs Bunt was living, and Annie at the greengrocers, she used to get beans and cabbages from her. She'd be sure to know. The girl needed help and advice, somebody to look after her. Her poor mother would have wanted that, expected it from the people of St Ruan. Here was true Cornish heritage at stake, and being denied to a true heir by treachery.

Through the kitchen window she caught a sudden glimpse of Matelot panting down the field path from the cliffs, the girl swinging along behind him. She had grown up, no longer a little maid Joanna used to watch leaping from boat to boat, but, as Nick said, quite a young lady.

CHAPTER SIX

Jack Lavelle nodded to the London taxi driver to keep the change, and followed the porter with his luggage into the crowded lobby of the Strand Palace Hotel.

"I have a reservation," he said at the desk. "The name's Lavelle."

The receptionist lifted her sleek auburn head to meet his glance.

"Mr Jack Lavelle?" she asked, a flicker of recognition behind her smile. This was the American, the one who had telephoned from Marseilles to confirm his booking. She remembered taking his call. London was full of Americans over for the Coronation; they came from New York, Boston, Chicago, but an American from the South of France – that had a romantic sound to it, not easily forgotten. "Of course, sir. Would you like to register?"

"A pleasure, ma'am," he answered, reaching for the pen.

"You're in Room 112 on the first floor," she told him, and turning to the keyboard, produced, with his key, a small yellow envelope. "And there's a telegram for you, sir."

"There is?" He took it from her quickly, leaving the key on the desk. "I guess this is what I've been waiting for," he said, tearing it open.

The girl eyed him approvingly, liking his looks; He was tall, well built, with crisp curly hair brindled black and silver. Not old though, she decided, mature would describe him better. The crinkles in his tan probably came from scowling into sunshine – sunshine, by the look of his well-cut clothes, he could easily afford. His taste was good, too; the blue of his tie toned exactly with the fine weave in his blue suit. He looked the kind of man who would always have exactly what he wanted, the eyes said so, the long firm mouth was too hard to give in to refusals.

Lavelle was oblivious to her interest. He was too busy studying the strips of ticker tape pasted across the telegraph form, news from the private eye he had engaged in Marseilles.

It read:

RACHEL IVES LEFT TREFOY FOR LONDON WITH DAUGHTER 1944 STOP SHE RUNS DRESS SHOP CALLED THE SALON 96 DALTON ROAD FULHAM TELEPHONE FULHAM 0385 STOP DAUGHTER STILL WITH HER STOP THEY LIVE OVER THE PREMISES STOP

LISETTE.

"I hope the room will be to your liking, sir," the girl was chatting on. "We're pretty full. Everybody is; with the Coronation, you know."

He nodded. "I guess so. The room will be just fine, but say, do you have car rental facilities?"

"There's a firm here in London who do it. Godfrey Davis, I believe. But you're not going to see much of the Coronation from a car."

The hall porter, overhearing, moved to his elbow, quick to break up the girl's overtures for a chat up. "They are first class cars, sir," he said, "Ford Zephyr, six cylinder engine. Would you like us to make the arrangements for you?"

"I sure would," said Lavelle. "How soon?"

"First thing in the morning?"

"Great. Then you will need my driver's licence"

"If you have it, sir. Thank you."

Lavelle slid his hand into his inside pocket and produced his international licence and, with a ten-shilling note tip, handed it to the man.

The porter beamed. "Thank you indeed, sir. I shall have you notified immediately the car arrives."

The girl at the desk sighed. He'd be an ex-GI, looking up 'old flames' to make the most of the Coronation week, she deduced, and disappointedly watched him follow his luggage to the lift.

Once in his room, the door closed behind the porter, Lavelle read the telegram again. The message had sharpened his curiosity, intensified the trace of unease that had first prompted him to make the enquiry.

So Rachel was right here in London. She must have packed up and left after D-Day, maybe when she got word her husband had been killed. Well, he supposed, that would figure. What would there have been for a woman like her once the forces had moved out? But it did not support his earlier belief that she might have made her peace with the old man and sweet-talked him into changing his will in her favour, or perhaps that something might have happened to Charlie, leaving her stepmother in direct line for the inheritance.

But the wire said that the girl was still with her. They lived over the shop premises. So what the hell was going on? Why was there no mention of Charlie in the newspaper report?

He propped up the telegram on the dressing table in a place where he could see it, then turned to unlock his suitcase. On the top of the neatly packed shirts and underwear was a folded newspaper. It was a copy of the South Cornwall Gazette; given to him by the young Cornishman he had hired to skipper his yacht. He took it carefully and put it on the bedside table, then slid off his jacket, lit a cigarette and threw himself down on the bed to look again at the story on the front page.

WEALTHY RECLUSE DIES.

Wealthy Cornish landowner, Silas Trevelyan died this week at the age of 92. He passed away quietly at the historic Pendowry Manor, the ancestral home of the Trevelyan family since 1775. where he has lived as a recluse for many years..

Mr Trevelyan was crippled as a young man after surviving the wreck of his father's schooner when the vessel sank in a storm off the Trefoy estuary in 1878.

Lavelle skipped over the following account of the Trevelyan family history, over the various references to the property and assets, until his glance reached the name Rachel Ives. The paper described her as the deceased's only surviving relative, the beloved second wife of his late nephew, William Ives, and it said that she was expected to inherit the Trevelyan family fortunes when the will was published. That was rich!

Lavelle's finger moved on down the column of smudged newsprint. What puzzled him was that she was the only mourner listed. There followed the names of friends, villagers and local dignitaries who had attended, the names of those unable to attend who had sent flowers, but he could find no reference to Bill's little daughter, Charlie, the real heir.

He felt a twinge of guilt. He should have been back years ago; assuring Rachel was doing right by the girl. That much he owed to Bill, the least he could do, since it had been his decision that had resulted in her father becoming a war casualty. Bill Ives should never have been involved in the D-Day departure. That night he was off duty. There were other pilots who could have provided safe passage for the flotilla of LCTs to the river estuary, but that foul night with the sea like a cliff, it was Bill he wanted on the bridge beside him, Bill who had been his friend throughout the months he had been stationed in Cornwall with the US Navy Amphibious Force, a guy who had been like a brother to him.

They had been buddies from the onset; maybe because they had both been losers, each going through a private hell of his own that had nothing to do with the war. Bill was having trouble with his wife. Rachel, already the Yankee sweetheart of the waterfront bars, was giving him a rough time. Bill was a man who needed to talk, unload his frustration...unlike Lavelle himself, who could find no words for his own locked-in grief, and was only too glad to shut out his own his misery by listening to another man's sorrow. At that time he guessed it did more for him than getting stoned or dating the broads.

He had welcomed that pre-invasion posting to the remote Cornish port of Trefoy, where he had been able to devote himself fully to preparing his men for action.

His work on the river had brought him into close contact with the pilots, especially Bill Ives who lived in the dried out creek the navy used for storing ammunition and landing craft, the deeply wooded banks providing a perfect cover against enemy reconnaissance. Bill had been the guy who asked him over to Sunday dinner at his creekside home, who had taken him fishing in the evenings, sharing the kind of peace there was to be found in those quiet backwaters, sharing each other's thoughts as they waited for the bass to bite, for the tide to come.

Bill had been concerned about the family fortunes; the land and property jealously possessed and guarded by his miserly old Uncle Silas Trevelyan, on whose death Bill would be next in line. For Rachel that had been the plum, her key to the land of plenty, once she had Bill's ring on her finger. After losing his first wife, widowhood had been a worry to Bill. He needed a woman's touch, a mother for his kid; not quite Rachel's idea though, and the honeymoon was soon over. As for Charlie, she got more mothering from the old neighbour across the creek than she did from her stepmother, and she preferred her dad's company to Rachel's any day. Lavelle recalled her, a fair-haired eight-year-old, who used to ferry them about in the dinghy and tag along behind when they tramped the coastguard paths. Poor little Charlie! She would be almost grown up now, but he didn't see her living over a London dress shop, not of her own free will.

He flung aside the paper and twisted his arm to see his watch. It was gone six. They'd be closed up now. Would she remember him he wondered, the one guy who never made a pass at her? Well, there was a telephone booth in the lobby downstairs where he would sure find out.

Her voice hadn't changed much, the raised pitch with a bleat in it answering behind the clonk of the coin going into the box.

"Rachel – Rachel Ives? Remember me? Jack Lavelle – Lieutenant Lavelle back in forty-four? Friend of Bill's when we were over here in Cornwall. You remember, the one they used to call Frisco?"

He waited for her to answer, the silence striking him cold.

At last it came, a thin shriek. "Frisco!"

"You remember me?"

"I'll say!" she cried. "Where are you?"

"Here in London."

"London!"

"Sure! Got in an hour ago. It's mainly a business trip, but timed nicely for the Coronation. How about having dinner with me? Maybe we could talk over old times."

"Frisco – I'd love to!"

"Then how's about I pick you up at the shop around nine?"

"That would be lovely," she answered, her voice curious and slow. "You apparently know where I live."

"I sure do," He sang out. "Put on something slinky and could be we'll do the town."

"You're on!" she cried.

His eyes grew cold as he put down the receiver.

****

Rachel Ives's room in the flat above the salon was not luxurious, but tasteful, with jade green walls, damask curtains and a deep pile carpet. The divan was covered with rose-coloured water silk, the cushions a deeper shade to match the bedside lamp and tiny wall lights.

Rachel had slipped into a claret-red robe and was seated at her dressing table when the telephone rang. She had been contemplating her reflection in the oval, gilt-framed mirror. Fridays usually left her drained, shadows round her eyes, gone the rose-bloom glow of youthfulness and the carefree look of her twenties, her sombre beauty more mature, the rich dark hair that had once fallen about her shoulders now drawn back into a bun. The style accentuated the high cheekbones of her face, giving her a certain elegance, until the day's end when the strands loosened untidily about her neck. This was the hour when she was glad to hear the shop door close on the last of the girls to leave and she could escape to her own quarters, bathe, relax and repair the damage the day had done to her looks.

Now seated before her pots of creams and lotions, smoothing away the weariness, it was gratifying to know that these days of drudgery would soon be over and she could contemplate the leisure and luxury she had always wanted. It was incredible to think that in just a few weeks so much had been achieved; Charlotte safely out of the way, a buyer turning up for the salon, the purchase likely to be completed by the end of July, loose ends all tied up in readiness for the inheritance Richard had so cleverly secured for her. The thought sent her pulse racing, but more from unease than excitement at the thought of what they were doing. Guilt, she supposed, remembering Charlotte. But there was no need for remorse. It was for the girl's own good, she would benefit eventually. In her name the money would only have gone into trust, and been lost to them all. Not that Charlotte would have cared, she only wanted to get back to that stagnant Cornish backwater and not make anything of herself. This way she would see the world, broaden her mind, and with luck, Rachel hoped, be off her hands for good.

She drew a sigh. What she herself would have given for such a chance at her age! What she would have given even now! The Pendowry inheritance might be worth a fortune, but the disadvantage was what – or rather who- went with it. Richard Ellis round her neck for the rest of her life. That thought was another reason for her unease, together with the underlying dread of the consequences should something go wrong. The scandal would ruin her. No picking up her career again as she had when Bill died. Her trade centred around a handful of Kensington ladies, many widowed in the war and unable to afford haute couture prices. Nobody, they said, copied a Worth original like she did. They may not be so kind if she were to return to them fresh from stitching mailbags.

But she must stifle such thoughts. Richard knew what he was doing. Nothing would be left to chance. She must trust his confidence. Hadn't he told her she would be a millionairess? The idea gave her a sudden lift. Quite an achievement for little Rachel Higgins, of Golders Green, who left school at fourteen to work those long hours in her uncle's sweat-shop.

She remembered how she'd looked out from the top of a bus on passing limousines going into the West End, debs. with rugs over their knees in the back, a chauffeur up front. How she envied them as they stepped out of their cars at Harrods, their lives radiating wealth and self-assurance! They didn't have to stitch raincoats for a living.

"You want to be rich? Then marry well," her mother told her. "Make the best of yourself and look for a way into the rich man's world."

Following her mother's advice she had taken a night school course in dressmaking and fashion design, training in skills that were to land her a job in the West End – until the war came to spoil it all. A whisper in her ear when she was dancing at the Hammersmith Palais tipped her off to find a dependant – if she wanted to dodge the call-up. She did, and set off for Cornwall to nurse a bedridden aunt.

As a young girl she had sparkled with vitality, her looks fresh with a beauty fashioned in the era of Dorothy Lamour and Rita Hayworth; masses of glossy dark hair worn on bare shoulders, suiting the swing of her dirndl skirts and long brown legs. She was a girl every GI had an eye for and she won them in droves with her beckoning smile.

There had never been any shortage of men in her life. She thought of them now with a certain wistfulness, those she wanted and those who wanted her, those she could have loved – if they'd had any money.

Her marriage to Bill Ives had been useful until his damn fool heroics led him to his doom and left her stranded in that Cornish creek with his confounded child. In those days Richard had meant relatively nothing to her, but she had always been flattered by his constant attention and the way he wormed her way so cleverly into her company. A man with such ingenuity was always worth a second thought. They were the kind who usually made the grade, but she had no intention of becoming a solicitor's wife in a remote Cornish port. Yacht Club teas and the Women's Institute was not her!

Some of the Americans she had known in those days might have given her a good life, but she'd heard nothing more from them after D-day. The letters promised never came, the gifts from Paris, the invitations back to the States. But Richard Ellis, he had outstayed them all. He knew what she wanted – to be rich. So that was the ploy with which he chose to manoeuvre her into his life.

Now, taking down her hair and brushing it out over her shoulders, she found herself thinking about him more with irritation than pleasure; the dull life he would expect her to lead, certainly not the toast of the London social scene she would have liked for herself. He didn't share her love of London. On those rare occasions when he'd come up to town to meet her for a meal, he always seemed to be withdrawn, and uncharacteristically nervous. She supposed it might be due to some war memory – he never talked about the war. But she would miss the West End when they went abroad.

She had wanted him to come up for the Coronation, book them both into a hotel on the Royal route, with a balcony spot to watch the young Queen go by, but he'd made an excuse. Well, if he wouldn't take her to the Coronation, there were others who would. Hadn't Arthur Jenkins offered her a balcony seat in the building over his office at Ludgate Circus? Not quite the same as the Waldorf and he'd expect to be invited back to her flat, but with Charlotte away and Richard in Cornwall she might as well make the most of her freedom. She had been pondering over the idea of popping round for a gin and tonic with him in the Crown when she'd heard the telephone.

Now back in her room, she stood flushed and dazed, unbelieving. Frisco! He was the last one she would have expected to call her.

Her mind went back to the war years, Trefoy teaming with Yanks, the faces coming mistily; Tex from Houston, Ben from Cincinnati, Gary from Brooklyn...any one of them she would have expected to look her up, but not Frisco, the quiet Lieutenant, who never dated, never made a pass, who spent all his free time mooching around in the creek, fishing with Bill. It couldn't be him! Yet he'd been the one she had fancied the most, the one she could picture more clearly than any of the others; hard, handsome male, towering tall in his officer's uniform. Everybody knew she had a crush on him.

But of course! That was it! This would be a joke, somebody having her on, one of the old gang here for the Coronation, turning up to date her. That was more like it. Taking off the Lieutenant was just typical of their sense of humour. If it had been Frisco he wouldn't have been making remarks about a slinky dress and nights on the town. All he would have wanted was to give Charlotte a day out at the zoo.

She frowned, struck with a sudden thought. But suppose it was him, here to snoop! Suppose he'd heard about Uncle Silas passing on, about her coming into the money, but he couldn't have. It was only the Cornish papers that carried the story. Besides, if, in respect for Bill, Charlotte was his concern, he wouldn't have waited nine years to come back, he would have been over straight after the war.

What the hell anyway if it was Frisco? He was a man. She would handle him. With a confident toss of her head she swept to the wardrobe to choose an evening gown; the scarlet chiffon, no, the black crepe. She was going to look elegant.

She was smoothing on her best silk stockings, when from the depth of the salon the doorbell rang. The sound shocked her into haste. Wriggling her toes into her black court shoes, she gathered up her skirts and teetered across the landing. She was half way down the second flight when the bell sounded again.

Reaching the hall she flung open the door, a ready quip on her tongue for the clown who thought he could fool her. Then the fun died on her lips as she saw framed in the doorway, big, broad shouldered and just as handsome out of uniform, Frisco, giving her his smile, his tanned features greenish in the blue mercury arc lighting from the street.

"Rachel!" His arms were wide. "You look great!"

She stepped back in astonishment, a sharp breath caught in her throat as for a moment, she could only stare open mouthed at him. Then she grabbed hold of his hands and pulled him into the hallway to look at his face.

"My God! It *is* you!" she gasped, "I thought somebody was having me on! Come on up, let me give you a drink!"

Lavelle called back to the cab driver to wait and followed her up the two steep flights to her flat.

CHAPTER SEVEN

"Now, what is it to be?" she gushed, "Scotch? Gin? I'm sure we've time for a gin and tonic."

"We sure have," Lavelle answered. "I have a table booked for nine-thirty. A place I know just off Sloane Street."

"Lovely," she enthused.

He sank down into a soft armchair and surveyed the room; reasonably well furnished, but not particularly well kept; dead flowers in a vase on the window table, dirty ashtrays and trashy magazines scattered about the chairs. Cheap prints of London scenes looked down from walls bright enough to have been newly decorated, but he saw no framed photograph of Bill's fair-haired daughter, in fact, there was nothing in the room to suggest her existence. It was all Rachel.

"How's Charlie?" he asked.

"Charlie? Oh, she's fine!"

He couldn't see her face. She had her back to him, making herself busy at the cocktail cabinet, full of sudden haste, snatching at bottles. He sensed he had touched a nerve.

"I bet she's quite a young lady now," he went on, probing. "Where is she? At college, maybe?"

"Not college –on holiday," Rachel said, without looking round. "I'm sorry, but I haven't any ice."

She was tipping the gin clumsily into the glasses, her mind in turmoil. She might have known he would be asking about Charlie. Would it be wise to admit the girl had been sent off to Australia? He must know something; otherwise he wouldn't be here. Why should he suddenly turn up after all these years? Could he have heard about the will? But *nothing* was published yet! There was speculation, of course, in the local papers, but nothing in the nationals. *Had* he been in Cornwall listening to pub talk? Of course not! She was jumping to conclusions. This was just panic. It was more likely that he was simply trying to be nice to her after what happened to Bill.

He was taking her in slowly. Still some dame, her fine figure enhanced by the black crepe of her tight fitting gown. He noted the wide thrust of her hips from a flattened belly, the long slender thighs, the peep of a shapely calf from the slit skirt.

She turned with the glasses, smiling, more at ease now, a glitter in her eyes matching the diamante earrings dangling above her bare shoulders. "Well, this is a surprise! How long is it? Nine years?"

"Almost to the day," he said, making room on the sofa table for the drinks.

"So it is!" She took an opposite seat and gave him her smile; the same old sparkle, although he could detect a flinty hardness in it now and, despite the heavy make-up, the lines round her eyes and at her throat gave away the years.

He raised his glass, giving her a toast and for a moment they drank in silence.

"Rough about Bill," he said quietly.

"Wasn't it?"

"I felt like shit after it happened. If I hadn't called him out…"

She cut him short. "No need to blame yourself," she said curtly. "Bill was a fool. He could have easily passed your call on to another pilot. The truth was there was nothing he wanted more than to get stranded aboard your landing craft. He liked heroics –it was his own damned fault he got killed." She swallowed back her gin and tonic and added, brightening. "But I got a very nice letter from your commanding officer."

Lavelle nodded, raising a smile to veil his disgust. Her attitude revolted him. But he was here for information, not for a fight. Having to suffer the woman was part of the price.

He groped for a way to change the subject. "So you haven't gotten yourself married again," he said, offering her a cigarette from a gold case.

"No," she answered cautiously, bending to the lighter flame, the halter neckline of her dress offering a deep view of her cleavage. "And you? Don't tell me you are all by yourself in London."

"I guess so."

She leaned back in her chair, studying him thoughtfully through the smoke haze. "How on earth did you find me?" she asked.

"The telephone directory – Rachel Ives, couturier – I guessed this must be you."

"But how did you know I was in London?"

"I didn't figure you'd stay on in Cornwall after the war. You came from the big city –I guessed you'd be back."

She smiled. "And here is me thinking you could have been in Cornwall and got my address from somebody down there."

He shook his head, quick to reassure her. "No ma'am! I guess I saw enough of the place during the forties." And anxious to disguise the real reason for his visit, he went on. "For the short time I'm here I have to be in London. And I wanna see the Coronation and take in a few shows before I go back to Marseilles."

She gave him a quick glance. "You're not over from the States then."

"Hell, no! I didn't go back after the war. Like a lot of other guys I stayed on in Europe. For a while I was just bumming around, then I got lucky and now I have my own business in Marseilles."

"What kind of business?"

"The cigarette trade." He gave her a steady glance; "It's quite lucrative. I live in style on the Cote d'Azure, a swell apartment, my own yacht."

"Really! How marvellous!"

He saw her neatly arched eyebrows raise a fraction. Same old Rachel, show her the colour of your money and you were halfway there.

"And fancy you remembering me!" she said, warming to him. Now she no longer believed he was here to quiz her about the will, she was ready to enjoy his company and amazed to discover that he was not only just as good looking but *rich!*

Of course, he looked older, his lean face lined, time scarred by war, by life, but it was his eyes that excited her, the look in them luminous with intrigue.

"Who could forget you?" he cried. "The American Forces sweetheart! You were the one gal in Trefoy every guy had an eye for!"

"Every guy except you," she said, with a provocative little smile.

He slowly shook his head. "Don't you believe it. I thought you were swell. But Bill was one of the pilots. I needed his help. I would have been crazy to make a play for his wife."

"Excuses, excuses!"

"But we were buddies!" Lavelle argued. "He took me fishing, had me over to dinner. Why should I louse it all up for a one-night-stand? But you, Rachel, you *were* a temptation."

"Was I?"

She was hardly able to hide her elation. So he'd had a fancy for her after all; aloof, laconic, unapproachable, but his feelings had still been aroused. He'd been as susceptible to him as the rest of them, even to the point of finding his way back to her after all these years. But of all the times to choose to re-enter her life, just when she was committed to Richard.

She smiled, meeting his gaze. "I always thought you were anti-social," she said. "You didn't go much in the pubs and hardly ever showed your face at the camp dances on Windmill Hill."

"How can you say that? I remember dancing there with you."

She nodded. "Once you did. It was an 'Excuse Me' quickstep and I cut in."

He grinned. "So you did" He had a sudden vision of her swirling figure, head held back, laughing, the long dark hair swinging behind her, and Bill's face like thunder because she been avoiding him all evening.

She looked wistful. "Then we had a slow foxtrot together before you marched me over to Bill. That was lovely, it was *Moonlight Serenade....*"

Her eyes met his, the look in them deliberate, coquettish, remembering.

He rose smiling, and reaching for her hands, drew her to her feet, his grip fervent, his gaze full of promise. "Come on," he said softly, "let's go to dinner, and maybe we can get the band to play it for us again."

The sudden warmth, the pressure of his palms, sent an internal quiver through her, inflaming quelled passions, awakening a need, a hunger for him. Why not she thought, for the hell of it! One last fling before she finally became just another property asset possessed by the Trefoy lawyer.

"I'll get my wrap," she whispered, twisting at his fingers as she broke away.

They dined by candlelight. They chose fillet steak with Béarnaise sauce, asparagus and a good burgundy, followed by a creamy desert, coffee and Benedictine. Rachel could not remember ever dining so well. About midnight they went on to a discreet little night-club in Mayfair, where they drank champagne and danced into the small hours to a dreamy quartet.

She felt intensely aware of him, the nearness. His breath warm with whispered words, brought in her a relaxed sensuality, and when they sat out, looking at each other over the champagne bubbles, he talked about his apartment overlooking the Mediterranean; the fine schooner he owned, large enough to sail the world if the fancy took him. He talked of London, the taste he had found for the city during the war years, lately revived, and how he was even considering buying a house opposite Hyde Park –if one day he should find the right woman to share it with him.

Rachel sighed inwardly, filled with anguish to think he had come back into her life too late, a man who could give her not just wealth but real happiness, a man whose eyes excited her, whose touch swept her with tides of wanting. Richard was an ape beside him, a blundering ape, cold and dull, a man she was only tolerating because of the fortune he was procuring for her through fraud and treachery. She was only accepting it because it was all there was. The youthful years of opportunity were now behind her, the dazzling front of sweet sophistication wearing thin, the machinist from Golders Green –stepped up to a Fulham dressmaker- was showing through.

"You're still a hell of a beautiful woman," he told her, as though reading her thoughts. "The years in London sure haven't changed you much. A little mature, maybe, less flighty, but I like it better."

"You're flattering me."

"The hell I am," he told her, clasping her hand across the table. "I still don't understand why you've never married again."

"A grown up daughter can sometimes be a little off-putting."

Lavelle tensed. Was the champagne loosening her up at last? Not once during the evening had she mentioned Charlie. Her conversation had been centred entirely on herself, her reminiscences of the war years in Cornwall, the hard work it had been building up a clientele for the shop in London. Not a word either about Silas Trevelyan and the fortune the papers said he'd left to her, news if it were true, he'd have thought she would have been only too thrilled to discuss. But it was a delicate area; one he'd noticed back at the flat when he first talked about the girl. Any move to stir the conversation back in that direction and she might latch on to it that he knew something. Now here she was doing it for him.

"How come?" he asked softly.

"Charlotte has never been an easy child. Bill had completely spoilt her, all that running wild on the waterside, it all came back on me. She was continually hankering to go back there, running away from home."

"Charlie a rebel! I don't believe it!"

"Oh, you don't know the half of it, the trouble I had with that girl! So wilful –just like her father. Sometimes I feel sorry for that woman who has taken her to Australia…"

She broke off, aware of making a slip, groping mentally for direction, her brain fuzzed by the champagne. She was drinking too much, but what the

Hell! He wasn't interested in Charlotte, he was interested in her, too busy looking into her eyes, she decided, and she went on to talk about her stepdaughter's sea cruise.

"It'll be a marvellous experience for her," she lilted, as he began to re-fill her glass. A chance to see the world, meet people with money, a life I could never have afforded to give her."

"So you're all by yourself in London."

"Aren't I?" she giggled, her eyes sparkling again."

"For long? When does she get back?"

"Never I hope," she said recklessly. "She only sailed last week – the Orion – Richard says it's like a floating hotel."

"Richard?"

"Oh, he's just a friend."

"Now it comes," he teased her, "I guessed a gal as irresistible as you would never be short of someone to go under the bed covers."

Her eyes sparkled again, the thought pleasing her.

"You're probing my love life."

"You bet I am."

The chat was automatic. His mind was elsewhere, fraught with a suspicion he needed to conceal. He had been right to worry about the girl. She'd been shoved off out of the country to keep her nose out of the pie. Rachel was behind it, but who was *this* behind Rachel, this Richard guy? Lavelle needed to know more about him, but she was being evasive again, cleverly veering the conversation back to Cornwall, romancing about the old times with her Yankie Sweetheart bedfellows.

"Do you ever go back there?" he asked, hoping to catch her off guard.

"Never," she lied, drowsily drunk.

"Not ever? You did have a house there?"

"*I* did? You're joking! That cottage belonged to Bill's flipping Uncle Silas, every damned stick and stone of it."

"Uncle who? Oh, sure, I remember! The old guy who lived up the hill, the one who hated your guts. Whatever happened to him, for Christsakes?"

She lowered her lashes. "Oh he died," she said, off handedly. "Years ago – deep in debt. What there was left of the ruins he lived in was sold off to settle it all up. So Richard told me. He lives in Cornwall."

Lavelle drew hard at his cigarette, his eyes narrowed against the smoke. He liked the way she substantiated her lies, by coming up with answers before they could be put, and so quick to inform him that the information had not been gained first hand. And here was this Richard turning up again – and in Cornwall, where she said she never went back!

He gave her a little inquisitive smile. "Who is this Richard? Do I have a rival?" he asked, topping up her glass.

"Oh, he's a dull solicitor," she said, watching the fizz dancing up.

Lavelle was suddenly thinking back. Could this be the lawyer Bill didn't trust, the one seeing her? If this was the same guy, then maybe there was a fiddle going on. Was this why they'd got rid of the kid?

Her voice came though her thoughts.

"Actually he's been fond of me for years. Always coming up to London to take me out. In fact, I'll tell you a little secret."

Lavelle switched his attention back to her, sharply. "Yeah?"

"He wants to marry me."

"He does? Has he any money?"

"Oh, quite a bit. He was the one who set me up in the salon. He's been pestering me for years."

"But you don't love him."

She wrinkled up her nose. "He's alright. But I'm always hoping I might do better," she said, with a meaningful lift of her lashes.

For an answer he slid his hand over hers, squeezing her fingers encouragingly.

She sipped her champagne, the confidence it induced bringing a liquid flow to her words, and she found herself talking more freely. Not about the will of course, that was her close little secret, but about herself, about Richard not wanting to live in London and not coming up to take her to the Coronation. Frisco was such an easy listener, the kind of man who generated a feeling of dependence, a man with whom she felt she could bare her soul.

They danced, his lips against her ear, wooing, teasing, jealously playing Richard down. To think he wouldn't take her to the Coronation! He was leaving her all alone in London on that wonderful day! What about that? Well, if Richard wouldn't take her, then he would. She was just the gal he wanted to do the town with, have beside him to see the Queen go by. Seats? He could get seats. To hell with the cost! They'd have the best position on the route.

"Frisco, darling! How wonderful!" she cried.

He gave her a tight squeeze, pressing kisses into her hair and wondered how many more promises he would have to honour before he could get her to completely open up? With luck it could all be resolved when he took her back to her flat and raped the truth out of her.

"Shall we go?" he suggested, holding her close to him.

His mouth plunged down over hers the moment they were in the cab, his tongue working, his hand sliding behind her, pressing her body into his, and they rode across London seeing nothing of the of the lights and the bunting swinging over the streets.

This time he didn't ask the driver to wait and she led him, trembling in her urgency, up the stairs to her room.

He took her with a crushing forcefulness, brutally thrusting his way into her, fired with a passion that came from anger and frustration more than endearment, but she swelled to him readily, glad of the burning, searing sweetness that brought tears to her eyes, arising in her a tiger-like ferocity. They fought like young animals, their naked bodies thrashing in the darkness, the watersilk coverlet slipping from the bed. The more he abused her, the more impassioned she became, spreading herself to be taken, giving herself to his iron embrace, wanting no escape from those long rapacious spasms of passion. She closed her eyes, matching herself to his rhythm, feeling herself dissolving into him, the delicious sensation of drifting as one being, riding a huge tide, spiralling to impossible peaks of ecstasy.

Later, lying with him, still wrapped in his body, languorous after the euphoria, she found herself thinking of Richard. In comparison he was nothing. This was a man in her arms, a man who could bring her on so beautifully, who could take her beyond any bounds of joy she had ever before encountered. But here, as she lay in his arms, breathing the sweetness of him, basking in his warmth, her mind was already wrestling with a way to escape from her commitment to Richard Ellis. But not for long, sleep was soon to envelop her, denying Lavelle the pillow talk and the answers he wanted.

There was a milk float standing in the street when Lavelle left the flat and he had to walk to Fulham High Street before he was able to pick up a cab. He was exhausted, depressed, but not defeated. He would have the truth out of her. It was only a matter of time.

CHAPTER EIGHT

Cornwall was having one of its dazzling blue days, a flag-flying breeze and sundance on the water. The ripples against the anchor chain of the *Cape Columbo* lifted her gently to the slight harbour swell. On deck Charlotte lay back, closing her eyes, drowsily listening to the tinkle of the halyards and the chatter of the tide.

These first few days in Cornwall had been sublime, magical days, everyone her friend, and even if there were still problems to be resolved, at least she now had Nick to help her overcome them. He treated her like a kid sister, and she had found in him the dependability of an older brother. She had become part of his family, accepted into his home.

Squinting through her lashes she could just see him on the foredeck. He was splicing some rope; the sleeves on his dark jersey rolled up above brown arms, furred with fair hair. Feasting her eyes on him brought a pinch inside, a flood of gratitude at what he was doing for her, especially his allowing her to stay aboard the yacht. Of course, this was only until they could locate Granny Bunt, whose whereabouts were still a mystery. Nobody seemed to know precisely when she had left the cottage or where she had gone. But Nick assured Charlotte that there was sure to be news of her soon. Meanwhile, she might as well make the *Cape Columbo* her home and, to protect her reputation, allow people to think she was the owner's daughter.

Charlotte loved the role and filled it with a certain confidence, busying herself about the yacht, adding a woman's touch on the furnishings. She polished the woodwork, laundered the settee covers and chintz curtains, and put freshly picked flowers in the galley. Nick had dug out some jeans and a Breton sweater for her and she spent four-shillings and eleven-pence on a pair of yachting shoes, completing the outfit.

Each morning she awoke with dusty beams of sunlight coming through the ports, making moving patterns on the cabin floor, but she was soon up helping Nick with the morning chores. In the afternoons they would take the dinghy and find a sandy cove to sunbathe, until she was tanned back to her original Cornish colour. Sometimes they would walk the cliffs to look for mushrooms and Matelot would bag them a rabbit to help eke out the Marney supper. But in the evenings they went fishing.

The good Whitsun weather had brought the mackerel shoals down the coast, and as the sun went down, the bay was dotted with local craft spinning and feathering for them. Some of the boatmen were even taking the visitors on fishing trips, and this gave Nick an idea, how he and Charlotte could raise some money for legal fees. Borrowing Jed's fishing boat, the *Flora Dora*, they soon had a regular trade, with Sally Stephens, the Trefoy Hotel receptionist recommending guests for fishing parties, while, Fisherman Luke offered his advice on where to head for a good catch.

Dusk would find them chugging homewards, Charlotte at the wheel, the taste of salt on her lips, her fingers sticky with mackerel scales and behind her the visitor's laughter lifting with the spray as they dipped and plunged over the harbour bar. Later, on the quayside, they would sit with the boatmen, selling their catch to the Trefoy landladies, and collect a small heap of shillings, plus enough fish to take home for breakfast.

Reflecting upon it now brought a glow of well-being, but at the same time, a twinge of sadness to think it could all end, if the owner of the *Cape Columbo* turned up or even worse – Rachel, on a visit to her lawyer friend across the water, should meet her face to face. But she mustn't think about such things, nothing must spoil the bliss of this lovely day.

Nick's voice stirred her from her reverie. "I hear they've got the bunting up for the Coronation over at Trefoy, archways of flowers, they say. D'you fancy going over to have a look?"

Charlotte sat up. "We could take Matelot for walk round the town."

The dog bounced up at the sound of his name and Charlotte went to bring the *Dipper* alongside.

"I hope Rachel hasn't decided to come down here to visit her boyfriend," she said, her voice raised as they skimmed across the water.

"She won't be down here this week – with the Coronation in London, where she can see it on television."

"She'll go up West to watch it. Get some bloke to take her to the celebrations. Him perhaps."

Nick grinned at her. "Well, you've a bloke to take you."

"Have I?" she said, feeling herself blush.

The ferry went by and the boat pitched as they crossed the bow wave, the spray coming up in their faces. Across the water came the peal of bells.

"Sounds like Sunday!" Charlotte cried.

"Bell ringers –practising for the big day," Nick told her.

The Trefoy quayside was lined with visitors and blue jerseyed boatman touting for business. Charlotte weaved the *Dipper* though their moored craft and two swans glided aside for them to nose into the jetty steps. Matelot leapt ashore as they tied up to the iron ladder. Up on the quay the town crier was swaggering about in his traditional costume, with cries of "Oyez! Oyez! Hear ye, hear ye!" much to the delight of the visitors, who were following him around with their box cameras.

Trefoy town was full of flowers, archways of them as Nick had described, ribbons and flags rippling above the crooked, overhanging streets, and there was the Queen's face smiling from every shop window. They strolled leisurely up the centre of the main street, as everyone did in Trefoy. At the newly opened gift shop, they stooped to throw pennies into the Wishing well, bubbling up from a spring in the corner. Charlotte looked down into the tiny pool and made a secret wish. Nick laughed and bought her a little brass Cornish piskey.

"To bring you luck," he told her as they left the shop.

They walked back to the beautifully decorated town square, its hanging baskets and flower murals, a dazzle of colour, but Charlotte was thinking of the home-made flags and wild flower displays she knew would be going up in St Ruan. How it reflected the wide division between rich and poor on the opposite sides of the river

Back on the quayside Matelot was dripping wet with a stick between his paws. He had found someone to play his game and now expected another round. Nick was about to throw it for him, when he paused, his eyes on three men standing apart from the crowd. One, who was doing all the talking, was tall, swarthy looking, with dark hair greying at the temples. As he talked, his two companions were looking out towards the mouth of the Pendowry creek across the harbour.

Matelot was bounding for the stick, but Charlotte had followed Nick's gaze as the three men now turned to walk slowly away from the quayside. The one doing the talking walked with a slight limp.

"Is that him?" she whispered to Nick. "Rachel's fancy man?"

Nick caught her arm, steering her away towards the steps. "Better keep out of his way. Rachel might have shown him your photograph."

Charlotte shook her head. "She didn't have any to show – not even the passport one. There was a recent school picture, but I gave that to Jenny."

Going back, Nick took the tiller. He was full of plans for the Coronation. How they could join in the celebrations on both sides of the river if they timed it right, and still finish up at the sailing club dance afterwards. They might even make a bit more extra cash by ferrying some of the revellers home across the water in the *Dipper*. Charlotte sat in the bow, her eyes shining, and thinking how incredibly good life was here in the old port again, especially with a handsome skipper to take her to the Coronation celebrations.

"You're sure you don't want to take Sally Stephens?" she said, ribbing him about the pretty receptionist at the Trefoy Hotel.

"When I've got the girl from the *Cape Columbo*! You don't get rid of me that easy, my beauty."

She laughed and they shared a long smile together, until the moorings came up and she leaned out for the wet line and marker to haul aboard.

Later, when the sun had gone down, they went ashore to St Ruan for the Marney supper. The harbour water was still, a translucent green, with glossy ripples, hardly stirring on the surface.

"It's been another lovely day," Nick remarked. "But the glass is dropping. It could rain for the Coronation."

****

It did, but Rachel didn't get wet. She was tucked up in her fox furs, pampered with fresh salmon sandwiches and sips of champagne, while the steady drizzle beat down on the awning above her. Below, umbrellas were bubbling over the heads of the crowd lining the glistening strip of London macadam, a crowd bobbing with policemen's helmets and limp little flags and when the procession arrived to complete the picture, the cheers rose so loudly she could hardly hear Jack Lavelle's whispers against her ear. But she could feel him, the touch of his breath sent tingles down through her thighs.

No man had ever given her so much, been more attentive or more impossibly exciting. He was all verve, exhilaration. It breathed from him, throbbed from his voice, from his touch. He was blood and flame and fever heat, and he wanted her, could never have enough of her. She could hardly believe she was living it all, but she was. Confidence in him was mounting, braced by his desire for her, his worshipping smile. Dependence on Richard Ellis was withering away, no longer important. Yet the greed in her, born out of the hard years, still glowed at the prospect of her coming inheritance, the liberty and the power it could bring her, but it all turned sour in her mind when she thought of the commitment it involved, shackled to a man she did not love. There must be some way to withdraw from her promise to him without having to suffer the inevitable backlash of his retaliation.

It was guidance she needed, someone clever enough to show her how to match the lawyer's cunning, someone as shrewd to find a loophole in the plan. She could think of no one more fitting to do so than Frisco, whose experience and business acumen had obviously brought him the success he now enjoyed, and from the impression he had given her, it had not been without some measure of ruthlessness. Not a man to be over-troubled by such scruples as playing fair.

Dare she trust him, seek his help? Why not? If he was going to marry her, how could she keep it from him? She would still inherit the fortune. Richard was already in the process of obtaining probate, negotiating the realisation of the assets; when eventually that was complete, the money would be hers. But her promise to marry him, over that she still had control.

If she were to point out that she did not love him enough to become his wife, that she could only see their marriage ending in disaster, offer full reimbursement for his efforts and generous compensation for his disappointment, would he be reasonable, she wondered? Or would he be as merciless in his spite as she feared? Could he already be holding incriminating evidence to use against her; a letter, perhaps, her handwriting cleverly forged as the will had been forged? To combat such vengeance she would need a man like Frisco.

Somehow she believed he would understand. If she were to explain that Richard had more or less forced her into the arrangement by proceeding with his plan without her consent; that she could have hardly have quarrelled with him when she was dependent on him for her livelihood, since the business in Fulham was in his name.

After all, the legacy had only been denied to her by an old man's spite. Left to Charlotte it would have been locked away in trust for years. This way she could give the girl every possible opportunity in these critical teenage years.

She had composed, rehearsed and argued it out with herself and, feeling word-perfect and confident, was awaiting one of those dewy moments as he lay intoxicated by her love, to play the scene.

****

Charlotte didn't see the Coronation, but she heard the commentary booming above the crackle on the Marney radio set, sitting with the family in the dark little parlour at the front of the house. Every home in St Ruan was tuned into the ceremony. It echoed from the houses into the damp narrow streets, the voices of John Snagg and Wynford Vaughan Thomas reaching up to the rooftops and shouted down by the gulls.

The low cloud carrying the rain up country had been soon to lift and a fresh breeze from the sea was drying the streets – streets soon to ring in song and celebration. People stood on their doorsteps and leaned over their balconies to watch the town band come marching down the hill, the furry dancers skipping along behind them.

Looking on, Charlotte was touched with emotion; the bump of the bass drum, the cornet section traditionally off key, the bandsmen's eyes set sharp on their tattered scraps of sheet music. Then suddenly the sun came out, flashing gold on the brass, picking up the dust on the shabby red-braided uniforms, and memories flooded back to her, of standing in this same place holding her father's hand as she was holding Nick's hand now. He felt her fingers tightening over his, and sensing her feelings, responded by sweeping her into the dance, bringing laughter through the tears as they skipped along to become part of that thundering Cornish rhythm.

Later they sat on the quay wall with the Marneys, Fisherman Luke and more of their friends, drinking toasts in cider, with splash of the swell behind them as the ferry came in. The pub radio blared from an open window with another chorus of *The Golden Coach,* the popular song of the Coronation.

"Don't you wish you were seeing it all in London?" Nick asked Charlotte.

"Not one bit," she answered.

In the evening they went across the water to watch the Trefoy celebrations. Here there were gun salutes from the yacht club, dinghy racing in the harbour and at dusk, a torch lit procession through the town. They followed the trail of smoky flares up to Windmill hill to light the first of the beacons, then danced at the sailing club until it was time to ferry the revellers to yachts and up–river landings. Coming back by the China Clay jetties, the water lay like a dark mirror, so vividly reflecting the lighted freighters it was hard to discern image from substance. Gliding through made a weird passage, like sailing into a grotto, strangely unreal, like a dream.

Was it all a dream? Charlotte wondered, snuggling closer up to Nick.

Would she wake soon to the square of Fulham fog, yellow against her bedroom window? But the feel of the salt breeze faintly imbued with burning driftwood, and the squeeze of Nick's arm around her was no fantasy of slumber. It was real.

"Enjoyed it?" he asked her.

"Loved it," she whispered.

They moored up the *Flora Dora* and returned to the yacht in the pram dingy. Nick rowed and Charlotte lay back in the stern, trailing her fingers in the water, watching the sparkles of phosphorescence fizzing away behind. This beautiful day was over now, the riverfront dark but for a pool of gaslight on Trefoy quay, and all that was left of the celebrations was a drift of smoke on the wind, left behind from the firecrackers and the paraffin flares, and the only sound yet another rendering of *The Golden Coach*, drunkenly off key, from an overdue reveller rolling his way home in the heart of the town.

But there was one light still burning on the Trefoy waterside, hidden behind the thick velvet curtains in Richard Ellis' study. He had seen nothing of the Coronation or the local celebrations, only heard and been irritated by them all day long; the tramp of feet past his window, the screech of Cornish voices, the incessant boom of that confounded band. It might have been more enjoyable if they had changed the tune occasionally, instead of sticking to that dreary floral dance which barely resembled the delightful song of his university days, one his favourite baritone used to sing. The persistent chant and the splutter of fireworks had completely disturbed his day, a day he had purposely set aside for his work on the Pendowry estate and his plans for the disposal of its assets, without the astute eye of his secretary, Harriet Couch, hovering over his shoulder.

Now at last it was quiet, the song of the last noisy reveller fading away into the maze of the town. His pen scratched across the page, the papers crackling under his hand, warmed by the reading lamp glow spreading over his desk.

CHAPTER NINE

Jack Lavelle blew long funnels of smoke towards the white embossed ceiling, hazing it blue. He could feel her warmly naked against him, hear her voice, low, confiding, spilling over with secrets. He had waited for this, worked at it, wooing, screwing, lavishing his money on her, and now it came, the answers to confirm his suspicions, the full disclosure of the conspiracy he feared, the very worst kind of betrayal.

It had been almost daylight when she began telling him about it. This time they were not in her flat, they were in his hotel room. They had danced until the early hours in a pokey Soho club and she was heavily wined and yielding, but even so it had taken matrimonial overtures before the truth finally began to emerge.

He lay now, one arm cradling her to him, his hand possessively cupping her breast, his palm moving over the hard nipple, keeping her sweet. There must be no falter in the confessional flow. But he didn't find it easy to hold down the disgust he felt as he listened to her trying to justify her own involvement in the Trefoy lawyer's scheme.

"If it had been left to Silas, I wouldn't have got a penny," she told him. "He would have cut me out. Left it all to Charlotte to be put in trust. I wasn't Cornish, you see, I was a foreigner from London. Just damned prejudice, it was. All Richard was trying to do was to put things straight."

"By talking to Silas about it, advising him," he prompted.

"Silas wouldn't have listened if he had. Silas never listened. You couldn't reason with him. But Richard was determined I shouldn't be done out of what was really mine. After all, as Bill's wife, the Pendowry fortune should have come to me."

"So how did Richard persuade him to make the will in your favour?" he ventured.

"Richard is a patient man, and he's clever – used to be a solicitor in London," her voice lowered to a murmur. "There was this counterfeiter he knew, down in the East End."

Lavelle drew a breath. Here it came. He feigned surprise. "He didn't!"

"He did!" she cried, "And it's never been questioned. That's why we had to get Charlotte away from Cornwall, away from local gossip and Silas' influence. We couldn't have her growing up demanding her rights and spoiling it all. That's why she's had to be packed off to Australia, so that she would never find out."

Lavelle closed his eyes, hot rage fuming within in, but he must not to let it show. He waited for her to go on.

"Of course, he hasn't done it all for nothing," she admitted.

"I guess so," Lavelle agreed, "And when you come into the inheritance he wants to marry you – that's the catch."

"Of course."

"Well, too bad! You've found another guy. He must have known it would always be a risk. He can't make you marry him."

"Oh, but you don't know Richard. He hasn't waited nine years for his prize, to see me walk away with it – Scott free."

Lavelle didn't doubt it, but he said, "He can't do a damned thing. Isn't the will already going through probate?"

She nodded and went on, her voice becoming a whine, "But he'll never let me get away with it, I know he won't. If I back out now he might say it was me who had the will forged and produce enough false evidence to have me convicted. That's the way his mind works. He has this thing about foresight, about always being ready with a counterplan if things go wrong. And if he can't get me done for fraud, he'll have me pushed under a bus. I tell you, he can be vicious!"

Lavelle inhaled his cigarette and stubbed it out into the bedside ashtray. Vicious! She thought he could be vicious! He sighed out the smoke as her voice moaned on, going over it all, tears, and her shoulders beginning to shake. "But I don't want to marry him, Frisco, it's you I want...."

His mind was racing, searching for words of reassurance. He was close now, the way ahead coming to him. He tried to sound tender. "Here, take it easy! Look who you have on your side. Remember me, the tobacco runner from the Med.? Don't I have some goddamned contacts in the London underworld, enough to put the frighteners on him?"

She lifted her eyes to him, her face wet, not pretty. "Do you? Oh, you've got to help me, Frisco."

"And I sure will, baby. Trust me, we'll work something out. Do you imagine that after all these years I'm going to give up you for that bum lawyer. Let him spoil it all for us?"

He buried his lips in her neck, and feeling her sighs, he slid his tongue between her lips, then turned over on her, covering her with his body for another of those flaming, relentless passion trips she so enjoyed.

****

Afterwards she slept, but his mind was too full of the fraud he had uncovered, too sickened by it all to sleep. To think how they had treated Charlie; how they had plucked that little sea urchin from the waterside she loved, forced her to live in a city she must have hated, then shipped her off abroad with strangers because they thought she might get wise to their lousy game. By the time she had found her way back, they would be safe in the sun somewhere. They didn't care a shit what happened to her, either of them.

But hadn't Bill seen it all coming, Lavelle recalled as he lay watching the shadows lift from the room. Dawn was breaking, the early June light filtering through the net drapes covering the windows, reminding him of another June, another dawn, and almost nine years ago to the day.

Omaha Beach, June 6th 1944; spurts of small arms fire kicking up the sand, LSTs lurching in, assault craft, troops waving rifles above their heads as they charged through the breakers, scores of them dropping, riding in face downwards on the incoming surf. He remembered how the cries of the wounded had been lost under the roar of bombardment and how the damp sand had been churned up with bootprints where Bill lay, his jaw smashed, and too many damned holes in him.

They had been under fire from the German shore defences the moment their LCT came into the beach, a beach already jammed with wrecked landing craft and burning vehicles. Bill got it when he went to push ashore a stalled jeep that had been blocking the way of the DUKWs going off the ramp. Lavelle remembered seeing him fall, seeing the tank crew bending over him, one yelling for a medic. He remembered running through the shallows, his one thought to get him back aboard and beat to the hell out of it. Not that there would have been much chance. Minutes later, other LCTs coming in behind had rammed into theirs as one of them struck a mine, and some of the hulks, coming broadside on, had created a logjam, blocking any retreat back out through the beach defences.

Machine gun fire coming across from the high bluffs winged past him as he ran towards the jeep. Ducking down behind it, he saw Bill slumped on the ground, crewmen with him, crouched to avoid the crossfire overhead. He remembered how the river pilot had gripped his wrist, urgent in his need to communicate, but the injury to his jaw had made speech impossible and the only way to read his mind was from the expression in his eyes. Moments later Bill died, his last words unspoken.

Now, pinned down behind the jeep, bullets clanging and ricocheting from the steel doors, Lavelle had time to think of little else but his own survival. Close by, mortar shells were bursting along the beach, throwing up enormous sand sprouts which rained stones and debris down on them, while from the sea the fast coming tide was quickly washing up, showering them with spray. The tank sergeant was urging them to make a dash for the sea wall where others were taking cover, but the first tank crewman to make the move was whacked by a bullet that dropped him dead.

It didn't deter the sergeant. "Come on! We gotta take our chance! We can't stay here. We're sitting targets!" he yelled at them. "We got two chances. Either we get picked off by those motherfucking bastards or we drown!"

One of the soldiers was looking towards the sea, more assault craft coming in farther up the shore.

"Say! Here's our chance! When they draw the fire, be ready to move."

Lavelle remembered lying flat on his belly as he watched them come, struggling in through four-foot waves, encumbered by their heavy equipment. The surf racing in ahead of them was rolling in wet bundles, bodies lifted from the sand. That was where he saw his escape. He didn't belong up the beach with the soldiers, his way was back through the sea. Floating among the dead he would no longer be a target.

Fifty yards out was his own ship, jammed beneath the wreckage of other craft that had been blown out of the water when the LCT struck the mine. Most of it was already submerged, but one vessel had been heaved up on end, stern first, its load of tanks tipped into the heap upon which it had come to rest. Now its blunt-nosed bow poked out of the island of wreckage like a tower block. That would offer him cover from the beach fire and somewhere to climb from the advancing tide – if he could swim out there.

As the others made off he rolled over into the shallows and waited for the surf to thrash over him, lift him into the swell, where he tried to keep afloat with the carnage all around him, hoping to be taken for another corpse by the snipers firing at anything that moved. He didn't believe he would ever live through it, but he did. He seemed to be hours in the water, swimming for his life, but the sea was ice cold and rough and it was all he could do to keep his head above the breaking waves, the weight of his clothes dragging him under. Gulping for air, he would hold on to bits of debris, dead men, anything thing that would keep him afloat, but with the tide against him progress was slow. When he finally reached the wreck he was so exhausted, so numb with cold, that he only wanted to die.

He remembered dragging himself over an upturned hull, green seas crashing down on him, then sweeping him off, smashing him against a protruding bulkhead of another wreck. He remembered crawling, slithering over wet steel, looking for handholds, until he found a rail to pull himself up the near-vertical deck. Below he could see corpses still sprawled in their own blood over the wrecked tanks and cargo, the place reeked of diesel, vomit and burnt cordite, the wet wind leaving an oily shine on the twisted steel. Only the rattle of small arms fire and the crash of the seas intruded upon his isolation. Finding no one still alive he climbed over a hump of kitbags and slumped down against them.

He knew there would be a long wait for a boat to take him off. Landing craft coming in weren't stopping for survivors, any more than he would have done. Those had been his orders. All he could hope for was a rescue launch, medics looking for casualties. All he could do was lie there, wet and shivering, cursing himself for his misfortune. Why did things always have to go foul on him? He seemed to lose out on everything he did. Already he'd lost the woman he loved, he'd lost his ship, his men, his best friend. With that kind of luck what chance had he of survival?

Out there to the grey horizon lay the ships, hundreds of them, packed with troops to back up the invasion, in shore, yellow flashes of flame spat out of the smoke haze, fire that was throwing back the invaders. The tanks they needed to support them were lying useless under the debris of the wrecked landing craft, his own ill-fated LCT among them.

Nothing seemed to have gone right since he had left Cornwall.

After those long, warm days in May, June had come in wet; low scudding cloud and heaving seas, weather that had caused delays to the invasion plans, when embarkation at Trefoy was already under way. The US Naval

Amphibious Force had been scheduled to move out at 18.00 hours on June 3rd to link up with the convoy at Plymouth. His flotilla had been the last one to leave, after engine trouble had developed in his own craft causing him to put back into port. The engineer had reported a squeak in the gearbox that had to be investigated. As it had turned out there was no real problem, but by then the tide had turned against the wind, bringing up a big swell over the harbour bar. LCTs were not easy to hold on course at the best of times. Heavy astern, they rode bow high, and, lacking forward ballast, were light up front. With the winds building up to force eight he was going to need a pilot to get him safely out of the harbour to join the waiting craft in his charge.

"Tis as well you called me," Bill said, as he joined him on the bridge. "The glass is dropping. It could be nasty. Miss the channel and you could end up on the rocks. Have my boat made fast, Jack, I'll take her out for you."

It had been a relief to have Bill beside him on the bridge. Bill knew every inch of those waters, the currents, the hidden reefs, every mood of the weather, every trick of the tide. He was the best pilot on the river. Maybe that was why they didn't let him go to war. To him the sea was a challenge, and the more threatening it was the more he enjoyed matching himself against it. That night there had been a hint of a smile on his bronzed face, his fearless blue eyes alight with intrigue, as he took over the helm.

Dusk was settling in early as they moved out down river, thin rain spattering across the bridge windows, great hollows between the rollers coming in. Reaching the bar the LCT was rearing up on end, and coming down with a twist and a shudder that threw the second watch out of their bunks. He remembered yelling orders to man the pumps as huge seas streamed in over the gunwales, but up she came and Bill brought her round beautifully, right on course, the foam-rimmed rocks, sliding away behind them.

Off the point they met a long swell, lifting from it angry white peaks, just curling over, ominously. The wind was whipping the tops off them, leaving a metallic crinkle on the surface. Ahead were hills and valleys of white water, climbing up to the horizon, where they could just see the rest of the flotilla rocking, hove to, waiting, then to disappear as they dropped back into a trough.

It was after a big sea had thundered into them amidships that a cry went from the deck astern. Minutes later a sailor brought the news that the pilot boat had been swamped, and that Bill's boatman was in the water. He remembered taking the helm as Bill hurriedly left the bridge. The procedure was to lash the boat to the side of the ship and let it ride alongside until the pilot was ready to go ashore, but a freak wave had smashed the bottom out of it. The boatman seemed to have disappeared, but Bill was convinced he would have swum with the tide to the beach under the headland. His own plight, trapped aboard the landing craft, he regarded as a lucky break.

"It's fate," he said. "I was meant to come with you. And you'll be damned glad of me when half your crew are down with seasickness."

And so he was, glad of him to share the watches, to share his thoughts during those long hours of waiting at sea. It had been a time for confidences, both of them becoming introspective, talking of things neither would normally have admitted even to themselves; fears of the future, a future they had no way of knowing would be theirs.

Bill's concern had been for Charlie, her right to the Pendowry estate, which he had been convinced, would be denied her if Rachel had her way. It was an obsession magnified beyond all reason, it seemed to Lavelle. He believed prejudice was behind Bill's distrust in the family solicitor, since he was one of those seeing his wife. But he hadn't argued, he'd just let him go on talking, telling how he had persuaded Silas to leave Pendowry to Charlie, so that, should he die first, which was probable with his age and the dangers of his job, it would never fall into the hands of his unfaithful wife. But even that hadn't stopped Bill worrying about it; he was still uneasy, still searching for reassurances. He had already impressed upon Silas the importance of keeping the original copy of the deed safe, but really there had been no need. Silas had already made up his mind what he would do. Bill had begun to tell him about it that night in the rolling cabin of the LST. Through waves of nausea Lavelle had found it hard to concentrate, but he still remembered the river pilot saying.

"I shouldn't really be concerned. Silas has his copy hidden away where the lawyer will never find it, and only those close to him know where it's been hidden." But those in the old man's confidence Bill had never been able to reveal.

Lavelle knew now that despite Bill's efforts, Rachel and this Cornish lawyer had still outwitted him. But wasn't he the smart one? He'd figured exactly how to shuffle that fortune into his own court, how to manipulate Rachel into doing just what he wanted. It must have been in his mind when he first took up with her in forty-four, behind Bill's back. He must have had his eye on the old man's gold then. And he had waited year by year, watching, as those who stood in his way passed on or maybe were carefully eliminated from the game – like little Charlie. Bill would have crucified him.

This fraud had to be smashed. Already the lawyer was preparing to strip the assets and sell up the old home that had been in the family for centuries as was his right as executor to the will. Once probate was granted he would be at liberty to go ahead and administer the estate. He had to be stopped, the will contested, the whole damn thing put in the hands of a good solicitor. But there would have to be evidence, grounds for dispute, something more significant than the drunken ramblings of the woman he had taken to bed.

What he needed was hard down-to-earth proof; like the original copy of the will that Silas had carefully put someplace. But did it still exist? The lawyer could still have found and destroyed it. It seemed inconceivable that he would proceed with the forgery knowing the original document was still around, unless, of course, he was confident that it could easily be retrieved from the old man's possessions after his death. Maybe right now he was worried sick because he'd discovered it was missing, and in a sweat to get the forged will through probate before somebody unearthed the original. Even though nobody had turned up with it at the funeral, it could still be hidden. The trusted friend may be unaware of Silas' death or could it be little Charlie, on her way to Australia, who knew the secret. He would have to get on to Lisette to bring her back.

In the meantime, he had better get down to Cornwall, meet up with his yacht, make it his headquarters. It would provide just the cover he needed for further investigation without raising the lawyer's suspicions. He might even chat him up over a beer in a bar, show interest in the property and be shown over the Pendowry Manor. He had the time, he had the money to mess around, and this guy was in limbo anyway. He couldn't do damn all until the will was through probate. One thing about law procedure, it was slow. It might take weeks, months to wrap it all up; time he needed to dig up enough evidence to slam on his own lawyer's desk.

After breakfast he was going to be busy. He would need to tie up his business in London, phone his office in Marseilles to say he was taking a longer vacation, and maybe, call in on P & O Lines to check out sailings to Australia. As for Rachel, he would have to nurse her along with promises. She could still be a valuable source of information, a mirror into the lawyer's mind. He would get her some orchids wrapped in cellophane and take her somewhere grand for dinner to soften the moment of parting.

He slept then, at ease with himself, his plans resolved.

After breakfast he took her back to her flat. The mail was behind the door, and among the assortment of fashion circulars, was a picture postcard. She waved it at him triumphantly.

"Here we are!" she cried. "It's a card from Charlotte. Posted in Lisbon. A picture of the *Orion* –that's the liner they're sailing on." She passed it to him. "Read me what she says while I put on the kettle."

He glanced at the picture of the white liner against a blue sea background, and flicking it over, saw that it was written in pencil. He read out. "Dear Rachel, Having a wonderful time. The sea is perfect and Aunt Millicent is all you said she was. Thank you for making it all come true for me. Charlotte."

From the kitchen came Rachel's laugh. "I've made it all come true for her!" she shrieked. "How do you like that?"

Lavelle didn't answer, his mind still on the message, was baffled by the enthusiasm. Somehow, it didn't sound like the Charlie he remembered. His brows creased thoughtfully, and he turned back to the picture of the liner, noting the name of it. Rachel was already chattering on about the coffee, about other things; she had already forgotten the card, probably wouldn't even bother to read it herself. He slid it into his jacket pocket and went into the kitchen for his coffee.

****

"But darling! So soon? Surely you could manage just a few more days."

She had dressed to please him, a taffeta gown of old rose, cut lasciviously tight, with the low cleavage exposing the jutting swell of her breasts. Her ringed fingers reached for his hand across the table, her glance pleading. But he was shaking his head.

"Baby, I wish I could, but if I'm going to settle over here in London, I first have to sort out my affairs in Marseilles, get my business organised to transfer to some offices over here. It also means I shall have to wind things up in Tangiers, where I also have commitments."

"How long will you be away?"

"Two, three weeks, maybe a month, I guess. But say! You're going to be busy with the estate agents, finding some place for us to live in London. Must be somewhere grand, overlooking the park."

He had chosen an expensive Mayfair night club, with soft lights and pampering waiters, a taste of the good life that he wanted her to know would be hers once they were married. It would count with her, strengthen her devotion. Her alliance was too valuable to discard at this stage.

"I wish I could go with you."

"And what if Richard should call and you're not around? I thought we'd agreed to keep things just as they are," he said, leaning towards her, his voice lowered. "We have to take it slowly. Let him go ahead, get probate, get your million. That way it's all clean and legal Once you have the money safe in your own bank, that's time enough to tell him you've changed your mind. He won't argue. By then I'll have enough on him to turn his hair white."

"To be hoped you have," she said, and gulped down some champagne.

Lavelle brought out a small leather bound notebook, and drew out a thin-stemmed pencil from the sheath. "I'm going to need some details about Richard," he said, pressing a clean page open to write. "Now, he's Richard Penrose, you said..."

"Penrose was the partner," she corrected him, "Richard's name is Ellis – Richard Ellis."

Ellis! The name had a familiar ring, Lavelle thought, as he scribbled it down. An English name he'd heard some place – from Bill maybe... "And his office?" he asked.

She gave him the details readily, freely volunteering a wealth of information that she gathered he wanted to pass on to some private eye. Much of it was irrelevant to Lavelle's own enquiries since the exercise was a mere facade to substantiate the lies he had told her, but it would all serve as background knowledge. Finally they moved on to her arrangements in London.

"So what happens when your new owners take over the salon? You'll need somewhere to live."

"Of course I will! Richard's idea is for me to go down to Torquay for a long holiday, but I'd rather stay in London. I want him to fit me up in a furnished apartment – perhaps in Belgravia."

His smile met her eyes. "That looks good. Somewhere for me to bed down when I get back from Marseilles"

She grew radiant. "Why not?"

He bent to kiss her fingers. "I guess we should drink to that," he said and hailed the waiter for another bottle of champagne.

About midnight, drunk enough, he drove her home to her Fulham flat and screwed her until dawn, using every trick he knew with tongue and penis to leave her pining for him for months. But he didn't stay for breakfast. He made an excuse about an early flight and left at six. Driving away through the damp streets he felt a sense of liberation. The relief it was to be rid of her, her stale scent breathed away in gulps of clean air from the open car window as he headed back to the hotel.

By eight he had packed, checked out and handed in the keys of the Zephyr. He would need to have a car of his own for Cornwall. It could be sold before he left the country. In a second hand showroom off Tottenham Court Road he found a two-year-old Ford Consul which looked likely to hold her value, and after a spin around the streets and some shrewd hard bargaining, settled the deal in cash for £36O. By one thirty he was heading through the London traffic for the Great West Road.

CHAPTER TEN

Charlotte leaned against the wheelhouse of the *Flora Dora*, her hand on the wheel to keep a steady course across the bay, her gaze resting contentedly on the sun going down behind the Dodman Point. Astern, lines trailed, spinners glittered below the surface, and now and again there came a shout from the visitors as another mackerel came aboard.

It had been a perfect evening for fishing. With the wind off the land, the water was milky calm, swayed occasionally into long slopes of a dying swell, and strewn here and there with patches of green weed. Gulls swooped, some coming to rest and paddling around them, they too alert for the mackerel shoals.

The engine of the little green fishing boat was grinding and spluttering to dead slow, fish flapped and bumped against the box, and from time to time came the gulp of the lead weight sinker going overboard. Nick sat perched on the transom, working a line and chatting up the visitors, trying to inveigle them into booking another trip.

One was a girl in her mid-twenties, tanned brown from long afternoons on the sun terrace of the Trefoy Hotel. Her companions were older, two stockbrokers from Surrey. They would have enjoyed some more fishing, but they were already at the end of their holiday. Not so the girl. Linda Downing wanted to book again for the following week. She expected to be in Trefoy for quite some time, since she was here with her uncle, a property developer interested in the Pendowry Estate.

"My uncle wants to make it into a boating marina. Personally, I think it would a shame to spoil that lovely creek. But as he says, you have to move with the times."

Charlotte opened her mouth to protest, but she was cut short as a cry went up from one of the stockbrokers, who was excitedly hauling in his line.

"I've got another bite!" he cried, dragging at the fighting mackerel.

"It's a beauty!" Linda yelled, as the fish broke water.

Nick, glad of the diversion, went to help him take it off the hook. It would have to be the last catch of the day. Dusk was gathering, the land dark against the crimson sky, the still coves under the headlands deep in shadow.

"Turn around, Charlie, time we were heading back."

Charlotte obeyed and pointed the bow towards St. Catherine's light blinking at them through the twilight. Behind her the visitors were chatting excitedly as Nick strung up the fish, the following gulls squawking for the guts he tossed into the water. Soon came the harbour lights and the amber beacon on Whitehouse Quay.

Once the visitors had been put ashore and they were heading round to the town jetty, Nick joined Charlotte at the wheelhouse. "I know how you feel," he said, "but we can't disagree with the people we take out. We need their custom."

Charlotte nodded, "Linda would be on our side. It's her uncle who wants to spoil the creek!"

"A few home truths might put them off. I bet Ellis hasn't told him about the silt in the channel, the money it could cost to dredge and keep the tide from pushing it back."

"Or the adders in the woods and the curse on the watermills. That should put them off."

Nick regarded her with amusement. "You and your watermills," he scoffed. "Give 'em that old yarn and they won't believe anything we say."

"It's an idea though," she said, bending to cut the motor as they inched into the steps. She leapt ashore to make fast the painter, while Nick lifted the box, over-flowing with fish, onto the salt washed jetty.

It had been a major night for mackerel and trade was brisk, the quayside crowded with blue-jerseyed fishermen, cleaning fish. They lay at their feet in scaly heaps, mottled green, flashing quicksilver, flapping tails, shiny wet from the bay. Landladies and residents alike lined the rail, purses clutched in their fingers, waiting as the fish were strung into half dozen bunches and coppers changed hands. Tomorrow the town would have mackerel for breakfast, buttered and baked on the bone, a taste the visitors would remember to bring them back another summer.

Charlotte sat on the jetty steps counting over the takings with Nick. Her hair was tangled, her jeans soiled, sea water oozing from her shoes, but she was deliriously happy, happy just to be there with him. He had become a part of her life now, as had the river and the yacht. What had been before she wanted to shut from her mind, while she lived to the full each moment of this stolen summer. Nick had brought it all to life, made it sparkle for her; she found herself melting inside when she looked at him, a feeling that made her wonder if this brother and sister relationship might be developing into something more. Lately she had felt in him a certain gentleness; a protective arm, a look he gave her, as though he too felt the wanting, the need. But the feeling was young, yet still dormant, fragile, no more than an awareness she felt now as they sat together counting the heaps of silver he was digging out of his jeans.

He gave her a fond squeeze. "We've had a good night, Charlie. Worth celebrating. How much was that dress you fancied in Rhoda's window?"

She shook her head. "This money is strictly for the legal fees, remember."

He hugged her to him. "But I'm not taking you to the sailing club dance on Saturday all covered in fish scales, am I?"

She giggled as he pressed a kiss against her cheek.

"I'm going to wash them when I get back to the Cape."

Jed Marney, on his way to the Pirate Inn with Fisherman Luke, paused at the top of the steps.

"You coming up the pub, Nick?"

Nick shook his head. "I've got a couple dozen mackerel to take up to the Trefoy Hotel-ordered. We'll moor up the *Flora Dora* for you."

"Mind you cover the engine on her. Could be a heavy dew by morning."

"Don't you worry, Jed. She's in good hands."

Jed gave him a wink. "And don't keep Charlie out too late," he called back to them.

Just off the steps, old Jake Vardo took a rest from baling out his boat and gave them his toothless grin.

"Don't know what the boss of the *Cape Colombo* would say if he could see his daughter running wild with the riff-raff of St Ruan," he remarked as soon as Jed was out of earshot.

Nick jerked up his head. "And listen to the riff-raff of Trefoy who goes home with a wet arse every night because he's too damned idle to stop the leaks in his old pulling boat. You mind your own damn business, Jake Vardo!"

"Boat was right enough till 'ee borrowed her, you and your brother-in-law and that ole dog. Weighed her down to her gunwales ferrying yourselves back to St Ruan, you did."

"And got our arses wet!" Nick yelled back at him.

Charlotte giggled. "He's testy because Sharkie pinched his catch," she said.

"Call me names and he'll lose more than his catch," Nick said, gathering up the mackerel for the hotel.

"Leave some for our breakfast," Charlotte said. "I'll take them back with me."

He looked up. "You're not coming up to the hotel then?"

"I need an early night. Besides, I want to wash my hair and have a tub in the galley"

He grinned at her. "Sure you don't want me to hurry back and scrub your back for you."

"I reckon I can manage. I'm a big girl now, remember," she replied, feeling herself blush.

"You certainly are, m'dear," he said, handing her a string of gleaming fish. "Mind you hang them up high so Matelot don't have them first."

"I'll leave Matelot with you. It's safer," she said, climbing down the vertical ladder to the pram.

Feeling his eyes on her, she leapt aboard, and taking the scull, sent the dinghy skimming through the still moorings to the main channel. The river was a dark mirror now, reflecting the candlelit hump of St Ruan, with the riding lamps of the moored craft winking at each other out of the darkness.

****

The drive down to Cornwall had been an emotional one for Jack Lavelle, the A30 full of reminders of wartime postings; signposts to Salisbury, Southampton, Poole...place names that raked over the old wound, uncovering his grief for Margo. It was the base at Poole where her letters came, where his were posted, where he almost won his own private war for her, only to lose it at the eleventh hour to a limey slob in London.

The thought sparked anger, and suddenly he was stamping the accelerator, tearing up the miles, driving out his feelings with the roar of the road, taking the turnpikes blind all the way to Plymouth.

When he reached the Tamar Bridge the estuary lay like beaten gold, reflecting the setting sun. Beyond, the land was indigo dark, the distant hills remote, promising peace. He felt a sudden lift, a strength within him restored. He remembered feeling exactly the same the last time he crossed into Cornwall. That was in 'forty four' when he went to take over his flotilla at Trefoy. It had been a slow journey, cold, driving a windowless Dodge staff car; left hand drive, floor starter, double clutch, and the April rain pattering down on the canvas roof. Then, crossing the bridge the sun had come out, the salt wind had swept his face, lifting the gloom like a drug.

But how different the river looked today! No longer crowded with ships of war, destroyers, MTBs, landing craft. All he could see now was one minesweeper and two corvettes lying off Torpoint, silhouetted black against the sunset.

Leaving the bridge he took the winding road up the hill towards Liskeard. Still another forty miles. He needed a drink. The next pub, he promised himself. Just before Dobwalls he spotted a granite stone inn set back off the road. The rattling sign said The Traveller. Slamming the car door he stood, his gaze on the open moor, the dusk devouring the colours under the crimson sky and he tasted the upland breeze, clean and fresh and sweetened by peat and young spring herbage. It felt so good after London.

Inside the inn a log fire blazed in an open hearth; it was a room full of dark oak and polished brass, and out of the gloom a woman's face, smiling and nodding to his enquiries about food.

"We've some beef, sir, I can recommend."

It was rare, the sandwiches generously cut, the ale of local brew. Cornish voices drifted musically as he sat down to eat, his gaze wandering over the low beams, hung with hams and strings of onions. The firelight danced on the brass and glimmered against the dark oak table legs, the gleam just reaching to the faded pictures of Cornish storm scenes around the walls.

At the bar the locals were listening to an old farmer, who was forecasting a drought because of the bird behaviour on his land. Lavelle, interested, found himself joining in the conversation, and he might have been tempted to stay for another beer with them, but he still had to find out where his yacht was berthed. In the rush to leave he had neglected to tell the skipper he was coming down.

"Trefoy? T'is a fair drive," the farmer told him.

It was. With his headlights boring out tunnels of grotto-green, he followed the road south, the dark landscape broken only by some isolated farmhouse, glimmering through the trees. At last came the welcome Trefoy sign, and soon he was dropping into a twisting, narrow street, lit by gas lamps which hung out from the crooked walls of the houses, throwing a greenish hue on the shuttered shops and shadowed doorways. Through the open window the night air was warmly imbued with scents of pine and flower blossoms and smells of fish and salt from the sea.

Then he turned the corner and there it lay before him, the harbour, with the St Ruan lights shimmering in gold columns on the water; this was where he commanded his flotilla, bossed his men and prepared them for the Omaha landing that cost so many of them their lives. No sailors now along the harbour wall, no men from the 29th Division, just a toothless old salt, thin as wire, making fast his boat to the rail.

"D'you know where the *Cape Colombo* is berthed?" Lavelle asked him.

Jake Vardo glanced up curiously, his blue eyes pin sharp. "And what would 'ee be wanting with 'er at this time o' night?"

Lavelle sighed, too tired to suffer fools. "I just want to go aboard."

"Then you'd better come back in the morning and see the skipper."

"She's my yacht! I'm the owner."

"You – the owner?" The old man's white eyebrows crisped up to his knitted cap. "There now! So you be the owner. Jus' fancy that then! 'Twas not an hour back I was yarning with your daughter down here on the quay."

Not understanding what he was talking about Lavelle tried again. "I'm looking for the schooner, the *Cape Columbo*. Do you know where she's moored?"

Jake Vardo's eyes sparked from their slits. "I do, too, m' hearty, but you won't find the skipper aboard. He's gone up to the Trefoy Hotel, taken some fish to another of his lady friends. But if you wants me to ferry 'ee out to 'er..." He hesitated, watching Lavelle's hand go into his pocket to chink the change. "Then you'd better hang on and I'll bring my boat round to the jetty steps for 'ee."

It took longer than Lavelle expected. Standing at the rail he could hear plenty of splashing around, not from a paddle but a baling bowl – a discovery he was to make the moment he stepped aboard the old man's boat, straight into six inches of water.

It was a heavy pull across the harbour. The old man's conversation about the 'riff-raff' of St Ruan being no fit companions for 'unchaperoned maids' made little sense to him and he was glad to see his yacht loom up out of the shadows. After all these weeks she was a heartening sight, the familiar rig, the rakish flare and thrust of her bowsprit. It was good to be home. But for the dim lights over the companionway she was in darkness. Drawing alongside he reached for the ladder, holding onto it as the tide bumped them against the hull, then pressing half-a-crown into the boatman's hand, he swung himself aboard.

The first thing he saw when he switched on the galley light was a pair of wet jeans hanging to drip over the sink and half a dozen mackerel strung up in a bunch beside them. The galley looked cleaner than he had ever seen it before; soap and a dishcloth, a clean tea towel. The cracked crockery and chipped enamel mugs had disappeared. In their place was a neat row of blue and white Cornish beakers, hooked from tidy shelves lined with kitchen paper. *Was* this guy domesticated! The saloon too had been fixed up swell, fresh washed drapes at the ports, a smell of polish on the seating, a white table cloth ready for supper. Lavelle smiled to himself. The place had a woman's touch, he decided, as he moved amidships to his cabin.

The moment he opened the door he knew it was occupied; the darkness had a scented, human warmth. He tensed, listening, and caught a faint sound of breathing. Oh, no! Not somebody in his bunk! So the skipper was aboard after all. How do you like that? The nerve of the guy! Using his quarters.

Keeping his eyes on the shadowed bunk he flicked on the light and took two strides into the cabin, his intent to yank down the bed covers and boot the bastard out. Then he pulled up short. What the hell...? It was a girl's face against the pillow, dewy in sleep, youthful, strands of fair hair swept back from a sunburnt brow.

Lavelle felt a sting of annoyance. Not that he gave a damn that the skipper should want to shack up with a local broad, that he could understand, but why dump her in his bed? What was wrong with his own – in the forepeak? And where was he anyway? Aw! It was too bad!

He backed away but collided with the doorjamb, noisily, and heard her stir.

"Nick, you've wakened me," she murmured sleepily, rubbing her eyes and squinting at him. Then she sat upright, startled, and he noticed she was wearing a man's Hawaii shirt for a nightdress. It had the same design as one he had bought in Tangiers. It *was* the one he had bought in Tangiers. He recognised the tear on the shoulder, ripped in a scuffle with a guy over a payment.

Charlotte was staring back at him, round-eyed with shock and dismay. "Who are you?" she cried, pulling the bed covers up to her chin as she suddenly realised she was looking at a complete stranger.

He was a big man, his dark hair bristling with grey, a London look about his clothes, but there was also something disturbingly reminiscent about his features, belonging to the past. He was a detective! Sent by Rachel to collect her, take her back... take her back to Fulham.

She stared at him in horror, her face crumpling, and the expression defiant. "No!" she cried, "I'm not going! You won't make me. I'll drown myself first." Her voice rose in anger. arms round her knees, hugging herself. "Nobody is ever going to take me back there. This is where I belong...here...this is my home...I've every right to be here.."

He stared at her dumbfounded, her face puckering up, shoulders hunched, the tears brimming. Had that dumb old sea tramp put him aboard the wrong yacht after all? But he couldn't have! The cabin was full of his own belongings; his books on the locker top, his brushes on the dresser, his slippers... but what for Christsakes was she doing here, this girl, staking herself out in his cabin, and all broken up because she thought he was here to uproot her?

"What..," he began, stepping forward, but she stiffened up like a cornered animal braced for attack.

"Don't you dare come near me!" she screamed at him. "I'm not going back. I won't!"

She ranted on, her face hot with anger and tears, and he could only stand, gaping at her, failing to make any sense out of what she was saying. He tried shouting against the outburst, and it was not until she finally paused for breath that his words hit the silence.

"Who the hell are you? Aboard my yacht, in my bunk, wearing my shirt...?" He heard himself yelling at her.

For a moment she looked at him stunned, then with a catch of breath, her hands shot up to her face.

"You're not the police," she breathed, her voice dropping to an awed whisper. "You're the owner of the *Cape Columbo...*"

"Right sister, you got it."

"Oh, no," she whimpered, and flinging back the bed covers she slid down from the bunk, his South Sea Island shirt reaching a prudent length just above her knees as she stood self-consciously sniffing back the tears.

He took out his handkerchief and handed it to her. She accepted it meekly, smothering her face into it, then peeping at him guiltily above the folds.

"Oh, I'm so sorry. I thought you were somebody else," she said faintly.

"You thought I was the police," he said, scrutinising her. She was just a kid, hardly out of high school, probably with folks worried sick about her. What could Nick be thinking about? Unless she was his kid sister. "Just what have you been up to? And where's my skipper, Nick Bonet?"

"He should be back any moment. He's only taken some fish up to the hotel. I should have gone with him, but my jeans were full of scales and – and I wanted to wash them and have an early night." She was talking quickly, bright eyed, scarlet faced, "You must be tired after your journey. I'll make some coffee."

"Forget the coffee."

"It's no trouble," she said, tripping barefoot from the cabin. "Then I'll move my things and find some clean sheets for your bunk."

"Will you listen to me!" he protested, following her into the galley, where she was already busy putting a light under the percolator, and keeping him at bay with a barrier of small chat.

Watching her scurrying around, reaching for mugs and spoons, setting a tray, taking charge, brought a stab of recollection, something about her that was nagging at his memory. She reminded him of Bill taking over on the bridge, not listening, doing it his way, indifferent to the book.

"We're a bit short on milk," she said, draining the bottle into a jug.

"I said forget the coffee."

"Nick will want some," she rushed on. "I think that's him now. I thought I heard *the Dipper*– the engine gives a little splutter as it slows. Do you take sugar?"

Before he could answer there came a scuffle behind him and swish of air down the companionway. He swung round to be enveloped in the sudden embrace of brown and white fur and a wash of a hot tongue round his face.

"Down Matelot!" cried the girl. "Mind your manners."

The dog sank to knee level and banged a sea-wet tail against his legs.

"He's quite friendly," she assured him, "If you go into the saloon, he will follow you, and in a moment I'll bring in the coffee."

Speechless, Lavelle moved to obey just as Nick came plunging down the companionway, cap in hand with apologies.

"Why didn't you tell us you were coming down? I'd have been over the quay to meet you..." his voice trailed off, appalled to see Charlotte scantily clad in the boss's shirt. He hastily took the coffee-pot from her and pushed her out of the galley. "I'll do that. You go and get dressed."

Lavelle stepped aside, watching dumbfounded as she made her escape amidships and disappeared into his cabin. Then he turned questioningly to Nick, more in amusement than anger.

"What the hell's going on around here? What cradle did you snatch her from?"

"I can explain..," Nick said, picking up the tray and carrying it into the saloon.

Lavelle followed him, the questions he wanted to ask lost under the skipper's rush of assurances – assurances not about the girl, but about the yacht, the voyage, the moorings... typical Cornish strategy for evading the issue, washing over the truth with irrelevancies.

"Okay, Nick, let's have it," he broke in. "Quit fooling around! Who's this girl you've got aboard? You realise she's under age."

"You're getting it all wrong, Jack."

"Then put me right, for Christ's sake."

"She's had a lot of trouble, see, and my family are trying to help her sort it out."

"What kind of trouble? She thought I was the police."

"Not that kind of trouble. She's done nothing wrong. It's what somebody is doing to her. That's why we thought it best for her to stay aboard with me, and let people think she was the owner's daughter."

A flicker of enlightenment came into Lavelle eyes, at least the meaning of the boatman's remarks was becoming clear. "Go on," he urged, "I'm intrigued."

"It was only supposed to be for a few nights – until we could find out where her old granny had gone to live, but nobody seems to know, and since there was no sign of you coming back, I just let her stay on. What else could I do?"

"What about her folks?"

"Her real parents are dead and her stepmother has been making her life hell. That's why she'd think you were the police arriving to take her back."

"So she's run away from home."

Nick heaved a sigh. "But there's more to it than that. This stepmother is a real bad lot – a proper tart. She's been sleeping with this lawyer and now they're trying to cheat this little kid out of her great grand-uncle's will....."

Lavelle gulped his coffee. "What!" Either this kind of thing was a fashion in these parts or he was having some kind of a dream.

Nick might have gone on, but the girl had appeared in the doorway. She was looking more subdued and even more irritatingly familiar in corduroy trousers and a navy blue seaman's jersey. Her blue eyes were fixed thoughtfully on Lavelle.

He gave her a welcoming smile. "Come on in, honey, come and have some coffee," he said warmly.

But she remained, still staring at him, drawing in her brows curiously; unaware of how her blue jersey was reminding him of her father.

"I know you, don't I?" she said, coming slowly into the saloon. "You're an American. You used to be here during the war."

"I sure did."

His heart beat with hope. But how could it be her? He had the card in his pocket, posted from Lisbon. It was a delusion, the consequence of a tired mind.

"I knew the moment I saw you," she said, "that I'd seen you somewhere before, a long time ago. You're the Lieutenant, the one they used to call Frisco, my father's friend."

Lavelle looked at her, still not believing, even though he recognised the determined tilt of the chin, the look of Bill in her eyes...

Then Nick said. "You must have known Charlie's dad, Jack, when you were stationed down here. He was one of the river pilots."

Lavelle stood up then, his arms wide, and she ran to him to be enclosed in his great embrace, warm and tight and full of loving like it used to be when he came to dinner at the creek house. He brought her candy and they went fishing, him and her dear old dad.

Suddenly she was crying again, but this time there was laughter in her tears.

CHAPTER ELEVEN

Charlotte stared first at the picture of the liner, then at the message on the back of the card, her face radiant.

"And she believed it!" she cried. "She really thought it was from me?"

"She sure did, honey," Lavelle told her.

"But it's your handwriting," Nick said, taking the card from her.

"'Course it is," she laughed, "I got the card from the travel agents and wrote it for Jenny to post back to Rachel, to show I really was on my way."

"Some move," Lavelle applauded.

They were sitting round the saloon table, the coffee pot drained, the conversation wandering back and forth over the fresh disclosures, as the full facts of their separate stories slowly came to light.

Nick was greatly relieved at the outcome of events; the awkward situation of having Charlotte aboard the yacht resolved, and his boss, as a friend of her father, now committed to dealing with her plight. Now he knew why Lavelle had been so interested in his newspaper and why it had shocked him into action. But being aware of the man's shady Mediterranean background, Nick hoped the motive was nothing more than a genuine concern for Charlotte.

Lavelle was hardly able to believe his luck. Charlie here in Cornwall! Aboard his yacht and incognito! But the more he heard of her story, the less it surprised him. Rachel had not one hell of a chance against this little lady. She'd been way ahead, waiting, with all Bill's cunning, for the chance to escape, and with all Bill's guts to follow it through. He marvelled at her ingenuity; to get another kid to take her place, to mimic her looks on the passport picture!

"How did you do it?" he wanted to know.

"Facial expressions," Charlotte explained, "The idea came from a play we were in at school. We were supposed to be twins and had to practice looking alike by narrowing our eyes and pursing our lips. And it worked for the passport pictures."

They wanted to hear more, but Charlotte was stifling a yawn. "I've still to find some fresh sheets for your bunk," she told Lavelle.

"Forget the sheets, honey," he said. "I'll use the starboard cabin tonight. Tomorrow we'll do some switching around and fix you up with a cabin of your own. Right now, you go get some sleep."

Charlotte, lifting her eyes to him, was again reminded of another time when he had worn a smart uniform and peaked cap with a badge on the front. He looked older now, but happier, more self-assured than the quiet Lieutenant her dad used to know.

"How do you like that?" Lavelle said as she left the cabin. "The kid I went London to find! Right here on my own goddamn yacht! I guess this calls for a drink. You know where I keep the cognac."

"How could I forget?" Nick said, remembering their last drinking session aboard the schooner."

“Now tell me,” said Lavelle as he tipped the spirit into the glasses, “I wanna know all about this Richard Ellis guy; who works for him, who he goes around with, where he hangs out.”

Nick did not have all the answers, but from local hearsay and his own observations he was able to draw a fairly accurate profile of the Trefoy lawyer. How Ellis kept much to himself, living alone with just a daily woman going in. At weekends he was usually seen on the river in his cabin cruiser and sometimes fishing in the bay. No men friends, no other woman, and he regularly visited the pubs where he liked to entertain his clients.

As they went on to discuss the conspiracy in more detail, Lavelle was soon revealing much of his own involvement with the Ives family and those months stationed in St Ruan before D-Day. As he talked Nick became aware of the great respect his boss had for the river pilot, who had been trapped aboard his landing craft. When he went on to describe how he’d watched Bill die on a Normandy beachhead, trying to communicate that last message, Nick was in no doubt about Lavelle’s sincerity towards the girl. It was obvious his only concern was to see the legacy go to her, as was her right, a debt he believed he owed to her father.

They sat up long after midnight going over it all, the river damp stealing cold through the saloon, the gentle sigh of the water running under the stern. Beyond the steamed up ports most of the shore lights had blinked out and the brandy was low in the bottle when they finally retired to their cabins.

Inevitably, Nick slept late and Charlotte already had the mackerel frying when he reached the galley. He found Lavelle on deck, taking stock of the river and looking around for reminders of the war. His gaze was resting on the boatyard jetties, above them the cranes and the tall sheds, their sloping corrugated iron roofs, the place ringing with the echoes of a riveter’s hammer.

“That’s where they used to build the landing craft,” Lavelle said.

“It’s now my brother-in-law’s yard,” Nick told him. “But it was Jed’s father who was there during the war.”

“I remember him,” Lavelle said. “Heavy guy, apple faced. That yard was booming then.”

Nick nodded. “Jed’s old man did well, made a packet, but he’d gone through most of it by the time Jed was demobbed. No idea about business.”

“Is he still around?”

Nick shook his head. “’Didn’t live long after he retired. Drank too much.”

“Don’t we all?” Lavelle said wryly.

His gaze followed the stone slipway that reached along the St Ruan shoreline towards the mouth of Pendowry creek. It looked bare without the navy boats. “So what do they build over there now?” he asked.

“Various craft,” Nick replied. “But they don’t get the big orders like they got during the war – or the profits. Now it’s all dinghies and fishing boats, refits and repairs.”

“Maybe we can put some business his way,” Lavelle suggested. “How about the Cape? She needs a re-fit, her bottom scraped, a coat of new paint. You guess they could take her on over there?"

"I'm damned sure they could," said Nick, "We'll go over later and see Jed."

"Sure! I guess I owe your folks plenty after all they've done for Charlie."

They strolled on across the deck, Lavelle taking stock of the river craft moored around them, his interest dwelling particularly on the stripped out hulk of an MTB, and he remarked on what good ships they were, their speed and sea worthiness. Nick smiled to himself. Since these were the craft used by the tobacco runners, it crossed his mind that Lavelle could be speaking from experience. Across the water Trefoy basked in the morning sun, and Lavelle's glance now moved to the long white terraces gleaming in their elegance.

"So which is the lawyer's house?" he asked.

Nick indicated with his hand. "You see Whitehouse quay where the ferry is just coming out," he said, "see the houses above, well his is the one with the patio and the steps down to the foreshore."

Lavelle nodded. "I got it," he said.

Then came Charlotte's call to breakfast and they went below. Afterwards they brought their coffee up into the cockpit and sat around in the sunshine to resume their discussion.

"Charlie! Just try to think back," Lavelle said again. "Did Uncle Silas ever talk to you about his will?

"Not really," she replied. "He once said that one day I would reign Queen of Pendowry, that was all."

"Ever give you anything to hide, a letter, a book, maybe?

She shook her head. "Never."

"Before you left for London did you go to see him to say goodbye?"

"I wanted to, but Rachel said he was shocked and ill, and I wasn't to go near."

Lavelle drew at his cigarette and tossed the end overboard. "So who was there he would have trusted? What about the servants?"

"Servants!" said Charlotte, "They hardly had any at all?"

"Not even a manservant?"

"There used to be Carter, but he joined the navy."

"And nobody replaced him?"

"Nobody would stay. Uncle Silas was always rude to them. The cook walked out in a huff, then the housekeeper, until there was only Hiram Bunt left."

Lavelle tensed. "Hiram Bunt," he said thoughtfully, "Rachel mentioned him. One of the witnesses to the will. But he died."

Charlotte nodded grimly. "He'd gone into hospital for an operation and he didn't survive the anaesthetic. I remember Granny Bunt being very upset. After he died she used to go up to the manor house every day to look after Uncle Silas. She never took any notice of his ranting and raving. 'Said it was only to be expected the way he was confined so much to his chair. She would have been the one he would have trusted his secret with, I'm sure."

"Then let's go see her!" cried Lavelle.

"She's the one who's missing?" said Nick, "The old neighbour who lived in the creek cottage we've been trying to find. Ellis turned her out."

Lavelle frowned. "What had her cottage to do with Ellis?"

"It was owned by the estate," Nick explained. "He would have been acting for Silas."

"Didn't they have an estate manager? There had to be! There were tenants up river. Somebody had to collect the goddamned rents, keep the properties in repair."

"There was Digby," Charlotte said. "He used to live up at Watergate. Then I think there was a row and he moved away up country. After that my father took over the estate management."

Lavelle grew thoughtful. The picture was becoming clear, a rich old man, crippled, lonely, getting sore with everyone around him, until he had driven them all away. The lawyer, seeing the potential in the dependence he could create, beginning to take over. Once Bill was out of the way and the old neighbour moved out, Silas was powerless. The manor house would have become his prison and Ellis his keeper until he died.

"So who'd been looking after him since Mrs Bunt moved away?" he asked.

"They got a girl, Lucy Gribble, to live in," said Nick. "We've been finding out about her, too. A big buxom Cornish girl, but backward, lives in a dream world."

Lavelle groaned. "That's sure some help."

"Granny Bunt would be the one to talk to," Charlotte insisted, "Uncle Silas would have confided in her, she was like one of the family. She could tell us so much, if we could find her."

"Has anyone asked Ellis where she is?" Lavelle enquired.

"Yes, Annie at the greengrocers," said Nick. "She told Joanna she couldn't understand why Mrs Bunt was no longer bringing her fresh vegetables and fruit from her garden. Used to bring it down to St Ruan in her boat. Annie thought perhaps she was ill and rang Mr Ellis to find out. He said she was no longer living at the creek cottage, her son had been over from Canada and had taken her back to live with him. Very strange, Annie thought."

"She didn't go along with it?"

"Not when the boy from the dairy said he'd seen Mrs Bunt leaving her cottage with two rough looking men in an open lorry loaded with some of her furniture. When they saw Dick – that's his name, they stopped and Mrs Bunt told him not to leave her any more milk because Mr Ellis had found her somewhere else to live. Before she could say any more the lorry moved on. Everybody then thought it more likely that Ellis had turned her out and lied to save his face."

"So who lives in the cottage now?" Lavelle asked.

"Nobody. It's near derelict. There's still some of her furniture there, the heavy stuff, the dresser, a wardrobe upstairs."

"We went to have a look," Charlotte said sadly. "It was a sorry sight, mould and damp everywhere. All her clothes had gone though, pots and pans, too, and her old rocking chair."

Lavelle sat in quiet thought, staring seawards, his mind in study over the findings, then suddenly he rose, stretching, his eyes on Nick.

"Okay, so lets get moving. First we go over to meet Jed, then I guess to Bodmin, get some food and stores bought in for the yacht and some things for Charlie. If she's going to be the owner's daughter she has to look like her. Some sweaters, new sailing shoes – oh yeah, and sleeping gear so I can have my old shirt back."

Charlotte caught her breath. "You don't need to-"she began.

Lavelle waved away her protests. "I owe it to your old man to look after you, and I mean to see this thing through. And you can quit scrounging meals from Nick's good folks. We'll have them over to eat with us some time. Get in a ham and some beef steaks, I'll have the icebox gassed up for storage, and with all the seafood around here we should live well aboard."

"Better not mention beef steaks in front of Matelot," grinned Nick.

Lavelle scowled at the dog. "As for you," he said. "We get you some bones and crackers, fill you up plenty."

"I'd better take him over to the boatyard if we're going to Bodmin," Charlotte said, the dog at her heels as she went to bring round the dinghy.

Nick turned to Lavelle, frowning. "Why Bodmin? There are shops over Trefoy."

"At Bodmin," Lavelle said, "there are your administration offices, the county registrar, where I want to go while you take Charlie to get fixed up."

"The registrar?" Nick asked curiously.

Lavelle leaned towards him. "Before we start looking for Emma Bunt," he said, his voice lowered, "I guess it might be kind of useful if we found out if she's still alive."

"I hadn't thought of that," Nick said bleakly.

****

The registrar was slow, meticulous, and intent on going back through nine years of registered deaths before he was satisfied that Emma Bunt's name was not among them. He was a neat, impersonal little man, undisturbed by the number of people waiting to see him, waiting as Lavelle had waited for most of the afternoon, sitting on a hard wooden bench staring at pale green walls and reading out-of-date posters.

From there he went to Bodmin Post Office, where he made numerous calls to hospitals, private nursing homes and institutions, but none of them had any record of the old lady being admitted. But if she was still in Cornwall and as close to Silas Trevelyan as they said, why, Lavelle wondered, hadn't she turned up at the funeral? His death had been in all the papers, why hadn't she heard about it? Maybe Ellis' story was true; maybe she was in Canada.

This was a job for Lisette, he decided; have him check it out with immigration, go into records at Somerset House. He was the guy to dig up the facts, find out for sure what had happened to the good lady.

Lavelle had known Tony Lisette during the war. He was a British officer stationed with him at Poole. They had met up again in Marseilles five years later, and luckily Lavelle had kept his business card. He'd call him, maybe tomorrow evening when the guy was home for the weekend.

Before he left Bodmin Lavelle decided to look in at the office of the South Cornish Gazette. The clerk was helpful and he came away with several copies that contained references to the Pendowry Estate.

Somewhere in the town a church clock was chiming five, prompting Lavelle to return to the town hall where he had left the car. Nick and Charlie were waiting, loaded with their parcels.

Lavelle waved away Nick's apologies for spending most of the money Lavelle had given to him. "So what! Just as long as you've got Charlie some new jeans and sailing gear, the right stuff? I want her looking good when we take the Cape out."

"The Cape! When?" Charlotte cried excitedly.

He pushed her into the car. "Soon honey, but right now I guess we'd better go and eat some place. Come on, let's go."

The following evening Nick and Charlie stood by their obligation to take Linda Downing out fishing, but with the promise to Lavelle to hand over the dues to Jed for the use of the boat, together with any fish left over for sale. Since Lavelle had now made Charlotte his responsibility and was pledged to fight her case, there was no need to raise funds for legal fees.

It had been a day of activity aboard the *Cape Columbo*; Charlotte's quarters fitted out, Jed coming aboard to work out estimates for the refit. Lavelle had gone back to the yard with him, a place which, with its many wartime associations he had found fascinating as he rooted out relics from the scrap pile. Left alone that evening on the yacht he had spent some time cutting out references to the Pendowry inheritance from the newspapers he had brought from Bodmin. Finally, he set out in the dinghy for Trefoy, where later he had arranged to meet Nick for a beer, and maybe get a look at the lawyer.

Now, leaning against the sea wall, enjoying a cigarette, he watched the little boats returning from the evening fishing. There was a destroyer in from Plymouth and the quayside was swarming with sailors, the local girls rushing to touch their collars for luck. Nothing much changed, Lavelle thought; put a few black MPs among them, some slouching GIs, guys in fatigues with the white stripe on their helmets and it would be like old times. Only the visitors in their holiday clothes spoilt the illusion.

Then at dusk he saw the little apple green fishing boat dipping over the bar, Nick at the wheel, a girl sitting astern with Charlotte. Time to walk up through the alleyway to the Ship Inn, and make that call to Lisette before Nick joined him. It was a warm night and people were standing about the square, talking in small groups, some of them local dignitaries just out of the council meeting. Then he pulled up, staring.

There were two men on the steps of the inn, one of them heavily built, with a beer belly and a balding crown, but it was his companion who had caught Lavelle's attention... the dark face, with brooding eyes, a face he knew from the forties. Even after all these years the memory of the man was still astonishingly vivid; a man in a dark suit, amongst the shadows of the London blackout, the darker days that followed.

It must be an illusion, of course, triggered off by seeing the sailors, recalling the war years. When he looked again there would be no resemblance. He straightened up, lifting his eyes through the smoke haze of his cigarette, and saw that the man was still there, talking quietly; the same face, a little older, maybe, but either it was the same face or the man had a double.

"Jack!"

Lavelle turned, startled, and saw Nick hurrying towards him.

"What are you doing lurking in the shadows, I thought we were meeting inside?" said the skipper.

"Sure," Lavelle muttered, coming together at the thought of a drink.

"Well come on..," Nick began, then he caught sight of the two men talking outside the Ship and clutched Lavelle's arm. "We're just in time," he said, dropping his voice. "That's him – that's Ellis. There on the steps, just going in."

"The fat man?" Lavelle asked.

"No, no, Ellis is the other one."

"The other one!" Lavelle halted, staring, "That's Ellis, the dark, swarthy guy?" His voice fell to a whisper.

"That's right," said Nick "The other man is Ian MacDonald, the property developer we've been telling you about."

Lavelle stood back, no longer hearing. Ellis! Of course, Abrahams and Ellis! Neil Street, the smoking rubble where the office block had been, all that was left of it the brass plate sticking out of a heap of debris. Abrahams and Ellis, solicitors. His partner had been called Ellis.

They couldn't meet now, not until he was sure it wasn't just a likeness. He would need to find out first if Abrahams' partner was called Richard. Another job for Lisette.

The thought jerked him into action, and, nudging Nick, he turned to move away down the alleyway. "Come on! Let's go back to St Ruan," he said, "I have to make a 'phone call. We can get a beer over at the Lugger."

Nick stared after him, mystified. "I thought you wanted to have a beer with *him*," he said, following Lavelle back to the quay.

Lavelle didn't answer. He looked as if he had seen a ghost, and it wasn't until they were aboard the dinghy that he would bring himself to offer a further explanation.

"I got a hunch I know that guy. Before we meet, I have to be sure. Where was he before he joined Wilfred Penrose, where did he come from? You know?"

Nick frowned, and struck by Lavelle's urgency, aware of something being amiss, he wanted to be helpful. "Jed might be able to tell you," he said. "He'll be in the Lugger. We can ask him. But you could have seen Ellis when you were stationed down here. He must have been around then."

"No, it was before that – in London. I think this was a lawyer who had one or two handy sidelines in the black market. More than that he was a crook and he ripped me off."

Nick's eyes widened. "So why should he be down here?"

"London got too hot for him, I guess."

Nick shot him a glance. Startling revelations, but not altogether surprising coming from Lavelle, judging by the people he moved around with on the Med. Life wasn't as sleepy as it would seem on the Trefoy riverfront either.

At the Lugger they found Jed in the corner of the bar drinking rough cider from an earthenware mug while he waited for Fisherman Luke to join him, but it was the barman, George Cobb, who was able to give Lavelle the information he wanted. George had worked at the Ship during the war while awaiting conscription and he well remembered Ellis' arrival in the town.

"It would be March 1944, I reckon, just before my seventeenth birthday. I remember he stayed over the Ship until he found suitable lodgings on Bull Hill. Oh yez, he came from London, you could tell by the way he talked."

Lavelle swallowed down his brandy and left to make the telephone call to Tony Lisette.

As the door closed behind him Jed looked inquisitively at Nick. "What's with him tonight? He's just downed three doubles!"

"Thinks he's recognised Ellis as a crook he knew in London," Nick whispered.

Jed's eyes sparkled. "Has he now? I reckon that boy's been around,"

"You bet," said Nick, grinning over his glass. "In with all the tobacco runners, arms dealers, knows 'em all. Don't worry me though – just as long as he does right by Charlie."

There was a sailor in the telephone box. Lavelle used the time he had to wait, deliberating over what he would do if his hunch were correct. As much as he would have enjoyed the satisfaction of beating Abrahams into pulp, this was not the time to settle an old score. Better to come up with enough evidence to have him convicted of fraud and British justice would do it for him.

Lavelle stood, watching the lights shimmering in columns on the water, the night wind lifting his hair. It wouldn't be easy, seeing him around and holding back the anger, inflamed afresh to discover he might still be alive. But to make an appearance at this stage would only complicate the situation and might impede the investigation. Lavelle supposed that no pain he could ever inflict on Abrahams could compensate for the hurt, the loss, the shattered hopes he himself had suffered through this man's greed.

But there were other ways, Lavelle decided, to screw the bastard and make him sweat. Torment could be a cruel weapon, harassment could wear a man down, undermine his judgement. Pushed too far he might make a mistake.

The sailor came out of the telephone box. Lavelle went in.

"I'll check with the Law Society," Lisette told him, "But if this chap does turn out to be your Mr Abrahams, you'd better watch your back. After nine years of steering a fortune his way by methods fair or foul, he's not going to risk having the past catch up with him on the eleventh hour."

"He won't recognise me – not when I've grown my beard again. I've decided to go incognito – like young Charlie."

"Then you had better use your business name down there. A yacht owner called Lavelle might nudge his memory."

"I guess so. Then mail my letters to Jack Breton, c/o, The *Cape Columbo*, St Ruan Post Office."

Lisette grunted his approval. "Well, give me a few days, Jack, and I've have something for you, both on Abrahams and the old lady."

A week later Lavelle got his report. The records at Somerset House showed no record of Emma Bunt's death, but that of husband, Hiram, was recorded, Cornwall August 1944, and that, too, of her son Herbert, who apparently had been killed in action on February the 20th 1945. So she certainly wasn't with him in Canada.

According to the Law Society Mark Abrahams was killed on November 18th 1943, when the office block in Neil Street, Whitechapel, was bombed. His partner, Richard Ellis escaped, and in March 1944 he joined the firm of Wilfred Penrose at Trefoy, Cornwall.

Lisette's report went on to say that there had been no cases pending at the time, no complaints from clients, in fact, it looked as though the firm of Abrahams and Ellis was on the point of winding up, judging by the interest shown in the business after the bombing.

That same evening Lavelle sorted through the cuttings he had taken from the South Cornish Gazette, until he came across a legal notice which he supposed would have gone into most of the papers. This he pasted on to a postcard and put it into an envelope with the letter he had written to Lisette, instructing him to send the card to Richard Ellis at his address in Trefoy, and to make sure that it was posted in Whitechapel.

CHAPTER TWELVE

"It docs make you look different!" Charlotte said, contemplating Lavelle's four-day beard.

"Not recognisable? Then I guess I'll go over to Trefoy to mail my letters, they go earlier from there."

"I can take them after breakfast," Nick offered, helping himself to another slice of toast. "I have to go to the chandlers. We need some new spinners for the fishing lines."

"You going fishing again?"

"Friday. Why don't you come along with us and meet Linda? She's been asking about you."

"And what did you tell her?" Lavelle enquired.

"Don't worry," said Charlotte. "We said your name was Jack Breton, that you're an American who married my mother after my father got killed in the war, but the marriage broke up. Now you live in Marseilles and I live in London with my mother. You've come over to give me a holiday on your yacht until I go to college in the autumn."

"And she believed it all."

" 'Course she did."

Lavelle grinned at her, satisfied. "Okay! We go fishing Friday," he agreed.

"How did you go on with Lucy Gribble yesterday?" Nick enquired, remembering that Lavelle had been over to Watergate see the servant girl who had last cared for Silas Trevelyan. "You found the place all right?"

"Yeah!" said Lavelle, finishing his coffee. "After a hell of a walk up to the farm. She sure lives in a dream world. Got this dumb crazy idea that Silas was a Captain of a ship, and how she used to bring his meals up from the galley, and sometimes she would join him for tea on the bridge with the Bo'sun. It was all crazy talk about the ships they had in port. She had a scrapbook full of them, picture cards of ships in ports all over the world. When I asked her how she came by them, she said she got them from the sailors. I don't see Silas ever trusting her with a secret."

"What did I tell you?" said Nick.

"Maybe we'll do better with old Mrs Bunt when we find her. After lunch I've fixed to go see the boy from the dairy who saw her leave. He lives at a farm at Lantaglos, Jed says."

"We could all go," Charlotte suggested. "We could take the boat up the creek with the tide, then walk up through the Pendowry woods. Matelot would enjoy a run."

"Great! We do that," said Lavelle,

Nick rose from the table and reached for the two bulky letters Lavelle had ready for the post. "I thought you'd written one to Rachel," he said, glancing at the addresses.

"It's in the package to Marseilles. I'm getting a guy I know there to mail letters back to her," said Lavelle.

Charlotte laughed. "You've pinched my idea!"

****

Across the water at Trefoy, Richard Ellis turned off the Esplanade to walk down through the town to his office. The church clock bell was already ringing out nine o'clock, but he didn't hurry. His secretary Harriet Couch, would already be there, going through the mail. It looked like being another warm day. The rooftops reflected the cloudless sky, sunlight glared from the lime-washed alleyways, where the still air held faint drifts of chimney smoke above the prevailing smell from the drains.

The bell, an accompaniment to the noise of the gulls, ceased as he reached the crooked hill to the harbour, and he descended slowly his knee giving way to his limp; it was more noticeable these days, due, he was sure, to years of jarring the joint up and down these steeplejack streets. But not for much longer. Before the year was out his association with this town would be over, behind him as he made a fresh start with his new found fortune. The thought brought a faint smile to the hard line of his mouth, and he even managed a good-humoured nod to passers by. He walked on past the chandler's shops, the bank, the Quayhouse Hotel, where wet bathing suits lay draped from the sills of the upper windows and the aroma of morning coffee drifted from an open doorway. Then he was turning the corner of the Albert Quay and mounting the stairs to his office.

"Good morning, Miss Couch. Come in, please, when you are ready."

Harriet Couch lifted her eyes above the rims of her reading glasses and returned his greeting from her mountain of mail.

She was a spinster in her late fifties, with crisp grey hair cropped short and a taste for tweeds and Wolsey twin sets. She had been engaged by Wilfred Penrose after the previous secretary, Mabel Stephens, a lady of long service, had fallen tragically to her death down the backyard stairway. A leaking gutter, the veranda slippery with moss, the handrail rotten had all contributed to her 'accidental death', the verdict returned by the Coroner. The outside stairway down from the balcony, had been installed years ago as a fire escape, and Miss Stephens, who lived in a flat just across the backyard, would insist on using it as a quick way down from her office on the top floor, despite repeated warnings from her employer that the veranda could be dangerous.

Ellis remembered ruefully how, earlier that same day, he had almost suffered the same fate himself. He had been running when he slipped on the greasy surface and crashed into the handrail, his weight cracking it in two pieces. For several terrifying moments he had hung by his hands to the planking, aware of the thirty-foot drop to the yard below. Somehow he had found the strength to pull himself back on to the walkway and sit there, shaking, contemplating his escape. His first thought had been to call the joiner to make the veranda safe at the man's earliest convenience, and to warn Miss Stephens.

It was precisely when he saw how the broken ends of the handrail fitted together and remained in place that he realised how a forgery of the Trevelyan will could be achieved. Mabel Stephens was the surviving witness and the only real threat to such a plan. The first witness, the gardener, had died only months after the signing and Penrose was already on borrowed time, but not so Miss Stephens; apart from the usual Cornish rheumatics she was a picture of health, and likely to remain with the firm until retirement. Unless on a dark night like this, if, on leaving the office, she were to reach for the broken handrail and fall to her death.

Here was a rare opportunity, he remembered thinking, and all he had to do was to say nothing about his own mishap.

At first, he had dismissed the suggestion as unthinkable, altogether too dangerous, but was it? Penrose would be bound to say how he had warned her about that slippery veranda, how one day she was going to break her neck if she persisted in using it. It would simply be passed off as an accident. He remembered how he'd fought with his conscience throughout the afternoon, avoided her eyes when she brought in his letters to be signed, and had even been on the point of uttering some word of warning. He almost wished he had when, at precisely five-thirty that rainy December day, they'd heard the scream. At the inquest the Coroner had no doubts whatsoever. It was plain the handrail had broken under the deceased's weight as she slipped, and Wilfred Penrose stood up in court and told under oath how he had warned her time and time again of the dangers.

Ellis smiled to himself. Lucky she hadn't managed to hold on as he had, lucky she had never recovered consciousness.

So Harriet Couch came into the firm, not a local woman, but fresh from Saltash, unacquainted with the Trevelyan family background. She had previously been with a firm of solicitors in Plymouth, but a disagreement with her boss about holiday leave prompted her to look for another job. With the thought of eventual retirement in Trefoy the post had appealed to her. She was highly efficient and meticulous in her office routine, but it was her quiet, retiring personality that suited Ellis. A lady who liked to spend her leisure reading or listening to music or walking the cliffs with her corgi, was unlikely to listen to gossip, and she had too many scruples not to respect office confidences in her keeping.

Entering his office Ellis sank down in the great-carved chair where Penrose used to sit spluttering over his pipe and lifting the litter of desk papers with his cough. These days there was more order, the desk cleared down to its green leather top and the pad of blotting paper, clean and free from doodling. The files for the days work in hand stood ready, topped by the bulky Trevelyan folder, thick with documents for his attention.

The sight of it excited him, raising a tremor in his hand as he reached to turn back the cover. It was all falling together perfectly, not a hiccup. He thumbed slowly through the pages, mentally totalling the assets, his eyes flicking greedily over the figures, indulging in a calculation of what he would be worth one day.

The Pendowry estate ran into thousands of acres, the lands reaching inland as far as Lanreath and extending south through the river valley to the sea. There was a large acreage of productive farmland, apart from the woodlands, brush and open moor, whilst the various properties included both farms and hamlets of cottages, most of which he had ensured were tenanted and kept in good repair. Some, in the more isolated places which had fallen derelict might have to be demolished, but not so the watermills. These, having some historic value, might be partially restored to serve as tourist attractions for overseas visitors, an idea that would add interest to the boating marina project. This he was already negotiating with Ian MacDonald, a big shot with the Taylor Ross Organisation, an international firm of property developers, presently down in Cornwall looking for sound business investments in tourism.

As Ellis had already pointed out to him, the Pendowry estate offered many possibilities. The historic manor house, shabby and overgrown as it was, could with a decent conversion become a five star hotel. Fell some of the trees to make room for terraces, tennis courts, a swimming pool; convert the creek house and old cottage on the quay into a smart sailing club, linked by pontoons for easy anchorage, and what an attractive holiday resort it would be!

Ian MacDonald had been impressed, so much so that he had requested his surveyors to come down and file a report to take back to London.

Ellis saw no real snags. The expense of dredging the silted up creek would be no problem to a firm with the Taylor Ross resources. The river authority would welcome any scheme to keep the waterways open and there would be no opposition from the local council. His influence with them was strong, built up through the years with advice, with the waiving of fees and by carefully conditioning those he knew into a progressive attitude towards a scheme to bring the tourist trade to Trefoy. With this one, Trefoy may even overshadow the larger resorts like Newquay and Falmouth. He supposed there would be some opposition from the St Ruan shore, but with the river authority on his side, it would be bound to be overruled.

But if the disposal of the estate looked profitable, it would be a mere pittance compared with the accumulated wealth from the family stocks and shares in gilt-edged securities. These had been accumulating interest for many years, and according to the London stockbrokers acting for the Trevelyan family, were all sound and on a rising market. They could be worth around a quarter of a million – and this was without the liquid capital in Silas Trevelyan's personal accounts.

Death duties, of course, were likely to take an enormous whack but with careful manipulation of the way in which the estate was realised, they could be reduced to a certain extent. But the purchasers were still going to get their hands on a lucratively promising investment, so what the hell! For him there would be a substantial sum to transfer into Rachel's London bank. This, with his own personal capital and the proceeds of his property on the waterfront and the practice in Fore Street, should ensure a very comfortable future for them both.

Into his reverie came a small throat-clearing sound, alerting him to the arrival of Miss Couch at his desk. He greeted her cheerfully as she placed the mail before him, remarking on the glorious day it was and making small talk while she responded chirpily, with a downward glance at the appointment book resting on her arm.

"And what do we have on the agenda for today?" he asked.

Miss Couch traced her pencil down the page. "You have two appointments this afternoon. Mr Berwick over that property at two, Miss Pimm again at three – oh, and Mr MacDonald rang- just after you left yesterday."

"Did he?" Ellis beamed.

"He would like you to have dinner with him on Friday evening at the Trefoy Hotel. Apparently his niece is going fishing again and he sees the opportunity to get down to some serious talking."

"Ah!" Ellis could hardly contain his pleasure. "Dinner, eh? That does sound interesting. You had better see if you can get hold of another box of those Corona cigars for me."

"I will make a note of it, Mr Ellis."

"Very good," he replied, his eye on a bulky envelope sitting unopened on the top of his mail.

"That one was marked for your personal attention," she said.

Ellis made no move to open it, guessing the contents to be the box number replies from the property advertisement. "Anything more, Miss Couch?" he asked, with a note of finality.

She hesitated. She was holding in her hand a plain postcard, eyeing it with a puckered brow.

"Just this," she replied. "I wasn't sure whether to give it to you or to toss it into the waste basket. But it does seem rather odd."

"Odd?"

"Yes, you remember that Trustee Act Notice we put out in the newspapers regarding the Trevelyan will. Months ago?"

Ellis looked up sharply, a shadow crossing his countenance. The Notice had been published merely as a matter of procedure. No claims were expected. How could there be? "What about it?" he asked abruptly.

"It appears" she answered curiously," that somebody has cut the Notice from a newspaper and pasted it on this card. It came with the morning mail addressed to you."

"They have done what?" he demanded, vexation replacing his good humour. "Here! Give it to me!"

He snatched it from her and sat with his eyes fixed upon it, brows drawn, the printed words mocking him.

Notice is hereby given pursuant to Section 27the Trustee Act 1925 that the Personal Representative of Silas Trevelyan, late of Pendowry Manor, St Ruan, Cornwall, who died on the 25th of February 1953,intends to distribute the estate of the deceased.

Any person having any claim in respect of the estate or any part thereof is hereby required to send particulars of his claim to the undersigned.

There was no name, no message, just the newspaper cutting stuck on to the blank card. What was this? A joke?

He flipped the card over to look at the datemark and saw that it had been posted two days ago at 4.30 pm in London E.1. Instantly he thought of Whitechapel.

"It is rather peculiar," Miss Couch's voice seemed to come from a long way off. "They can't know you very well otherwise they wouldn't have made a mistake in the former name of the firm. We used to be Penrose and Ellis!"

He steadied his hand against the desk to read the address. It was hand written in blue ink, the script rounded, anonymous.

Mr Richard Ellis,
Richard Ellis, Solicitors,
Formally Abrahams and Ellis.

He sat motionless. This was not a mistake or a coincidence, this was a warning. He had been rumbled.

The office was suddenly airless. Close by, beyond the open window, a gull swooped, screaming into the silence, the anger of its cry voicing the blasphemy he longed to rage upon the sender of the card. But Miss Couch was still at his desk, waiting in that ear-ringing silence.

How to keep calm. The newspaper cutting on the card implied that the sender knew about the will! The only person in the East End of London who knew about that was its author, Sol Brodsky, and surely Sol wasn't in such a tight spot that he had to stoop to blackmail!

Harriet Couch's throat clearing reminder broke into his thoughts and recovering himself, he threw down the card and snapped at her.

"Right. Enough of this nonsense. Let's get to work. I want you to get me a London number. There's a man I want to talk to at the Liston Press, Back Court Street, Whitechapel. You'll have to go through to Directory Enquiries for the number."

"Certainly, Mr Ellis," said Miss Couch, somewhat disturbed by his pallor and his sudden change of mood.

As soon as the door had closed, Ellis reached for a cigarette and sparked at it impatiently with his lighter. Once the sharp smoke touched the back of his throat, he reached for the card again, scrutinising it, without, now Miss Couch had gone, making any effort to conceal his alarm.

If it was money Brodsky wanted, he could have it. The demands would be met, within reason, of course, but only for the immediate future. After that he would need to devise something quite deadly to snuff out this little enterprise before it really took hold.

The telephone rang on his desk. He grabbed the receiver. It was Miss Couch to report that Directory Enquiries no longer had a number for the Liston Press.

"Perhaps, if you would give me the name of the gentleman you want, Mr Ellis," she said.

"The name is Brodsky, Mr Solomon Brodsky," he told her. "Try the Rose and Crown in Bow High Street. He used to have a room there."

"I'll try right away, Mr Ellis."

"Thank you, Miss Couch."

He put down the receiver and sat waiting to pick it up again, his fingers beating a sharp tattoo on the desk, oblivious of the gulls' cries, the river sounds, the drowsy sunshine pouring across the room. All he could see before him was Brodsky's hooded eyes and those rubbery lips breaking into that faintly devious smile.

It was several minutes before the telephone rang.

"Mr Ellis, I have a Mrs Ida Benson on the line, the landlady of the Rose and Crown at Bow. I wondered if you would like to speak to her yourself. Apparently, Mr Brodsky died about twelve months ago of a heart attack."

Ellis stared. Sol dead – a year? Then it must be someone else who sent the card, who was trying to put the finger on him. But how could it be? Nobody else knew. .

"Would you like to speak to her if I put you through?" came Miss Couch's voice.

"I – er – not just now," he muttered. "But do offer my sympathy, and say how sorry we are to hear of Mr Brodsky's death, will you?"

He laid down the receiver, his eyes glazed, and sat, the shock of it leaving him weak.

Somebody knew, somebody had rumbled him. But who?

That was a question he was to ask himself over and over for the rest of the day, to lie awake brooding over most of the night, probing back through the years, searching every half-forgotten pocket of his mind. But there were no answers, no reasons and no logical explanation to bring him peace...nothing, but the gnawing worry of the unknown.

CHAPTER THIRTEEN

Richard Ellis was not enjoying his dinner at the Trefoy hotel. His host Ian MacDonald, had chosen a well appointed window table with an enchanting view of the river estuary, bathed now in the golden evening light. He had been fine during the cocktails, able to muster a bold front, full of his usual verve. It was only when they took their places at the table that his depression returned and his appetite deserted him.

The waiter was bending over him. "A little cheese, sir? We have some excellent Stilton, some water crackers perhaps?"

Ellis shook his head impatiently and gulped some more wine, hoping his refusal would go un-noticed by his host.

He need not have worried. The other man appeared to be too busy enjoying his own meal, with too much to say between courses to notice the appetite of his guest.

Ian MacDonald was big and hearty looking, the picture of affluence. He was not particularly well educated, but despite all the fork waving gestures, he was a good talker and all the time his astute brown eyes, gleaming at Ellis, gave nothing away.

"His company, of which he was the board chairman, had done well out of the war on government requisition orders, cleverly switching to post war development within hours of the armistice being signed. Now they were looking towards investment in tourism to reap the profits from the years of recovery.

"Today," he told Ellis, "people want something more than piers and proms. On holiday they want a beautiful coastline, places to see, a perfect setting for their hotel. If we are to bring tourism to Britain this is what we shall have to provide – plus amenities above the standard they get at home. Here we can't always depend on the sun, so when it isn't shining, we must provide facilities; craft centres built around your old water mills is the sort of thing I mean. On the Cornish Riviera, that is what they should be getting, not an eyeful of that shantytown across the water when they come down to breakfast."

Ellis took another deep gulp of his burgundy.

His host bent closer, his voice lowered to a husky whisper. "Your creek up the river could become a gem of a resort tucked away in those woods, but it's going to cost, really cost before we can get it off the ground."

"But think of the profits you'll reap when you are pulling in the crowds," Ellis reminded him.

"We would hope so," MacDonald said, with wry smile. "I grant you, the potential is there, but we have to consider how much we shall need to put into the project, what pitfalls await us round the bend of that sludgy creek. And to be blunt, that is all it is at the moment- sludge! God knows how many fathoms of it."

"With modern equipment it can easily be dredged."

"True, but how many man hours before we touch the rocky bottom, that's what I need to know, and when we've got over that, how do we keep the tide from sweeping it all back in again?"

"With today's technology –the technology we got out of the war, your engineers should be able to come up with a method to reduce the build up of sand, and sieve the tidal flow. I was only reading about being done somewhere the other day," Ellis informed him, quite untruthfully, but hopeful of inspiring some research into the subject.

"If there is a way round it, we have the means and the men for the job," said the property developer, confidently. "I took my niece up there yesterday the high tide. We hired one of those self-drive boats. I must admit the trip set my mind reeling with fresh ideas. As you yourself pointed out, we could have platoons for easy anchorage in the yacht basin and private houseboats along the shore line, backing up to a road for their own vehicles. Once we've lashed down that spread of trees to the waters edge, there could be room for holiday bungalows as well."

Ellis nodded approvingly. "How soon do you expect your architect down here?" he asked.

"Wednesday next. We should have his report, together with that of his engineers, by the end of the month. Frankly, I don't see any reason why the project shouldn't go ahead. That's why I asked you over to-night so that we could talk about drawing up the contract and perhaps to arrange to meet your client."

"That won't be necessary," Ellis said quickly. "Mrs Ives has put the disposal of the estate entirely in my hands. She detests Cornwall and has no wish to be bothered with the details of the transaction. That I get her the best deal is her only concern."

"She lives in London, I take it?"

"When she is not abroad," Ellis lied, "At the moment she is somewhere on the French Riviera, where I understand she hopes to make her home."

The waiter was bending over them again. "Would you the gentlemen care to take coffee in the lounge?"

MacDonald mopped his chin with the linen napkin. "On such a lovely evening we would prefer the terrace, I think," he said.

"Certainly, sir, as you wish."

MacDonald rose from the table and led the way round to the French windows, where lounging chairs were set out beside white painted wrought iron tables. With the evening sun setting behind them, long shadows lay across the veranda, throwing pin sharp patterns from the balustrade, and although it was still warm from the heat of the day, the air was cool for from the sea.

"You'll have some brandy?" MacDonald pulled out the chairs. "And perhaps I can try one of your excellent cigars."

"Indeed," Ellis replied, choosing a place where he could easily avert his eyes from the St Ruan squalor.

Smoking, the coffee and brandy beside them, Ellis followed his host's gaze seawards, where the fishing boats were dotted about beyond the harbour mouth.

"My niece is out there to-night fishing," MacDonald said from his cloud of cigar smoke.

Ellis nodded. "It's a popular pastime here, even with the ladies."

"She's just happy being on the water," MacDonald said. "Reminds her of California, I suppose. That's where she has spent the last few years."

"Really?"

"She was a war bride. Married to an American flier. Sadly he was killed in Korea last year."

"Oh, dear," Ellis said, respectfully, but shortly. He was eager to draw the conversation round to business again, but his host was in no hurry.

"That's why I've brought her down here with me. Where better in all this peace and quiet to collect her thoughts and decide on her plans for the future?" He lifted his hand. "Ah! I believe that's her boat out there now –just off the point. Can you see the green fishing boat? She's out with those people from the cream schooner."

Ellis nodded. "The Frenchman. I've noticed it," he said, trying to think of a way to steer the conversation back to the property.

Then suddenly there was no need as MacDonald turned to him, his beaming smile veiled in cigar smoke.

"So what are you asking for the Pendowry estate –manor house, watermills, land, the lot?"

Mellowed by the brandy, Ellis' confidence returned, and while they sipped and talked, the green fishing boat drew farther and farther off the point, until eventually it was no more than a dot on the horizon.

****

Away from the lee of the land, the northerly breeze was whipping up a short swell, lifting the bow of the *Flora Dora* and see-sawing her over the wave crests. Charlotte, never more at peace with herself than when she was in charge of a boat, was enjoying steering into them and watching the spray rip up against the wheelhouse.

They had hit a mackerel shoal back off Gribbin Head, caught a dozen, then ran out of them again. But nobody minded, least of all Linda Downing, whose white silky dress appeared to have been chosen more to impress the owner of the *Cape Columbo*, than for catching mackerel.

For Lavelle it was a relief to rest his brain from the tedium of the enquiries, asking the same old questions and getting the same goddamn answers. Their visit to Hogg's Farm had been disappointing. Dick Hogg had found little more to add to the story he had already given to the postmistress. Emma Bunt had stopped him to cancel the milk because she was moving away, that was all. Even his description of the two men in the truck had been vague; but he did remember that the vehicle had smelt of fish.

This point they mentioned to Fisherman Luke, whom they met in the creek, on their way back. He suggested the truck could have come from Polperro, where according to the dentist in Bodmin, Emma Bunt might just be living. Fisherman Luke's wife had visited the same dentist the previous day, after breaking her bottom teeth, and he told her that he had done a similar repair to Emma Bunt's teeth just over six months ago. When Mrs Luke enquired about her new address, the dentist was unable to help. It was a stranger, he said, who brought in the repair. Apparently the good lady was unable to come into town herself because, with her arthritis, she had difficulty in climbing the long hill out of *Polperro.*

Fisherman Luke then told them he now intended to find out her full address from the Polperro boatmen. Relieved to hear they were finally getting somewhere, Lavelle decided he could afford to take time off the problem and enjoy a fishing trip with the girl from the Trefoy Hotel –that was if the kids didn't louse it all up with their campaign to disrupt Ellis' property deal.

"Not his to sell?" Linda Downing looked more quizzical than surprised.

"So it is rumoured," Nick told her.

She smiled at Lavelle. "I don't think these two want my Uncle to recommend Pendowry Creek for development," she said, "Last week they told me the wood with ridden with adders, the land full of treacherous bog and that there was a curse on the watermills! Now it's a dispute about the ownership."

Lavelle grinned. "They don't want anybody muscling in on the worm they dig out of the silt back there. They need it for fishing."

"Oh, that's it, is it?" she said, smiling, "Opposition from the local fishermen."

"You got it!"

"I thought you'd be on our side!" Charlotte said, giving him a resentful glance.

"You can't hold up progress, honey."

"Even so," Nick said, "your uncle should look very carefully into what he's buying – especially when he's dealing with a man like Richard Ellis."

"Don't worry," she assured him, "Uncle Mac would have done that already. He is a very astute businessman. He never takes anybody at face value. In fact, he's wining and dining the man this evening, no doubt to analyse him. That's his way-"

She broke off suddenly and began tugging in her line. "Oh, I've got one! I felt it pull!" she cried, hauling excitedly.

They all turned to watch as the spinner came sparkling up through the backwash, but only lightly and easily, no jumping fish breaking water.

"You've lost him," said Nick disgustedly.

"She never had one," Lavelle said in her defence. "We've come too far off shore."

Nick turned, glancing back at the thin blue line of the land, St Catherine's light blinking distantly. "Indeed we have. You'd better turn around, Charlie, unless you're planning to take us to supper in Le Havre."

Charlotte altered course and the little craft rolled into a trough until they came round with the wind and the seas were coming up against the starboard bow.

Linda was trying to re-wind her fishing bale. Lavelle bent to help her. "Let me do that," he said, taking up the tangle of dripping line. "You're going to spoil your pretty dress."

She looked up at him gratefully, pleased at his attention. She had been intrigued to hear that Charlotte's stepfather was an American, and had been looking forward to meeting him. Now his accent and mannerisms were reminding her of Mel. Like him, he was a big, towering yank, with the same dry, laconic way of talking, but quite different in looks, his face older, more bruised by life, the thin growth of beard giving him a rakish appearance that excited her.

"I'm not much good with fishing lines," she said, watching his long fingers pulling out the tangles.

"I guess I ought to be," he said, without looking up. "I was doing this when I was knee high, coming from a family of fishermen."

"Really? Not here in Cornwall?"

He shook his head. "No, over in the States, in San Francisco, where I come from."

Her eyes widened. "You come from San Francisco?"

"I sure do," he said, meeting her glance.

"What part?" she asked curiously.

"Downtown. I was born in an apartment just off Grant Avenue. I spent my early youth down on the wharf where my uncle ran a fleet of boats."

She nodded, smiling. "Near the Embarcarddero? Where you can buy crabmeat and sourdough bread, where the cable cars start?"

He gave her a broad grin. "Say! How come you know San Francisco?"

"I should. It's where I live."

"Where *you* live!"

"I married an American pilot in forty three."

He saw her glance away seawards, her eyes sad, filmy in the last of the light. "He was shot down in Korea seven months ago."

"Gee, that's tough!"

"That's why I'm back with my parents in London. It's easier over here to give way to my grief–to come to terms with it. I have to for Joey's sake"

"Joey?"

"My small son. He's over at Pacific Heights with Mel's people. I would liked to have had him with me, but he's settled at school."

"You don't plan to bring him to live in England then?"

"My parents want me to but I'm not happy about it. We have a small charter firm in Sausalito and a lovely home overlooking the sea. I want to hold on to it if I can. It's not having Mel around that spoils it all."

"You'll come through," he told her gently, "In time the hurt heals. Not that it can ever be the same, but one day you will find it will be easier."

"You sound like one talking from experience."

He twisted the line over the bale, snapping the knot. "I guess so, but it was a long time ago," he said quietly.

For a moment she expected him to go on, become confiding, but he remained silent, his brows drawn into a tight lined frown. She supposed it must be something to do with his relationship with Charlotte's mother. The war left behind many marriage complications, faded hopes and broken dreams. The war had, but for Lavelle it was not quite the way she imagined.

He dropped the bale in the box with the rest of the fishing tackle and slid down on the transom seat beside her.

"You cold?" he asked.

"A bit," she answered, resting against his sheltering arm, the feel of him felt good, the manly warmth, so like Mel.

The little craft was picking up speed, smacking into the short seas, throwing up sea spray. Nick had squeezed into the wheelhouse with Charlotte, pressed up against her as she steered. They were in a carefree mood, singing together to the noisy accompaniment of the engine, the breeze carrying away the words of their lusty sea shanty in the gathering dusk.

Lavelle turned to smile at the girl beside him, her cheeks deep rose under her tan. The breeze was whipping back her hair, the youthful boyish cut glistening under the light of the sky.

It was almost dark when they slid into Trefoy harbour; the quayside still crowded with visitors standing under the gaslight. Charlotte had suggested they all went up to the Toll Bar for a nightcap to which Lavelle readily agreed. The pokey little café in the twisted high street didn't serve the kind of 'nightcap' he had expected, but it wasn't disappointing. They all four had fun sitting up on the bar stools, sipping frothy malted milk and biting hungrily into fresh lobster filled rolls, and joining in the local talk about dinghy sailing.

Later they took Linda back across the dark waters to Whitehouse jetty below the Trefoy Hotel, and she stood waving to them as they chugged homewards, Charlotte and Nick still singing at the wheel.

Lavelle stood astern with his cigarette, looking back at her, watching the breeze dragging her skirt, shaping her thighs beneath the thin folds of her white dress.

CHAPTER FOURTEEN

Jack Lavelle waited all weekend for Fisherman Luke to turn up with Emma Bunt's address, but all he got was a pipe-puffing nod from the old man as he went by in his boat. Nick was not surprised.

"He's not a man to be hurried," he told Lavelle. "He's probably waiting until he has a glut of fish to take to Polperro fish market. That's when he'll see the boatmen."

"Then why don't we go talk to them ourselves? How far is it up the coast? Six miles?"

"You mean take the Cape?" said Nick, with sudden enthusiasm. It was just the day for a sail, a blue sky, a fair wind and the barometer steady.

"Sure! Why not?" said Lavelle. "Jed's men don't come aboard until Wednesday. And I guess it's about time we took Charlie sailing."

Charlotte, overhearing as she came up the companionway, gave a whoop of joy. "Sailing! When?"

"After lunch," Lavelle said. "Maybe, if the wind's okay we might let you sail her back from Polperro."

"Me!" she cried, her face glowing with pleasure.

"Fancy you can handle her?" Nick joked. "All these tales we've been hearing about how you used to sail with your dad."

"I used to hold the jib sheet," she cried, her mind going back to the little gaff rigged cutter they used to have at Pendowry. She looked excitedly at Lavelle. "Polperro! Does that mean we've found Granny Bunt?"

"Not yet, honey, but I sure hope today will be the day."

So it was with some optimism that soon after noon they slipped their moorings and slid out of the harbour on the tide. A north-westerly breeze filled the red sails and the sunshine put a champagne sparkle on the water. Soon the river was broadening into the estuary, the headlands slipping by with the white houses and wooded cliffs.

At sea they took the wind on the starboard quarter for the first tack, then changed course for a broad reach to take them across the bay to Nealand Point and a short close hauled leg into Polperro. They found anchor at a buoy and rowed ashore, Matelot sitting up in the bow, tongue hanging. Then through a forest of masts came the sleepy hollow of whitewashed cottages overhanging a harbour colourful with fishing craft and noisy with gulls. As they climbed the wooden ladder up to the jetty, Matelot made his own way by leaping from deck to deck across the trawlers tied up alongside the quay, then took a dive overboard for a short swim to the muddy strip of beach.

Lavelle laughed. "He sure knows where he's going."

"To make a nuisance of himself," said Nick, "having the visitors throwing sticks for him all afternoon."

Picking their way around the heaps of rope, crabpots and drying nets, they followed the long jetty to the inner harbour. The heat of the day lifted from the sunbaked stone with an effluvium of fish and tar smells. Below, the still water shimmered with oily reflections, the surface spattered with colour like a half finished canvas, the tranquillity broken only by the gulls, whose cries echoed back the emptiness. This was the idle hour, before the pleasure boats brought swarms of visitors to trail the narrow streets and drool over the quaintness of Cornish squalor.

The Polperro boatmen were sitting in a row on a jetty bench, the ash from their pipes dusting their blue jerseys grey, their peak caps half shadowing their copper bronze faces, but faces into which came no recognition when the name Emma Bunt was mentioned. Even so there was plenty of jaw-stroking puzzlement behind the pipe smoke, much debate on who to ask, who would know, but like all the Polperro folk whom Lavelle stopped to question that long afternoon, nobody in the town seemed to have heard of the good lady.

"You could try the vicar," suggested a pirate-faced old salt. "If he don't have her in the Parish, the chance is he'll have her in his graveyard."

"I guess we should try the post office first," Lavelle said, as they moved on towards the clutter of streets out of the harbour.

The Polperro houses appeared to Lavelle to be propped up on top of one another, their chimneys craning over the rooftops for a glimpse of the water. Below, courtyards overhanging with balconies were taking turns for a share of the shade, while washing fluttered between alleyways hardly wide enough for the gutters to run. Somewhere, a brook from the hills babbled away under the houses on its way to the sea.

The post office was a double-fronted shop; its tiny windows crammed with bottles of sweets, tins of tobacco and dusty birthday cards. Inside was dark and airless, hinting a smell of lamp oil. The postmistress was a big fleshy woman with a pale pudgy face, scored with age lines; her sleeveless bag of a dress sheltered a heavy bosom and revealed massive arms more fitted to kneading bread than selling postage stamps.

"Emma Bunt," she repeated after Lavelle, then proceeded to name and describe all the Bunts who lived in that part of Cornwall, none of whom seemed to bear any resemblance to the old lady from Pendowry.

"You got the electoral roll?" Lavelle asked.

"Somewhere I have," she said, and shuffled off behind the counter to look for it.

They spent more than an hour going through the yellowed sheaf of typewritten pages, but although they explored every street and hamlet listed, there was no record of Emma Bunt.

The vicar wasted even more of their time. They found him scything away the long grass in the churchyard, a paunchy little man, growing pink from the exertion, and glad to hand over the job to Nick while he gave some study to their enquiry.

"I certainly haven't buried her," he assured them, and paused, waiting for Nick to swing the scythe into action. Then he went on to reveal that the only

Bunt he knew was a postman at St Neot, who used to walk twenty miles before breakfast to deliver the mail.

He droned on, carried away by his reminiscences, while Nick scythed lustily at the thistles and Timothy grass, perspiration breaking hot from his brow. Charlotte, losing interest, soon wandered off to read the names printed in lead on the gravestones, while Lavelle remained, a patient listener, alert for some inadvertent slip of the tongue which might hold a clue worth following. But the vicar's verbal flow was deviating farther and farther from the issue they had come to discuss.

Finally they made their departure and returning to the harbour found Matelot having a tug-of-war with an old gentleman and his walking stick. Nick whistled shrilly. The dog let go and came sheepishly towards them with a waggle and a shake of wet sand. Charlotte scolded him, and Lavelle made some humble apologies for the dog's behaviour.

Charlotte looked downcast as they walked away. "It's all going wrong, isn't it? Matelot disgracing us, no trace of Granny Bunt."

Lavelle slung his arm around her. "Take it easy, honey, we'll find her. She has to be around here someplace."

"But if the vicar doesn't know and she's not listed on the electoral roll."

"All that means is that we could be right about the lawyer. He's found her a hideaway, maybe with someone he's paying to look after her."

Nick scowled into the sunshine and slowly repeated the clue Fisherman Luke had been given. "She couldn't climb the long hill out of Polperro. But which hill? There's the one up to Crumplehorn, the one up to Raphael. They all go up and up and up!"

"Then what are we waiting for? Let's get on our walking shoes and go up and up to look for her," Lavelle said. Then he lifted his glance to the ice cream parlour across the street. "After we've had ourselves an ice cream soda. Okay?"

Although with fresh optimism, they walked up hill after hill from the Polperro waterside, nobody they met could help them.

Returning to the harbour they stopped to buy produce from the cottage gardens and as Charlotte hung back, still seeking a whisper from the local woman pulling the lettuce for her. The two men drifted ahead, voicing their doubts in undertones.

"Not here, is she?" Nick muttered.

"Could be penned up some place," said Lavelle, "where she won't see the papers or hear the local gossip. He can't risk any hassle from her, the wife of one of the witnesses. Once the will's through probate and he's off to the sun, he won't give a damn, either about her or the folks he's landed her with.."

"So how do we find her?"

"We keep looking. Sooner or later we'll stumble onto something – like the clue from the dentist. I guess I'll go over and see him myself. Try to get some kind of a description of the guy who took in her teeth to be repaired."

They dined aboard the *Cape Columbo* moored up to the buoy off the outer harbour. Lavelle had bought a couple of lobsters from one of the Polperro fishermen and Charlotte made a salad with the lettuce, radishes and some of Jed's early tomatoes. Hungry from hill climbing, their faces tingling from the sun-salt air, they tucked in heartily to the sweet white fish scooped from the pink shells, washed down with a bottle of French wine brought up from the stock Lavelle kept cool and undeclared in the bilge.

The meal, the wine, soothed away the strain of the day's search, but for Charlotte, even more intoxicating was the sail home, slanting away into the sunset with the roar of the wind in the canvas and the swish of the seas against the bow.

Despite the strong tide and the freshening breeze off the point, Lavelle kept his word by allowing Charlotte to take the helm, and once they had gone about and were safely set on a broad reach homewards, he moved over for her to take his place, with a nod to Nick to remain watchfully behind her.

The schooner was going easily with the wind on her beam, careless of the short choppy swell meeting them off shore, the waves lifting her up and plunging her down again as the seas sank away beneath the bow and leaving behind a mane of fizzing foam.

Charlotte, the wheel firm in her hands, was radiant; her sunburnt cheeks blushed to a deep rose, her eyes shining with pleasure. She could feel the power of the harnessed wind, hear the creak of the ropes as it came, feel the yacht heel as she put the helm down just a teeny bit closer to windward, the thrill of it stirring dormant passions, the old lure of the sea that was in her blood, awakening old ecstasies.

"Oh, she's beautiful!" she cried, the wind carrying her voice away.

"Keep her just like that, honey, you're doing fine," Lavelle said, sheeting in the jib and making it fast round the winch. Then he sat back, lounging in the cockpit with his feet up on the coaming, smiling a thin, secret smile. He was thinking about Rachel and how that rouged, creped face would pucker into fury if she could see Charlie now, up at the helm of his yacht, and living as she wanted to live, here in Cornwall. He tried to catch his skipper's glance to exchange a grin, but Nick was too deeply absorbed in Charlotte himself, a tenderness for her bursting over him as it did so often these days, warming to her now with sudden pride to see her up there, holding the yacht on course. She felt for the sea as he did, the pull of it strong like the tide, felt its challenge, its call for courage, its restlessness and moods. It satisfied a longing, a need like love, an understanding no words could describe. All he knew was that he belonged as she belonged, gripped by this compulsive urge for it.

They were making good speed, the long reach taking them far west of the Trefoy estuary, and beyond the Gribbin headland Charlotte could see the lights of Mevagissey against the dark shadow of the distant land. Southwards to port, the blue crinkled sea reached to the far horizon, the waves picking up a metallic glitter from the pink sky. Now and again white spray lifted from the bow, showering the foredeck, leaving it wet and gleaming.

"You'd better let me take her now, my love, we're almost ready to go about," Nick said, moving up to the helm.

"I'd hoped you'd let me try," Charlotte said, as he slid into her place.

"Not this trip, honey," Lavelle said. "Watch Nick this time, see how he eases her gently round. You can be ready to tack when I give the word. Okay?"

"Proper job!"

Nick, now at the helm, was looking for a smooth patch of seaway.

"Right," he said suddenly. "Ready about!" Then "Lee oh!" as he put the helm down, the signal for action, and over came the main boom with a creek of ropes and timber. For a moment the schooner steadied herself and the wind in the canvas seemed to pause for breath, then as the decks heeled, took up its roar on the other tack. Charlotte, half flung, half scrambling, made a dive for the jib sheet, the weight of the sail almost carrying her away with it, but she hung on with both hands.

"Pull, pull!" Lavelle roared at her. "Put your back into it! Good girl – sheet her in! Now make her fast round the winch. Watch your fingers. Snap for home."

"Well done!" Nick commended, the pleasure in his face as this time he caught Lavelle's glance.

"Some of the old sea dog in her."

"You bet," agreed Lavelle.

Charlotte hardly heard. She was completely absorbed in it all, sea and sky and sun-warmed wind, the bowsprit pitching into the swell and lifting white wings of spray from the seas. If only life would stand still, let these precious moments last and last, these recaptured joys, but it was all too beautiful, too fragile, too soon to crumble in the hurry of time, just as this stolen summer would one day if they didn't find Uncle Silas' copy of the will to prove her rightful heritage. She pushed the thought from her mind, determined that nothing should spoil this exquisite moment, one she would always treasure however dark the days to come.

They were sailing close-hauled for the Trefoy estuary, the gunwales awash. Soon the headlands were outstretching their rocky arms to embrace them, St Catherine's light blinking its welcome as they crossed the bar. The great yacht righted herself, canvas flapping, red sails coming down and Matelot, his rump arched in a long stretch, yawned his content to be back in port.

Up on the terrace of the Trefoy Hotel, Linda watched them come in, her eyes searching for the handsome American among the tumble of sails. Then she saw him, his arms raised to the main sheet, tan shirt billowing in the wind, his face darkened almost black by his new beard, and within her came a pang of longing, awakened by that one glimpse.

Would they come ashore for a nightcap in the Toll Bar? Would she meet them if she were to walk casually down to the town quay? Chance meeting – would it look that way?

She stood only a moment in hesitation. Something stronger than her own will was leading her down the terrace steps. Dusk had gathered over the gardens, dew in the grass and heady scents of the tobacco plants lifting against the warm evening breeze. She hurried, descending into the Esplanade, and caught a glimpse through the Cornish palms of a dinghy leaving the yacht.

They were coming ashore.

Her sense of wellbeing soared, impatience quickening her stride through the draughtless streets, where the thick white walls of the houses still radiated the heat of the afternoon. Down on the quay she felt the breeze again softly on her face, a land breeze, flower scented and sweet. The water lay mottled green and moving with gleaming reflections from the shore.

The quay was crowded. There was a destroyer in from Plymouth, the sailors out-numbering the visitors. Revellers, reeling against each other, spilled down the steps of the Pirate Inn, their outbreaks of song shouted down by a tight group of German seamen chorusing *'Deutschland, Deutschland'* under the gaslight.

Linda edged her way to the jetty rail and saw the dinghy alongside, someone bending over to make the boat fast. It was Jack. He was on his own.

She backed away, lest he should think she had been waiting there, to waylay him, then feeling as she did so a sudden grip from behind.

"'Ello, ducky! Looking for a Jack Tar to buy you a drink?"

She spun round, catching a whiff of beery breath, and found a lobster-pink face, peeling with sunburn, coming close to hers, glassy blue eyes and an HMS navy cap tilted from a damp fringe of ginger hair. She tried to pull herself free, but the sailor's grip tightened.

"Aw, come on! Lemme buy you a port and lemon! That'll make your eyes shine, darlin'."

"Let me go!" she shouted at him, bringing a whoop of catcalls from his mates looking on which suddenly faded into silence.

"You heard what the lady said, brother," came the American's deep, easily recognisable voice behind her. "Beat it! Scram! Before I kick your front teeth in."

Linda saw the colour deepen in the sailor's neck, but after one glance at Lavelle, tough jawed, broad shouldered, white threat in his eyes, the sailor backed off, as Linda, Lavelle's sheltering arm encircling her, was swept quickly away.

"What the hell were you doing wandering around with that bawling mob?" he demanded jokingly .

"I wasn't wandering anywhere, I was being molested," she protested laughing.

"And so you ought to be, straying from your swank hotel!"

She grinned up at him. He looked as pleased to see her as she was to see him.

"I saw your yacht come in. I thought you might be coming ashore for a night-cap – like last Friday."

He raised his eyebrows. "Sure! Why not? I came ashore to mail some letters."

"At this hour? The post went hours ago."

"I guess so, but this is the first chance I've had all day." It was a lie, of course. He could have mailed the letters in Polperro, but the truth was he needed a Trefoy datemark on one particular item of mail. He gave her a warm smile. "So where's your Uncle Mac tonight? Dining with his lawyer friend again?"

She shook her head. "He's gone back to London for a few days. Business. He'll be back at the weekend."

Lavelle nodded. "Come on up to the post office with me, then I'll walk you to your hotel and buy you gin and tonic. Okay?"

"Lovely!" she cried. The clasp of his hand, big and warm, sent her heart soaring. What a perfect ending to that long wait for his yacht to come back to port.

"Did you enjoy your sail?" she asked as they set off.

"Sure. We've been teaching Charlie helmsmanship. She's been coming along just fine. I guess we shall go out again soon if the weather stays good. You fancy a trip with us?"

She caught her breath. "Oh, I'd love it." Then she lowered her eyes, trying not to show her eagerness. "You're sure I wouldn't be in the way?"

"Like hell." His hand squeezed over hers. "How's about Saturday? I'll have Nick come over to pick you up. Would noon be too early?"

"Perfect," she said, the joy of it singing through her, hard to repress.

They had reached the post office and he quickly pushed his mail into the box. Among the letters was the postcard of the ocean liner, the old stamp steamed off and replaced, Charlotte's pencilled correspondence erased and re-addressed.

CHAPTER FIFTEEN

Ellis received the picture postcard of the *S.S. Orion* thirty-six hours later. Harriet Couch handed it to him with the mid-day mail. Although the card had arrived by the first post she had been wrought with misgivings and tempted to toss it into the wastebasket, but was not prepared to suffer the agonies of conscience as a result. Instead it had stared up from her blotter all morning as she wavered with indecision.

At first glance it looked like a holiday card, a colour picture of the luxury liner – until she flipped it over and saw the correspondence section was blank. No message, no signature, just her employer's name and address hand-written, a heavier stroke of the pen than before.

Another anonymous card to upset him again, put him into one of his moods. Could somebody be trying to blackmail him, she wondered? Somebody with a grudge seeking to dispute the Trevelyan will? Wasn't that what the last card was about? Even so she had no business holding it back. It would have to go in with the next mail.

Hers had been the wrong decision. She knew it the moment he looked at the card; she saw it in his face, the downward drain of colour to the tight line of his mouth, the anger in his eyes when he looked up to dismiss her; an utterance of blasphemy as she closed the door behind her. Afterwards it was very quiet, a silence so tense she found herself speaking in undertones to people who called. As she expected he skipped lunch and stayed shut up in his office for most of the afternoon, taking and making no calls, except a London number he asked her to get for him, then changed his mind before she was through to the exchange.

Ellis' day was in ruins. He had a brief to prepare but the shock of receiving the second card had left him numb and he could only sit, staring at it on his desk. His first reaction had been of anger because again the card had been sent, not to him personally at home, but to his office, for his secretary to see. Last time he had been able to pass it off as a joke, the work of a crank, but now Harriet Couch would be bound to suspect that he was being blackmailed. She was much too sharp to be twice deluded. She would want him to tell her about it, that fixed look of expectancy on her face.

He sat, playing with the card, turning it over, scrutinising the postmark, and trying to read from the very pressure of the pen some clue to the sender. The card had been used before, there were India rubber smears and faint markings in the stamp area, but unreadable, telling him nothing. Even so, whosoever the sender was, obviously knew too much.

The last card, sending him the newspaper cutting of the Trustee Act notice, had really been no more than an expression of contempt, mockingly suggesting corruption. This one was a real threat because it indicated that the sender was fully acquainted with his plans for Charlotte. It was blackmail, no doubt about it, and since the first card was posted in London and the second in

Trefoy, it looked as though the onset of the pressure was imminent, the usually heavy demands implying the rest.

Ellis sat, tense, his cold eyes narrowed as he searched for answers. Where did he begin to look for the blackmailer? Somewhere back through the years, along the course of his carefully made plans, something had been missed, one small mistake. Names, faces flashed across his mind, people who had been relatively close to Silas Trevelyan, neighbours, tenants the old man might have told about the will. Nonsense, he never left his chair, he saw no one. Of friends he had none, his irritability had driven them all away – except the Bunt woman who washed and cleaned for him. There was no need to worry about her. Where she was she wouldn't be wagging her busy tongue to anybody. As for her successor, she was too simple-minded to be of any threat.

Harriet Couch, Ellis felt, was beyond suspicion. Committed secretary as she was, she knew nothing of the origins of the Trevelyan will. He was certain of it. The townsfolk, of course, were not to be trusted. Affable as they were to him, in their Cornish way, Ellis knew he had never really been accepted. His upcountry breeding stirred in the native's strange resentments and prejudices, no matter the number of years he had lived in the town. But Ellis doubted there being much more to their antagonism than petty spite and whispers behind his back. Blackmail was an art, he reasoned, it called for an astute, criminal nerve.

No doubt about it, this had the smell of London, the consequence, maybe, of a word dropped inadvertently by Rachel. No secret was ever safe with a woman. But it would surely have needed more than just the odd word, and after all Rachel was constantly worried about being detected.

He stared down at the card, twisting the corners forcefully until they began to flake between his fingers. It had probably come from P & O's head office in London-or Southampton? Was Charlotte behind this? He had worried about the girl from the onset. That was why he had engaged private detectives to make sure she was definitely still on the boat for Australia. Which reminded him – he hadn't received the report yet, so perhaps they were having trouble tracking the sea voyagers down. Rachel always said the girl was wilful, hell bent on getting back to Cornwall. Perhaps she had been secretly communicating with the St Ruan clan and was aware of what had been going on. Rachel maintained she had always kept the girl well under control, but how did she know she hadn't been steaming open letters and listening in on telephone calls? And who was to say, once out of Rachel's reach, the little brat had not confided in this Australian woman, blurted it all out and won her confidence? Still, if this had been the case it wouldn't be blackmail, it would be a showdown, the woman storming back to London with the girl and looking for immediate legal action.

He closed his eyes, trying to think it out clearly. He would need to ring Weller, find out what was going on. Damn it, he was paying for the information! It was too bad he hadn't received some word by now.

He snatched up the telephone. Harriet Couch was on the line promptly – almost too promptly, almost as though she had been anticipating his call. He gave her the number but regretted it as soon as he had put down the receiver. No, no. He couldn't have her listening to his conversation with Weller. Good God, no! A call to him must be made from home. He dragged off the receiver again and cancelled the call.

For most of the afternoon he moved like a robot through his work, quite unable to put his attention to his brief and finally surrendered his jottings in crumpled balls of paper to the wastebasket. Then he locked his desk and set off for home. He had to ring Weller, catch him before he left his office. Ten minutes later Ellis was striding quickly through the house to his study, his brow gleaming with perspiration from his sprint through the heat of the afternoon. Crashing down his briefcase, he lifted the telephone and waited for the operator to answer. Another exasperating wait, listening to the ritual of exchanges before the distant tone of the London number began to ring.

At last, Weller's voice, answering him.

"News for you, Richard? Not good news, I'm afraid. We've been having problems. That woman, Mrs Millicent Potter and the girl, left the *Orion* at Gibraltar."

"Left?" Ellis heard himself repeating. "But they were going on to Sydney!"

"So they were, but according to the man I put on the job out there, they left the boat at Gib., apparently because the girl had been very sea-sick, so they had decided to make the rest of the journey by air."

Ellis gaped. Sea-sick? Bill Ives' daughter seasick!

"You're sure he's got the right woman?" he asked weakly.

"You must be joking! He's got the right woman all right."

"So where are they now?" exploded Ellis.

"We're not sure. According to the hotel where they stayed overnight, they left Gibraltar in a hired car. There was talk of them touring on through Spain to Madrid and taking a plane to Sydney via Rome. This woman appears to be lousy rich so she might think the girl needs a holiday to build up her strength after all the sea sickness."

Ellis was no longer listening, his mind was flashing back through the years and an image of Bill Ives heading down the river in the pilot boat, the child sitting up on the transom beside him, the boat plunging into steep seas at the harbour bar, spray lifting over their heads. That girl seasick! Never in a thousand years. She was born to it. There was something wrong, something dreadfully wrong. They wouldn't have left the ship because the girl was sea sick, that would have only been an excuse, a cover up. Nor would they have any intention of touring through Spain and flying to Sydney later. They had only hired the car to head back to England. They were in London last week, Trefoy this, looking for evidence to contest the will.

Weller's voice was crackling urgently from the earpiece.

"Richard! Are you listening to me? Is that all you need or do you want me to make further enquiries? Do you or don't you?"

"Yes," Ellis muttered, recovering himself. "I want you to check out for sure where they went after Gibraltar. Try the airports and check all the passenger lists. Not just Madrid, but Lisbon and Barcelona. It's imperative that I should know. Do you understand?"

"It'll cost, Richard."

"Never mind the cost – just do it!"

He slammed down the receiver and sat with his hand closed over it, the knuckles showing white. The girl had found an ally in this Australian woman, aroused in her enough curiosity to head back to investigate. First to London to engage the services of a private detective – the best her kind of money could buy, a professional, able look up records and to probe into his background. On to Cornwall to search for the one person likely to be any help to them, Emma Bunt. But they would need time to look for her – that was the reason the cards had been sent. It wasn't quite blackmail, more like harassment, a ploy to undermine his confidence, distract him from the business of disposing of the estate. They wanted to slow things down while they put a case together against him. If they were to find Emma Bunt he was finished. There was only one way it could now be resolved. There were no alternatives. No time even to wait for further information from Weller.

Ellis shook his head. If only he could watch these people as they were watching him, but how did he recognise them? The only memory he could bring to mind of the girl was a grubby eight-year-old sculling her father's dinghy. She would be in her teens now, grown up. The only description he had of the woman was that she was stout, rich and middle aged like hundreds of the summer visitors. It had only been his constant reassurance that had persuaded Rachel to conspire with him at all. Suppose she were to panic, now back out, turn on him, mess it all up. That would be no good. But it might not do any harm to ring her, see if there had been any word, any new developments. Again he lifted the receiver.

Rachel seemed pleased to hear from him. Yes, there had been news from the voyagers, a card from Charlotte posted in Lisbon. She had meant to post it on to him, but had mislaid it. No problems though, the girl sounded happy enough. Then before Ellis could get a word in edgeways, she was rushing on to tell him at great length about some flat she'd found in Belgravia, an ideal place for her to live after the new owners took possession of the salon next month. For that area, it was a snip, and would be easy to re-sell once the inheritance was settled and their wedding plans finalised.

He offered no opposition. He was only too glad Rachel had received the card from Charlotte and it told her nothing one way or the other.

When Rachel had rung off, he had the sudden urge to escape from the study, the house. To walk, think and to work out a plan. Leaving the house he headed for the coastal path, striding as though in a trance, hardly aware of where he was going or how far, and he didn't stop until he reached Polridmouth Cove four and a half miles away. There he stood for a long time, staring through the pines to the wash on the shore, going over it all in his mind.

Eventually he returned home, and collapsed on his bed. There he lay, exhausted, sweating under the heat of his clothes, no strength left even to undress. Long into the night he remained wakeful from thought, and when he finally slept, his dreams were full of the girl. He had no idea what she looked like, but saw her as a youthful, female Silas Trevelyan; the same piercing eyes, the same sneering, crackling laughter. Then suddenly the sea was coming in over the patio, a huge wave crashing against the glass of the French windows, smashing clean through it, engulfing the room, and within it the girl's laughter, mocking, screaming like the gulls...

It was the gulls, their morning cries following the fishing boats out, that brought him back into the reality of another day and the problems to be faced.

Eventually he went out onto the patio, the salt wind cool on his face, the St Ruan 'monument of despair' drably garbed in its morning light. He glanced away towards Pendowry Creek, the silhouette of the French schooner blackly etched against the rising sun. For a moment he looked at it absently, his mind elsewhere, then he began pacing the patio, backwards and forwards, on and on. Today he would have to go out to see Emma Bunt, satisfy himself that she hadn't already talked to the enemy and devise the means to ensure that she never would.

He paced on, unaware of the eyes behind the Zeiss lens watching him from a porthole of the *Cape Columbo*, Jack Lavelle's wide mouth twitching into a smile.

CHAPTER SIXTEEN

"So you didn't find Emma Bunt the day you went over to Polperro then?" said Fisherman Luke, cutting himself a slice of tobacco.

"Not a trace," said Lavelle. "We got nothing."

"Didn't think you would," said Luke.

He was sitting on an upturned pulling boat at Jed's yard, where Lavelle had gone with Nick to discuss work being done on the yacht, and by the slightly derisive look the fisherman gave them as they approached, they suspected he might have something to disclose. They waited, watching, as he stuffed the tobacco into the bowl of his pipe and struck the match to light it.

"You did say a long hill out of Polperro?" Nick prompted.

"That's right, my handsome. That's where she be."

Lavelle shook his head. "We went up along and down along every goddamn one of them. She just wasn't there."

Luke drew at his pipe, his eyes sparkling behind the blue haze. "But did you go up over headland to Talland?"

"Talland!" Nick exclaimed, puzzled.

"Can you think of a longer hill going up out of Polperro than the one what goes through Talland?"

Nick put his back to rest against the woodstack and frowned in concentration. "You mean the long hill that goes down to Talland Church?"

"Goes farther than the church."

"To Pelynt Farm!" Jed said, arriving with a tray of enamel mugs, the steam coming up from the coffee.

"Further than the farm," said Luke, "That lane goes down to the bay and then along the coast to Polperro. 'Tis just before you comes to Talland beach you sees the cottage."

Jed set down the tray down on the top of the woodstack and nodded for them to help themselves. "Where Josh Hawkey's old father used to live. Died there," he said. "The place has been derelict for years."

"Years ago it was," said Luke, between pipe puffs. "But how long since you was in close enough to notice? Since anybody was? 'Tis a treacherous place; shallow, hidden reefs, full of weed."

Jed nodded as he stirred his coffee. "And you think that's where we'll find Emma?""

Luke sucked thoughtfully at his pipe. "'Twas something I saw t'other day," he said mysteriously. "Lately there's been some good pollack off the point there and I've been going inside for them of an evening, see. That was when I saw the smoke rising straight up from the cottage chimney. Going in close I could see curtains at the windows and a touch of colour about the garden. Somebody living there now, boy!"

"But you don't know that 'tis Emma Bunt," said Jed. "Could be anybody – one of Josh Hawkey's sons, taken himself a wife at last."

"Oh, my good God!" said Luke. "Not much hope of that with both of 'em retarded."

"'They the people at Pelynt Farm?" Nick enquired, sipping his coffee.

"That's right. The rundown place this side of Talland Church. You'll see the Hawkey boys down on Polperro quay – when they have a lobster to sell. No harm in Matt, mind, just backward, that's all, but that big ape of a brother of his, Reuben, he's as maze as a coot."

"Think I've seen him," Nick said. "Built like a bull and just as testy."

"Tis true," Luke agreed. "When he flies into a tantrum, better you're not in reach of his boot."

Lavelle dragged at his cigarette, impatient at the local gossip. "So let's get back to the cottage. What makes you so damn sure its Emma Bunt who lives there?" he asked Luke.

"Because t'other evening I sees an old woman down on the foreshore. I sees her limping along on a stick and dragging a bag of driftwood. I watched her all the way up to the cottage. "Could have sworn 'twas her."

"You recognised her!" exclaimed Lavelle.

"I'd swear 'twas her – and it would answer."

"Why would it answer?" Jed asked, spooning his coffee.

Luke pulled thoughtfully at his pipe. "D'you remember years back a shooting at Pelynt Farm?"

"Do too," said Jed. "Josh Hawkey's wife found dead in the barn yard, shot in the stomach. They said 'twas awful! Not that she didn't have it coming, mind. She was a tyrant, ruled 'em all with a rod of iron. Reuben would stand up to her and 'tis said there were fights, but it was Josh they sent to the assizes, though 'tis my belief he was never within a yard of that gun. 'Twas Reuben he was shielding. Thought the world of that boy, prepared to hang for him."

"But who was it who got him off?" Luke's eyes were sparkling with intrigue. "Wasn't it Mester Ellis who had down a fancy barrister from up country? And didn't he get a verdict of accidental death, brought in on account of the gun going off while Josh was cleaning it?"

Lavelle relaxed. Now they were getting somewhere. These were just the people who could be harbouring the old lady. What a neat set up! Josh Hawkey was deeply indebted to Richard Ellis, who had seen to it that he was aquitted on a murder rap. It was quite feasible that the imbecile son had shot the mother and Josh had taken the blame to protect him. Knowing the full story Ellis would have seen the isolated cottage as a hideaway for Emma and used his hold on the family to obtain it for her, maybe by threatening to produce fresh evidence and having the trial reopened, should they fail to keep her under wraps. It figured.

But it was Luke 's next disclosure that really gave a kick to the theory. Enjoying the drama he was making out of his findings, he had, of course, saved the plum fact for the finale.

"I was out there yesterday," he went on, "Drifting, just under Downend Point, my rods out, my pipe filled, when I sees a boat going straight into the bay. I looks hard and see 'tis that white cabin cruiser Mester Ellis keeps up on his moorings."

"I knows it," said Jed. "Takes it out fishing Saturdays."

"It was *him?*" cried Nick.

"No other," Luke replied. "Went straight across the bay and into that little quay where the Hawkey boys land their lobsters and I sits with my pipe and watches him tie her up; then he goes up the beach to the cottage. Could have stayed a good half hour before he heads back to Trefoy."

All three men looked at Lavelle, who was slowly nodding his head.

"We go over there," he said. "Soon."

"Pity we can't take the Cape," Nick murmured, stirred at the thought of giving Charlie another sailing lesson.

"You couldn't take a big yacht in there!" cried Jed. "'Twould tear the bottom out of her. You'd be better with the *Flora Dora*."

Lavelle sat thoughtful, his brows drawn. This would call for a casual approach, visitors off on a picnic, maybe.

"Forget the sea route," he said. "We go by car, make like we're tourists from the States looking for a way down to the beach. Nick can leave his peaked cap behind and we'll get Charlie into a dress – yeah, and Matelot on a lead."

"I'd leave him behind," said Luke. "I hear tell the Hawkeys have a savage dog down there that would eat Matelot. And likely have the arse out of your pants should you venture into their yard."

"Or having you ducking Reuben's gun!" Jed teased.

****

They chose the following afternoon for the visit to Talland, using the morning for making plans, Lavelle conducting the preparations with his usual naval officer authority.

"Now remember," he said as they drove off the ferry at Bodinnick and into the steep ferny lane at the start of their six-mile journey. "Just you remember if we run into the Hawkey's you leave me to do the talking. We're American tourists, okay?"

"That won't be difficult," Nick muttered, fingering the slick navy blue beach shirt he had been made to wear with lightweight trousers and suede shoes. He would have been much more comfortable in his jeans and jersey than dressed like a visitor. But he had no complaints about Lavelle's choice of clothes for Charlotte. She looked gorgeous in a blue floral dress and a shady hat, the ribbons streaming down behind. Nick found it hard to take his eyes off her, as they sat together in the back of the car with the map on their knees.

Lavelle drove fast, the road winding between the hedgerows, the old trees sleeved in ivy, the leafy foliage jealously screening the landscape as though from alien eyes, keeping Cornwall secret from the traveller.

Soon there were signposts ahead. Lavelle began to slow down but Nick was directing him to go farther on.

"Not this turn off – it's the next, There's the sign! See! Talland. Two miles."

"I got it," Lavelle said, indicating to go right and suddenly they were burrowing into a deep lane so narrow that the greenery pattered against the windows.

Then it was widening out into a junction, a track branching off to some cottages, while the lane ahead tunnelled on down the hill, but parked across the dividing triangle of grass was a pick-up truck, the driver loading milk churns onto the back.

"This the farm?" asked Lavelle.

"Not yet," Nick said. "This is just a hilltop hamlet, but that could be the Hawkey truck. This will be where they leave their milk for the dairy to pick up. Looks like Matt collecting the empty cans."

Lavelle slowed down as the man turned from the truck to hail them.

"Jus' where you be to?" he asked, in a crusty tone.

"We're looking for the beach," said Lavelle cheerfully.

"There'm no way down," said the man, shaking his head.

He was thin, consumptive looking, with dark brooding eyes. "You won't get no farther than our farm. You'd best turn around an' go to Looe."

Lavelle was glancing towards the truck. He could see the name Hawkey on the cab door. "How do we turn around with your truck in the way?"

Matt Hawkey hauled aboard another milk churn. "Then I reckon you'm have to back up, won't 'ee?"

"Oh, brother! You have to be kidding! Back up all the way to the main road – round those bends?"

"You'm no choice, boy. I have to see to my traps a-fore I goes down. I could be gone awhile, so you back up. Bleddy foreigners! Shouldn't have come down 'ere!"

He slammed back the tailboard, slid in the pins, then turned, his thin shoulders hunched as he walked towards the field gate. They watched him go through and disappear into the meadow.

"Now what?" Nick said flatly.

Lavelle sat with his arms over the steering wheel, his gaze on the truck partially blocking the downhill lane ahead. "Wheels in the ditch, I guess we could just about scrape through," he said.

"He'll come after us."

"So we make it tough for him," said Lavelle. He flung open the car door. "Come on! We let the air out of his tyres!"

"You can't!" cried Charlotte, her hand to her mouth.

"Watch us," Nick grinned, as he leapt out after Lavelle.

Minutes later they were on their way, behind them the truck resting on its wheel rims, the hedgerows flattened and Matt Hawkey on his way to his traps.

"That should keep him busy for an hour," said Nick, "and even longer if he has to walk down to the farm for a pump."

Lavelle looked at his watch. "I guess that gives us until about five o'clock," he said.

For more than a mile the road descended steeply downhill, winding between high banks hewn from rock and earth, lowering only occasionally for a passing glimpse of the valley. Above the banks the age-old trees leaned towards each other across the lane, their embracing boughs shutting out the sky except where, through the thinning foliage, the sun poked its dusty beams. Round another bend the incline dropped even more steeply, burrowing down, down, down as though forever.

Lavelle slowed the car to a crawl, craning cautiously ahead.

"Oh! Isn't it spooky," Charlotte said. "Are you sure this is the road?"

"Hold on, honey," he told her, swinging the wheel for another corner. "Can't be much farther. Isn't that the church just ahead?"

The lane was widening. There were signs of habitation; a stony track branching off into a field and farther along an old house set back in the trees. The Spartan dignity about the place gave it the look of a vicarage, and there beyond was the church, half hidden by a gnarled old oak standing sentinel over the graveyard, the headstones barely visible in the long grass. Blue granite steps, smooth as marble, offered a leisurely ascent to the lichen dusted gates sunk deep into the weeds.

Lavelle stared, his foot on the brake.

"You'd have thought they'd have built the church at the top of the parish instead of tucked away down here," he remarked.

"Years ago," Nick said, "This was the top of the parish. Talland was a fishing village down on the shore, but the sea came in and claimed all the houses. All there's left of it is the church, Hawkey's farm and the old stone cottage at the foot of the hill."

"How about that!" Lavelle exclaimed. Then he turned his gaze to the lane leading on down the hill. It looked rough and overgrown. "What say we leave the car here and walk the rest? I sure wouldn't like to get stuck down there."

They agreed. He locked up the car and they set off, following the church wall, where creepers trailed and plants flourished in the dry earth between the stones, where a running ditch, overgrown with nettles, gurgled its secret way through the undergrowth. Soon on the opposite side of the lane the outer wall of a barn or outbuildings replaced the banking. Then came the stone posts of a gateway leading into dung-stained yard and they could just see the farmhouse beyond, long and low and smothered in ivy. Milk cans stood outside the porch and pails were stacked beside the pump, but apart from the clucking hens scratching up the dust and the drone of flies above the midden, there was no sound or sign of life. At least until they became aware of the dog.

He was a large, shaggy coated Alsatian, head resting between his paws, and eyes half closed in slumber, until the crunch of their footfalls alerted him and he sprang up on all fours, barking ferociously, teeth bared like a wolf.

Charlotte drew back, startled. The dog was coming towards them, but soon to be stopped by the length of chain clanging behind him. They saw that it led back to a stone dog kennel behind the wall, and was clipped into an iron ring.

"He's tethered," Lavelle said, against the din the dog was making.

"But not short enough for us to get by," said Nick.

They stood looking into the lane beyond which was narrowing again and dipping even more steeply into another tunnel of trees, but barred to them now by the dog, whose jaw-snapping growl threatened anybody who tried to pass the gate.

Judging by the efforts that the Hawkeys were making to deter strangers it looked as though they just might have something to hide.

Lavelle drew up short. "Ah – ha!" he said, "We got company,"

Two men had appeared at the farmhouse door and were advancing across the yard. They came slowly, their heads lifted in curiosity, their sunburned faces the same dun brown colour as their clothes, in their eyes the same threatening stare as shown by the dog. The ageing, greying man was obviously Josh Hawkey; his balding crown freckled and shining above a face wizened with worry lines. He was stockily built and wore cord breeches, his collarless striped shirt of bolster cotton, unbuttoned and laying bare the scrawny emaciated neck, speckled with grey stubble. The younger of the two was a giant of a man, brutish, with a rawhide face and cheekbones set high under slitted eyes; and by the cat-like stance and the loose gaping mouth, they knew this could only be Reuben. Like his father, he wore a collarless shirt and corduroys, but with a red spotted neckerchief, leather jerkin and heavy lace-up boots. Tipped back from his brow was a stained felt hat, oily black hair peeping from beneath it.

The dog cowered to the ground when it saw him, stifling its growls to a grumbling, whimpering sound, half fear, half anger.

Reuben, head up, jaw hanging, came through the gateway, peering at them, beady eyes in slits behind a beaked nose, but it was Josh, behind him, who spoke first.

"You people lost?" he asked in a husky, reedy voice, and gave them a sudden gummy grin with one yellowed front tooth.

"Guess not," Lavelle said brightly. "We're on our way to the beach."

"You can't get this way," he said, coming out to bar their way.

"The sign at the top said to Talland."

"Yes, but 'tis rough, see, dangerous, all crumbling away. The lane's gone. You can't get down to the shore no more."

"'Tis!" Reuben agreed.

"Gee! That's too bad," said Lavelle. "We'd have sure liked to have taken a look at the bay. But if we can't get down I guess it'll have to be your old church back there. It looked kind of interesting when we came by."

"Oh, 'tis a handsome old church. You be better off looking in there. There's nothing down Talland Bay no more."

"Good of you to warn us about the lane," Lavelle said. Then he turned pointedly to Nick. "I guess that's what the guy back there was trying to tell us about, the one with the broken down truck...."

The farmer looked at him sharply. "Broken down truck, did 'ee say? Not a green pick-up."

"Yeah!" cried Lavelle. "Milk churns on the back. The guy wanted to know if we got a foot pump. He had a flat tyre!".

The two men looked at each other, startled, and Reuben broke into a nasal jabber of disgust, accusing his father of not putting the pump back into the pick-up where it belonged.

"'Tisn't true! I never had it!"

Reuben turned on him angrily, his thick mouth drawn up over broken teeth, eyes blazing.

"You'm a bleddy liar!" he shouted. "I saw 'ee with it just afore cock-crow in the straddle barn. You'm borrowed it to pump up the postman's bike."

They turned towards the gateway, grumbling at each other, then began to walk across the yard, Reuben to an antiquated looking tractor and Josh to the straddle barn, presumably to fetch the foot pump. Lavelle, nodding to Nick and Charlotte to follow, turned to lead the way back up the lane towards the church. Behind them they could hear the tractor starting up and they waved as it came crawling past, puffing smoke from its long funnel, but the Hawkeys were too busy arguing with each other to notice them.

Nick turned away, his shoulders shaking with laughter, Charlotte covering her face to hide her giggles, while Lavelle muttered warnings for them to restrain themselves; but once the tractor had moved out of sight round the bend, they turned quickly to retrace their steps back to the farm.

"The speed they're moving I guess it'll take them a half hour to get up there," Lavelle said. "And that's before they start on the tyres."

"But how do we get past the Alsatian?" Nick wanted to know.

"I'm working on it," Lavelle said.

The dog had taken up sentry duty in the middle of the lane, sulky head on his paws, upper lip lifted threateningly above his teeth, eyes narrowed peevishly as he watched them, and as they began to move forward a growl gurgled warningly from his throat.

"We'll never get past him!" cried Charlotte.

"We don't have to," said Lavelle and stooped to pick up a piece of dry bark from the grass. "Here catch!" And with a sporting gesture he tossed it to Nick, who caught it and tossed it back.

The dog sat up, his interest aroused as he watched them enjoying a game of 'catch'. Charlotte looked on, laughingly anticipating what was to come as Lavelle swung round on the dog, the stick raised in his hand for a throw. The dog was on his feet, the pleasure in his eyes, the chain jangling.

"Fetch, fella!" Lavelle cried, tossing the stick through the yard gateway. The dog sprang after it, and was just able to reach the stick before he came to the end of his chain. But Lavelle wasn't waiting for the retrieve. Instead he made a dive for the gate and dragged it closed, shutting the dog in the yard.

"He'll jump it!" yelled Nick as the dog raced back.

Charlotte caught her breath, her hand raised, but Lavelle stood his ground.

Back came the dog with the stick in his mouth, measuring his stride to leap the gate, but as he lifted himself for the take-off, the chain, trapped beneath the bars, pulled him up short. He stood, meeting their gaze, the peevish look back in his eyes again, the growl gurgling in his throat. Then with a sigh of defeat, he sank to the ground and proceeded to vent his anger on the stick.

"Come on!" said Lavelle, leading off down the lane.

The track descended into a tunnel of green. Tree trunks smothered in ivy spread their mossy boughs into a roof of drooping foliage. Ferns sprang shoulder high into the ever-narrowing pathway as it spiralled deeper and deeper, dark but for occasional rays of sunshine spearing through the branches. The air was heavy with the stench of wild garlic, the silence broken only by tinny birdsong and the crickets chitter-chatter in the grass.

Suddenly they could hear the sea. Ahead, a lumpy white-washed wall of the cottage was coming into view, the chimney stack rising stark against the sky and through the trees came the first glimpse of the blue bay, curving out from a white sandy beach to meet a dark headland.

Charlotte, unable to contain her excitement, hurried ahead, to plunge from the shade into yellow sunlight where, beside the cottage, washing was swinging across a cobbled yard. There was a porch overhung with honeysuckle, looking out on a garden, gay with summer flowers. Bending to tend them was someone in a floral pinafore, worn over a long black dress, someone with wispy white hair gathered back into a bun.

Startled by Charlotte's cry, she lifted her brown, lined face, her grey brows drawn together with sudden curiosity, staring at them, completely dumbfounded as they came into view.

CHAPTER SEVENTEEN

It was Emma Bunt. There was no need to enquire. The answer was in Charlotte's face, suddenly pink and crumpled; eyes moist, bright with emotion. She stumbled forward, her hand outstretched.

"Granny! Granny!"

The old lady looked at her at first without recognition, her astonishment at the appearance of strangers from the overgrown lane still occupying her concentration and she could only stare, her face upturned. The face suggested character, an inner strength; a lined face, burned dark like a gypsy, yet kindly; a warmth about the mouth, intelligence in the pin sharp brown eyes, and a certain dignity in the lift of her head, turned now thoughtfully to one side as her glance rested on Charlotte. There was a likeness in the girl's face which sent her thoughts searching back to the tight-shut recesses of her memory; the splash of ducks in the still waters of the creek, a child sculling, ripples on the surface ever widening in the green depths.

Her hand fell to her side, the flowers she had been holding slipping to the grass at her feet and her eyes were suddenly wide, the pupils dilated as though she were seeing a ghost.

Charlotte crept forward, reaching for her. "Granny, you remember me, Charlie, pilot Bill's daughter?"

The old lady opened her mouth, her breath coming heavily. "But Charlie died!" She cried. "My little maid, Charlie, she died up country."

Lavelle was shaking his head. "That was all talk, ma'am, rumour. Take a look at her – can't you see Bill?"

The old lady drew a sharp breath, her glance fixed on Charlotte's face, recognising now the determined Trevelyan chin, a familiar tenderness about her mouth, and there was no mistaking the eyes, blue and intense, the eyes of her father.

"My love!" she cried, her voice raised shrill.

Charlotte, speechless with emotion, fell into her arms and the old lady held her with closed eyes, her joy so deep it was almost like sorrow, her work-worn hands feeling into the girl's shoulders, as though to assure herself she was real. Then suddenly she found control, biting back her lower lip against the sobs rising to her throat, she held Charlotte back, looking at her, agape with wonder.

"Oh, my love, 'tis good to see you, to have you back."

Charlotte responded fondly and for a little while they hugged each other, until she turned to introduce her friends.

A few prompting reminders of the war days and Emma was soon recalling Lavelle as the naval lieutenant who used to go fishing with the pilot, and although Nick was a stranger she remembered his sister, Joanna – and their mother from Newlyn.

"She was a good soul. Used to buy the red currant jam I made for the

Institute when she came to St Ruan. Oh, how I longs to see some of they ole faces again! Syd, the postman, Nora over at the bakery and Essa Luke coming loaded up the hill with the washing she took in from the Trefoy hotels. Tis only when they'm gone, you misses 'em, don't 'ee. But here's me chattering on, let's go inside and have a cup of tea."

She reached for her stick and they followed as she led the way into the cottage, ducking under the honeysuckle growing down over the porch, the scent of it drifting in to meet the woodsmoke from the fire.

Nick immediately made himself busy, reaching down cups from the cupboard while Lavelle took the poker to the driftwood embers to raise a flame under the kettle, soot black on the grate. But Charlotte stood aghast, struck by the shabbiness of the place, remembering the creekside cottage at Pendowry. Here, there were no pretty chintz covers, no ornaments or family photographs, and despite the scrubbed clean look it was dingy, the fagged floor covered with strips of thready carpet, the colours washed out of the curtains and faded from the cushions upon the hard cane chairs. The thick uneven walls were almost bare but for a sepia print of a storm scene, and the large commemorative picture of King Edward VII and Queen Alexandra, framed behind cracked glass, had probably been there since their Coronation.

Even so there were flowers in stone jars; cowslips and sea pinks, arranged with sprays of fern, and there was a warm smell of strawberry jam bubbling in a black pot on the hob.

When they were seated round the tea tray and Emma Bunt was handing round the soft bread splits to eat with the jam and a bowl of crusted, clotted cream, Charlotte asked. "Why did you leave the cottage at Pendowry, Granny? Why did you allow Richard Ellis to move you down here?"

The old lady sighed. "Twas only s'posed to be temporary, while he had the cottage roof repaired. The damp was doing my arthritis no good and Mester Ellis thought it would be better for me down here on the coast for a spell. He don't charge me a penny rent, mind! But can be bleak in winter though when the sou'westerlies bring in the weather, and there's none of the comforts I had at my ole cottage. No room for my stuff. 'Been in storage so long I worry it might be rotten. But I think 'tis the loneliness what grieves me most. Down here I never sees a soul, not even the postman. Not that I ever get any answers to my letters. Given up writing 'em. Out o' sight, out o' mind, s'pose 'tis."

"A long climb to go post a letter," Lavelle suggested, watching her thoughtfully over his teacup.

"Oh, I don't post they. Josh does that. Won't have me climb that hill for nothing, says 't'would cripple me to try."

"So how do you shop?" Nick asked.

"Don't. Josh brings me stewing bones and a bit of beef for pasties or maybe mackerel when the boys been fishing. And Fridays there's a box of groceries sent by Mester Ellis – paid for out of my pension, mind, which he keeps safe for me. 'Taters and greens I grows down the garden at the back. Buried though I be, I reckon I don't go short."

Lavelle nodded, deeply aware of the lawyer's strategy. Keeping her content would keep her quiet. "Is that lane back there the only way out of the bay?" he asked her.

"Oyez. Part of the lane over to Polperro has crumbled into the sea. Only way round is up the hill which you came down. Farthest I gets is up to the farm gate when they forgets to bring down my milk, but there's no getting by that ole dog. Lately I've been giving him bones, but 'tis no good, he still won't let me by. 'Tis a wonder you weren't savaged."

"His chain was trapped under the gate," Nick told her, with a remarkably straight face.

"There now!" She said, her eyes wide. "I reckon you was lucky. He'd have gone for you. He'm a mean ole dog."

Lavelle found himself glancing uneasily towards the open doorway, half expecting a shadow to cross the triangle of sunlight thrown across the flagstones, half listening for footfalls on the path, but the only sound was the twitter of birds and the distant beat of the surf on the shore.

Emma Bunt was pouring out more tea and fluttering like a mother hen around her unexpected company. It was a rare occasion for her to have visitors.

"Oh, 'tis lonely down here," she told them. "But you gets used to it. I finds that 'tis better that I don't dwell on what I had, but on what I've got, bit though it be. Of course, I'd have been back when the cottage roof was done, but then ole Mester Tevelyan took bad and proper nursing staff had to be called in. 'Course, he wouldn't have them living up at the Manor so they had to have my cottage, see. T'will have to end sometime though. Mester Trevelyan is an old man. He won't live forever and one day they'll be gone and I can go back as Mester Ellis promised I should."

They exchanged glances. Nick opened his mouth to speak, but it was Charlotte who said in a quiet, small voice.

"Granny, there's nobody living in your cottage."

Emma Bunt stared at her, puzzled. "Nobody living there!" she repeated. "But there must me. T'was needed for the master's nurses! That's what Mester Ellis told me."

"He lied to you, ma'am," said Lavelle. "There are no nurses."

"None?" Her wrenched brow drew into a frown. "So – so who looks after Mester Trevelyan? Somebody has to..."

"Uncle Silas died, granny," Charlotte said gently.

"Died! The master dead! Oh, my good God! When was this then, maid?"

"Last February."

"Last February!" she echoed. "But that was back winter. 'Can't be true, Mester Ellis would have said. Only down here Tuesday. Never seen the likes of him since primrose time. I thought 'twas funny him coming, but he never said nothing. 'Fact, when I asked after the master he said the old gentleman was fine and still banging with his stick for attention. I don't understand! Why should Mester Ellis lie to me?"

"There's plenty you don't understand, ma'am," Lavelle said. "That's why we're here, to put you straight."

Charlotte nodded. "Its true, granny. Uncle Silas is dead and your cottage has been empty since you left; no repairs have been done to the roof, it's just derelict, the gate is off the hinges, the garden overgrown. We could show you. It's all been left to rot."

The old lady looked from one to another, lips apart, a pinkness lifting to her cheeks.

"Left to rot!" She looked hurt. "There now! Well, I suppose if I wasn't wanted back, perhaps he didn't like to say. But even so, I should have been told of the master's death. I should have been at the funeral. Mester Trevelyan would have wished it." She turned sharply to Charlotte. "Was it a big funeral, maid?"

"I don't know," said Charlotte. "Rachel wouldn't let me go."

The old lady drew a quick breath. "Wouldn't let you go!" she cried. "But you're his heir! Everything is willed to you!"

"You know that?" Lavelle said sharply.

"'Course I knows it, everyone knows it. 'Twas the master's wish always was. You can ask Mester Ellis."

"Granny," Charlotte said firmly. "Uncle Silas's lawyer has been deceiving you, he's been deceiving us all."

Nick sitting forward in his chair, joined in. "He's had a new will forged so that it all goes to her stepmother, Rachel Ives."

"Rachel! To her? That hussy!"

Emma Bunt's mouth had dropped open, horror in her face, and she sat uttering little gasps of dismay as she listened to their disclosures, of how Charlotte was being cheated and Pendowry sold up for development. At first she found it all too incredible to believe. Richard Ellis had always treated her with the utmost respect and kindness, appearing to go out of his way to make her life easier. All the same, her years on the Talland shore had not been entirely without questioning, without moments of doubt when the solitude seemed to be a coincidence too strange not to have been contrived. Why had there been no answers to her letters? Why were there always obstacles whenever she expressed the wish to visit Bodmin or St Ruan? There had been no logic to it, not until now.

They watched her lined face harden and her eyes grow cold as she listened to them, then, as though to give some vent to the anger within her, she took up the poker and began to dig into the fire.

"Never did I hear of such treachery!" she said. "The master would turn in his grave. 'Tis wicked! You'll have to stop them."

"For that we need proof that Charlie is the true beneficiary," said Lavelle grimly.

She shot him a glance. "And so she is! The true heir! I knows it. Didn't my dear husband, Hiram, witness the will?" she said fiercely.

"And Silas had a copy?"

"He did, too. And tis kept safe."

"You know where it is?"

For a moment she did not answer, but went on poking at the fire, chipping at the glowing wood, sending sparks back against the soot lined grate. "Oyez, I knows," she said.

They waited for her to go on, but she was taking her time, holding back with little irrelevancies.

"'Tis funny you should say Master Bill never trusted the lawyer because neither did the master. Apart from old Mester Penrose, who'd always been the family solicitor, he didn't have a good word for none of them, least of all Mester Ellis. When Mester Penrose died, Master Bill wanted to go to a firm in Bodmin, but the master didn't want to bother. Said they were all in league with each other. T'would do no good. Funny, but I always got along with the master. I used to bring him sticks to whittle. 'Twas his hobby, see, carving the tops and shaping them into figureheads. Beautiful." She tapped the stick at her knee. "This was one he carved, made for me specially, a good heavy one to carry my weight. Made me real proud, the master giving it to me. I reckon 'twas because I always admired his work, and since he'd lost Master Bill I'd always been a friend to him."

Lavelle was sweating with impatience, anxious for her to go on before the Hawkeys came looking for them. "You were telling us about the copy of the will, ma'am," he prompted her.

"So I was."

She sat back in her chair thoughtfully; memory putting lights into her eyes, and for a moment there was no sound but the hum of flies from the open doorway. Presently she began, her voice lowered in reverence.

"The day the word came that Master Bill had been killed in France, 'twas me who had to go up to the manor house to break the news to old Master Trevelyan. Never will I forget that day; the rain teeming down, choking the land with mud, streaming down the windows of the conservatory where the master sat, almost as though it was weeping for him. He couldn't, poor soul, he just stared and shook, his face like a ghost. Master Bill had been like a son to him.

"Then later that same summer, the master calls me to his side, all secretive like, and he tells me that one day when his time comes there was something I had to do for him. He wanted me to deliver the details of his last will and testimony to the Probate Registry at Bodmin. And that I must see no other but the officer in charge and tell nobody, least of all Mester Ellis, what I had done. Then he told me where I would find it. I was to go up to the thirteenth watermill, and I would see his old sea chest. And with me I must take his stick, the one he always kept by his side, and that I was to give the lid a good whack – the only way to open it. T'was stiff, see. And there I would find a package hidden, with thirteen pieces of silver, with which I was to take the bus to Bodmin. That was the master's wish. But now since it's come to this, I shall need help to get there. That's why I've told you."

They looked at her without speaking, the excitement showing in their faces, but Lavelle's appraisal was not without scepticism. A crazy place to hide it, up in some old watermill. And would it still be there? Ellis would have been all through those properties.

"Did the lawyer ever ask you about Mr Trevelyan's copy of the will, ma'am?"

"Regular. But he never got to know nothing from me."

"What about when he came to see you on Tuesday?"

She shook her head. "Didn't ask me about it then, too busy asking me about other things."

"What for instance?" Lavelle enquired.

"Oh, the usual," she answered. "Asked after my health, the garden, anything I wanted special, if I'd had any visitor's – that's what he always wants to know. Tuesday he asked me three times if anybody had been down to see me, kept on coming back to it, asking if there'd been a middle aged lady, rather stout, to see me? The only stout lady down here is me, I told him."

Charlotte and Nick, seeing no significance the lawyer's enquiry, laughed at her joke, but Lavelle knew at once what lay behind it. Ellis had received the picture card, he'd got the message and his number one suspect was Rachel's Aunt Millicent.

"Can you remember anything else he talked about?" Lavelle asked her.

"Not much, sir. After he'd done asking questions it was my turn. I wanted to know about the cottage and how the blackcurrant bushes were looking. And to think of it," she said disgustedly, "every answer he gave me was a lie, even to promising to take me over in his boat to see the cottage. 'Couldn't have had any intention!"

Lavelle frowned. "Promised to take you over in his boat!" He exchanged a sharp glance with Nick.

"When was this to be?" Nick asked her.

"He said 'twould have to be when the Hawkeys were next up at the cattle market at Liskeard. They don't like him landing here, see. 'Gets peevish about it – so he says! So 'twouldn't do for him to bring the boat in again so soon. They'd see from the farm, but not when they'm away at market. 'Said he'd have me over there and back and they'd never know I'd been."

Oh, sure, Lavelle thought to himself. Nobody to see him come or see him leave. Nobody to connect Richard Ellis if her body was ever washed up. This guy was getting desperate. It was a wonder he had spared her so long. If she did know the old man's secret, she could blow his plans sky high. Yet he had gone to great lengths to keep her mute, isolate her from all communications, using lies, blackmail, collusion. Why had he done this? Maybe to tread softly, avoid any coincidence with another death. He was shrewd enough to have suspected all along that, with Bill gone, Silas would have confided in Emma. Could be Ellis was relying on the fact that providing she remained ignorant of the old man's death, the document would not come to light and he would be clear of suspicion. But now it was different. The pressure was on; somebody was wise to him. He couldn't risk them getting to her. So he had decided she would have to go.

Lavelle understood immediately that his provocation of Ellis with the anonymous postcards had driven him to this. Seeing his plans under threat, his past catching up with him, he was manning his defences and stopping a gap. It could cost the old lady her life if they didn't get her away from the cottage.

He sat tense, his eyes on the door. Decisions would have to be made – fast. Before the Hawkeys got back.

Emma was still complaining about Ellis. "All he ever told me was lies, lies, lies. But not no more," she said, bending to the tea tray and beginning to collect the cups and saucers. The haste, the clatter she made reflected her wounded pride, her indignation at being deceived. Charlotte rose to help her, carrying away dishes to the kitchen. But the old lady remained, holding the tray, her knuckles white on the handles, and for a moment she stood deliberating. Then, her face suddenly grim with resolve, she set the tray down and turned to Lavelle.

"How did you come down here – walked?" she demanded.

"From the church. We left the car back there," he answered, glancing uneasily towards the door again.

She frowned. "'Tis a long climb, but reckon I'm game if you was to take my arm, sir. I don't stay here no more, not after what I've just heard, I don't. I'm going back. I have to see that package reaches the Probate office in Bodmin," she cried, rising from her chair.

Lavelle was on his feet, struck with sudden alarm. They couldn't have her barging into the Hawkey bothers. He reached out to put a comforting arm round her shoulder. "Here now, ma'am. Let's not be too hasty. First we have to think this out."

"I don't hold with thinking," she told him, "Not when I've made up my mind."

She picked up the tray and limped away to the kitchen, where they could hear her making plain her intentions to Charlotte.

"But we can't leave her here," Nick said in a loud whisper.

"Too damn right we can't," said Lavelle, moving to the door. He had to satisfy himself that the Hawkeys were not on their way. All through the old lady's story he had expected them to suddenly come barging in, but not wanting to alarm her he had been awaiting the right moment to take a look up the lane. The sun was warm on his face as he stood now, alert for voices, footfalls, the distant throb of a tractor, but there was nothing, just the chirp of grasshoppers and the hum of bees.

Coming back into the cottage, shaking his head to Nick's questioning glance, he went on to the window and stood thoughtfully looking out over the bay. The tide was out; the reefs bared like giant jaws of broken teeth, standing stark from the silvery grey sand.

Nick joined him. "I don't like the look of it, do you?"

Lavelle shook his head. "There's a hell of a lot of deep water out there, Nick, enough to lose her overboard."

Nick shot him a glance. "He wouldn't go that far!"

Lavelle turned to him, his eyes narrowed. "Wouldn't he?" he said bleakly. "You don't really know Ellis."

Nick stared at him, detecting a deep animosity Lavelle had towards this man, a grudge that went back much farther than the lawyer's involvement with the Pendowry inheritance. But if Lavelle was speaking from experience Nick was in no doubt about taking him seriously.

"You think we should go to the police."

Lavelle spread his arms. "How do we go to the police? No crime has been committed. Ellis could say he moved her out of the cottage on Silas Trevelyan's instruction. Hadn't the old guy a reputation for getting rid of his staff?"

"But not when they've heard what she has to say and we have the will to prove it."

Lavelle gave him a sidelong glance. "Hang on, buddy! We have haven't found it yet. How do we know Ellis hasn't got there first and destroyed the goddamn thing?"

Nick lifted his eyes. "Christ! I hadn't thought of that!"

Lavelle asked quickly. "When is the cattle market at Liskeard?"

Nick frowned. "It's on a Friday – but that's tomorrow," he said in a hoarse whisper.

"Then we have to get her away from here – tonight."

"But how?" Nick demanded. "Suppose we run into the Hawkeys. They might set their bleddy dog on us."

Lavelle shook his head. He had no intention of risking a confrontation with the Hawkeys. Word would go straight back to Ellis and provide clues to their identity. At this stage it was important that they should continue to remain anonymous, leave as they came, beach intruders the Hawkeys were being paid to keep out. Even though Lavelle was now in some doubt that the will would still be in its hiding place, the search for evidence would have to go on, the fraud smashed. Too long had this man been allowed to violate the lives of others; it had happened to him, to Charlie, and now to this defenceless old lady. His mind went back to her cottage at the creekside, the furniture she believed in storage, rotting, covered in mould, while she had been condemned to live in isolation to preserve her silence. Now the bastard was planning to kill her for his own peace of mind.

But like hell he would!

Nick's voice broke through his thoughts. "So what do we do?"

Lavelle nodded towards the shore. "We take her out that way," he said. "We come back after dark. In the *Flora Dora*."

"In through those reefs – in the dark?" Nick cried, his glance on the fangs of rock.

"There's a way through, there has to be, otherwise how would the Hawkeys and Ellis have got in? You can just see the little quay out there, up under the headland. See! There's their boat! I guess we ought to go down there before we leave and take a look."

"That old Kelvin we have in the *Flora Dora* makes a hell of a din," said Nick doubtfully. "They might hear it up at the farm."

"Then we cut the engine at the head of the bay and pole in with the tide."

Nick nodded, the adventure of it appealing to him; a secret landing, night their cover, stealth. Poling in with the tide was a good idea. By midnight there would be plenty of water and time enough to pick up the old lady and pole back again. Of course, it would be out of the question taking her back to her cottage, the state it was in, but he supposed Joanna would put her up.

Lavelle didn't agree. "Too near home," he said. "We don't want her meeting up with Ellis. What about your old ma in Newlyn? Used to be old friends, didn't they? What do you say we drive Mrs Bunt down there for a visit? Nice surprise for your old lady to see her again, take her in as a paying guest. You think she'd go for it?"

Nick bit his lips together thoughtfully. His mother liked a bit of company, someone to go shopping with and take to the whist drives. And there were raspberry canes and gooseberry bushes all along the back terrace. Emma would like it there. He gave Lavelle a firm nod of approval, then grinned, his glance towards the kitchen where the good lady was still raging on about the lawyer and the rousting he would get from her the next time they met. "But first we'll have to bring her round to our way of thinking."

"I guess so," Lavelle said, with a sigh.

But Emma was easily persuaded that a plan of cunning was better than a clash with the Hawkeys and the risk of being savaged by their dog. She welcomed the suggestion of a holiday down at Newlyn with Nick's mother – just until the legal problems had been resolved, Charlotte promised. Then if all went well, her cottage could be renovated and she could go back to live on the creekside where she belonged. This brought tears to Emma Bunt's eyes and she hugged the girl fondly again.

"Tonight, I shall put the lantern in the window and keep it burning 'til you come," she told Lavelle. "Like I used to do in winter for the Hawkey boys when they was out fishing after dark. Used to give 'em a bearing for coming into the causeway between the reefs."

Thanking her they rose to leave. Outside, with still no sign of the Hawkeys, the two men went to make a quick reconnaissance of the landing place. It was no more than a strip of stone jetty leading along the cliffside towards the headland. At one time it must have been part of the old fish dock, for at the end they found a winch and an iron capstan. Here too, tucked in between the boulders was a little quay of deep water, where lying at anchor was a dilapidated fishing boat, the once white paint flaking, the gear red with rust, and, rubbing against her old tyre fenders, was a pulling dinghy in no better condition. Rope and lobster pots were heaped untidily about the jetty.

Nick wanted to go out over the rocks to see if he could spot the causeway, but Lavelle was anxious to get back to the car before the Hawkeys appeared. Waving their goodbyes to Emma Bunt they began the long climb back up the hill, their ears straining for the sound of the tractor or the truck, but when they reached the farm and the dog sprang up to bark ferociously at them, his chain was still trapped under the gate.

Nearing the car Lavelle broke into a run and he was already revving up the engine as Nick and Charlotte scrambled into their seats. Gravel spat from the tyres as they roared up the hill.

The truck was at the junction, ready to be away; Josh at the wheel, but the brothers seemed to be having an argument. They were standing face to face, shouting insults at each other, Reuben pointing angrily towards the tractor. Lavelle pipped for them to move so that he could get by and they walked on without looking up, still continuing their dispute, apparently over whom was to drive the tractor and who was to ride in the truck.

As the car drew level Matt Hawkey suddenly recognised them and let out a shout, but Lavelle accelerated hard to the main road, only one thought on his mind, to rescue Emma Bunt from her imprisonment that night.

CHAPTER EIGHTEEN

Harriet Couch looked down at the letters on her desk, the afternoon post waiting to be signed by Richard Ellis. Nearly four o' clock and he still hadn't summoned her into his office. Just two hours ago he had told her he wanted to study the architect's report on the Pendowry estate and was not to be disturbed. The Pendowry file came before everything. He was obsessed with it. She put her elbows on the desk and rested her chin on her knuckles, exasperated at the delay. The letters were going to miss the post. She had a good mind to ignore his orders and take them in.

If she had done so Miss Couch would have been startled to see the architect's report cast aside unopened and her employer sitting bent over his desk, pencil in hand, scrawling drawings and diagrams all over a single sheet of paper. There were mooring buoys, frape lines, a wharfside, with a dinghy sketched in, and in the margins jottings on tides and currents. Outside the office window the sky had clouded over and a damp breeze whipped back the curtains, chilling the room, but Richard Ellis was oblivious to it as he diligently planned an excursion by sea to settle some business in Talland Bay.

Now with the likelihood of a search being made for Emma Bunt, he had no alternative but to get rid of her. Even though the chances of her being found were slim, it was not worth the risk. Once she knew she had been deceived, then he would be in trouble. Her evidence would be invaluable to those seeking to dispute the validity of the will.

Emma Bunt had been too close to Silas Trevelyan, indeed to the family. Her husband, Hiram, was one of the two witnesses and his perfectly copied signature now endorsed the forgery. Even more disturbing was the possibility that the old man's original copy might still be in existence and, he suspected, in Emma Bunt's possession. At the time of the forgery Ellis had not expected that copy to pose any problem. Locked up in the desk at Pendowry it would have been a simple matter to retrieve and destroy after Silas' death.

But after Penrose died Ellis noticed a change in his client. Silas was becoming more and more hostile towards him, though for what reason he could not imagine. Therefore, to leave one copy of the will at Pendowry with Silas in his present state of mind had seemed extremely inadvisable. Suppose the old man should decide to dispense with his services? On more than one occasion he had threatened to transfer his affairs to Proctor and Penhaligan in Bodmin, and only over some conflict of opinion.

But all efforts to induce Silas to hand over the deed, on whatever pretext and however plausible, had only met with opposition. He always had excuses; either the key to the desk had been mislaid or the wrong one produced and, then after much grumbling and a half hearted attempt at a search, the old man would lose patience and tell Ellis to come back another day.

Then Ellis had returned, only to find the study blackened, the desk charred and the old man's private papers in ashes. Apparently, in one of his tantrums,

Silas had knocked over a candelabra and set fire to the desk. He would have burned the house down, had not Emma Bunt seen the smoke and raised the alarm.

Silas had seemed badly shocked and so distressed about the loss of his papers, that he announced his intention of making a new will. Eventually he had been persuaded that there was really no need; it was only a copy that had been destroyed and that the original was safe in his lawyer's vault. Although his concern appeared to be genuine and the incident too nearly a disaster to be other than an accident, Ellis could not help intuit a touch of Trevelyan cunning. Had he deliberately started the fire after first removing the document and passing it into the safe hands of his servant, Emma Bunt? Had it all been contrived to avoid handing it over to him? And since Silas had not asked for another copy for his files which Ellis first feared he might, there seemed little doubt that the document was still in existence.

It was a theory Ellis had carefully investigated – and without a question being asked. If Silas had taken Emma Bunt into his confidence there would be no question of that trust being betrayed. The Cornish kept their secrets well. Instead Ellis made regular visits to her cottage while she was up at the Manor, sifting through her belongings with meticulous care and thoroughness. He had also explored the manor house from cellar to attic, taking apart the panels, the pictures, the furniture, but had found nothing. He had made a careful examination of the charred Georgian desk. There had been legal documents there, among them the remains of an envelope incredibly like the one which had contained the copy of the will. It should have been enough to satisfy him but he could take no chances. If there were but the slightest possibility that Emma Bunt had that copy, he would need to make sure she was never to learn of Silas Trevelyan's death.

But now she had become a threat, an obstacle to be removed.

He had given much thought to how it could be done. The sea was the answer. The rope-strewn wharfside offered him the means. The seclusion of the Talland shore would provide the privacy he would need for her disposal; the coastal paths, crumbling, untrodden, the bay overlooked only by woodland and heath, the Hawkeys away at Liskeard market.

He would start early, the breakfast hour, the fishing boats gone to sea, the pleasure craft still in the harbour, few people about to notice him leave Trefoy. Once round Downend Point and into Talland Bay, he would be out of sight of the coastguard. Nobody to see him land except her. She would be delighted, ready and eager at the prospect of going to see her old cottage, glad to take his arm as they stepped over the ropes on the wharfside to reach his waiting boat.

He would have made all the necessary preparations before he went to the cottage; hauled up the mooring iron, fastened to it a second length of rope with a noose on the end, the noose he planned to guide Emma's foot into as he helped her across the jetty. Then the pause, bending as though to move the rope from her path. One jerk of his hand and the noose would snap fast round her ankle and before she had time even to recover from her astonishment, he would heave the mooring iron over the quayside. For a moment or two, the loose line would snake across the quay, then as it drew taut, she would be snatched off balance, and be hauled sideways to plunge after it with a sickening dive to the bottom. It would be over in seconds. No screams, just bubbles. When they had settled he would take his boat and tow the mooring iron, with the body floating from it, to the deep water from where he had taken it. Then drawing in the line, he would cut free the rope holding the body, so that it would float out with the tide. Raise no suspicions, and it may take months before her body was found. By then the only suspect would be Reuben.

Before he left Talland he intended to make a thorough search of her cottage to assure himself the copy of the will was not among her belongings, there for somebody else to find. Even with Emma Bunt out of the way, there was still the girl and the Australian woman to be reckoned with, no doubt busily fortifying themselves for battle on the speculative gossipings of the St Ruan townsfolk. But they would need more than just gossip and hearsay to successfully contest the will. They would need new evidence, which they did not yet possess, otherwise he would have already heard from their solicitors.

At the moment it was clearly a game of nerves. The watchers were trying to intimidate him with a campaign of harassment by those threatening postcards, but he would go ahead and call their bluff. The danger was that their meddling might bring about an enquiry and he might have to defend himself. It was imperative that he dealt with them swiftly, and resolve the problem before it took hold.

A timid knock on the door raised him from his reverie, and remembering Miss Couch, he slipped the paper away under the blotter, picked up the architect's report and called her in.

He left early that evening, unable to give his mind to anything until tomorrow's operation was over. The weather was changing, the mist creeping in, obscuring the sun, and the quiet waters, gently whipped up by the vaporous breeze, were beginning to look like crumpled satin in the pearly light. Sea fog would have been ideal for his plan, but in Cornwall's unpredictable climate, not certain to last until tomorrow, a pity.

****

At the Trefoy Hotel, curled up with a book on the terrace, Linda was also watching the mist rolling in, but with a sense of disappointment. Jack had half promised she should go for a sail with them that evening and she had been waiting for his call. Now with fog about she doubted whether they would think it wise to venture out.

She had been looking forward to another trip aboard the *Cape Columbo*.

She was still glowing from the last one; an unforgettable evening, slanting through sunset waters, the gentle breeze barely enough to fill the sails, but there had been no hurry. It had been almost dark when they had returned to the harbour. He had rowed her ashore for a drink at a waterside bar, just the two of them. They had talked, endlessly, about San Francisco, about the war, about her – but not so much about himself. He never spoke of Charlotte's mother, but then neither did Charlotte. There were no little family references one would have expected. In fact she treated him more like a friend than a father. Linda sensed a mystery in their relationship. They were close – even the skipper, as though there was secret all three shared, a confidence that drew them together.

Linda had not wanted to pry. Her relationship with the American was young yet and she was still feeling her way, just glad to be with him, glad of the reassuring hug of his arm around her, the warmth of his kiss. She could only hope that his feelings for her would blossom and mature.

All afternoon the book had been open on her knee, but although her eyes had followed the lines on the page, her mind was too full of him to take in the meaning of the words. Every now and again she had felt the urge to allow her gaze to wander towards the *Cape Columbo* moored in the river. The yacht looked deserted, not even Matelot patrolling the deck. She believed they were all ashore somewhere since the *Dipper* did not appear to be on the moorings. She was right because a little later she saw them returning, Charlotte wearing a dress and Nick in his Sunday best. Jack had his back to her; his head bent to the motor.

She lifted her hand to wave, but they did not see her. The patchy mist was sweeping down, taking the tops off the headlands and the breeze felt wet on her face.

They wouldn't be going sailing, but perhaps he would call...

****

Later that evening Jack Lavelle had more on his mind than making social calls on Linda. He was worried about the weather. He had watched the mist drifting like smoke over the river, the shore lights smudged behind it as darkness fell.

Nick shared his apprehension, the thought of that tooth-rocked passage into Talland Bay was quite daunting enough in darkness, without fog an added hazard.

"We won't see the light from the cottage until we get right in and by then we could have hit one of those hidden reefs," he said.

Lavelle nodded, his brow furrowed. They were sitting round the saloon table, the charts out, the coffee going cold.

"Once we leave the point we have to have a compass bearing."

"We could do with some advice from Luke," Charlotte suggested.

Lavelle looked at his watch. "It's gone ten. Where will he be at this hour?"

"In the Lugger," said Nick, "Settling into his brown ale and pickled egg."

Lavelle rose to get his coat. "Then let's go find him. I could sure use a drink."

"Take Matelot with you," Charlotte cried as the dog shot up the companionway before them.

The mist had thickened, a shroud over the harbour that left a layer of wetness on everything it touched; deck, coaming, the paintwork of the pram dinghy as they scrambled aboard. The colours too, were lost in the greyness, the moored craft passing like phantom shapes as Nick sculled ashore, the dampness glittering up from the pitted stone as they scraped into St Ruan jetty.

Above them blue puff balls of light marked the inn across the quay, where a chorus of "*You Make Fast the Dinghy*" lifted above the pre-closing time hubbub of voices. Lavelle shouldered his way in.

Fisherman Luke, squeezed up in a corner of the bar, beamed at them. From the new urgency he saw in their faces, he guessed their mission to Talland had been worthwhile. His eyes twinkled as he listened to their plan to bring Emma Bunt out by sea, applauding the idea and waving away their fears about the mist.

"'Tis nothing," he assured them. "'Tis for heat."

"We don't want a weather forecast, just how to get in there without tearing the bottom out of Jed's boat," Nick snapped.

Luke stroked his stubble. "Then I reckon I'd run along the coast till you comes level with Ula rock off Downend Point, then steer North by N'east. Look out for two lumps of rock marking the reef. The causeway goes in between them. Head straight then till you sees a big tooth of rock. From there you may see the light from the cottage that'll take you into the Hawkey quay."

Lavelle ordered some more drinks, and they talked in lowered tones, keeping to themselves in the corner of the bar. When they rose to leave Luke was still optimistic about the weather.

"It'll be cleared by midnight," he promised them as they went out into the cobwebs of drizzle.

Nick whistled to Matelot and they hurried, with him on their heels to the jetty. "We might as well pick up the *Flora Dora* and be on our way," he said, as they pushed off from the wharfside.

Lavelle nodded. "I guess so." His eyes rested on the *Cape Columbo*, the hazy glow of the cabin lights, where Charlie waited for them. The thought of involving her in this brought him a sudden twinge of disquiet.

"I don't like it either," Nick admitted, when Lavelle voiced his view. "but just you try leaving her behind."

"I guess we had better put her in charge of the boat while we go to the cottage. Any trouble with the Hawkeys and she'll be out of it. Okay?"

Nick agreed.

Within the hour they were all three aboard the apple green fishing boat, chugging out of the harbour. Charlotte, muffled up in one of Lavelle's heavy Aran sweaters and Nick's sou'wester pulled over her head, was all aglow with excitement and not at that moment sharing the tension and anxiety felt by her two companions.

Ahead the dark shoulder of Pencarrow Head dipped into the silver shimmer of the sea, the white mist floating in wispy veils above the cliffs. The swell was long and languid, stirred only by their own bow wave frilling up for'ard and fanning out behind. Out of the fog at sea came the hollow toll of the bell buoy off Udder Rock, its eerie moan a lost soul warning of peril. In just over an hour they reached Downend Point and the fog swept reaches of Talland Bay, where they could feel the pull of the tide that was to take them in.

Lavelle switched off the lights and it was suddenly very dark, with just the dim glimmer of the compass dial and the glow from his cigarette. Nick went astern with an oar, ready to pole them in. When Lavelle cut the engine, the silence was death-like, not even a swish of wash against the bow.

They crept in with no sense of time or distance, and it seemed to Charlotte, shivering against the wheelhouse with the fog against the glass, one eternity before that great eye-tooth of a rock loomed up to starboard.

Then, just as Luke had promised, they saw an orange candle-glow beckoning from Emma Bunt's window.

CHAPTER NINETEEN

The waiting seemed endless. Charlotte had wanted to go with them but they said they needed her to stay with the boat, to alert them with a blast of the horn if the Hawkey brothers should appear. It was nonsense, of course, just Nick being protective. If there was going to be trouble it was more likely to be up at the cottage than down here on the jetty.

They had tied up to the iron capstan on the derelict quay and there was nothing for her to do but to sit on the gunwale and wait for them to return. It was worse, the waiting, the not knowing what was going on, worse than whatever else there was to face. She had been excited on the cruise down, thrilled to be taking part, but now the eeriness of her surroundings inspired fanciful fears being busy would have averted; Reuben Hawkey waiting with his gun at the cottage, the savage dog off the leash, Granny harassed and frightened, in need of comfort.

She sat alert, her ears straining for the slightest sound, her eyes tired from peering into the darkness, peering at the amber smudge of light from the cottage window. When she saw it go out she would know they were on their way back with the old lady.

Eventually, stirred by her own restlessness, she ventured along the jettyside. There was a reek of seaweed, the water mottled with oily ripples, black, bottomless it looked, prompting her to take care as she picked her way over the litter of rope and nets at her feet. A stony track led to the beach and she could just see the lacy frill of surf, hear the beat and rattle of it on the shingle. Beyond the shore mist wrapped the land in darkness, cupping the hilltops in smoky cloud, but thinning out above, wisps of it veiling the high sailing moon silvering the sky.

She returned to the boat and stood looking back, her eyes resting on the cottage. There wouldn't be any trouble, it was too quiet, but she wished they would hurry. What could be keeping them? To be hoped Granny hadn't changed her mind about leaving, afraid to venture to sea in the mist.

Charlotte stared at the window, watching the glimmer of light. Suddenly it went out. Her heart leapt. They were leaving. There was a clink of an iron gate. Then somewhere, beyond the fog and the darkness came the sudden, startled bark of a dog.

Charlotte caught her breath. The Hawkey dog had picked up the sound. She stood, head on one side, straining to listen. The barking broke out again, louder, the sound ringing hollow across the bay.

"Hurry! Hurry!" she found herself saying, hardly able to control her impatience, but they were coming. She could hear the scrape of their shoes against the stones and the tremulously raised voice of the old lady above the muffled growl of the men. She peered into the mist. A figure loomed up – it was Nick. He carried a cabin trunk on his shoulder; his back bent to the weight, hurrying, his breath coming hard. A little behind, Lavelle had a bulging carpet bag and he was helping Emma Bunt over the rope littered jettyside as she poked forward with her stick.

Charlotte turned quickly and, leaping aboard, heaved on the line to bring the gunwale level with the jetty side.

"Good girl!" Nick said, loading the trunk astern. "Hold her fast while we get Granny aboard."

"I can manage. Brought up with boats," Emma Bunt cried as Nick reached for her hand. She was bubbling with excitement.

Lavelle bent towards her, his voice soft. "Quiet ma'am! We have to keep our voices down or they'll hear us. Sound carries like hell over water."

"I knows it does," she said, dropping her voice to a whisper. "Trouble is I'm all so agitated 'tis hard to keep within myself. You got my handbag, dear?"

"Sure, I got it, ma'am," Lavelle said, as they helped her over the gunwale.

She was wearing a long black coat with an astrakhan collar and a dark woollen shawl draped over the felt hat pulled down over her brow. The clothes flapped as she landed, bringing a whiff of lavender and mothballs into the boat with her. They guided her to the seat on the engine box and piled up some cushions behind her.

"You'll be warmer here under the wheelhouse," Nick told her. He took her stick and stowed it away under the port seat, while Charlotte brought a rug to tuck round her knees.

Lavelle was glancing back inland where, behind the bank of fog, the dog's persistent barking was now joined by men's voices, shouting. They all paused to listen and Nick whispered thickly.

"What d'you reckon? We start the engine and make a run for it."

Lavelle shook his head. "And put them on our scent! They don't know we're here, so let's keep it that way. If we pull out along the causeway, we can lie doggo under the mist." He turned to give Emma Bunt a warning glance. "Not a word, ma'am. Okay?"

She nodded her head affirmatively. her eyes bright and twinkling. She was thoroughly enjoying the adventure.

They cast off, and with Charlotte steering, the two men used the oars to propel the boat silently between the narrow gauntlet of saw-tooth reefs. Even with the tide full and slack water, it was a hard pull against the current and progress was slow, but gradually the little quay began to slip away, fading into the shroud of fog, and the only bearing they had were the humps of granite marking the causeway entrance from the open sea.

Once clear of the reefs, Nick, carefully, without making a sound, lowered the anchor, and it was there with the white mist swirling round them that they waited, listening to the dog barking and the shouts from the Hawkeys, the sounds strangely muted. Somewhere a gull, disturbed, gave voice to its haunting call, others taking it up. Once there were voices, close enough to have come from the jettyside, and they waited, holding their breath for the throb of the motor boat, but they heard nothing to indicate that they were being pursued. Presently the voices died away and distantly a door slammed, the sound echoing back across the hollow crater of the cove.

Then for a long time there was silence, broken occasionally by fretful barks from the dog. Emma Bunt, settled against her cushions, was looking drowsy.

The two men glanced at each other, judging the danger to be over. It would appear that the Hawkeys had found nothing amiss on the jettyside and with Emma Bunt's cottage in darkness, had returned to their beds.

The mist was drifting in patches, carried by the freshening breeze and now and again came a glimmer of moonlight on the rippled water. By the seaward drift of the boat they realised the tide had turned, and as all was quiet ashore Lavelle told Nick to weigh anchor.

Emma Bunt had already nodded off, her chin sinking into the folds of her shawl, her lips apart, expelling a tiny snore, and she did not waken when the anchor came aboard or when Nick stepped over her on his way down from the foredeck.

With a whispered word to Charlotte about the compass bearing, Lavelle joined him at the oars and the two men, their backs bent to the effort, began to pull the boat out into the bay.

Charlotte at the wheel watched the tiny compass dial, her eyes lifting from time to time to look ahead into the mist sweeping against the windscreen. She was cold, her shoulders ached, her eyes pricked from tiredness, but she glowed inside to know that Granny Bunt was safe, they hadn't holed Jed's boat, the Hawkeys were none the wiser to their plan.

Then quite suddenly the mist was clearing, falling away behind them in a dark cloudbank and ahead was the stark black shoulder of Downend Point set in a glittering sea, backlit by the moon.

"We've made it! We're clear of the reefs!" she cried, turning in triumph to the men at the oars.

Nick swung round, his lifted oar dripping with phosphorescence. His shoulders were heaving, his breath smoking, but there was laughter in his eyes as he looked at her with pride.

"So we are, you've brought us clear, and safely." He turned to wink at Lavelle. "Have to hand it to her, Jack, not a bad bit of seamanship!"

Lavelle nodded "You bet!" he agreed. But the girl's natural skill did not surprise him. It was almost like having Bill up there at the wheel again. He gave her a broad grin. "Okay Charlie, I guess we can start her up now and head on out of here."

Charlotte obeyed and the old Kelvin kicked into life, the vibration shaking them all up, but not enough to waken Emma Bunt. She slept on, half smiling in her slumber.

"Don't disturb her," Charlotte said to Nick as he came into the wheelhouse. "She's done in."

"And so are you, m'love," he said, his arm straying tenderly round her waist. "Losing your beauty sleep. We should have left you back aboard."

"I'm not a bit sleepy," she lied.

"Aw, Come on!" Lavelle said. "At two thirty am?"

She jerked up her head, suddenly excited. "Two thirty? Then its Thursday – my birthday! I'm seventeen today."

They stared at her. "Your birthday?"

Lavelle gripped her shoulder. "Honey, why didn't you tell us you were going to have a birthday? We'd have planned some surprises, presents."

Charlotte nodded towards the sleeping old lady. "That's the one birthday present I wanted, finding Granny, bringing her safely home."

Nick hugged her close and pressed a kiss on her cheek. "Happy birthday, Charlie. We'll think up a special tea for you."

"We sure will!" Lavelle said, but his smile faded to see how tired she looked, and Nick, too, beside her, the sweat of exhaustion on his face. "I'll take over now," he told them, moving in behind the wheel. "Charlie, you get your head down on Nick's shoulder and try to get some rest. It's going to be around four before we make port."

And Charlotte didn't need any persuasion as Nick led her to the seat astern.

Lavelle, the collar of his reefer jacket pulled up against the draught, bent to the throttle and put the boat full ahead for the point. Off shore a light breeze was freshening from the north-west, bringing a slap of swell against the starboard bow, lifting the spray. After the hard row across the bay he found the change of motion pleasantly invigorating. Unlike his companions, the stress of the night's endeavour had not left him exhausted. He was more geared up to it than they were, used to making clandestine landings under the cover of darkness, of being hunted and pursued. He had been trained for it during the war; the skills he had developed had brought him through, helped him to survive, the experience equipping him for the peacetime conflicts on the Mediterranean.

This trip reminded him of wartime, of night manoeuvres farther down this very coast at Downderry, where they used to practice beachead landings in preparation for D-Day. The thought triggered off a train of memories; Plymouth, Poole, Portsmouth, London.....back home, San Francisco and that unforgettable embarkation leave.

Margo.

The thought of Margo twisted knots inside of him; her eyes shining through her tears, the tremble of her mouth against his kisses in that final, crushing farewell. There had been no words between them, just that heart-tearing explosion of emotion, transmitting through them as though they were of one blood, one breath, one beating heart. How he'd loved her! How hard to bear the parting, even harder the final cruelty which fate had in store for them.

In his memory he saw her eyes again, the hope in them when he assured her all would be well. If she would have the faith, the courage, he would find the means. He had given his word she wouldn't die. It had seemed hopeless at first, he didn't have a buck saved, but back in England at the naval base there were enough high earning rackets around to see him through. But the time it had taken, those long tormenting months. He was almost there, compassionate leave granted, help for her in sight. Then to be fleeced by that shit of a lawyer. The thought brought his blood up, the veins in his temples throbbing, his knuckles standing out white as he clutched the wheel. If he'd known then that Abrahams was still alive, he would have beaten him bloodless, but they'd told him the guy was dead, buried under the ruins of his building in the East End of London.

Lavelle sighed. Afterwards he had gone to war ready to die, all he deserved for failing her. Miraculously he had survived where others had perished; he had come through, forced to live on with his grief and his conscience, blaming himself for not recognising Abrahams as a double-dealing bastard he should have known better than to trust.

If Margo had lived how different his life would have been. They would have had so much together; the beach house they planned at San Mateo, family; maybe a boy and girl, grown up now like Nick and Charlie. Instead he had drifted without purpose, living by wit and cunning, indifferent to danger, the direction he had chosen a token of defiance, retaliation against the bruising he had taken from life. But it had left him without roots, deadwood cast adrift, his only love the battered schooner he had first found deserted and dragging her anchor after the landings in Southern France. She had become his bolthole, sometimes from the law, mostly from himself – until the day a newspaper story had nudged his memory, his conscience, beckoning him back.

He had returned to find life going on simply, beautifully, where kids grew up, fell in love and dreamed of a future together – like those two astern, he guessed, dozing in each others arms. It had started that way for him, misty waters, sailing with Margo in his uncle's boat; her dark brown hair blowing across her face, a shining, happy face, the tears in her eyes only from laughter. The boat anchored off the reef they had swam ashore, ran hand in hand, leaping the wavelets, their bare feet sinking into the soft wet sand as the surf raced back. Up on the dunes the sand had been hot under their bodies, the sun warming their backs, as they loved. It was forever, they told each other, nothing could ever spoil it, nothing. In those tender, precious moments, they had not reckoned on the stamp of fate.

It had been a long time since had brought himself to think of her, open up the hurt again, to bear to do so without wanting to lash out or just give way to his grief as he often had in the wakeful hours of dawn. No sir, stick your toes in brother, hold on, you're in great company! They know nothing of your private ache. That's yours to live with, alone. Who Goddamn else would understand? Yet here he was, thinking about it, without hang-ups. What got him on to it? That gal from the Trefoy Hotel, he guessed, talking to her in the bar the other night about Sausalito, Fisherman's Wharf, all the places back home still vivid with Margo. Yeah! Talked about it, without wanting to kick her teeth in for bringing it up! How'd you like that? Maybe she reminded him of Margo, those warm brown eyes, the way they looked at him. But she'd lost someone, too. Guess that made it easier.

She had been talking out her feelings, her hunger for San Francsico. One big part of her needed to return, to go back to the kid out there, but how could she face it without the guy who made it mean something for her? He knew exactly how she felt, knew how it hurt, how it tore at those inescapable memories and made them into nightmares.

He had felt a genuine desire to comfort her, take her, love away the tiny frowns from around those warm brown eyes, but it would not have been for her comfort but his own. She wasn't a cheap portside whore to be picked up for his pleasure, she was the kind of woman you made your life with, to whom you gave everything you had.

Why couldn't they have met in different circumstances, some place else where he didn't have to live a lie, involved as he was in this business of the will?

He thought of her now as they rounded the headland into the wide harbour mouth, thought of her sleeping, her long smooth legs under snow white sheets, up there in the Trefoy Hotel. Looking up he eyed the tall Victorian edifice towering above the waterfront, it's tawny stone glimmering in the pale dawn, picking up the dim glow from St. Catherine's light.

And then he remembered. He had promised to call her to go sailing with them. It had gone completely from his mind.

****

Something had wakened her. She stirred and lay on her back, listening. A motor boat chugging by, a fishing boat. But it was still dark – and silent. The early morning mackerel boats were usually accompanied by screaming gulls, the sound that always wakened her.

She slid from her bed and stole to the open window, drawing aside the net curtains. The fog had gone and dawn was breaking over Pendowry creek into a cobweb-like haze. In the grey light she could see the boat was coming in, not going out. It was the *Flora Dora.* A heaviness sank over her. They must have gone fishing after all, been lost in the mist and were only just coming in. But they were not heading for the *Cape Columbo*; they were going over to the Trefoy quay.

She could see the boat clearly now, Jack at the wheel, half in shadow. Nick and Charlie were sitting astern, arms round each other, heads close like lovers and there was somebody else sitting against the wheelhouse, a stooped figure in dark clothes.

How odd, she thought, at this hour!

She watched until they were out of sight, the rooftops on the waterside obscuring her view, but she could still hear the chugga-chugga-chug of the engine idling by the jetty. Then the sound quickened and hanging over the sill she watched the boat come back into view again, but this time Charlotte was at the wheel – alone...and she was heading for the boatyard. Perhaps she would be mooring up and returning for them in the *Dipper.* But when the dinghy pulled away the bow was pointing out towards the *Cape Columbo.* Charlotte was not returning to the quay for the others.

Linda waited by the window until she was chilled and shivering, but she did not see Jack or Nick return. Later, out of curiosity she took a stroll down to the quay and discovered their car had gone.

****

Richard Ellis had also heard the motor boat, but he had been too busy in his study finalising the details of his plan to concern himself with early morning river traffic. He had been awake most of the night with last minute doubts. Old people could be unpredictable. Suppose she had changed her mind? Suppose she wanted to leave it until another day? He had to be prepared for an alternative way of getting her down to the jetty. A crack on the head from behind would have been positive, but she was a heavy woman and he didn't fancy having to drag her body so far. Some other means of force would be needed.

At four a.m. he remembered the small Beretta pistol Wilfred Penrose had kept as a protection against intruders. The thought of it in the top drawer of the bureau had brought Ellis, on rising, straight down to his study. Now he stood cradling it in his hands, a gun slim and light, easy to conceal in his pocket. He checked the magazine and discovered it was loaded. Good enough. If the worst came he might have to fire a shot to frighten her into submission.

Satisfied he walked out onto the patio and breathed deeply the sweet morning air. It was coming light and all there was left of the mist hung in a gossamer veil above Pendowry.

CHAPTER TWENTY

"What have you done with her? She's gone!"

Richard Ellis' voice bellowed across the lane and for a moment even the dog's frenzied barking was silenced.

Josh Hawkey stood, the hen crate he was unloading from the truck clattering to the gravel.

"Gone..?" He stared, round eyed at the lawyer, only half understanding.

"Gone!" Ellis roared at the top of his voice. "She's not in the cottage, not on the shore, the jetty! Where is she?"

Josh gave him a glassy gaze, his mouth trembling as he began to speak. "C-Couldn't have. Matt took her milk." He turned, appealing to his eldest son, who had slid down from the cab to join them. "You took the milk this morning, didn't you, Matt?"

"Certainly I did!" A look of indignation had come into Matt's bony face.

"Did you see her?" Ellis demanded. "Speak to her?"

Matt shook his head, his eyes shifty. "Only just gone cockcrow. She was still a-bed, the curtains drawn over the windows."

"And so they are still," Ellis said bitterly. "And she's not there."

"She mightn't have 'eard 'ee. Could be taken bad. Did 'ee knock hard enough?"

"Knock!" stormed Ellis. "I broke the bloody door down!"

Reuben crept out from behind the truck, advancing sheepishly, mouth agape. For a moment he stood contemplating them with his head on one side, then as it occurred to him what the fuss was about, he began pointing down the lane excitedly. "They people! 'Twas they people! They took her – not we!"

"What people?" The lawyer's voice dropped to a harsh whisper.

Josh looked at Reuben in disgust. Knowing how touchy the lawyer was about having the old lady disturbed, he had not intended to mention the visitors. Now here was the boy weaving all manner of bad into it. Josh did not believe the visitors would have let down the truck tyres. That was more like one of Matt's pranks so he could go rabbiting instead of bringing back the churns for milking.

"What people?" Ellis repeated to Josh.

The old man raised a sheepish smile. "They was only visitors, come down to look at the church."

"Not the church, 'twas the beach they were to," Matt corrected him. "I told 'em they couldn't go, that's why they let down my tyres. 'Twas three of 'em. Two men and a maid..."

"You mean a girl!" Ellis looked at Josh with fresh alarm. "Not a woman – rather stout."

"Just a maid with two men," Josh insisted, "One was older – her father I would say."

All three were nodding their heads.

"How did they get past the dog?" Ellis roared.

"His chain was fast under the gate and he couldn't reach 'em. But there was no harm done, Mister Ellis..."

"Harm done! She's gone, hasn't she?"

"I reckon she went in the night," Matt said darkly. "Somebody must have come in by sea and fetched her in the fog. 'Must have been why the dog was fretting all night. None of us got no sleep."

"And you didn't investigate!" cried Ellis.

"'Course, we did," said Josh quickly. "We came out to him but 'twas thick mist. You couldn't see a hand a-fore you. But 'twas all shut up at the cottage and nothing amiss on the jetty."

Ellis dropped his head. It was them. They'd found her. The older man would be a private investigator engaged by the aunt. They must have been down in the afternoon to draw up a plan, then cruised in during the night under the cover of the fog. But only somebody with local knowledge would have dared to venture beyond those eye-teeth reefs after dark and in such weather. It must be as he suspected. The girl was in league with the St Ruan clan, people who knew the coast.

Now they had Emma Bunt, the copy of Silas Trevelyan's will might already be on its way to their lawyer. Searching her cottage had been a waste of time; it had gone with her, with her clothes in the cabin trunk missing from her room.

He began to sweat. He could expect trouble now with every knock on his door. But there would be no question of giving in. He was too far committed not to fight. Now he would have to find a way to disprove their allegations, defend himself as he had defended others. There was no question of resigning himself to defeat, as his father would have done; not when, with some careful manipulation of justice, he might slither out of it relatively unscathed.

"Twas none of our doing, Mister Ellis," Josh was whimpering.

He left them then, satisfied that the threat of his ferocity would hold their silence. He took the boat across the bay at top speed, his blood up for battle, despite an underlying trepidation generated by the thought of what might await him on his return to Trefoy; detectives on his doorstep, Harriet Couch looking pale and distraught.

But these fears were unfounded. All was well when he arrived home, nothing unusual had happened at the office, no calls, no messages, and Miss Couch's voice over the telephone impassively reassuring.

He poured himself a brandy and carried it out with him onto the patio, his eyes resting darkly on the tatty watercolour of St Ruan. Somewhere in that hotchpotch hill of houses his enemies lurked, watching as he had returned from Talland.

Nick had seen him, from the porthole of the *Cape Columbo*, Charlotte from the deck as she threw scraps to the gulls, neither of them thinking twice about it, but Lavelle, noticing the white cabin cruiser missing was from its moorings, had had been watching for it all afternoon, as he sat with Linda on the terrace of the Trefoy Hotel. He first spotted it rounding the point at the harbour mouth, but as his gaze followed it into the estuary, his eyes gave nothing away, as Linda listened to his excuses for the broken date.

"You had to pick Nick's mother up from Polperro – I thought he said she lived in Newlyn?"

"Sure, but she'd been over to see her sister, and the bus home hadn't shown up because of the fog," he explained. "Nick got a message to pick her up by boat where she could catch the train at Par. I'd expected to be back in time, but we had engine trouble. It was after four am before we got in."

"I'll believe you!"

"So how's about tonight? You and me driving over to the Rashleigh Arms at Polkerris? Watch the sunset over a gin and tonic."

Her face lit up, "Why not?" she said, meeting his glance.

Aboard the *Cape Columbo* Charlotte stood against the rail watching the gulls rocking and banking, wheeling above the mastheads, soaring away into the sunless sky, vanishing into low cloud scudding over the hilltops. But she was only half aware of them, their cries, the river sounds; the persistent knock-a-knock of the caulking mallets from the yard, the hum of passing motor craft, their backwash of wake against the schooner's hull. Her mind had not yet surfaced from the night's adventure, moments still returning, the daring, the triumph, but sweetest of all the passage home, Nick's shoulder to cushion her head, being drowsily warm in his arms.

It was not what had been said, they had said nothing, there had been no need. Their feelings expressed it all, a tenderness radiating a glow between them, beyond words. The wind had been cool on their faces, the moonlight painting silver patterns on the seascape; sparklets where its light touched the ripples, touched the dew on the coaming, the wash on the bow. Granny Bunt had been deep in slumber, Frisco humped over the wheel, lost in his own private solitude and she'd had Nick, so close, so precious.

All too soon had come the homing glow of St Catherine's, the shadowy shore of the Trefoy waterfront taking shape, reality breaking the spell. Nick had drawn her to her feet as they came into the jetty, his hands gripping her waist, and there in the pastel light of dawn he had kissed her as never before. It was a kiss to still her heart and in that moment she had seen his eyes, luminous with love for her.

She looked up now to see him coming up through the hatchway, solid Cornish, his face dusky with sunburn, the quiff of hair below his cap bleached almost white like the knees of his jeans. A man her dad would have wanted for her, she decided. She observed him quietly as he moved down the foredeck with Jed Marney, pointing out loose planking in need of attention, and she found herself swept with waves of fondness for him, but not without a little knot of anxiety for the future. Her life was so interlaced with complications, her freedom still restricted by her age, and she was only too aware that her stepmother, should she discover her whereabouts, had every right to take her back to London. Despite Frisco's assurances that he would protect her, Charlotte knew there was little they could do until the conspiracy had been proved in court.

A shout from Nick broke into her reverie and recognising the familiar kick-kick-kick of the *Dipper*, she turned to see Frisco bringing the boat alongside, and then she laughed as Matelot came bounding aboard with a large pink crab clasped between his jaws.

"Just look what he's got!" she cried, as the dog sheered off aft and disappeared down the companionway.

Lavelle was grinning as he swung himself over the gunwale. "He bagged it off the quay while Sharkie Flint was selling them to the locals. He had it in the boat before I could stop him."

"Sharkie'll have your guts" cried Jed.

"The hell he will!" Lavelle said, "I gave the goddamn guy half a crown for it – crab sandwiches for Charlie's birthday tea."

They cheered.

Half an hour later, round the saloon table, Jed acquainted with the all the details of the Emma Bunt rescue, they were discussing the whereabouts of the thirteenth watermill.

"Must be at Lanreath. That's the last one up the valley," Jed declared.

Charlotte was shaking her head. "It's lower down, near Peakswater," she said, with some authority. "There's Tredowr, then just below, down by the weir there's Tryun. That's the thirteenth watermill."

"What makes you so sure?" Lavelle asked, he was already having doubts about the usefulness of this latest excursion. He sensed more fantasy than fact in the old lady's story.

"Because of the name," Charlotte explained, "in the Cornish language 'un' means one and 'try' means three. Toss the two figures and you have thirteen, an omen of ill luck."

"You have to be kidding!" Lavelle groaned.

The men laughed and Charlotte went on. "I remember going there once with my dad. You go up through Pendowry woods to Watergate, across the fields to Trevada then take a steep track up to the weir. It's a good walk."

"I bet it is!" said Lavelle, recalling the last time he had walked his feet into blisters after taking her directions up to Hogg's Farm. "So I guess that settles it. We go by car. We can drive up as far as Peakswater and work our way down to it, following the river from Tredowr."

****

The winding lane twisted round another blind corner, dipped between banks of thick brambles and up again for a straight narrow run ending in a T-junction. The signpost said Lanteglas Highway to the left and Lansallos to the right.

Nick swore softly as Lavelle jammed on the breaks. "We're back where we started again".

"We're being 'pisky' led'," said Charlotte.

Lavelle behind the wheel squinted at her in puzzlement. "If that means chasing around in circles, you can say that again," he said.

It was how they had spent the last hour; driving the maze of lanes to the south of Lanreath in search of the Pendowry river valley and always finishing back at the same place.

Nick studied the signpost. "Lansallos will take us too far south, so I reckon we should go left for Lanteglos Highway, then left again at that unmarked lane we passed last time."

"Left it is!" Lavelle sang out, as they set off for another snakes and ladders run, as Charlotte called it. Easier to have followed the river up from Pendowry.

The unmarked lane was like a rabbit warren, plunging beneath the roots of the trees; down, down into a deep clough almost surrounded by humpy wooded hills. At the bottom the road forked, one way swinging back to the left, the other going on over a stone bridge before it wound away, disappearing into another an archway of greenery. The warm air coming in through the open window was dank, humid from the heavy vegetation, and they caught a glimpse of bright water to the south where the clough, clothed thickly in brush, sloped away south.

At the bridge there was an old man, dressed like a farmer in breeches and leggings, green jersey over his flannel shirt. He was flattening himself against the wall to let them go by, a basket of eggs over his arm, but Lavelle slowed down and leaned from the window as they drew level with him.

"Are we okay for Tredowr?" he asked.

"Tredowr?"

The farmer looked at them suspiciously, his brow tightening into tiny frowns. "'Tes nothing at Tredowr – only my place on the hill and a couple o' cottages down by the mill stream."

"Is it far?" Lavelle asked.

The farmer nodded up river. "Over there – right of the hill."

"Then this is Peakswater," said Nick, getting out of the car to look over the bridge. Lavelle joined him and they gazed down at the shallow river splashing over the slabs and boulders, to course on down the valley, curving away between the hills.

"That's right," said the farmer. "Goes all the way down to Pendowry creek and the sea."

"So the next mill down there must be Tryun," Lavelle said.

The farmer stared at them, his face grim. "Tryun! You don't want to go down to Tryun. Tis an evil place, surrounded by swamp. Wouldn't get me down there. 'Tis said there's a curse on it, ill luck befalls all who venture there. Has always been so. There was a whole family wiped out with diphtheria back in the thirties, then a miller drowned in the mire, and one of his men was struck dead by a grinding stone. A seafaring man, who once lived there, told me he thought the place was haunted."

"Nobody living there now?" Lavelle asked.

The farmer shook his head. "Nor likely to be. The place is derelict, dangerous, rotting away – like all they properties down by the river."

"We only wanted to have look at the mill," said Nick. "How do we get there? Is there a road from Tredowr?"

"Not from Tredowr," said the farmer. "You'd have to go to Langtaglos Highway and look for the turning to take you to Trevada. Up alongside the mill you'll see the old lane up to Tryun, but 'tesn't fit for motors, no more. Over grown with thistles and bracken."

"That was the way my dad took me," Charlotte said, as they drove on. "We called at Trevada Mill. They had some geese and a goat with a bell."

There were no geese or goats to be found wandering in the Trevada mill yard that day, no tinkle of a bell to break the empty silence, only the hum of flies and bees among the thistles which had sprung up between the cobblestones. The place had a sad, desolate look, forgotten and neglected. The water wheel stood dry and rusted above the conduit, where the river had once been recoursed to power it. The millpond was choked with weed and inhabited by mallard, fluttering and squawking in the bulrushes.

Lavelle locked up the car and they walked along the bankside, and saw that the pond had been fed from a weed-hung culvert, the stone tunnel still shining wet and rich green with algae. A stony driveway climbed above the culvert and they could now see the wooded clough coming down through the fold in the hills, marking the course of the river. Immediately ahead was a thin copse of spruce and oak, and beside it, winding away round the bend of the hill, was the steep cart track Charlotte had told them about.

Lavelle groaned. This was crazy. Silas would never have expected an old dame like Emma Bunt to make it all the way up here? Either she had misunderstood him or there was something more cryptic in the message he had given to her.

He was now having serious doubts about the whole exercise, a feeling that they were wasting their time, but Charlotte and Nick were already up ahead, ducking under trailing creepers and overhanging thorn. No use damping their enthusiasm – not yet. As the woodland dropped away behind them, the rutted lane dwindled, hedgeless, leading them up through the clough. Here they could see the river, broad and shallow tumbling over the stones; hear it burbling round the boulders, and up ahead as the gorge narrowed, the low roar of it coming down over the weir.

Just before the foot of the waterfall, it branched away to the right round a rocky outcrop, the track still climbing. There, against the skyline, they could see the boundary wall sweeping down along the ridge of the hill and dipping away into the gully close to the weir. Reaching it, they saw it was high and solid, partly clothed in ivy, the crevices abounding with dry, weedy plants and yellow lichen. There was a gate, but it was shackled in brambles, so thick and high, that not even Lavelle standing on tiptoe could see over the other side. Then they noticed the stepping stones of a stile, half hidden in the bracken.

Here from the top of the wall they could look out on a wide terrain, the land sweeping down through woodland and furze, to a flat expanse of marshland with tracks of yellow bog and still pools of swampy water shining ominously among the rushes. The river came round the shoulder of the hill from Tredowr and Peakswater, cutting through in a wide curve towards the weir.

Immediately below them was the mill dam, the steps of the stile leading down to the path beside it. The glassy pool lay almost still, except where the dusted surface glided silently towards the brimming rim of the weir. There, mirrored dark and green within its depths, was the blackened, crumbling remains of the thirteenth watermill.

CHAPTER TWENTY ONE

They stood, aghast at its dilapidation. It was almost as though the elements had turned upon it with wrath and scorn for its greedy intrusion on an over-worked river; as though it had been relentlessly thrashed by winter rains, battered by the north wind tearing down the valley, eroded by the constant torrent against its foundations. But still it stood, stubbornly implanted, tottering tall above the water, the blind eyes of its mullioned windows lit in defiance as they reflected the glow from the afternoon sun.

Yet for all its pride it looked a sorry sight; the roof sunken, slats showing through, a residence for bats, nesting places for swallows and martins. The walls were creviced and crumbling, the wheel arch gone, the gaping hole it had left behind laying bare the rusted workings. They appeared to be leaning outwards, dragged by the water wheel now slumped, half submerged in the stream. The buckets were slimed and rotting, useful only to rats looking for landing places to scuttle into the mill. All that was left of the gantry was a bare post sticking out of the mainstream, trailing a spar of planking into the current.

They looked at it, awe-struck, the desolation reducing them to silence as they crossed the stone bridge over the dam to the mill yard. From this angle the whole edifice seemed to have shifted sideways towards the opposite gable end which had collapsed, taking the corner of the building with it. The remaining wall bulged dangerously, and in one place had already broken out, spewing a heap of powdery stones into the grass beneath it. Now they could see, through the gap in the masonry, the outward shift of the mechanism inside the building. Part of the upper floor had gone and the spur wheel at the top of the shaft, the wallower still attached, appeared to have fallen against the front wall and now lay at an angle above the demolished part. The grinding stones looked as though they had slid free and crashed down, thrusting the pit wheel forward against the sloping wall beam, now braced to take the whole weight of the mechanism.

"Holy Moses!" Lavelle muttered.

"Bleddy dangerous," Nick commented.

They eyed it gravely, the bend of timbers, strained and taut.

"When that beam goes," Lavelle said, "the whole place'll tumble like a pack of cards."

Charlotte stood back. "We can't go in there!" she said, but the two men were already on their way round the side of the building looking for an easy entry. She followed them, uncertainly, picking her way gingerly over the rubble.

At the back of the mill the walls were in better condition, although blackened and stained where the rain had streamed from broken guttering. Here would have been the living quarters, the windows looking out on a square of mossy cobbles. Beyond were outhouses and a gate leading up into a field, suggesting a short cut up the hillside to Lantaglos Highway. The air was still, oppressive, the reek of age, the silence broken only by the haunting whoo-hoo of wood pigeons in a nearby copse.

From the high arched entrance into the mill one great barn door hung drunkenly, the other was down, nettles springing up through the rotten wood. Sweeping round it was a dry drift of river sand leading through the doorway, the mens' footprints sunken into it. Charlotte trod through and found herself in a lofty interior, hanging with broken spars from the half collapsed first floor on which, amidst the tangle of machinery, spears of light picked out gold from the rust.

The men were standing, surveying it, and trying to ascertain the cause of the collapse.

"You can see what's happened here," Lavelle said, pointing to the drift of sand and pebbles banked up against the wall. "It's water erosion. Flood damage."

Nick nodded. "A lot of water comes down this valley after the winter rains, nothing to stop a swollen river. See! That's where it's broken in, through that gap under the front wall. It's loosened a way through the stones. See the green slime."

"Sure," Lavelle agreed. "Come the whole way down, washed away the foundations. Look at the heap of rubble there!. I guess that lot must have been supporting the main beam." His gaze followed the slant of timber to the opposite side of the building where it rested upon a stout stone buttress set into the wall. "Those supports would have been built to take the strain of the beam under all that weight of machinery. Now that one goddamn buttress is holding up the whole damned building."

"Is it safe?" Charlotte asked, round-eyed.

For an answer Lavelle made his way round a fallen beam for a closer inspection. Nick followed and they bent to examine the lower part of the buttress, kicking away the river sand from the base until they could see the condition of the framework.

"It's not too bad," Lavelle said, and grinned at Charlotte. "I guess it'll hold long enough for us to take a look up in the loft."

He moved on towards the back of the mill, where a door swinging ajar revealed a flight of steps. He didn't think there was a hope in hell of finding the hidden document here, but the dilapidation of the building intrigued him, stirring him with curiosity.

Charlotte hung back but Nick gave her an encouraging grin. "Built of Cornish granite, last another hundred years," he said, "Come on!"

He grabbed her hand and they followed Lavelle up the stone staircase to the first landing.

There, through a doorway, they could see where the floor had given way, and paused to look down on the devastation, then upwards, contemplating the condition of the floor above. The wooden ceiling glistened with dampness and in places bulged ominously, as though it was about to come down. They saw the reason for this when they reached the upper storey. Green grass and young corn was growing from mounds on the floor, probably the result of burst bags of grain that had mouldered into compost. Watered by the rain coming through the gaps in the roof, the seed had sprouted and flourished, then withered, refertilised itself and come up green another season, but beneath it the floorboards would be slowly rotting away.

"That area we avoid," Lavelle warned.

He turned, peering into the gloom on the opposite side of the loft. Cobwebs, thick and black with accumulated dust, hung from the worm-eaten beams, but the floor looked dry, sound, even though it creaked under their tread as they crept to explore. Above them, birds fluttered from under the eaves and a rat scuttled into the shadows. They ventured gingerly, picking their way round empty barrels, a broken wheel and box full of rusty tools. The whole place had a sweet sour odour of fustiness and decay, which gave up from everything, that was disturbed.

Suddenly, Nick halted. "There it is!" he said, pointing across the loft to where a grimed window let a dim shaft of sunlight into the gloom. They followed his gaze and saw there was an old sea chest half hidden under a heap of rotting sacks.

Charlotte caught her breath, her hand on Nick's arm. "It's the chest!" she cried.

"This I don't believe!" Lavelle drawled, as he went to help Nick drag it out from decayed layers of hessian. It was heavy, solidly built of oak, the wood blackened with age, bound in iron and studded with brass, indestructible, and not easily moved.

"So what we got in here?" Lavelle asked, straightening his back.

"Pieces of eight?" Nick quipped.

"Sure!" Lavelle said bleakly, as he watched Charlotte, impatient with excitement, trying to help Nick to prize it open. There must be oak chests like this in all the old attics in Cornwall.

"It's locked," Nick said flatly.

"Just stuck," said Charlotte, "We have to whack it with something – a stick. Remember what Granny told us."

Nick turned to hunt around. Lavelle picked up an iron rod lying at his feet, and arming him to stand back, cracked it smartly across the lid of the chest. The blow lifted a few splinters, but the lid remained closed.

"Harder!" cried Nick.

Lavelle stood back, braced himself and with the rod in both hands, brought down a shattering blow that rang the metal and shuddered the building, and debris began dropping from the rafters.

"Don't!" cried Charlotte, raising her hands as they listened to dislodged slates slithering down the roof. "We're going to have the whole place down!"

"We sure are," said Lavelle, casting a wry glance upwards, and lay down the rod.

Nick, coughing from the smoking dust, nodded grimly. "I told you it was locked. We'll need the key to get in it."

Lavelle picked up a splinter of wood and began poking the dirt from the keyhole. "You got a bit of wire?"

"Might be some among the tools," said Nick, going to rummage in the box and produced the ideal strip for picking locks. For a while Lavelle poked and probed expertly into the keyhole. Then, suddenly a delicate touch produced a promising click and the lid shuddered loose.

Nick pulled back the lid, and an effluvium of must and mildew lifted into their faces as they peered inside. It appeared to be crammed to the rim with old books.

Lavelle stood back as Nick helped Charlotte to drag them out, her face flushed with excitement. "These must have belonged to Uncle Silas when he was a boy. This must have been his secret place."

Lavelle, loath to dampen her spirits, knelt down to examine them. Many were heavy bound volumes of The Boy's Own Paper. Others related to military history and early century shipping. It was the sort of stuff old Silas would have hoarded, but he could find nothing hidden between the pages, no sign of the package containing the silver pieces Emma had described to them. But he had not expected that he would. Even if the chest did belong to Silas Trevelyan, this was not the hiding place.

"That the lot?" he asked, as Nick, bent double, groped into the bottom of the trunk.

"That's it. That's all there is."

"No packages down there? An envelope?" Charlotte asked, disappointment bringing a weariness to her tone.

"Nothing," said Nick, "Perhaps Richard Ellis has been here before us, 'praps that's why the trunk was locked. He could have the key."

Lavelle looked down wearily on the empty chest, the books stacked around it. Sure, Ellis would have been there, searched every inch of the place, just as he would every other Trevelyan property, every stone unturned to find that document. But as for the chest Emma Bunt was talking about, he did not believe this was the one. There was some deeper meaning to the old man's directive that Emma Bunt had failed to understand.

They stood, without speaking. A despondency had settled over them, the optimism gone, their mood matching the gloom of the sagging, worn out building. A puff of breeze wafted in from a gap in the roof, smoking the dust across the floor and some dislodged debris began a slow slide from somewhere above.

Lavelle started for the stairs. "Come on," he said, "Let's get to the hell out of here!"

Outside the sun was warm, flies whining by, and after the fustiness of the mill the air felt sweet and clean on their faces. Walking back to the yard nobody was inclined to pursue the subject further, at least, not verbally, looking instead for little irrelevancies. On the bridge they paused to watch the river bubbling over the stones, watch it sweeping beneath them under the archway into the dam.

"The time I came here with my father the water was swirling down here the noise was deafening. Today it's nothing but a trickle," Charlotte remarked, a forced cheerfulness in her voice.

"You forget," Nick said, "We've had a long dry spell, unusually dry for Cornwall. But for that drizzle we had the other night, there's been no rain for weeks. The earth is parched."

"Guess that old farmer was right," Lavelle said thoughtfully.

"What old farmer?"

"One I met in a pub the night I came down here. He was forecasting a drought. Said he knew by the way the birds were behaving."

Nick nodded. "He was right. Look how dried up and brown the marsh is. Bet if you were careful to walk round the pools you could get right across that swamp."

"I guess I'll take your word for it," Lavelle said wryly.

His gaze was taking in the lay of the land, observing how the river came round the shoulder of the hill, its course cutting sheer under the bankside. To the east were the marshes, dense with reeds and tufted grass. He noticed how they lay in a shallow depression, bordered to the north by an oak wood, beyond the hills sweeping down, and how to the south, the high-banked perimeter wall running down to the weir, formed a barrier, holding the boglands back from the valley.

"I guess there's quite a lake up here when the rains come and the river floods," he remarked.

Nick glanced towards the weir. "It all drains away to the sea."

Charlotte began to move on. "Come on," she said. "This place gives me the creeps."

They drove home in silence, all three preoccupied with their own thoughts. Charlotte was thinking about her old home by the creekside, Granny Bunt's cottage, the risk of the bulldozers moving in, now so much closer. Nick, deeply aware of how she felt, was considering the prospect of their life together, and how her youth, her inheritance was complicating it all.

But Lavelle was not looking forward to having to tell the old lady their mission had failed. She wasn't going to believe it. She might even demand to be taken there to look for herself. How was he to convince her the watermill was almost derelict and the lane inaccessible? Somehow he'd have to induce her to tell him more, have her search back through her mind for some small detail that might answer where they had gone wrong. But she was such a dogmatic old dame. She might easily take umbrage if she thought he doubted her integrity.

Even so, she was still their only means of finding the document. And what had they without it? Nothing but his own testimony based on what Bill had told him and what Emma Bunt had said to qualify it. The rest was hearsay. He supposed they could have Rachel served with a subpoena. She might crack in the witness box. But Ellis would fight. Well versed with every trick of criminal law, he would offer a faultless defence, justify his treatment to old Emma as a kindness when her cottage was derelict. Hadn't he provided her with another property, rent free at Talland, groceries delivered, the Hawkeys to take care of her needs?

With his long years of respectability in the town, what hope had they of bringing him to justice? The only real evidence that would convict Ellis of fraud was to produce the original copy of Silas Trevelyan's will in court. And where was it now? Maybe already found and destroyed by the lawyer.

But it was a theory soon to be rejected by fresh disclosures, which emerged when Jed and Fisherman Luke came aboard the schooner that evening, eager to hear the outcome of their visit to Tryun.

"If Ellis had already found that copy of the will, why was he was searching for up at Talland yesterday, rummaging through Emma's cottage on the shore?"

"Ellis was?" Lavelle asked, suddenly alert. So that was where he'd been in his boat yesterday. "Tell me more."

Jed turned to his friend, nudging him with his elbow. "You tell 'em, what you overheard the Hawkey brothers saying. You tell 'em what you told me."

The attention turned on him; Fisherman Luke began to puff thoughtfully at his pipe. "'Twas yesterday I was out 'Talland," he began in his usual long-winded fashion. "Been pulling good pollack all evening, staying under the cliff out of view of the Hawkeys. Then just on dusk I sees the boys, taking the boat out to their lobster pots. Didn't see me, though, I'd crept in behind Ula rock, but I could hear 'em shouting above the noise of the engine – you knows how voices carry over the water. I could hear every word that 'twas said. How Ellis had been to Mrs Bunt's cottage while they was away at market and pulled the place apart; emptied the drawers, the cupboards, even dragged the pictures down from the walls... left the place a shambles."

"He was looking for the will!" Nick cried.

"What else would he be looking for?" said Jed.

Luke's blue eyes were twinkling as he went on. "Course, Reuben thought he was searching for Emma in the cottage. But Matt believed she'd been taken away by sea because somebody had been tampering with the mooring lines."

"Ellis must have gone to pick her up," Lavelle said quietly, "Did they say how he got in there – we locked up before we left."

"Smashed the door down!" said Luke. "I heard Matt say so."

Lavelle sat back thoughtfully against the divan, his shrewd eyes fixed on the river lights flicking past the portholes. So Ellis did suspect Emma Bunt had that copy. It was why he kept her in isolation. Providing nobody got to her, the document would be safe. The postcards had worried him, he believed someone had uncovered the truth. Now the soft touch was over, it had to be force. When he'd found her door locked and the curtains drawn, he must have burst in thinking something was wrong. Finding nothing amiss, he'd think she was down the beach getting wood for the fire and time for him to look for the will before she got back...then he'd see her trunk gone. That must have turned him cold. It had been late afternoon when he returned in his boat which suggested he had waited for the Hawkeys to come back from market before he left.

Lavelle mulled it over in his mind, going through the findings. But Silas Trevelyan was no fool, a devious old man, who trusted nobody. Had he really trusted Emma Bunt? Were the instructions he gave her all eyewash for her to feed back to the lawyer? The old lady's story had same ring of incredibility more attuned to one of Charlotte's legends. Or had it just accumulated a touch here and there of fantasy, as it remained secret so long in her mind?

He heaved a sigh. Was he missing something? Some clue planted by the old man and known only to his nephew Bill, who died with the secret?

CHAPTER TWENTY TWO

London was hot. The temperatures had been pushing up into the eighties all through August; people walking coatless to work, picnics in the parks and queues at Victoria and Waterloo for tickets to the coast. But Rachel Ives had no desire to escape from the city – not for one day. Happily installed in Belgravia, she was feeling like a new woman, life was good, London was hers to enjoy.

She watched it all, gazing blissfully through the window of the cab taking her home from shopping to her own little flat off Eaton Place. Richard had agreed she should take it, just for a month or so until the money came through. Then she would have a husband to take care of her. And so she would, Rachel told herself gleefully, but it wouldn't be Richard, it would be Frisco.

The thought of Jack Lavelle brought a flush of excitement as she sat clutching her parcels. She had been to Harrods to choose something chic and expensive to please him when he returned from Marseilles. He would have been back ages ago but for his yacht needing a re-fit. He was having it done specially for their honeymoon in Corsica. He had written about it so much, and had enclosed a photograph of himself on board, stripped and sun-tanned, leaning against the mast.

It always took him ages to answer her letters, but she knew he was busy winding up his business before he could settle in London with her. His letters were full of it, full of questions, too, many of them about Richard. Had he telephoned her? Had he asked her to go down to Cornwall? Poor Frisco! He was jealous, afraid she might change her mind, the little niggling worry of it in every letter he wrote.

In a way, it was the same with Richard. In his letters, a reoccurring concern about Charlotte. Had she written? Was there yet no word from the aunt? And these were always the first questions he would ask when he telephoned as though he was expecting to hear that the girl was about to arrive back on the next plane. Of course, it was eleventh hour nerves, fear of a last minute hitch, understandable after all the trouble he had taken, the years he had waited to get what he wanted. But it was not to be, it wouldn't have worked. What she was doing was for the best.

Arriving at the terrace of Regency houses where she rented her flat, she tipped the driver generously and flashed him her smile. She felt good, dazzling, and looked it as she teetered up the steps, the scarlet chiffon scarf and bright lipstick vivid against her white linen dress.

There was a letter on the mat. Must have come by the afternoon post. Not from Frisco, but news from Richard about the inheritance. Probate was through, formally granted, making her Silas Trevelyan's sole heir and he would be sending her a copy of the will in the near future.

With a whoop of joy she danced into the kitchen, the letter waving in her hand. After supper she would write to Frisco and give him the good news.

****

Three hundred miles away in Cornwall Jack Lavelle had already heard. Everybody had. It was all over the front page of the local newspaper,

THE PENDOWRY CREEK DEVEOPMENT TO GO AHEAD
TREVELYAN HEIR NAMED

The outcome had been no surprise to him. He already knew from Linda that The Taylor Ross Organisation was prepared to make the purchase and the contract had been drawn up, ready for completion once the will was published and Rachel established as the new owner. But it had not taken as long as he expected and the evidence he had hoped would disprove her right to it still to be found.

Once he suspected that Ellis did not have the original copy in his possession, Lavelle had decided to delay his proposed visit to Emma Bunt. He needed a few days to consider the best line of questioning. He knew he would have to handle her with tact and diplomacy. He had reached the conclusion that it might be better to say nothing about their expedition to Tryun Mill. Tell her that before the search could begin he would need her to clarify Silas' instructions. Go through it all again with her and ask her to recall any details she might have overlooked. That way he could interrogate her more closely, use a psychological approach to draw her out, and glean from those mists of memory some vital clue.

Better too, not to rush the meeting, allow her time to settle in with Nick's mother, get over the trauma of the last few days. Now she was out of Ellis' reach, there was no hurry. It might be months before probate was granted to Rachel, plenty of time.

The right strategy in place, his plan had been to sail down to Newlyn for a few days. Invite her aboard, and have some time alone with her, while Nick took his mother off some place with Charlie.

But there had been a hitch. Jed had found urgent hull work to do on the *Cape Columbo*, and they needed the schooner up in the yard. At the most it would only take a week, he promised, but closer inspection in dry dock pointed to major repairs; serious stress cracks and spewed caulking, and delays finding replacements had kept her on stilts through most of July.

He supposed he could have gone down by car to Newlyn, but he believed tea on the big schooner, still gleaming from her re-fit, would be more likely to mellow the old lady's mood. The decision he made was to wait.

Meanwhile, there could be further visits to Lucy Gribble, try to read some more into her wanderings, and maybe seek out others who had once worked at the manor. It would also give him time to develop his relationship with Linda, who he hoped would be there for him when all this business was through. But with her uncle's connections so closely involved with Ellis, keeping her happy on the outside of their affairs was not easy. Charlotte had already had let it out about the crumbling Tryun Mill, and he had been obliged to promise Linda that she could come with them on the next trip. Once the repairs on the schooner were through, they would have more time.

But it was well into August before the yacht was ready for her sea trials. The same week the newspaper headlines, indicating the completion of the Pendowry Estate being imminent, brought a new urgency. The time left now to find the will was running out. The trip to see Emma Bunt would have be his next priority.

It was decided to give the schooner its trial run down the coast to Lands End, Jed sailing with them to attend to any adjustments, and on the way back they planned to make for Mounts Bay and call in at Newlyn.

It was evening when they made port, the fishing jetties crowded with French crabbers, but they were able to find a convenient place to tie up.

It had been agreed that Nick and Charlotte should go ashore and prepare the way for Emma Bunt's proposed visit aboard the following day. The last thing Lavelle wanted was to be drawn into his proposed discussion at a family gathering.

"Just don't mention it" he told Nick, "Dodge the issue. Tell her tomorrow that all will be revealed. Okay? Even if she tries to quiz you."

"I'll be prepared for that," Nick promised, joining Charlotte on the jetty.

But none of them were prepared for the unexpected revelations they were about to uncover.

Lavelle and Jed were still on deck, when, after only a short time ashore, the two were seen heading back, their faces radiant, flushed with excitement.

"We got it all wrong!" cried Charlotte, as she followed Nick aboard.

"Got what all wrong?" Lavelle demanded.

"Silas' copy of the will."

Lavelle shot Nick a hard glance. "Thought I told you not to mention the will."

"We weren't going to," Nick began.

"Neither of us were," cried Charlotte, "but it was what she said."

"What she said?" He looked puzzled.

"As soon as we walked in she asked. 'Did you go up to the house for the master's will?' And Nick said, 'But you told us to go up to Tryun!"

"And she said," Nick chimed in, a touch of triumph in his voice, "What did you have to go up to that old watermill for? The chest was up in his den."

"Oh, my good God!" muttered Jed.

Lavelle sank down on the cockpit seating, his head in his hands. "But she didn't tell us that. She said it was up in the thirteenth water mill."

"And so she did," said Charlotte, "But she didn't mean the Tryun Mill."

Lavelle groaned. "Don't tell me its some other goddamn mill."

"It wasn't in any mill," said Charlotte. "The Thirteenth Watermill was a picture on the door of Uncle Silas' attic den."

Lavelle's jaw dropped. "You don't say," he drawled, with a glance at Jed.

"He used to tell the servants," Charlotte rushed on "that nobody must ever go beyond The Thirteenth Watermill. That was his private domain. It became a nickname for his room. Granny thought I would have known about it."

"So we had to tell her then," said Nick, "about finding the locked sea chest up at Tryun. It *had* once belonged to Silas, she knew about it. The chest up in his den is just like it, except that this one won't open unless you whack it with a stick."

Jed looked at Lavelle. "There could be some mechanism in the lid the crack of a stick would release."

Lavelle nodded. "It would figure." He grew suddenly thoughtful, his mind going back to one of his visits to the Gribble cottage. "Lucy said that Silas spent much of his time whittling sticks and 'making things' in his workshop. And when I asked her if Silas ever went up to the thirteenth watermill, an old crippled guy like him? Y' know what she said? *That he'd take it steadily up the stairs.*' I thought she was crazy!"

Jed was shaking his head. "But if he had hidden the will up in his den, Ellis would have found it," Jed pointed out.

"Sure! The first place he'd look," Lavelle agreed.

"But Ellis didn't know how to open the chest, that you had to whack it hard with a stick," Charlotte argued. "Only granny Bunt knew that."

Lavelle heaved a sigh. "Well I guess, maybe we'll learn some more when she comes to aboard tomorrow," he said, still not altogether convinced.

Nick lowered his head. "She's not coming," he said bleakly.

Lavelle shot him a glance. "Not coming!"

"She says there's no time to waste – that we must get back there and find the will. We must leave at once. She says she can always come aboard to tea some other time, when we've found it."

Lavelle opened his mouth to protest, but Charlotte was nodding her head. "And we'd better do as she wishes," she said. "She was all for coming back to Trefoy with us until we talked her out of it."

"And what does she expect us to do? Break into the old house? Lavelle snapped. "Get ourselves done by the law?"

"Not down here," said Nick; "People go in and out of each others houses all the time, especially the visitors. They're always poking their noses into our boathouses, and any cottage with an open door. 'Twould do no harm just taking a look."

"That place will be bolted like a fortress."

"There's a way in," said Charlotte, "Through the water tunnel – down by the river".

"Water tunnel?"

Jed nodded at Lavelle. "She means the old conduit leading up from the river. It was built to bring the water supply into the house in the old days. It leads to a stone tank under the cellar that fills up with winter rain and remains stored for summer."

"There are steps up to the wash house door," Charlotte said.

"That will be locked," said Nick.

"But I know where the key is, "Charlotte said quietly, "Granny gave it to me so that I could visit Uncle Silas secretly without Rachel knowing. It's probably still under the stone where I kept it."

Lavelle was slowly shaking his head. More Trevelyan cunning. It never ceased to amaze him. Only a fool would underestimate the resource and ingenuity of the Cornish.

They were all looking at him, eyes bright, waiting for his decision.

"Okay," he said finally. "I'll think about it. We head home. We'll leave on the tide."

****

Ian MacDonald nibbled greedily at the bar top olives. He had invited Ellis to the hotel for an evening drink. "So your client will definitely be in London by the end of the week."

"Definitely," said Ellis. "I shall go up to see her myself."

He stood, stooped over his glass, black hair Brylcreemed flat, his thick brows raised in confidence. He was well satisfied with the week's events. His dream was now in sight; probate had been granted, the disposal of the assets complete – but for the signing, and he hadn't heard a dickey-bird from his unseen enemies, not for weeks.

Ian MacDonald swallowed the last of his brandy. "You having another?"

"No – please let me!" Ellis said quickly, and turning to hail the barman caught a glimpse of Linda pushing through the crush towards them. "Ah! Here comes your niece! What will you have, my dear?"

Linda shook her head, smiling. She had changed from her dinner gown into a silky, floral dress, the rosy design matching the blush of pleasure under her tan.

"Thank you, Mr Ellis, but I only came in to say goodnight." She turned to her uncle. "Jack's back. He's just rang from St Ruan. He's coming across in the dinghy. I'm going down to meet him."

"Which means," MacDonald said, with a wink at Ellis, "that I shan't be seeing her until breakfast."

Linda laughed back at them as she made her departure. Ellis glanced enquiringly at the property developer. "Your niece appears to have an admirer then?"

"She would like to think so."

"But you see no future in it?"

MacDonald fidgeted, screwing up his face. "It's an odd sort of affair. He's the owner of that French schooner, divorced, but he seems to want to spend more time with his daughter, always off somewhere with her, while my niece sits, eating her heart out for him."

"Oh, dear!" Ellis tried to appear interested.

"I welcomed it at first, thought it might help her to get over her husband. Now it looks as though she could be heading for another broken heart." He took a sip of brandy and went on. "Could be another woman in tow Remember that night we had the mist? That was when Linda saw him bringing someone home in a boat at four o' clock in the morning. She said it was an old lady with white hair. More like a platinum blonde at that hour, I'd say."

"Undoubtedly," Ellis agreed.

MacDonald shrugged. "Ah well, we shall see! But to get back to business. Do you think your client might be persuaded to come down at all on the derelict properties? That old mill by the weir will need to be demolished. According to our architect it's bloody dangerous. There's only a crumbling buttress holding the whole thing up."

"Tryun you mean?" said Ellis, "I shouldn't think you'll do too badly out of that one – think of all the scrap iron you can salvage! But we might agree to throw in the antiques at the manor house, despite the fortune they might have brought on the American market, since my client is anxious to get the sale over with, I think..."

Ian Macdonald blinked back his astonishment. The house contents had not originally been included in the purchase price and were to have been sold by auction. Now and not for the first time in the recent weeks, here was the lawyer making another very generous concession to see the transaction quickly completed. It had not always been so. MacDonald remembered how, at the start of the negotiations he had found Ellis a tough man to bargain with, but now rather disturbingly, he was ready to give it all away.

"Talking of the Manor, you did promise to let me see the original deeds of the old part of the house," Macdonald reminded him, as they continued their discussion.

"'Course I did," said Ellis. "Actually they are still locked away in Trevelyan's study. But I'll see that you have them this week."

"Be glad if you would, Richard. Let me get you another brandy."

Ellis shook his head. "I had better not. I have some notes to prepare on a case coming up at Bodmin on Wednesday."

Walking back along the Esplanade, Ellis took his time, his mind going back over the conversation, not about the property deal, but about the man from the French schooner. Bringing someone home in a boat at four o' clock in the morning, an old lady with white hair! His eyes narrowed, and he paused for a moment to look at the yacht in question as she lay at anchor in the harbour. Registered in Marseilles, she was. He had seen the owner about town, bearded. Looked a bit big for a Frenchman. His skipper was a blond lad and they had a young girl on board. But then that yacht had been here all summer. There couldn't be any connection.

He walked on trying to dispel the thought from his mind, but it left behind a sense of unease, spoiling the splendour of the day.

CHAPTER TWENTY THREE

The creek was still with silence, a deep breathless silence, the tall woods looking down on the brown water strangely hushed; scarcely a flutter, not even a note of birdsong, except for those eerie sibilant whispers passing through the branches. It was almost as though the creek was gripped by a premonition of the devastation about to befall it, as though it knew and feared, Charlotte thought, what was to come. Already there were signs; ugly caterpillar tractors parked by the gateway of Granny Bunt's cottage, a barge moored in the deep water under the trees, and stacked on the jettyside timber sections of workmen's' sheds, ready for construction. Apart from the threat of the development, the long summer had taken its toll; the foliage which had crowded thickly to the water's edge was thinning now, the oak leaves brown against the tawny, autumn tints of bronze and gold, while the air had a dry parched taste of dead bracken.

They had come up in the Dipper on the falling tide, and beaching on the shingle, had lingered awhile, the men wandering towards the jetty, speculating on the development plans. It was another scorching hot day; too hot even for Matelot to go chasing sticks. He sat on the grassy bank, tongue hanging, as he kept them in sight with a whiskered eye. Charlotte stood on the slipway, watching the mallard with her ducklings. How they had grown since that spring day when she first saw them, baby chicks swimming in formation, now almost as big as their mother!

The water was draining from the mudflats, leaving them smooth and shining, swarming with flies. A few oystercatchers had come down to feed, and farther upstream a heron stood, motionless on one leg, a thing of grace. She turned away to join the men, who looked ready to set off for the manor house.

They were waiting for her on the bridge, their brown arms resting against the warm stone as they looked down at the river. The drought had left the pebbles dry, and the flow down from the hills was no more than a shallow trickle, finding its way lazily round the rocks and boulders towards the mouth of the creek. Farther upstream the reed beds were touched with yellow, the overhanging willows, straggly, their brown roots exposed; only the cedars stood cool and green against the blue sky.

Nick eyed it all with some misgivings. "Everywhere's thirsty for rain," he said.

Lavelle nodded, his mind elsewhere. Unlawful entry was not usually a problem to him. But this time he was in the process of upholding justice and he was mot prepared to put the case in jeopardy with underhand methods. If they were discovered there Ellis might hold it against him. But the hiding place in the den had to be searched. Once Rachel had been paid out, there would be little time left.

Charlotte too was silent. The thought of seeing the old house again was already beginning to overwhelm her, and at that moment she was too full of turbulent emotions to trust herself to speak. Watching her Nick was filled with a sudden longing, to hold her and kiss away the sadness he saw in her eyes. He ached to get near to her, but the strength he sensed in her held him back She had no mind for him yet, not while this Pendowry cloud hung over her, hung over them all.

But Matelot, trotting along ahead, ears pricked and carrying his tail like a pampas plume, had no cares.

They followed the trackway Charlotte had taken up the creekside that first May morning. The spring flowers had gone, but the verges were full of campion and foxgloves, and wild garlic reeked under the blackthorn.

The iron gate was down on the ground, wrenched off its hinges; beyond, the ferns had faded into gold and were trampled into a pathway, the dried mud indented with workmen's' boot prints.

"Watch out for adders!" Charlotte warned as Nick went ahead, widening the way through the thick undergrowth. They followed him, heads down.

Then the path flattened out and there was the house, crouched over its portico; the ivy thick and green against its granite walls, its creviced turrets and steep sloping roofs encrusted in lichen. Some of the overhanging creepers had now been torn down from the windows, the brambles and weeds stripped away, to give better access to the great oak door under the portico. Grass lay in withered heaps where a clearing had been scythed from the wilderness of the garden.

Beside the house where once green lawns had sloped by the woods to the river, the flowering grasses stood high; tawny yellow where the ragwort flared, bronze where the bracken had faded, while thistledown floated slowly by and bees were busy among the purple teasel heads. The drive, curving away round the spinney was overgrown with brambles; suckers of wild plum, blackberry and sloe had been thrown out from behind the iron fence holding back the thicket and young saplings had struggled up through the leafy shale with the thistles and the moss. It was all incredibly still, as though it had slept undisturbed for centuries, left to the seasons and the dictates of time.

They stood, taking it in without speaking, abruptly aware of trespassing, not upon the keepers of the domain, but upon the house itself, as though it lived and breathed its wrath upon them, a presence personified by the old man who had lived there and perhaps left something of himself within these granite walls and narrow latticed windows.

They advanced upon it slowly, trampling furrows through the weeds, lifting dry smells into the warm air, of pollen, wood mould and crumbling stone. Charlotte led the way round to the flagged yard, past the basement stairs and under an archway. It lead into a small walled garden at the back of the house, the lawn a jungle of weeds overlooked by a tiled veranda, and a conservatory full of dried up plants, laced with spiders' webs.

Then her face crumpled suddenly with pent up emotion.

"That's where Uncle Silas used to sit," she said, nodding towards the veranda.

She felt Nick's hand in hers, and squeezing his fingers led them under an archway to the rear of the stables, where the land swept down towards the river. Matelot rushed ahead, his nose down, sniffing for rabbits. Soon the bracken was shoulder high, dry as rust, and they pushed through it until they came across a rocky track, dropping steeply to the riverbed.

"This way," Charlotte said, clambering down.

They picked their way over the dry pebbles, the mainstream gurgling along beside them, the water clear and sparkling in the sunshine. Matelot splashed through the shallows, stopping here and there to drink, lapping noisily, jaws streaming and then showering them all as he shook himself dry.

Just ahead they could see the back wall of the house towering above the embankment, and under it was the water tunnel, hewn from the rock like a cave, the narrow entrance hung with creepers and abounding with ferns. Inside it was pitch dark, ice cold and stank like a drain. Nick groped for the torch he had brought with him and when he switched it on they could see the passage burrowing away to the right and hardly high enough for Lavelle to walk upright without bumping his head. Underfoot their shoes sank into soft mud, slowing them down, but Matelot squeezed past them inquisitively and they soon heard him splashing up ahead, the sound throwing back hollow echoes.

After curving for a few yards the tunnel ran straight towards a stone built archway. Passing beneath it, they found themselves in a small chamber looking down on the sunken pond Charlotte had described to them. It lay gleaming under the torchlight, a slimy square of ominous looking grey silt and hanging above it an ancient wooden bucket, tied to the end of a rope which came down from a trapdoor in the ceiling. Nick played the torch beam over to the right where a stone stairway led up to the cellar door. Matelot was already there, scratching excitedly to get in.

"He's heard something!" said Charlotte, and they paused to listen, their glances raised to the high wooden ceiling, where there was a muffled sound drumming across the floor of the room above.

"Rats!" said Lavelle. "If we get the door open Matelot will go scatter them."

Charlotte was already feeling between the stonework for the key. It was red with rust but it twisted easily in the lock. The door fell open as Matelot pushed though, bringing a great warm whiff of animal odour against their faces.

They stood back, astonished to see a moving mass of sleek brown fur; loppy ears, bright eyes, flashes of white behind, bounding away in all directions, lifting a haze of dust into the torch beam.

"Not rats! Look, they're rabbits!" cried Nick, swinging the light around the cellar.

Matelot stood in the centre of the floor, poised on all fours, at loss where to spring, ears pricked, jaws apart, gaping his amazement. He had never seen so many rabbits before. The sight overwhelmed him and he could only watch, whimpering grievously as they romped away from him.

For one moment they were everywhere, peeping from behind tubs, scrubbing boards, ducking away under a great iron mangle with wooden rollers. Then quite suddenly as though some kind of telepathic communication had passed among them, there was a gathering stampede for the far corner of the outer wall. Nick held the torch steady and they saw loose earth rising as the rabbits kicked back, crowding to enter the burrow under the crumbling foundations. But the sudden rush was too much for Matelot. He plunged into the mass, lifting dust and fur down, to finally emerge engaged, with his nose to the powder puff of a large buck. For several seconds they raced in thumping, bumping pursuit round the cellar, then the rabbit spotted a way of escape through the doorway behind the intruders, and streaked for it, thudding away down the steps. Matelot, hanging tongue and flying fur, rushed after him, almost knocking them off their feet. They turned aghast to watch him disappear into the darkness, his claws clattering against the stone, then just echoes coming back as he splashed off through the tunnel. Then the sound had gone, leaving a vacuum of silence, and when they looked back into the cellar they saw it was bare, not a rabbit to be seen, only sparklets of dust raining down through the torch beam, falling to rest on the brown carpet of decomposed droppings covering the floor.

"They must be using this place as a warren," Charlotte said, lingering, but the two men were already on their way up the stairway leading into the house.

Daylight dissolved the torch beam as Nick opened the door. They saw they were in a large kitchen, with cupboards reaching to the ceiling and ovens along the length of the room. The black Cornish range was crowded with sooty pots and pans, and on a hob stood a giant kettle, cold and dead-looking without the perpetual puff of steam. The room was tidy, with signs of a recent clean up; the table had been scrubbed white, the floor streaked from mopping and although there was still a faint smell of Jeyes fluid, it failed to disguise a lingering fustiness. There was evidence, too, of a cleaner's presence about the sink, where a tap dripped into an overflowing enamel bowl, and on the draining board were cloths, a tablet of carbolic soap, hard and crystallised, and a packet of Rinso.

They began to look around. A door opened into a pantry, the shelves bare, another led into the dairy where milk churns and cider barrels were stacked under a long stone bench. A third door took them into the servant's hall, a shabby room with tall dressers and a large open fireplace. Crockery had been packed into tea chests and linen into bundles. Against the far wall was a carved oak settle, dark and shiny with age. Charlotte paused beside it, resting her hand tenderly upon the arm, as though touched by some memory it stirred. Then she moved on, the two men following, curiosity luring them on through the rest of the house.

What they saw astounded them. They were appalled at the decay, the neglect. So much that had once been beautiful had been left to rot, just as the garden and the rest of the estate had been left for nature to plunder. They saw how the silver had blackened, how the porcelain had become almost unrecognisable under the dust. Fortunately most of the exquisitely carved furniture had been covered by dust sheets and protected from the falls of plaster crumbling away from the moulded ceilings, but in places, where the covering had slipped, there were powdery heaps on the red velvet seats of the high backed chairs. Lavelle shook his head to see so many priceless pieces; a rare mosaic table, a jardiniere stand and an elegant ormolu clock.

They found Silas Trevelyan's downstairs quarters at the back of the house, a suite of rooms with access to the veranda and the conservatory they had seen from the garden. The study was small, the walls oak panelled and lined with books, but here some of the furniture belonged to a later period, like the leather armchair and the fairly modern roll top desk, closed and locked.

The drawing room was more interesting. Here were the ships Lucy Gribble had been talking about! They were in the pictures on the walls, the *Constantine,* the *Mary Combe*, the *Dauntless*, and not only pictures, but scaled down models of old sailing ships, each with its own delicately carved figurehead, indicating the old man's passion for working with wood. This was further endorsed when Charlotte took them into his little workroom off the veranda, and showed them a soft-lined box on the bench where he kept his cutting tools; gravers, spitstickers and scorpers, all with the same smooth mushroom shaped handles. Against the bench were his crutches, in the corner his wheel chair, a Cornish tartan rug folded across the seat.

In these rooms the old man's presence was strong, reminders of him everywhere, his art work and wood carving. Crowded into an umbrella stand was a unique collection of walking sticks, their knobs and handles beautifully sculptured, depicting birds and animals; a snake's head, a sea serpent, a rose, but it was the stick propped up against his chair that drew their attention. It had been carved into the shape of a clenched fist and was so lifelike it looked almost threatening.

Lavelle took it in his hands, examining it curiously. "The sure kind of knobstick to bat someone with..," he remarked, with a wry glance at Nick.

"We'll need it for whacking the chest," Charlotte said, taking it from him.

Out on the veranda Lavelle was reminded of Lucy Gribble again and how she had spoken of joining Captain Trevelyan for tea on the bridge with the Bo'sun. It was all here; the white rails, the ships' lamps, the brass compass on the chart table and the figurehead above the drawing room doorway now giving vivid meaning to her ramblings. Lavelle stood, deep in thought, trying to recall something she had said that might suggest a direction, but at that moment nothing came to him. Maybe as they moved through the house it would.

They had reached the front hallway. Sunlight, filtering through a tall stained glass window, fell in dull shafts over the dark oak staircase. It swept up majestically to an open landing, the wall lined with portraits, all the past generations of the Trevelyan family, courage and defiance in their blue, rebellious eyes. So like Charlotte's, Nick thought.

Lavelle led the way to the top of the house, but the passageways took them into the servants quarters and they had to descend to another level before they came across the narrow stairway up to the old man's den. They knew they had found it as soon as they saw the pictures of the watermills, pen and ink drawings in passé partout frames, hanging on either side of the stairway. The titles were in copperplate, signed by Silas Trevelyan, and, mounted on the door at the top, was larger picture, it's title printed boldly beneath it – like a warning.

THE THIRTEENTH WATERMILL

The door was slightly ajar. They followed Lavelle into a garret room. It had a wide sloping window, a desk top the length of it, heaped with pencil sketches, old photographs and scribblings, the papers ash grey with dust. Round the walls were more drawings, of ships again, below them well stacked bookshelves and cupboards, inks and various art materials crowded against the glass doors.

Standing in the centre of the floor was the oak chest, a replica of the one they had found at Tryun Mill, but there was no need to whack it with the stick. It was already open, half the contents heaped on a chair beside it.

They stood staring at it, their faces blank with disappointment.

"Ellis!" Nick muttered.

But then he was on his knees, Charlotte beside him, dragging out the hoard of old books and papers still inside.

Lavelle stood watching them flatly. It was as he expected. This was all too easy. Ellis would have figured how to open the chest, been into it before Silas was cold. And since only half the contents appeared to have been tipped out, maybe he had found it.

But if that was true, why did he have to worry about Emma Bunt? Keep her banged up at Talland? Why wait until the heat was on before he decided to silence her? Maybe he suspected Silas had given her the document to keep safe, and she'd taken it with her when he moved her out. No need for him to worry, as long as it remained hidden with her at Talland.

Hang on! Then why did Ellis search her cottage? He surely didn't expect she would leave it behind. So why smash the door down and ransack the place? Wasn't that what Luke had heard the Hawkey's say? He heaved a sigh. Or was this the Cornish weaving fantasy into fact again? Could be, Ellis, finding the curtains drawn, thought she'd had a heart attack. Hell! What was there next to think?

Charlotte, sorting through the papers, suddenly caught her breath. She had come across a photograph of her father. Lavelle bent to look. It was a group picture, taken in the walled garden. There was Silas in his chair, with Bill behind him and a man Charlotte suddenly recognised as a visitor to the house.

"He used to come to see Uncle Silas when I was just a tot. Brought me sweets. I think he lived somewhere up river, he might have been the man we went to see at Tryun Mill."

"You remember his name, honey?"

She shook her head. "It was such a long time ago."

Nick came to join them. "Look! Here's another one of him," he said, handing the photograph to Lavelle.

It was a half plate portrait of a man in navel uniform. He looked younger than the visitor in the snapshot, but the features were the same. Lavelle flicked it over and saw scrawled across the back: *'The copy I promised you. The Bo'sun, Tryun Mill, Lantaglas. August.1935.'*

Lavelle frowned. The Bo'sun. Another grain of truth emerging from Lucy Gribble's fantasies.

"Granny Bunt might remember him," Charlotte said, then added, "There might be more pictures in the study downstairs. Come on Nick, let's look!"

"Take the stick with you," Lavelle said, "Put it back where we found it. I'll be on down shortly."

As the door closed, Lavelle moved to the desktop, and spread out the photographs under the light from the skylight. The group picture looked jovial, Bill and the Bo'sun grinning at each other, even Silas looking pleased with himself. Who took it? He wondered, hardly Rachel. Maybe it was earlier, when Bill's first wife was alive.

He put the pictures into his inside pocket and lit a cigarette. The Bo'sun! If he was family friend, Silas might have confided in him. Wonder if he's still around someplace? The farmer they met on the bridge at Peakswater! He spoke of a seafaring man, who once lived at Tryun? Might be smart to go back there and talk to that farmer.

He stood smoking, thought absorbing him, his mind working feverishly for a new direction which had to be found before it was too late. Finally he crushed out his cigarette into an ashtray and went back down the stairway.

The house had become oppressively hot, the rooms baked by the heat against the closed windows. Time to get out of here. Descending into the gloom of the house, he could hear Charlotte's voice, and on the bend of the stairs, and saw her standing before one of the portraits, her chin lifted in pride, as she described one of her ancestors to Nick. This one was an oil painting of a seafaring man in a tricorn hat and a brass-buttoned coat, a telescope on the table beside him.

"This was Brig Trevelyan," she was saying, "He was a fair trader. He didn't hold with the family's fancy for working the rivers and tearing up the earth with the plough. He believed the Trevelyans were born to live off the sea and would thrive from it. When his father Jonathon Trevelyan decided to build a thirteenth watermill, Brig swore it would bring ill luck. They quarrelled and later Brig was betrayed. They hung him at Bodmin and as they placed the noose around his neck, he laughed in their faces, screaming a curse on the family, promising they would suffer his wrath for centuries, until a day when the heavens would open and all the Trevelyan gold would be washed away with a great torrent into the sea, and people would drown...."

Nick turned as he saw Lavelle. "One of her yarns," he said, and as his smile fading added "Nothing here, is there?"

Lavelle heaved a sigh. "Not a goddamn thing," he said gloomily.

They had almost reached the foot of the stairs, the panelled hallway dim now the sun had moved from the window. Opposite them was the heavy oak door that opened into the portico at the front of the house. Lavelle tensed. There was a sound behind it. He stood, staring, his gaze resting on the keyhole.

Suddenly it clacked, the sound breaking upon the stillness and in a chord of echoes, the door came swinging inwards, light streaming into the hall, breaths of sun-warmed air against their faces.

They stood transfixed, to see standing on the threshold, looking in upon them in utter disbelief, the man they hated; briefcase, clerical grey suit. It was Richard Ellis.

CHAPTER TWENTY FOUR

In that first suspended moment Ellis could only gape at them in astonishment; the question, the demand set stark in his face, the anger in his eyes turning slowly to wonder as he recognised the intruders. The people from the *Cape Columbo*, the people whose very presence in Trefoy he had already been viewing with suspicion. Now at Pendowry – here in the house, and not only grimed from rummaging, but wide-eyed with guilt and dismay at being discovered!

He advanced curiously into the hall, his shoulders bent to his stoop, chin raised enquiringly.

"May I ask just what you are doing in this house?"

The question was directed at the man with the beard, a man who glared back at him, his eyes strangely luminous, a malice in them that Ellis found disturbing. Equally disturbing was a likeness about the fellow, a sense of knowing him from somewhere – somewhere in the past, in court perhaps.

Nick felt Lavelle stiffen, felt the antagonism, the heat of it. He reached out, ready with a restraining hand, but Lavelle didn't notice. He was caught in a blood-rush of shock at finding himself face to face with the man he hated, but he knew he would have to control himself.

He felt Nick's grip then, but shrugged him off and descended the stairs with a spread of his hands, smiling his apologies.

"I guess we shouldn't be here, but we just had to take a look around this great old house, all these paintings! What a place you have here!"

Ellis, unimpressed, looked at him with suspicion. He had not expected to hear an American accent from the owner of the French schooner. "Just where did you break in?" he demanded coldly.

"We didn't break in," Nick hurried to say, "We – we just walked in."

"Walked? I don't begin to understand you."

"We came in through the cave by the river," Charlotte said, with a touch of defiance.

Ellis turned to her in astonishment. "You mean the water conduit! You came in through there!" he exclaimed, his eyes widening as he looked at her. There was something vaguely familiar about her, too, the way she raised her head at him. And the insolent young miss was actually carrying one of Silas Trevelyan's walking sticks.

Lavelle, in an attempt to draw Ellis' attention from Charlotte, said quickly. "Which ever way we came in we've done no harm! We've just had a walk around, admiring your fine old place? If you're sore about it, then we're sorry, okay?"

His words trailed off under Ellis' withering stare. The man's close scrutiny was making him sweat. The lawyer opened his mouth to speak, ready with a tart rebuke, but Lavelle decided he had humbled himself enough. Time to get to the hell out the place. An arm around Charlotte and Nick he ushered them towards the doorway. "Come on! We've intruded enough on the gentleman's property," he said, no longer attempting to conceal the contempt in his tone.

"Wait a minute!" roared Ellis, the sudden outcry halting them. "You had better leave that walking stick behind – unless you want me to have you charged with theft."

Lavelle pulled up. He hadn't noticed Charlotte still had the stick. "Hand it over, honey," he said softly. "We can't expect to take souvenirs."

Charlotte, tight-lipped walked back to the hallway, and slapping it into the lawyer's outstretched hand, turned on her heel without a word.

The two men fell in beside her and Ellis stood watching as all three walked away down the drive, observing them with even more curiosity.

Without any doubt this was the trio the Hawkeys had seen at Talland Bay. They fitted the description perfectly; the older man Josh had talked about, the girl, who looked like his daughter.

He could be the private detective the Australian woman had hired. He was posing as the girl's father and conducting the investigation from the yacht. This was a blind. The skipper, a local lad from St Ruan, who knew the coast, probably in their pay, and that white haired old lady Ian MacDonaold's niece had seen in their boat, must have been Emma Bunt.

So where were they hiding her? Probably Mrs Millicent Potter was keeping her out of sight in some swank hotel down the coast.

He watched the intruders until they disappeared down the woodland path, then he went into the house to collect the property deeds.

Evidence of the intrusion was everywhere, fingerprints in the dust, doors left open, sheets covering the furniture disturbed, not a room left untouched. And they had been rummaging in that old sea chest in the den, dragged out the contents – just as he had done more times than he could remember.

He threw the walking stick onto the settle and stood, fuming silently. No doubt about it. It was that copy of the will they were after. The Bunt woman would have told them it was in the house somewhere, but it didn't look as though they'd found it, judging by he state of the place and the hours they must have been here. And if they had, they wouldn't have been smoothing over their intrusion with apologies, they would have simply marched past him, with that 'see you in court' look on their faces. Instead they had sloped away sick to their boots. He knew losers when he saw them.

Ellis relaxed. So either Emma Bunt had given them the wrong directions, or typically of the elderly had clean forgotten where Silas had told her to look. But that was the easy answer, and too much was at stake to assume it was the right one. Again, he was not absolutely certain that Silas had even confided in her. The house search could just have been her suggestion. How was he to tell?

He drew in his brows, brooding over it. He would need to know more about these people. If that copy was still hidden and for them to find, there would always be a threat. They might question Emma Bunt again, interrogate her, and something might just jog her memory. Too much was at stake to allow this incident to pass.

He would make some tentative enquiries, perhaps from the harbourmaster – or better still, Ian MacDonald's niece. She knew this man, and at the moment she was feeling a shade neglected by him. She might be encouraged to open up. It was worth a try, he decided, as he went into the study to look out the papers for her uncle.

Before he locked up, he made his way to the kitchens. It would be advisable to make sure that cellar door was bolted on the inside. There must be no more visits through that river tunnel. It was as well that he did. The door was wide open. Using the torch they had left on the kitchen table, he made his way down the steps. The place smelled like a midden, the floor covered with droppings from the vermin inhabiting the place. It couldn't have been used for years. Pushing aside the overhanging spiders' webs, he went across to door leading down to the tunnel. It had a heavy brass lock. Swinging the torchlight he saw that the key had fallen out onto the top step. As he bent for it, a sound alerted him, a splashing sound, coming from somewhere beyond the chamber below.

He straightened up, listening. There was something coming along the tunnel, probably a rat. No, not a rat, here it came! It was a dog, a shaggy brown and white mongrel, coming, rushing towards him up the steps. He was carrying a rabbit, but before Ellis had time to stop him the dog had shot past him into the cellar and was racing up the steps into the house.

"Come back here!" Ellis roared, waving the torch. "You can't go up there!"

But the dog had already disappeared into the kitchen. Ellis stumbled after him, encumbered by his gammy leg, and saw when he arrived at the top that the dog was down on his haunches before the Cornish range, munching into the rabbit.

"Out! Out!" Ellis thundered at him.

The dog picked up the rabbit and made off with it into the servant's hall. Ellis, staggering after him, was just in time to see him shoot straight under the oak settle and continue to munch into the blooded fur.

"Out I said!" Ellis went on, pointing towards the door.

The dog lifted a glance to him and unconcernedly went on with his meal. Exasperated, Ellis reached for Silas' stick and struck the top of the settle with it in an attempt to frighten the dog out, but he simply refused to budge.

"Blast him!" Ellis thought and began to wonder what on earth had brought the dog barging in through that tunnel. Suddenly it occurred him. He belonged to those damned people. Coming to think of it, he'd seen this longhaired mongrel out in their boats with them.

His anger flared afresh and he began to prod at the dog with the stick, trying to push him out from under the settle. There was a watery growl as the dog felt the stick against his rump, and he sprang out and began prancing around Ellis, ready for him to throw. Ellis, not used to such boisterousness, tried to hold the dog off with the stick, but he leapt for it, and, grabbing the end between his jaws, sank down on his haunches for a game of tug-of-war.

Cursing the animal, Ellis, tried to wrench it off him but the dog growled threateningly, and Ellis, afraid of being bitten, felt compelled to let go. Immediately he did so, the dog took another hold on the stick half way up the stem, then turned and made off with it down the hallway.

Ellis, red faced and sweating, decided he wasn't going after him. He'd had enough. He picked up the torch again and went back down into the cellar to lock the door to the tunnel. When he returned there was no sign of the dog – or the stick either. He had probably cleared off with it through the front door.

****

Charlotte dragged behind as they walked down through the clough. As she allowed the men to stride on ahead of her their voices, low and intent, drifted back to her. They were all still stunned after their encounter with Ellis, but she was particularly angry to have been humiliated by the man's rudeness, up there in the family home. It left her bitter, outraged at the unfairness of it all. What he was doing to them, a feeling not even the peace of her surroundings could dispel.

The air was cooler now, autumn on its breath, and as she dropped down to the bridge she could see the tide had crept up, filling the creek; the banksides brimming, the branches trailing the water, like they always did, and the patterns on the surface as the early evening sunlight flickered through the trees. Two swans with a grown up cygnet glided by, their reflections mirrored in the still green depths.

Nick had brought the *Dipper* across from the jetty pool and was standing holding the painter as she drifted back into the current. Lavelle, sitting on the bankside, was idly watching the lapping tide lifting the flies from the pebbles.

"We'll just give it a few more days," he was saying as Charlotte reached them. "See if we can find anything on this Bo'sun guy. Maybe Silas confided in him."

Charlotte was hardly listening. She was still cross about having to give up the walking stick. "It's so unfair," she complained, "Uncle Silas would have wanted me to have it. I think the clenched fist was a symbol of Brig Trevelyan's anger."

"It'll be yours one day," said Lavelle, rising from the bank, "That I promise you. We'll see if we can track down this Bo'sun guy, and if he can't help. Then I'll get the best attorney I can find."

Charlotte reached for his hand. "I know you will, Frisco," she said.

Nick was looking round for Matelot. "Where's that old dog be to?" he said. "I've not seen the like of him since he went chasing after that rabbit." He put two fingers in his mouth and whistled shrilly. They waited, the ducks quacking in the silence, but Matelot did not appear.

"Don't say he's got himself lost," Charlotte said.

"What Matelot?" Nick asked. "More like got fed up of waiting and gone home down the creek path. When we get back he'll be on St Ruan jetty, wet through after chasing sticks."

He pulled the boat alongside the slip and they hopped aboard, Lavelle taking the seat at the tiller. She started first time and he swung her round into the channel. Charlotte, sitting up in the bow, was looking back up the creek, her eyes still searching for Matelot. She had an uneasy feeling about leaving without him. It was a feeling that was to intensify when they reached port to find he had not yet returned,

"He's after rabbits," Nick said, unconcerned. "If he's not back by morning, we'll go up and root him out."

****

Linda was sitting in her favourite place on the veranda when Ellis found her, the coffee tray on the white wrought iron table beside her.

"Hello," she said, smiling at him. "You've missed my uncle by about five minutes. He's gone over to the station slip with the foreman, there's some machinery arriving."

"Oh, has he?" said Ellis feigning surprise. He knew perfectly well where Ian MacDonald had gone. He had watched the foreman pick him up from Whitehouse Quay and take him off down the river, leaving his niece at the hotel. Ellis had waited three days for this opportunity. He set down his glass on her table. "Would you allow me to buy you a drink?"

She shook her head. "No, thank you. It's coffee for me at lunchtime. But do sit down and enjoy yours with me. It's such a beautiful day. I shouldn't think Uncle Mac will be very long. He'll want to do some sunbathing."

"You spend quite a lot of time here, don't you?"

"I never tire of watching the river."

He followed her gaze to the cream schooner across the harbour, where he could just see 'the intruders' sitting on deck.

"You know those people on the schooner, don't you?"

She nodded, smiling. "One can never keep secrets from Uncle Mac."

"Sees the lovelight in your eyes, does he?"

"You could say that."

"Nice yacht! French, isn't it?"

"Registered there, but Jack Breton, the owner, he's an American – from San Francisco! He has business in Marseilles."

"Really," Ellis said, sipping his brandy. "Actually I ran into the fellow the other day up at Pendowry Creek. He was with his daughter and the skipper."

She looked up. "Did you? When was that?"

"Friday afternoon,"

"Oh!" she said, "So that's where they got to on Friday."

Ellis looked at her a little sheepishly and said. "To tell you the truth I was rather annoyed with them. You see, they were trespassing up at the manor house and I'm afraid I rather showed my displeasure. They shouldn't have been there, you know."

"Oh, dear," she said. "That creek happens to be one of their passions. They are rather gone on the place. In fact they are quite against it being developed into a tourist centre. They're always throwing out hints about the problems that my uncle will have to face when the construction work starts. I think Charlie would have preferred your client to have sold it to the National Trust."

"Charlie?" Is he the skipper?"

"Oh, no, the skipper's called Nick. It's Jack's daughter who is called Charlie – short for Charlotte."

Ellis, feeling suddenly too warm under his office suit, brought out his handkerchief to mop his brow. Good God! The girl was called Charlotte!

"And where does she live? France or America?" Ellis asked, his fingers moist round the stem of his glass.

"I think she's been in London with her mother. But it's a broken marriage so they don't talk much about it. Charlie was already down on the yacht some weeks before Jack joined her."

Ellis was sitting forward in his chair, trying to choose his questions without appearing too inquisitive. "How did you get to know them?" he ventured.

"They took me fishing, then Jack asked me to go sailing with them and that was really lovely. He often takes me for a drink in the evenings, if he's back in time from one of their expeditions."

"Expeditions!" said Ellis curiously.

She smiled. "Oh, they're always going off somewhere, in the car, in the boat. Usually they are rather cagey about where they go, but one day Charlie let it slip that they'd been to an old watermill up the valley, a really spooky place."

"Really? Which one was that?"

"Its called Tryun Mill. It's almost falling down."

Ellis tensed. Tryun Mill? The place was near derelict. Ah, but wasn't there a sea chest belonging to Silas left up in the loft there? Nothing but books in that one either.

Linda was chatting on. "Charlotte said all the time they were exploring the attic you could hear the slates falling down the roof. "I shall see for myself on Saturday afternoon. They are going there again and this time they've promised to take me with them."

Ellis was tempted to ask for what reason, but he had lost her attention, her glance was straying back to the schooner, where the skipper was pulling in the dinghy.

"Looks as though your friends are coming ashore for you now," he said.

"I don't think so. They are rather worried about their dog. He's missing and they've been going out every afternoon looking for him. Jack may come over this evening though..."

Her voice trailed off as Ian MacDonald's plump, smiling face appeared from behind the glass doors.

"Richard! Don't tell me you've brought over those deeds at last."

"As a matter of fact, I've had them for you since Friday, but this is the first chance I've had to come over," Ellis said, untruthfully.

"You should have come earlier and had lunch with us," said MacDonald. "Allowed us to entertain you for all the trouble you have taken."

"Your niece has been doing that already, telling me all about her gentleman friend on the schooner."

MacDonald stiffened his chins. "The one we hear so much about and see so little of," he said, with a slightly reproachful glance at his niece. "Why don't you ask Jack to have dinner with us one evening, Linda. What about Saturday after you've all been out looking at the watermills."

"That would be nice," she said. "But will he come?"

"If he doesn't I shall be insulted. What about you, Richard, will you be back from London in time to join us for dinner on Saturday evening? Its Friday you go, isn't it?"

Ellis was about to decline the invitation, then he hesitated. He had intended to be away for the weekend with Rachel Ives. They were meeting at the George at Honiton. Now his brain was busy contemplating a change of plan. "Yes, I think you will be able to count on my company, Mac," he said. "I shall look forward to it."

Ian MacDonald chatted on and would have continued to do so, had not Ellis, desperate for some time to muse over his findings, made an excuse about having an appointment with a client at the office and quickly made his departure.

CHAPTER TWENTY FIVE

The Esplanade was crowded; bathers coming up from the beach, brown-legged children trailing buckets and spades and old men with knotted handkerchiefs protecting their bald heads from the sun. The town was teeming with trippers, pouring in from other resorts, car fumes filling the streets, and all along the sea wall holiday makers drooled over the sorry hump of the St Ruan waterfront.

Ellis, walking back to his office, saw none of it. His mind was a frenzy of thought. She was called Charlotte. It was her! He had been right. She had been wise to their plans all along, spying on Rachel, steaming open letters – just as he suspected. No wonder she had readily agreed to go to Australia. It had given her the chance to expose them.

But how did she find out about her inheritance in the first place? Either Rachel had let something slip or Charlotte had been secretly corresponding with the St Ruan clan, probably this young skipper, who after the funeral had put her wise. Astute enough to know she would need adult advice and guidance to prove her case she had probably sat tight awaiting her chance. The rich Aunt Millicent and slow cruise to Australia must have seemed a heaven sent opportunity to win an ally. It was a strategy the devious little miss seemed to have achieved with flying colours, since, by the time they reached Gibraltar the woman was sparing no expense to see her rights upheld. And now they were here, and looking for that one piece of evidence that would turn his dream into a nightmare.

He sighed heavily. But here he was weaving theories round the facts again. First he had to be absolutely sure, that this girl was Bill's daughter and to identify her positively there was only one way; that was to get Rachel to pick her out. But it would have to be damn soon, before those bastards could make another move. Couldn't be tomorrow though, he was in Court, and the case could drag on into Thursday. It would have to be Friday – damn! Friday he was taking the papers to London for her to sign. Forget that. He'd have her down here for the weekend instead

His step quickened. He would telephone her immediately Miss Couch left the office with the post.

****

"Rachel..," Ellis began. Her voice came excitedly over the line. "Richard! How funny you should ring! I was going to call you tonight. What d'you think? I've had a telegram from Australia."

"Australia?" His stomach turned over.

"Yes! From Aunt Millicent to say they've arrived safely in Sydney."

Ellis sat upright in his chair, for a moment unable to speak.

"You still there, Richard?"

"Yes, of course. D'you have the wire handy?"

"Want me to read it to you?" He heard the paper crackling. "She says," came Rachel's voice again, "Arrived Sydney today stop. Wonderful trip stop. Writing to tell you all about it. Charlotte fit and happy. Sends her love. Millicent Potter. So how's that then?"

Ellis opened his mouth without saying anything. If the wire were to be believed this completely knocked the bottom out of his theory. All along he had assumed that the Australian woman was behind it all, but was she? Suppose she knew nothing about it? Just suppose for a moment the girl she met at Westbury was not Charlotte, but somebody got up to look like her? It could have been one of Charlotte's friends, prepared to take her place. That would solve the mystery about the girl's seasickness. The young skipper of the *Cape Columbo* could have been her contact in Cornwall. Perhaps he had confided in his boss, this Jack fellow, who was obviously the brains behind the whole thing.

"Richard! Are you still there?" Rachel was asking.

"Yes, yes. Rachel, listen – I can't come to London on Friday. I need you to come down here instead. Get the Cornish Riviera Express and I'll meet the train at Par."

"Me come down there!" She protested, "Oh, you know how hate Cornwall. Why?"

"I can't make it, I'm in court all week. I've booked you a nice room at St Catherine's."

"What's the matter with the Trefoy Hotel?"

"They're booked up," he told her. He couldn't have her meeting up with Ian Macdonald. It had to be another hotel.

She began whining over the arrangements, but he cut her short, his tone brusque.

"You want your inheritance, don't you? I have papers here for you to sign. Buy your ticket tomorrow and ring me with your arrival time. Don't let me down, my dear."

He heard her sigh. She would come. Now he must devote some serious thought to the problem of disposing of the enemy, should his new suspicions turn out to be correct.

****

Jack Lavelle didn't have any trouble finding his way to Peakswater. It was his second trip that week. He now knew the farmer they had met on the bridge was called Amos Wilkes. His was the small holding on the hillside above the near derelict Tredowr mill, but when Lavelle first called he was away at a son's farm near Callington, according to the hired lad, who was looking after his hens for him.

'Back Wednesday,' Lavelle had been assured.

Now taking the right fork at the bridge, he drove slowly up the river valley looking for the cart track up to the hillside farm. This time Amos Wilkes was at home. Lavelle could see him scattering corn for some pullets in the yard. He looked up, giving Lavelle a nod of recognition as he approached the gate.

"Manage to find your way up to Tryun that day?" he asked.

"Sure did," said Lavelle, "You were right about the state of it".

The farmer nodded. "An evil place," he said.

Lavelle came straight to the point. "You talked about a seafaring man who once lived there," he said, "Would he have been the guy they called the Bo'sun?"

The farmer narrowed his eyes. "May I ask your interest?"

"Sure, He could have been a friend of a guy I knew in the war, who was killed in France – Bill Ives."

The frown of distrust faded. "You mean the late-river pilot?"

"You knew him?"

"Oyez, I knew him. And tes true, he was a friend of the Bo'sun. So was his uncle, Silas Trevelyan."

"So would you know the Bo'sun's real name?" Lavelle asked, finding it hard to hold back his impatience.

Amos Wilkes set down his bucket of corn and rested him arms on the gate. "He was Tom Constantine, a navy man," he said, "but he was also a scholar, used to write books about the old sailing ships, and Silas Trevelyan used to do pictures to illustrate them. Tom used to stay in the cottage at Tryun Mill to do his writing. Fascinated with the place, believed it was haunted. He was a solitary man, preferred it out here than living with his widowed mother in Plymouth. But then come the war and he was back in the navy."

"And he came through okay?" Lavelle ventured.

Amos nodded. "Oyez, Came back to Plymouth about '48. His old mother gone, he sold the house and bought a yawl. Lived aboard. My oldest son has a pub down on the Barbican where Tom used to go of an evening. That's where he met they people who owned the *Pandora*. She was a ketch, and old boat they'd been doing up all summer. They were planning to take her out foreign, the Middle East. They wanted the Bo'sun to skipper her, but he didn't fancy the work they'd done on the hull. Thought they should have let a good yard do it. Rotten timbers needed experts. Finally he agreed to join them on a sea trial to St Malo before he made up his mind. That was the last we heard of her. Gone. All hands lost."

"She went down?"

"Off Brittany. Wreckage was found all along the coast."

"When was this?" Lavelle asked.

"T'would say about two years ago. Wasn't much in the paper about it? Just a small report."

"Long before Silas' death? I wonder if he knew about it."

"Might have guessed, when the Bo'sun came no more to see him. I don't really know."

“Maybe that’s why Tom Constantine was not at the funeral?” Lavelle said, his mind going back through list of mourners.

Amos Wilkes was stroking his chin, “You might learn more about the wreck of the *Pandora* if you were to go over to St Malo, find out if his body had been washed up. My son always reckoned the Bo’sun was never one for drowning. Believes he would have swam ashore and found a hideaway in France, and is still writing a book about the adventure, as he did all his other shipwrecks.”

Lavelle heaved a sigh. Even if he was still alive, how long would it take to find him? Too long to be of any help.

“Would you like me to give my son a message for him, should he ever turn up?” Amos was suggesting.

“Sure,” Lavelle answered, and, feeling into his pocket, produced a business card on the back of which he scribbled his name and some telephone numbers. “I guess it’s a long shot, but I have to be due for some better luck.”

****

Ellis had always believed his best ideas came from deep concentration, and by dwelling on a problem, an answer would eventually suggest itself.

This one came to him early on Thursday afternoon driving back from Bodmin. He had lost his case, but that had been inevitable after the small space of time he had given to the brief. But what the hell, his client had been guilty anyway. For once he didn’t care. On the point of sweet retirement, why should he?

It was another blistering day, belonging more to August than September, heat haze shimmering above the tarmac on the road ahead. His mind had been dwelling on the dangerous state of Tryun Mill that his enemies planned to visit at the weekend. It was during these reflections that the first flicker of an idea occurred to him. This would be his chance.

He pondered over it until he joined the main road, and instead of making the right turn home to Trefoy, he turned left towards Lostwithiel for a route that would take him close to the Tryun Mill.

Just before he reached Lanteglas Highway he pulled off the road into a grassy lane and let the car run down the slope a little, to be out of sight of the main road. Leaving his jacket and tie behind he set off down the hill, hoping with his open necked shirt, he might be taken for a holidaymaker if he were to meet somebody.

The lane narrowed into an overgrown footpath that he knew would lead him down the hillside to the back of the watermill. It was a quicker route than the riverside track up from Trevada and less tiring in the heat. Beyond, the hills were blurred in hazy blue, the grass beneath his feet dry and slippery from rock-hard fields, and the ditch in the bottom gave up the same stench as the Trefoy drains.

Dust smoked from his shoes as he trudged through the dry silt banked up before the arched entrance into the mill. He noticed footprints, the distinctive dotted pattern of Dunlop plimsolls used by the yachting people. He followed them inside and once he had become accustomed to the gloom beyond the inner door, he was able to survey the wrecked interior of the building; the wheels silent, rusted, girders slanting, swinging from broken beams, the collapsed floor resting its debris amidst a tangle of machinery.

His gaze moved slowly along the main beam, noticing how it sagged as it took the strain of the building; it was holding though, at least while it still had the support of that wall buttress. He smiled thinly; the idea which had brought him there was already taking shape in his mind. Here was the perfect answer to his problem, an accident destined to happen. It was a pity MacDonalds's niece would be involved. He would probably grieve a little, but the he should have warned her about the danger. Hadn't he said himself the place was on the verge of falling down?

Of course, it would have be set up in advance, he couldn't wait for Rachel to recognise the girl, that would be too late, and if her answer was negative, he could always advise MacDonald that the building shouldn't be approached and to tell them to call off their visit.

The trail of footprints led towards the stairs. He tracked them up to the loft and on across the floor to the old trunk which must have been around since Silas was a boy. But how did they know it was here? Perhaps somebody had told them about the hidden compartment in the lid, but they'd missed it, otherwise there would have been traces of that fine white sawdust which puffed out everywhere when you released the catch. Perhaps, that was why they were coming back – to try again.

He stood, his mind on his plan. Why not go ahead now, get it over with, what better opportunity! He turned for the stairs. suddenly eager to make a start.

At ground level he went straight to the wall where the remaining buttress seemed to have become the last support before the building toppled. For a moment he stood looking up at it, his gaze travelling on along the beam which sagged noticeably under the weight of upper floor. Safe enough though, he decided, until damp or floodwater eventually eroded away the base of the buttress – which was exactly what had happened to the one on the opposite wall. All he had to do was to help it along. The thought sent his knees to jelly but he braced himself, shutting his mind against the consequences. It would have to be done, a problem resolved, like all the other problems which had stood in his way.

He began to poke at the crumbling stonework, the old mortar powdering under his fingers. Easy enough, he decided, and turning, he glanced back across the room to the inner wall, where the door leading out into the barn was slightly ajar. He contemplated it, nursing his chin. That door was the only way into the mill, the only access for anybody who wanted to view the workings or reach the stairs, and placed as it was only yards away over the rubble, so convenient for his plan.

He recalled to mind a case he had years ago in London. His client, a shopkeeper in Whitechapel, had been suing a firm of demolishers after a chimney they had been bringing down had fallen the wrong way and collapsed on his premises. Ellis had learned a good deal about the principles of demolition during that case. Now here was his chance to put his knowledge to work – with some slight variations, of course.

He began to hunt around for the materials he would need. Those two barrels over there would do nicely. He picked his way round the rubble and rolled them one at a time towards the wall. Then he lifted them one on top of the other a short distance out from the buttress and in line with the door. He would need a prop and some planks but most of the demolished wood was too rotten for what he wanted. There would probably be some better material in the carpenter's loft in one of the outhouses across the yard. The key was in a crevice under the gantry, left so that Ian MacDonald's men could inspect the tools and implements kept there.

The outhouses had been built at a much later date than the mill, and the loft was dry and in reasonable condition. All the tools he wanted appeared to be there, a sharp chisel, a roll hammer and a rusted but fairly decent saw. He would need some rope, too, and after a search eventually found a coil of strong hemp in a top cupboard. He took note of a stout post which would serve as a prop to shore up the buttress, but he didn't fancy the soundness of the planks lying around, – too far gone, so he ripped up one of the floor boards and cut from it the plank sizes he needed, one long, the other short. Lastly he must have a wedge of wood. He hunted around until he found one just the shape he needed in a box of off-cuts under the bench. Now he had everything he wanted. He could hardly believe that it was going so well.

The yard was in shadow as he returned to the mill, a stillness upon it, and inside the building it was so silent he found himself creeping about for fear of stirring the echoes.

Reaching the buttress he laid the wood down against the barrels and immediately set to work with the hammer and chisel to loosen a section of the stonework. Soon he was able to bring out enough of the stones to get a hole through the buttress to the wall behind it. It was not quite as simple as it looked because the stones were of different sizes and not easy to dislodge, but once they were free he was able to dredge enough mortar from the outer stonework to fit in his first piece of wood. He selected the shorter of the two planks and inserted it into the hole, hammering it firmly into the crevice. It now lay protruding out from the buttress and pointing towards the top of the barrels.

Next he had to set up the prop. He started by placing the longer plank on top of the barrels, so that it reached horizontally to the shorter spar of wood, under lapping it by a few inches. Holding it into position he reached with his free hand for the prop and placed it vertically under the planks at the point where they met. Then, allowing them to balance for a moment he took the wedge of wood from his pocket and slid it tightly between the prop and the longer plank. The prop was now firmly in position, set solid upon the stone floor ready to take the full weight of the buttress – and indeed, the beam. It was a precarious, unstable construction, delicately engineered so that when the longer plank was moved sideways, the wedge would spring out, the prop would collapse and then down would come the whole tottering edifice of the Tryun Mill.

He stood back, taking it in, a smile curving from the corner of his mouth, and then he reached for the coil of rope and tied one end to the longer plank. Finally, lifting a wary glance at the buttress rising above him, he took the chisel and began loosening the stones immediately beneath the protruding spar.

It was hard, backbreaking work, the stones were heavy and not easily dislodged, and he had to stop from time to time to ease the tension. He was sweating and the dust was rising in his face, making him cough. The deeper he dug the more aware he became of the weight of masonry there must be above him and he found himself glancing uneasily towards the beam as another stone gave way, thudding onto the one below. Once he thought he heard a creak of timber and had a sudden urge to dive for cover, but it was only the inner door swinging ajar.

The last stone was a chunk of granite, bedded in, hard to budge. He was frightened, almost reluctant to hack it out. Once that had been removed the buttress would then be resting on the spar, the prop taking the full weight. Would it hold, he wondered? Was the wood as sound as he'd thought it to be? Was his positioning accurate? One miscalculation and he might be initiating off his own burial. The thought was very frightening.

But there was no turning back – not now. He had come too far. There were too many years of waiting behind the many obstacles he had overcome. But now the goal was in sight, his dream about to be realised, and the desire for it too strong. No, not even the trembling fear within him was going to hold him back from that last tight-wedged stone.

With trembling hands he reached for his hammer, using it lightly at first, chipping at the edges, then harder striking up sparks of fire, ringing echoes through the building. He worked feverishly, breath coming hard, his face liquid with sweat. He was jammed up against the wall, the chisel hot under his fingers as he worked on the mortar on the back of the stone. It was coming, loosening; he saw it drop – an inch. His hands were in there now, dragging, he had it, free, and as it thudded down he felt the sudden shift of the buttress as it settled to the spar. He caught his breath, agape at the prop standing firm beneath the planking. Oh God, it was holding!

He drew himself up and stood back staring at it, shoulders heaving, hardly able to believe he had done it, he had made it work.

Now for the last bit. He crept for the rope which he had earlier fastened to the planking and watching where he put his feet – one slip could mean disaster- he carried it cross the rubble. Reaching the inner door he took up the slack until he felt a gentle pressure on the rope. Then pulling the door slowly towards him until he almost had it closed, he wound the rope round the handle and knotted it tight. It now hung above the rubble connected at the other end to the longer plank, which he had wedged between the prop and the spar.

Whosoever opened that door from the other side would be pulling on the rope. One small tug and the plank would slide side-ways, the wedge jump out and the prop collapse, bringing Tryun Mill down about their heads.

The thought brought a sudden urge to leave the place, be away before those walls closed in on him, struck him down for what he had done. Nervously he clambered over the rubble towards the gap in the wall, the only way out now. The drop on the other side surprised him, but he made it despite the pain in his leg and as he limped to the millstream to wash the dirt off his hands, the triumph soared inside him.

CHAPTER TWENTY SIX

"I'm sure I heard him bark when we were coming into the creek, somewhere across the mud," said Charlotte.

"Then why didn't he come when we called him?" Nick asked.

"Could be trapped somewhere."

It was Friday and they were sitting round the saloon table, finishing the evening meal. Matelot, so much beloved by all of them, was still missing; his own special place, hollowed out on the divan, conspicuously empty.

Although it was a full week since his disappearance, Charlotte refused to give up the search. Their fears for the dog's safety had completely overshadowed the importance of the inheritance, and had provided Lavelle with one more excuse for holding back on his decision to seek legal action. But soon he must, but at least that must buy them some more time.

"Jack! We're going up to Pendowry for another look for Matelot before dark," Nick was saying, "If you're taking Linda for a drink we could drop you off at Whitehouse Quay."

Lavelle nodded, "Okay," he said, stirred from his thoughts, and rose to follow Nick up the companionway. "I'll give you a hand to get down the hatches. This hot weather sure can bring a helluva dew after the dusk."

"It'll break soon. Luke says there's rain coming."

"Yeah! I guess he's right."

The harbour water was still, a translucent green, mottled with oily ripples as they nosed the *Dipper* into Whitehouse Quay. Linda had watched them coming across the water from the hotel, now she was on the jettyside as Lavelle leapt ashore, astonishing him with her beauty, her dress a swirl of pastel pink, enhanced by her dark hair.

He felt for her hand and drawing her close caught the warm fragrance of her. "Where d'you want to go? Down town?"

"There's no air in the town, let's find somewhere cooler," she replied.

"I know just the place," he told her, "A swell background to set you against in that dress."

"Dark green woods?"

"How about sand and surf and aquamarine sea?"

Her face lit up. "The hotel in the pines? Jack, let's go there!"

His hand slid to her waist, drawing her close to him as he steered her up the slope to the Esplanade. "Come on, we'll go get the car."

As they drove the scent of the pines came through the open windows. Walking across to the hotel they could feel the crunch of the dry needles under their shoes. They sipped their gin and tonics on the terrace and looked out at the sea, neither blue nor green, but a milky mixture of both. It lay almost still against the narrow strip of white sand, and across the pale sky there was one streak of pink left over from the sunset to match her dress.

She gazed at the sea. "Isn't beautiful! They say it's the china clay coming down from the hills that gives it that colour."

"Now don't you go spoiling the illusion," he said. "It's nature gone crazy with a palette of oils."

She turned to him and saw his eyes, lit with love for her. "I've hardly seen you all week," she said. "I've missed you."

He pressed her hand. "I've missed you, too, honey, but it's been one hell of a week."

"Still no news about the dog?"

He shook his head. "Nick thinks he may be away after a bitch someplace, but Charlie, she's worried. She's afraid he's gotten himself lost for good. But how about you? Getting some more tan, I see."

They exchanged some chat, then she said happily. "Guess what? I have an invitation for you – from Uncle Mac. He wants you to have dinner with us tomorrow night at the Trefoy Hotel."

Lavelle looked at her, lips apart to answer but quite unable to think of a good reason to decline. How could he possibly sit down to dinner with Ian MacDonald, accept his hospitality, just when he was on the point of bringing a case of fraud against the people with whom the guy was doing business? At a later date maybe, he would be only too glad to meet him, explain to him the reasons behind his activities in Trefoy, but before he had taken legal advice it might be embarrassing. Then as she went rushing on about the arrangements for the evening, came the disclosure that made the whole thing quite impossible. Ellis was going to be there.

She saw his eyes grow cold and realised it had been a mistake to mention the lawyer. "Of course," she said quickly, "it's not certain he will come. He was going to London and he may not be back. Honestly, I don't know why Uncle Mac had to ask him. I suppose it was out of courtesy really since he was there when the dinner party was suggested. You see, we had been talking about you."

He looked at her sharply. "Who was talking about me? Ellis?"

She lowered her glance. This was not really the moment to bring it up, but unavoidable now. "He came over to the hotel on Tuesday. I rather got the impression he was quizzing me about you. He'd seen you up at Pendowry Creek – trespassing, he said. Then he began asking questions, it was just small talk really."

"What did you tell him?"

"Only that we'd been seeing each other. How I'd been out fishing and sailing with you. Then Uncle Mac arrived and he suggested I ask you to dinner." She heaved a sigh. "You don't want to come, do you?"

He gulped his gin. Too damned right, but how did he make her understand? "Isn't it tomorrow we're taking you to see the watermill? I had thought maybe afterwards."

She was hardly listening. "It's the lawyer, isn't it? You don't like him."

He looked away to the sea. "After the other day at the manor house, I guess it could be embarrassing."

She shook her head. "That's not the real reason, Jack, there's something else. I've seen hate in your eyes at the very mention of that man's name. It's something to do with that creek, isn't it?"

He looked at her then, his expression dark, troubled. "The creek is only the half of it," he admitted, "I guess you're going to have to know the truth. I've wanted to come clean for weeks."

She leaned towards him, urgently. "I knew there was something, I've felt it all along."

"The secret wasn't mine to tell," he said, trying to find a way to begin.

"Something to do with your ex-wife, your daughter?" she asked, making guesses.

He took her hand. "Linda, Charlie is not my daughter. That was just a blind to stop her from being recognised."

Linda was staring at him. "If she's not your daughter – then who is she?"

"She's the true heir to the Pendowry fortune. The will that's just been published is a forgery."

She looked at him in disbelief. "A forgery! You don't mean it?"

"I sure do. It's this way," he leaned closer, his voice low, "Ellis is involved in a conspiracy with Charlie's stepmother, a woman called Rachel Ives. Once the deal with your uncle is through the two of them plan to clear off abroad with every red cent."

"You're saying his client is Charlie's step-mother, and she's the mystery woman behind the negotiations for the estate?" she said, her eyes widening.

"He's the one behind the negotiations. He's behind the whole damned thing. He set it up."

She sat, staring at him. But she was not altogether surprised. Rumours that the Trevelyan will was about to be contested had been going around the pubs for weeks. Her uncle had at first dismissed the idea as idle gossip and only to be expected in a place so opposed to change, but lately other rumours about the lawyer's methods of doing business had been causing him genuine concern. But fraud! Surely not?

"Jack, that's a very serious accusation."

"It happens to be true."

"What makes you so sure? Where did you get this from?"

"Do you really want me to tell you?" he asked. She would have to know sooner or later. Better to hear it from him now than for her to read it in a newspaper. "I got it from her –Rachel."

"*You got it from her*!"

"Yeah! Back in London before I came down here." He heaved a sigh. "Not that she's going to admit one goddamn word in court."

"It's going to *court*?"

He nodded. "Looks on the cards."

Linda grew thoughtful. If what he was saying was true and the legacy was in dispute, then no smoke without fire! Even though his own connection was not yet entirely clear to her, it certainly explained a good deal of his very puzzling behaviour.

"How did you get involved in all this?" she asked him.

He lifted his eyes to her, the dark, troubled look again. "I guess it's a long story," he said. He pressed her hand. "But hell I need to share it with you, Linda. I'm through holding back."

"We have the time," she said gently, "and I'm a good listener."

He knew then he would have her understanding, that he could count on her support. He began with the war days, talking of his relationship with the Ives family, of Bill's doubts then about the lawyer, and later his own when he saw the report of Silas Trevelyan's funeral in Nick's newspaper. He had expected that she would have been shocked to learn of the lengths he'd had to go to force the truth out of Rachel, but her contempt was not for him, but for the woman herself and the way she had treated her step-daughter. When he went on to describe how cruelly Ellis had deceived poor Emma Bunt, Linda was appalled.

"But at least her evidence should swing the case," she said.

Lavelle shook his head. "Not for sure. Ellis will claim he acted under the old man's instructions, maybe even produce a forged letter in court to prove it."

"He couldn't do that."

"Yeah? You bet!" He paused, and went on. "The guy's real name is Mark Abrahams. During the war he used to be a lawyer in the East End of London and up to his eyeballs in all the criminal rackets, including the black market. Maybe it got too hot, I dunno, but he cleared out when his office took a direct hit in a daytime raid in 'forty-three. Seems he'd been at the bank when the bombs fell. His partner was killed, and Ellis took up his identity to make a fresh start here. Very neat."

"How do you know all this?"

"How do I know?" said Lavelle hotly, "Because the fifteen grand the bastard went to the bank to collect in his suitcase was *mine*, that's how I know!"

"Yours?"

"My cut out of a deal he owed me. He was due to meet me that night to pay me out. But the bastard never showed up. He'd walked off with the lot, used it to get out of London, though he knew damn well I desperately needed the cash to pay for my wife's kidney operation….."

His voice trailed off. It was a part of the story he had meant to leave out, a part he had never before been able to discuss with anyone, but now with her, suddenly it was different. She cared about him. She wanted to know, wanted to share his grief.

"While I was stationed at Poole I got the news that she was sick. Four thousand miles away, loused up in a goddamn war, her sick and not a buck saved between us! My folks had put all they had into getting me into naval college and hers hadn't a nickel. So I got myself in on a nice little racket, run by a chief petty officer in the navy stores, supplying cigarettes for the black-market. There were so many comings and goings around that time that it was as easy as pie to fiddle the paper work, and it was paying off fast and big for a lot of guys."

"So where did Ellis come into it?"

"He was the middle-man who handled the consignments we delivered to an address in the East End. He paid out okay, but if we wanted, he'd hold on to the payments, letting them accumulate until they were needed. That way I guess he could use the dough or maybe pick up the interest, I dunno. But that was okay by me. I didn't want to touch a penny of it until I had enough to take back home to Margo."

He dropped his head in his hands. "I waited five hours for him that night. In the Savoy Hotel of all places. Next morning I went round to his office. It was just a heap of rubble and a helpful official told me Abrahams had been killed. I didn't believe him – even when he showed me the list with his name crossed off."

"Why didn't you believe him?"

"Because I was damn sure he wasn't dead. The bomb hit around three pm, and about five minutes before that I'd called his office and they said he'd just left for the bank. I reckoned he would have cheated death by a few minutes. I spent the rest of my leave walking the streets of London, looking for a sign of him, and then I went back to Poole. I was suicidal."

"But how do you know Richard Ellis is that same man?" she argued.

"Richard Ellis was the name of his one and only partner killed when the building fell in. A simple switch of identities. But there's no doubt about it because I recognised him the moment I saw him here in Trefoy."

Linda didn't speak for a moment; she just sat holding his hand, her face full of compassion. "And your wife?" she ventured slowly.

He turned his face to the sea and she saw his eyes were wet. "She died," he said softly. "I'd started trying to raise some more money, but just after Christmas I got the wire..." He broke off biting his lips together.

For a while he said nothing, battling within himself to overcome the emotion, fighting down the hurt all over again, but he could feel Linda, close, the warmth of her hand a comfort to him.

"Let's go for a walk," she suggested, "along the beach."

The sun had gone down behind the headland and the pink streak across the sky had deepened into crimson, but the air was still warm, the sea motionless, the wash no more than a soft beat and fizz against the shore, a relaxing sound that brought them a sudden sense of peace.

Clasping hands they began to walk along the sea edge, away from the hotel and the sounds of people. The ebbing tide had left a wet border, their shoes sinking into it. She let him talk as he wanted to. It came easier now and he began to tell her about his life on the Mediterranean.

"After D-Day we moved down to the Med. for the landings at Toulon and that was where I stayed for the rest of the war. I should have gone on to the Pacific, but landing craft were being used for transporting salvaged tanks and equipment, so I turned down promotion and stayed on to skipper an LST in the mopping up operations. When the war ended I refused my passage home and remained in Marseilles to team up with another couple of guys bringing in wrecks for salvage. The beaches were littered with stuff still being washed up and I guess we made a packet. Soon we were moving into the rackets going on ashore, shipping contraband cigarettes mostly, using old MGBs and such craft to out-race the customs boats. It was big business then and still is today, if you have the nerve and the know-how. But it wasn't the way I wanted to spend my life, living on a knife-edge, I wanted to go back home, see my folks again, but how could I face them? I was the guy who said he could raise the money to save Margo. And I'd screwed it up, let her die because I was damn fool enough to trust that shark of a lawyer."

"But that wasn't your fault, Jack! You can't blame yourself."

"But you know how I feel. Just as you can't face Sausolito without Mel, I can't bring myself to go home to memories of Margo."

She nodded. "In a way we share the same nightmare, don't we?"

"We sure do."

They had reached the end of the strand where the point jutted out into the sea, midst rock pools and broken reefs, and under the cliff was a tiny cove, the soft sand still warm from the sun. They sank down into it, their backs against the rock to watch the sunset, but the question of the Pendowry inheritance and the daunting prospect of having to fight Ellis in court was still uppermost in their minds.

"If only we could have found old Silas' will," Lavelle said, with a sigh.

"You think Ellis has it?" Linda asked.

"I dunno," he said, "How can we be sure? Kicking Emma Bunt's door down was no real proof he was looking for it. He might have already found it in the chest at the house where Silas told Emma to look. But those crazy directions he gave her, they keep bugging me. Whacking the chest with stick, fifteen pieces of silver – the bus fare to Bodmin, belonging more to myth and legend. But Silas Trevelyan was no fool. Surely he wouldn't have chosen the chest in his den as a hiding place. Okay – there was secret way to open it. That wouldn't have stopped Ellis. He'd have taken an axe to it. Smashed it to bits."

She nodded, "Why couldn't he have sent it to a bank or some other independent person he believed he could trust."

"I don't think he really trusted anybody except Bill – and perhaps a friend he called 'The Bosun' whose real name was Tom Constantine. We found a photograph, and yesterday I believed I was close to tracking him down. Then I heard he was last seen on a yacht which sank off Brittany, all hands lost. Finding him was my last hope."

Linda grew thoughtful. "Have you ever thought about going to see Ellis?" she said, "Having it out with him?

"He'd tell me to get lost."

She pressed his hand, "But listen, Jack. Ellis must know he's under suspicion. He must be a very frightened man. He caught you red handed searching the house. He would have guessed it was you who sent the postcards, who took Emma from Talland. That's why he's trying to rush these contracts through, knocking great chunks off the asking price, trying to get a quick decision. What really astonished Uncle Mac was when he offered to throw in the antiques at the manor house that should have originally been sold by auction. I think that's why my uncle wanted to make a foursome at dinner, another chance to talk about it over a drink with him before anything is signed."

Lavelle tensed. She was right. Ellis *was* worried. The harassment had really paid off. Now he was rushing the deal through at any price. Once Rachel had blotted her signature, he expected to be on his way.

Linda was saying, "Why don't you tell him you intend to contest the will. You have evidence, witnesses who will testify, tell him Rachel told you, show him some of her letters to prove it...."

"But he's not going to admit to anything. He's too smart."

"Listen," she said, "Ellis won't want to face a charge of fraud, spend months fighting it. If you were to offer him a way out, he might jump at it."

"What did you have in mind?"

"Come to some agreement – like having Rachel put the Pendowry estate in trust for Charlotte."

"Oh, sure! Can you see him doing that? Backing out on the deal?"

"But then there won't be any deal! Not when Uncle Mac hears about all this. He wouldn't touch it. Neither would his firm. A dispute over the ownership is likely to take months to resolve. The Taylor Ross Organisation won't want to hang about, they'll just pull out, move their equipment down to Salcombe where they already have another development under consideration."

He nodded. "Sure, they'd do that. I guess, I should have let you in on this from the start. I should have advised your Uncle."

She nodded. "But I can understand why you didn't. You were afraid he would have laughed in your face – or worse, put Ellis wise."

"You got it."

"It's only just recently he's had his doubts. There's been so much rumour and speculation – not just about Pendowry, but about Ellis himself. We've even heard his house on the Esplanade has been privately sold, and that practice in Fore Street is on the point of changing hands. Ellis dismissed it as utter rubbish, but it did make Uncle Mac uneasy."

"I bet it did."

He stared ahead, his eyes intent. She could be right. Going to court wasn't going to suit Ellis, it would louse up all his plans, and with the prospect of the Pendowry deal falling though, he might be only too glad to see the estate settled in trust to Charlotte, and out of his hair. The shock of Rachel's betrayal on of top all his other doubts might just swing it. Ellis wouldn't want to see her served with a subpoena. She wouldn't want it either. Already sore and humiliated after the fool she'd made of herself, anxious not to have her folly the centre of a public scandal. No sir! He didn't think they would have any trouble with Rachel, and without her support, what chance had Ellis?

He slid his arm around Linda, hugging her to him. "I think maybe I'll shave off my beard and give our friend Abrahams a visit when he gets back from London."

She rested her head on his shoulder. "Make sure you do it before you join us for dinner," she suggested. "Then he's bound not to come, and we can discuss all this together with Uncle Mac."

He pressed a kiss on her cheek. "Great idea. I'll do it."

The sands were darkening now, the colour of the sea changed to a silvery grey; the wet rocks glittered black against it, catching the light from the sky. Her face was in shadow, the last of the light behind her, touching her hair. A loose strand had fallen across her cheek. He moved it gently away with the tip of his finger. She was beautiful. He cupped her face in his hands and kissed her softly on the lips.

"You still love me?"

"I've been loving you for a long time."

He gathered her up to him, holding her. She started to speak but his mouth smothered the words, the kisses coming, bringing a prelude to their need.

He could feel her hands beneath his shirt, feel the soft silk of her dress under his fingers, the folds falling away; her skin smooth, warm, her breasts, her thighs, firm under his hands and he found himself drawn deep down into her. They made love there on the shore as the tide fell away and dusk fell.

It was almost dark now, no light left but a silver sheen on the horizon and far out to sea the patient blink of the Eddystone lighthouse brightening the night. They lay, spent, drowned in their love for each other, watching it.

"You're taking me home to San Francisco, aren't you?"

"Sure, I am. I need you to face it all just as you need me."

He buried his face in her breast and she stroked his hair.

CHAPTER TWENTY SEVEN

Rachel was bored. Her weekend in Trefoy had barely begun, and she was already wishing she were back in London. It might not have been so bad if she had been able to potter about the town. But Richard had called her at the hotel, insisting she came down to his house for coffee. Not out in the sun on the patio, but cooped up in his stuffy little sitting room where he expected her to remain until, she supposed, he was ready to take her to lunch.

He was in a damnable mood, curiously secretive, prone to wandering restlessly about the house or stopping to gaze in a preoccupied way at the yachts in the harbour, completely immersed in his own importance. The morning was slipping away and they had hardly discussed the inheritance. All in good time, he told her. First there was something he wanted her to see.

She had dressed so carefully to please him, fashionably to match her newly acquired wealth; a dazzle of canary yellow, the tight waisted skirt flouncing with net and petticoats, and set off with expensive accessories; high heeled ankle straps with tiny bows, earrings, bracelets, necklaces jangling, and a flowing gossamer wrap to hold on the impossible little hat she had bought from Harrods – all of it wasted on him though. She had set out feeling like Joan Crawford. Now she felt overdressed and uncomfortable.

Stifling a yawn, she rested her gaze on the waterfront. It was low tide and the river and the foreshore looked drained and unsightly, the brown rocks bared, ugly, dripping green. Gulls perched on them or pattered the mud, squabbling, their cries hollow like the riveting hammers echoing across from the boatyard. Then all the sounds were drowned by the foghorn blare from a coaster sliding by, dusted white and down to her gunwales in china clay.

The blast broke off suddenly and she could hear Richard calling her from somewhere below.

"Rachel! Come quickly! Come now!"

With an impatient sigh she rose from the window seat and made her way down to the study where the glass doors opened out onto the patio. He was waiting, his hands reaching out to her impatiently.

"Just come here. I want you to see something," he said, leading her out into the heat.

He was looking down river to where Whitehouse jetty curved out into the still quay of deep water. The little ferry was just leaving, half loaded for St Ruan, and a green motor boat was coming in, a girl at the tiller. He nodded towards it.

"D'you recognise anybody?"

She frowned, following his gaze. There were two men in the boat; one, in a white topped seafaring cap and a blue jersey, was reaching out to hold the boat steady as the other man stepped ashore. He had a long limbed swing about him that was familiar; cream trousers, navy shirt, tight curled dark hair bristling with grey. She watched him turn to say something to the other two in the boat and saw his face, the handsome line of jaw.... he looked like *Frisco*! Her heart plunged. Good God! It was Frisco! He was here in Cornwall. This would account for Richard's behaviour, the mood he was in. Frisco must have been to see him, shown his hand – already! The bloody fool! It was too early. She hadn't got the money yet. She didn't even know if the deal with the Taylor Ross Organisation had yet been completed. Good God! He might have waited until the ink was dry. And he could have given her forewarning! Now she had to face the ordeal with Richard all by herself – unless Frisco was on his way up here now, Richard expecting him, a pre-arranged appointment, with her present for the showdown.

"Well?" Ellis was asking, "Do you recognise the girl or don't you?"

Rachel jumped then as though he had struck her.

"Girl? What girl?" she said, utterly confused.

"The girl in the boat. Is it Charlotte or isn't it?"

"*Charlotte*?"

She started forward, gaping. Frisco was standing on the jetty, his hand raised to the two in the boat, probably thanking them for the lift. The engine was picking up, the bow moving round, the girl coming into view; fair hair, roped into two short pigtails, sun brown face, jean-clad knees – like she used to look. 'Am I going mad?' Rachel thought, 'or is it a bad dream?'

Ellis, glancing at her, saw the hot colour washing over her face, then draining, leaving behind small beads of sweat bubbling up from beneath the pancake make-up.

"What in God's name is Charlotte doing here?"

"You may well ask," Ellis said darkly.

Rachel glanced at him and saw the focus of his attention was on the boat, watching it lift to the slight swell rolling in from the ferry's wake. It occurred to her then. Charlotte was the one he was interested in. He wasn't giving Frisco a second glance. She would have expected a cutting remark, if not an outburst, but he was completely oblivious to him as though he was a stranger with no part in the intrigue. Perhaps he was totally unconnected and this was a complete coincidence. Frisco might not yet have approached Richard, but was merely on his way over, hitching a lift by boat from somewhere. If that were the case, there may still be time to warn him – if she could get to him first.

The motor boat was heading towards the harbour. The boatman had moved to sit with Charlotte at the tiller, his arm about her waist.

Ellis made a sound of disgust. "She's been living with that man all summer aboard a yacht. He's some oaf from St Ruan."

"But I don't understand. She's supposed to be in Australia," Rachel said weakly. She was keeping her eyes on Frisco, who was still standing on the jetty, watching the boat returning across the water. "I put her on the train myself."

"You were duped," said Ellis bitterly. "She had arranged for someone on the train to change places with her."

“Someone on the train?” Rachel repeated absently. She was not really listening. She was wracking her brain for an excuse to leave, waylay Frisco and prevent him from barging in at a time like this; Charlotte was a secondary consideration.

“Richard-” she began urgently.

Ellis, mistaking the tremble in her voice for fear, slid his arm about her. “Now listen, my dear. There is no reason to panic. This can easily be resolved. I already have a plan. After we’ve had lunch we shall take my cabin cruiser and go out to this yacht and collect Charlotte. She is under age. Any objections from this skipper fellow and I shall threaten him with a suit for abduction. Then this evening I shall then take you both over to the station slip where my car is waiting and drive you to Par to catch the Plymouth train overnight back to London. The rest you can leave to me.”

She was staring at him. “Back to London?”

“It will be better that way. Come along, we shall discuss the details over lunch at the hotel.”

She held back. They couldn’t leave for lunch. Not now! If they did they would run straight into Frisco coming up the street. She pressed his arm. “Richard? Isn’t it a bit early, and if I’m going back to London, I shall need to go to the chemist, something for my headache,” she said, edging her way towards the steps leading up to the Esplanade.

Ellis relaxed. “By all means, my dear. Better still, why don’t we meet at your hotel, say in about half an hour? Alright?”

“Yes, yes,” she cried eagerly, as he escorted her up the steps to the side door.

Ellis was inwardly relieved. This would suit him perfectly. He needed some time to himself to examine the situation. He had yet to decide what to do with Rachel now she was here. He had never had any intention of sending her back to London with Charlotte. That had been a bit of bunkum to assure her he had everything under control. The last thing he wanted was her going over to that yacht and demanding an explanation from Charlotte. The girl’s fate was about to be resolved when she went with her friends to explore the Tryun Mill. His only real concern was that there might have been a change in their plans, the excursion called off or postponed. Now the girl had been positively identified the element of uncertainty about the trap he had set bothered him. Too much about the operation depended on luck, whether they went to the mill as planned, whether they opened that door.

He walked slowly back into his study. He didn’t feel at all like having lunch with Rachel, putting on a cheerful face. Perhaps, he had better ring St Catherine’s and leave a message to say he was being delayed and for her to go ahead and eat without him. Remaining here, he could watch the comings and goings from the *Cape Columbo*, see the three of them meet Linda at Whitehouse Quay and set off together. Once they were safely away, he could then pick up Rachel and take her across to the yacht, feigning his displeasure to find them gone and suggest to her that they waited until the following day.

It might be an idea to ring Ian MacDonald and ask if he might bring Mrs Ives to dinner with him that evening. She had arrived unexpectedly from London. That should please him. Perhaps then they would all be together when the news of the Tryun Mill disaster came through.

****

Rachel hurried, her high heels clicking up echoes along the pavement. There was no sign of Frisco. He couldn't have reached the Esplanade yet. He must be still walking up the steep approach from Whitehouse Quay. It was uncomfortably hot, the sky heavy, a pinkish haze veiling the sun, and on the corner a warm puff of breeze caught her wrap, sweeping it behind. Careless of it, she held on to her hat and began to run down the approach, expecting to meet him coming up the steps. She stumbled on, perspiration wet under her dress, the breeze catching her petticoats, bringing them up above her knees. Where the hell was he? She rushed down the steps and on round the bend.

Then she pulled up short. She must not go any farther. Richard might be looking out from his patio. But she could see the jetty now, see it was empty. Frisco must have already gone! She hurried back to the Esplanade. People were returning from the beach, girls in shorts, youths swinging bathing towels. Rachel pushed past them, breathing hard, hair loose, hat clutched in her hand, the chiffon wrap trailing behind her in the dust.

At the top she looked both ways but he was not in sight. How on earth had she missed him? If he had walked towards Richard's house they would have met. He must have gone the other way towards the hotels.

She gathered up the wrap under her arm and set off in pursuit, needing to blow her nose but panting on, no time stop to reach for her handkerchief, her only thought to find Frisco.

****

If Rachel had gone right down on to Whitehouse jetty, she would have seen Jack Lavelle scrambling over the rocks, making for the pebbly strip of foreshore, already being lapped by the early flood tide. Above, against the cliffside was the iron stairway to Richard Ellis' patio. The sign hanging from the chain across the entrance said PRIVATE. He took a quick leap over it and went up, climbing stealthily to the gate at the top.

The crazy paving, the black wrought iron, geraniums and fuchsias in pots round the glass patio doors, were all unsurprisingly familiar. He had seen them before in the magnified circles of his binoculars.

"You do seem to make a habit of walking into private property uninvited."

The voice came from beyond the shadowed doorway, dark to him after the glare of the sun. When the dazzle cleared, he saw Ellis standing there looking out at him with cold hostile eyes.

Lavelle felt his heartbeat quicken, the anger rising, but he was determined to remain cool. "Yeah!" he answered. "I guess so."

Ellis advanced slowly from the doorway, his brows drawn in curiously. There was something about the build of the man, the swagger that reminded him of the Yanks during the war, and now without his beard he looked deucedly familiar. "Don't I know you from somewhere?" he asked.

"You sure do, brother!"

"Pray tell me? Where did we meet? I seem to remember your face."

"Oh, sure! Maybe you remember my face, but you didn't remember our appointment."

"Appointment?" Ellis repeated, his frown deepening.

"Eight o' clock. November the 19th 1943. The Savoy Hotel. London. You didn't remember that, did you, Mr Abrahams?"

The utterance of his real name sent shockwaves through Ellis and in that second came a rush of memory; the smoking rubble of his office building, another man's raincoat, another man's money in his suitcase. Good God! The American he owed for all those Camels and Chesterfields! He felt the hair follicles prick down the length of his spine, but outwardly he was handling it easily, he was too well practised from long years of bluff and deceit to betray his reaction openly.

"I think you're making a mistake," he said, with a faint smile. "My name is Richard Ellis."

He saw the American stiffen, his eyes narrow, the look in them threatening. "No mistake, Mr Abrahams. You remember me okay, Lieutenant Jack Lavelle, US Navy. My buddies used to call me Frisco. I was the guy whose money you were holding, the money I needed for my sick wife. You killed her, you sonofabitch, you know that?"

Ellis began to lift his shoulders, spread his hands, as though mystified, but the glittering menace he saw in the other man's eyes was suddenly disturbing. He had seen that look before, a danger he knew better than to disregard.

He eyed him shrewdly. This man wasn't here just to settle an old score though, otherwise he wouldn't have waited all summer to show himself. He was here for the other reason, here without any apparent representation from his lawyers, and alone. That had the smell of a compromise. Obviously he had failed to find the vital piece of evidence he needed to contest the Trevelyan will and was looking for a way out. As far as Ellis was concerned nothing could have been more appropriate, the chance to quiz the bastard about his plans for the afternoon, assure himself that his own plan had a chance of succeeding.

He raised his hands, apologies, enlightenment flooding his countenance. "My dear fellow! Do forgive me! Now I realise who you are. Of course! I should have met you. And I would have done- But please, do come inside, we must talk." He backed into the study, and, making a sweeping gesture for Lavelle to enter, moved away to take refuge behind his desk. It was solid mahogany, the top covered in red morocco leather and set out with Victorian paperweights and a cut glass inkstand set.

Lavelle advanced slowly, and, ignoring Ellis' invitation to sit down, stood sullenly taking in his surroundings. The room was furnished with the kind of elegance and good taste he would not have associated with the man he remembered from that dingy second floor office in Whitechapel. This seemed more like the home of someone with pride and dignity, who loved old things, treasures; the very fine mahogany breakfront bookcase, full of leather bound volumes, the black marble-cased French clock with side ornaments standing on the mantle shelf, the carefully chosen nineteenth century prints hanging from the wood panelled walls, the Chippendale, the Hepplewaite chairs...But there was nothing of Ellis; no clutter of belongings scattered about the room other than The London Illustrated News on a rosewood side table, no photographs in silver frames, no past.

Lavelle watched the lawyer turn to a small lacquered cabinet and bend for glasses from a shelf of sparkling crystal. On its top was a silver tray, holding a collection of good brandies; Hine and Charlottenburg, one probably obtained off German ships.

Ellis reached for a decanter and brought it with the glasses to his desk. "Let me give you a drink," he said obsequiously.

"Forget it!" Lavelle snapped at him. He needed one, but how could he bring himself to drink with the man?

With a sigh Ellis sank down into the elbow chair at his desk. "Look here! I never had any intention of reneging on our deal. But my office had been bombed!" he said, lifting his hands. "I'd lost everything, your money with it."

Lavelle drew back his lips. "Don't lie, you bastard! The dough was never in your office. You were out at the bank collecting it in cash. I know because I called you just before the raid. The guy I talked to – he was Richard Ellis. You used his name like you used my fifteen grand – to start a new life for yourself."

Ellis was white. This man knew more than was good for him. "Alright," he said, "perhaps I did, but, my dear fellow, I was desperate. I had some very unfriendly people on my tail. I needed to get out of London, but I always meant to make it up to you."

"Make it up to me!" Lavelle exploded. "How could you have ever made it up to me? I needed the money that night. My wife was dying. You knew that, you no good sonofabitch!"

Ellis allowed his face to fill with compassion. "I'm terribly sorry. You must believe me."

"Terribly sorry!" Lavelle mimicked. He was sweating, his knuckles clenched, and an almost irresistible desire to break the lawyers teeth.

Ellis looked at him helplessly. "What else can I say? I let you down. But for your money I would have been finished – probably found floating in the East India dock. I saw a way out and took it. You must understand that...."

"Save me the eyewash. I didn't come here today just to talk about my fifteen grand."

"No," said Ellis quietly. "Somehow I didn't think you did. I expect it's Silas Trevelyan's will you are here to see me about. Actually I have been expecting you. I realised what you were up to when I found you going over the manor house. You were looking for evidence to contest it, I suppose."

Lavelle dropped back into the leather chair behind him. "You got it," he said.

Ellis looked at him shrewdly. "Though I now know that girl with you was Charlotte, it's your connection with all this that puzzles me?"

"My connection is purely personal."

"Really?" said Ellis. "So what have you got? Testimonials from the St Ruan locals, who believe Charlotte to be the true heir?"

"And the rest of it. How you had the will forged in London, how you're planning to beat it abroad with Rachel – once she gets the money and you've disposed of the assets."

Ellis narrowed his eyes. "Where did you get hold of all this nonsense?"

"From Rachel," Lavelle coolly replied.

Ellis quivered. "Rachel!" he echoed in dismay.

"Yeah!" said Lavelle. "Before I came down here, I was having an affair with her. Not that she meant a damn thing to me, but I needed to know how much truth there was in Bill Ives' suspicions about you. So I fucked her stupid night after night after night" he cried, banging his fist on the desk, "until she spilled the whole damn story."

"You bastard!"

"In fact," went on Lavelle, "I left her so starry eyed, she's been writing to me all summer, pouring out her heart to me. Now she believes I'm the one who's going to marry her and share her fortune. Me, brother, not you! How's that for afters?"

Ellis' face was bloodless. "I don't believe you! You're bluffing!"

"Oh, yeah! How about taking a look at some of her letters? Here..." He reached into his back hip pocket and drew out a packet of the hand-written, sickly scented pages and tossed them across Ellis' blotter. "And that's only the half of them, pal! Go on, take yourself a look!"

Ellis stared in horror at Rachel's familiar pink notepaper, her unmistakable rounded hand, the address of her Belgravia flat in the corner. My Dearest Frisco one of them began.

He turned suddenly cold. The bitch! This was all her doing, ready to take off when the money was hers, leave him for a younger man. But then it didn't surprise him. He had always known she was a whore. It was his own fault for leaving her to her own devices in London. He shouldn't have been so naive to believe she would remain long out of another man's bed. But no matter, he would handle Rachel. She was too deeply involved to back out now, too vulnerable. The fear of being found out would soon bring her to heel.

Punishment from him would come later, when he was next in line for her money. Then she would pay the price for her betrayal, by God she would!

First he had to deal these other people, this smart-guy American, whose involvement with the family was still not altogether clear to him and his apparent association with Bill Ives somewhat disturbing, but no doubt with a little probing the connection would eventually come to light.

He looked at him curiously. "Tell me?" he said. "From where did you know Bill Ives?"

"We were friends during the war. I was stationed here before the D-Day landings."

"Were you, by God?"

Lavelle looked at him in scorn. "And lucky for you we didn't meet up then or your body *would* have been found floating – up river under the china clay jetties."

Ellis, deep in concentration, ignored the jibe. So Bill Ives was the connection. It must have been from him that Lavelle had learned about the contents of the will, but not where it was hidden or they wouldn't have been searching for it so long. But what other incriminating things might Ives have discussed with this man and may have put in writing?

He looked coldly at Lavelle. "Alright," he said. "Suppose we get to the point. Obviously you aren't here just to goad me about your affair with Rachel. So let's discuss your allegations, accusing me of fraud. But I have to confess I find your behaviour highly irregular. You arrive, uninvited, up from my private foreshore, and tell me you have reason to contest the Trevelyan will. You say you have evidence, witnesses, so why, may I ask, have I not yet heard from your solicitors?"

"But you sure will," Lavelle told him. "The moment you decide to turn down our proposals."

"Ah!" said Ellis, resting back in his chair. "Now we're getting to it, the reason for the clandestine visit. For all your evidence, your witnesses, apparently you are ready to settle with me out of court, cut yourself in for a share, and you think I will be glad to oblige to avoid a scandal. Now I begin to see the reason for your sordid little affair with my fiancée."

Lavelle shrugged. "Like it or not you're finished. I have the evidence."

"Have you?" Ellis sneered. "I doubt it. Apart from my altered identity I don't think you have one damn scrap of evidence worth considering, and you needn't get any ideas about trying to hold that over me either. When I knew you in London you were up to your neck in the black market yourself – and probably still are. What! Over here in a Marseilles registered yacht from a part of the world where illicit cigarette trading is still rife! Give me half an hour on the 'phone and I'll have enough on you to get you deported as an undesirable alien. Double quick time."

He was bluffing, of course, but from the shade of unease he saw in the American's eyes Ellis knew the point had been taken. With fresh confidence, he went on scathingly. "All you have is hearsay, empty rumours that have been circulating this town for months, and as for this rubbish Rachel has supposedly told you? How do you think you are going to get her to admit that in court, eh?"

It was just as Lavelle had expected. The lawyer wasn't going to admit anything and was even ready with counter measures should there be an attempt to expose his real identity, measures Lavelle didn't doubt could louse up all their plans. Unable at that moment to find an answer he was forced to sit through the lawyer's long and predictable ritual of disparagement about their chances in a court action, and finding it hard to control his anger tried to concentrate instead upon an English sporting print in a gilt frame across the room. The hope of a deal with Ellis looked slim. Nothing less than possession of a copy of the real will itself would accredit them in his eyes as opponents to be reckoned with, so why not bluff it out? What had he to lose? He looked up, suddenly full of defiance.

"Okay! You wanna know about this one piece of evidence we have been searching around for all summer? It's the original copy of Silas Trevelyan's will naming Charlie as the heir. He gave it to somebody to hide. Did you know that?"

Ellis looked at him, his glance narrowed with interest. "Really," he said, his pulsebeat quickening. He waited for Lavelle to go on, but the American's thin smile was implying the worst. He regarded the man shrewdly for a moment, then asked. "Are you trying to tell me you've found it?"

"You're damn right I am."

First bluff to me, thought Lavelle. The lawyer had not laughed in his face. It looked as though he was taking him seriously.

"You are just trying to provoke me," Ellis said icily. "If, Mr Lavelle, you really did possess that copy, you wouldn't be sitting here suggesting a trade. You wouldn't have to."

"I sure wouldn't," Lavelle replied. "If it was up to me I wouldn't have wasted a minute getting the case heard, but a court action is not what Charlie wants. She's a good kid. She doesn't want to see the woman who brought her up go to jail. She wants to make a fair deal with her."

Ellis hadn't thought of that. Rachel had always mothered the girl well, worked hard at that salon to see her well clothed and educated, and in difficult times, too. Perhaps there was more affection between them than he thought.

He looked sharply at Lavelle. "Alright! If you have this document, may I ask where you found it?"

"Up at Tryun Mill. Emma Bunt told us about this friend of Silas' who used to live there."

Ellis was sitting forward, his interest aroused. "So it *was* you who took her from Talland,"

"Of her own free will. She wanted to stay with some friends in North Cornwall. We got her back and put her on the train," he lied.

"And she told you where this copy was?"

He shook his head. "She only knew where this Bo'sun guy used to live, who she thought might know something. We went up there but the placc was derelict. He must have gone years ago. Then last week at the manor Charlie found a picture of him which jogged her memory, how her father had once taken her with him to see this man. She remembered he had a large envelope with him and they were hunting around the loft for a place to hide it. She was convinced it must be the missing copy, and she was sure right. Last last Monday I went up there, and I found it."

Ellis nodded. All very plausible, but he didn't believe a word of it. Nevertheless, any topic likely to lead to a discussion about Tryun Mill was worth pursuing. He might just drop a subtle hint to ensure that they did go up there for another search. He drew in a deep sigh and relaxed back in his chair.

"This is very interesting," he said, "The Bo'sun was a friend of Silas Trevelyan, he used to bring him books on sailing ships and naval history, an interest they both shared. The estate manager told me once he kept his books in an old sea chest that Silas gave him. It had a secret compartment in the lid, where he used to hide his money. I've often wondered what became of it, who bought it at the sale after he moved away."

He watched for the slightest flicker of interest in the American's eyes, but this time they gave nothing away. Anxious not to dwell on the point, Ellis went on quickly. "You say you found this document at the mill. I'm surprised it's still standing? I keep getting reports that it's falling down."

"You've not been up there lately?" Lavelle said.

"I haven't, there's no proper road up there. But about this document you are supposed to have found. I wonder if I might have a look at it?"

"You think I'm crazy? Lavelle asked. "That's stashed away in a very safe place and the first time you'll see it will be in court- unless, of course, we can come to some agreement."

"I see," said Ellis darkly. "If you really do have that document I shall want to examine it, for if it should, as you are suggesting, differ in any way from the will, which has just gone through probate, it could cause me a great deal of embarrassment. I wasn't the only solicitor involved with Silas Trevelyan's will; perhaps you didn't know that. If there was any infringement of the law, I have no wish to have my own good name tainted with it. Any variations or contradictions in the original deed copy would need to be investigated. On the other hand, you appreciate the time and inconvenience to me could prove, shall we say, unacceptable, and therefore, I might be prepared, once the document is in my possession to consider these proposals of yours."

The guy was clever. He knew better than to be taken in by words, and he was very careful with his own choice of them not to give himself away, even in the privacy of his own study, and without witnesses.

Ellis sat quietly as he listened to the deal: the Pendowry estate put into trust for Charlotte, a meeting to be arranged with both their solicitors, plans to draw up an agreement. He nodded his head, going through the motions, fully aware that whatever arrangements were made; he had no intention of keeping any of them. He had no need to, for with luck in a few hours time this man and his companions should all be dead and the whole business resolved.

From beyond the patio the river sounds came distantly. A warm breeze lifted the drapes from the open French windows, bringing in a drift of sun-dried velvet. Lavelle, anxious to quit the heat of the lawyer's study, rose to leave. The remark Ellis had made about the Bo'sun's chest and it's false lid bugged him. If that was where the guy kept his money, then it surely was a likely hiding place for the copy of the will. But how come Ellis should tell him about it? What motives could he have, Lavelle wondered? Bluff or double bluff? Was that where he had found the deed, or was it where he now wished he had looked?

Ellis followed Lavelle out onto the patio, and glancing over the waterfront he saw the green motor boat was back at Whitehouse Quay, the girl and the skipper aboard, and walking down the slip to meet them was MacDonald's niece. The lawyer felt a surge of relief. The party for Tryun Mill was gathering, ready for the afternoon excursion.

"Take the steps up to the street," he told Lavelle. "You won't be able to leave the way you came. The tide is coming in fast."

CHAPTER TWENTY EIGHT

Lavelle hurried down the steps to Whitehouse jetty. Linda, looking cool and lovely in a white dress, was coming towards him.

"How did it go?" she asked.

He slid his hand into hers. "Lousy, I guess, I'll tell you about it on the way to Tryun Mill."

"I don't think Charlie wants to go," she said, as they walked to the boat.

He nodded. "She's unhappy about the dog. Last night she had a dream he was shut up some place."

"It's not just because of Matelot," Charlotte said, overhearing them as they reached the boat. "Tryun Mill gives me the creeps."

"You fancy going for a sail, honey? You go with Nick while I take Linda up to the mill."

Charlotte lifted her glance, brightening. "Just the two of us?"

"Sure! Why not?"

"I can always go to see the watermill another day," Linda began, but Lavelle was already turning to Nick.

"Take the Cape out for a couple of hours, but keep your eye on the weather. The forecast wasn't too good."

Nick glanced at the sky. It was dull, but cloudless. "It's holding," he said, "and since Luke's gone fishing, there won't be much to worry about. We'll see you back in the harbour around five for tea?"

"Sure! Only first maybe you'll drop Linda and me off at the town quay to pick up the car," Lavelle suggested.

Linda leaned towards him as they took their seats in the bow. "Don't look now," she said. "But I think we're being watched. Mr Ellis up there on his patio."

Lavelle nodded bleakly. "Yeah, I know," he said, above the noise of the engine.

****

It was not until Richard Ellis had seen the green motor boat pull away from Whitehouse quay, that it came to him, the enormity of what he had done. Alone now, with nothing but the empty patio and the pulled back chairs in the study to answer him with their silence, a cold fear crept over him; doubts about certain imperfections in his plan, and a sense of his own vulnerability if it did not succeed.

He lifted the decanter and poured himself a stiff brandy, his hand shaking as he held the glass. He gulped it nervously, half–sitting against the edge of his desk, his head bent, echoes of the American's words racing through his head. That bitch Rachel must have seen the bastard from the patio as he stepped from Charlotte's boat and that was why she wanted to rush away. She couldn't wait to see him. Well, he'd better get her back over to the house to tell her the truth. He would enjoy enlightening her and she too could share with him the agony of the next few hours.

He picked up the telephone and dialled St Catherine's Hotel. It was already turned two-thirty. By now she would have eaten lunch without him and he'd probably catch her finishing her coffee in the lounge. But Rachel had left already. The receptionist passed on a message for him. She had gone to walk off her headache and would see him at tea.

Headache be damned! She was still looking for that blasted American. The heat of the study had suddenly become overpowering. He poured himself another brandy and carried it out onto the patio. Whitehouse quay was crowded, the ferry in, unloading passengers from St Ruan, people waiting to board it. He glanced along the line, looking for the yellow dress, but Rachel wasn't there.

He let his gaze stray across the harbour, then drew he himself up, stock-still, his eyes widening. The green motor boat was heading back towards the yacht! Don't say they had changed their minds about going to the mill! Wait, there was only two of them in the boat, the skipper and the girl. Perhaps they had forgotten the picnic or something. No, it looked as though they were staying aboard, allowing the motor boat to drift back onto its moorings. Surely, the whole plan hadn't fallen through! Unless the American had decided to go on his own with Linda to the mill. There was only one way to find out. See if Lavelle's car was still parked on the town quay. Ellis knew which one it was; he had once noticed the American taking parcels out of the boot.

He swallowed down the brandy, slammed shut the patio doors and went two steps at a time up to the street.

He reached the town quay, breathing hard. The sun had come out again and the crowds were gathering, waiting for the sailing races to start. He shouldered his way towards the line of cars, flashing scimitars of light and heat radiating from the metal. The space where the American's car should have been was empty; only Jake Vardo bending over his fishing tackle, the seat of his trousers wet from his leaky boat.

Ellis caught the old boatman's elbow. "The car usually parked here – did you see it leave?"

"'Ess," said the old man, his crafty eyes flickering over Ellis, watching for his hand to go into his pocket. "There's not much that goes unseen by me, Mester Ellis."

The lawyer brought out a handful of change and picked out a two-shilling piece. Jake Vardo's eyes gleamed as he took it. "T'was the owner of the *Cape Columbo* taking his fancy woman out."

"You didn't happen to hear where they were going, did you?"

"'Ess," said the old man, without looking up. "They was talking about some watermill."

Ellis' shoulders sank with relief. "I thought the girl and the skipper were going with them," he muttered, thinking aloud.

"Don't look so," said the old man cocking his white eyebrow towards the water. "More like they'm going sailing."

Ellis swung round and saw the French schooner was moving away from her moorings and heading out on her engine toward the bar, her red sails crumpled around her masts, ready for hoisting.

Going sailing! Usually they all went out in the yacht together. Perhaps that had been the original intention before the American picked up his hint about the chest's secret lid, and decided to investigate it with Linda.

A shade of doubt crossed his mind. Suppose it had, in fact, been the reverse, that the American had not been bluffing, that they did have the evidence they needed and the girl genuinely wanted a settlement out of court! The change of plan might have been a last minute decision. The American had claimed this morning that the copy of the will was in a safe place, so obviously it was aboard his yacht, and knowing he was dealing with a man who would stop at nothing to get his hands on it, perhaps he had decided to leave the two aboard as a precautionary measure, while he took his girl to see the watermill as he had promised. That could have been what the discussion was about on the quay before they left.

Ellis stood, watching the yacht going out, dipping to meet the slight swell at the harbour mouth. The breeze was off the land. They would need to head well off shore to fill their sails.

The sunshine had dimmed, the murky sky leaving a tarnished brightness upon the waterfront. The racing dinghies were grouped in the harbour, a host of white Bermuda sails, becalmed, hovering in formation, waiting for the futile crack of the starting pistol. When it came the sound ricocheted back and forth across the water, but there was so little breeze, they hardly moved.

"No bleddy wind," Ellis heard somebody say behind him. "'Been fluky all day."

"But not for long. Have you seen how low the glass is?" The question came from the coastguard, Michael Coombe, who had just moored up his boat. "Been talking to Pendeen. They say there's storms out in the Atlantic."

"To be hoped we don't get no storm here," said one of the boatmen, "Not with the high tide we have tonight. She's a big one! Up to five foot seven."

Ellis cast a glance to the heavy sky, yellowish towards the sea, and as he turned away he felt a splash against his cheek. Isolated raindrops were flopping, large as pennies, on the tarmac, drying as they fell, but by the time he reached the Esplanade, the shower had passed over.

He walked slowly back, alarm intensifying as an even more disturbing thought came into his mind. Suppose as they'd sped across the harbour the American had mentioned to the others the pointer he'd dropped about the chest. The real significance would only dawn upon them when the news came of the disaster. They'd be certain to repeat that remark to the police. Questions about the American's visit to his house would be inevitable; a thorough investigation of all his plans, including the disputed will...then they would produce their trump card! The original copy of Silas Trevelyan's last will and testament unearthed from its hiding place aboard the yacht. Up at the mill, the sawn up floorboards in the outhouse might easily be discovered, his fingerprints somewhere, even though he'd taken care to wipe the tools. And the charge would not be fraud but murder! He felt a clutch of panic and he realised that the pair aboard the yacht were now more of a danger to him than the American.

He arrived at the house in a muck sweat, fully aware of the awful consequences his plan could bring upon him. The only way it could work was to get rid of all four of them. For even one of them to survive, he was finished.

Slamming the door behind him, he went downstairs to the study and carefully stoppered the brandy decanter. No more to drink. He needed to think clearly now. There was no question of him giving way. No turning back, not when he was so close to winning! Somehow he had to brace himself for a final effort to achieve a resolution. He had always before found the strength and ingenuity to overcome the threat of defeat. He would do so now.

He sank down into his chair, his elbows on the desk. The problem he faced was every bit as difficult as his plan to get rid of Emma Bunt, and this time it was infinitely more dangerous. He'd had two hours to deal with the young people on the yacht. Precisely how he would do it in the time available to him he could not imagine.

He got up and wandered out onto the patio. The sun had gone in but the harbour glittered with a strange luminosity, hard and bright, cloudbanks building up to the west. Before the afternoon was out there would be a storm. Conditions could change suddenly, particularly at sea, squalls, poor visibility, a big swell, just the weather for losing people overboard. An idea was beginning to suggest itself. He had already set the scene for one accident, why not another?

His glance fell on his cabin cruiser, ready on the moorings. As the clouds gathered, the *Cape Columbo* would be running for port. Now, suppose he was to go out there and intercept her, think of a ploy to get himself aboard. He would not have fancied his chances of outwitting the American, but with a slip of a girl and the young skipper it might be different.

He looked out to sea. There was no sign of her, not a speck on the horizon. She would be quite alone out there. There wouldn't be a better opportunity! All the local boats were congregated just outside the harbour mouth either watching the racing or trawling for mackerel, as he usually did on Saturday afternoons. If he were to go out now, throw out his lines and head for the Gribbin, nobody would give him a second glance. Once round the headland and away from local waters he could troll seawards, in search of the schooner.

His heart thumped with excitement. He would need the gun for his own protection if his plan were to succeed. He was taking an enormous risk, and the chances of pulling it off would depend on nerve, good judgement and a lot of luck. The sea might be calm now, but if the wind changed, the storm broke... this could be highly dangerous. He pushed the thoughts from his mind. It was a gamble, one he would have to take, win or lose, for if he failed there would be only one choice left. To use the gun on himself.

He turned into the house for a sweater and deck shoes, the only hope left for his long cherished dream was that the watermill would bury the American and his girl, and he could arrange for the sea to depose of the others.

****

During the long wait for the Bodinnick Ferry, Lavelle had given Linda a full account of his interview with Richard Ellis.

"I just don't understand why he should have told me about it," he argued. "It was the only damned piece of information he volunteered throughout our talk. He just wouldn't admit anything, that he had the copy of the will or that he believed that we had it. So why should he should he bother mention the Bo'sun's chest?"

"Perhaps that was where he suspected it had been hidden all the time," she said, "but he thought the chest had gone to a sale with the rest of the Bo'sun's stuff and been lost forever. That's why he never bothered to go up there to look for it. And" she added, "if he had found it, why would he have agreed to discuss a settlement with you?"

"I dunno," said Lavelle, "But could be we're about to find the answer!"

The road from the ferry climbed steeply to the wide range of rolling countryside. Linda glanced through the open window. Beyond the ridge of hills to the right of them, the sky looked ominously dark. "I hope we get there before it rains," she said, "Charlie says it's a long walk up to the mill."

"Yeah, but just along this road past Langteglos Highway, there's a field path leading down – I found it on an Ordinance Survey Map."

Half a mile on he slowed down and parked up against the hedgerow. From a gap in the thorn a narrow grassy track dwindled away down the hillside. Following it, they were soon able to look out on the valley below; there was a flash of the river and the hills beyond, blue and clear under enormous gathering clouds. Suddenly, low to the land, where the towering cumulus was dark at the base, came a blue and white spark of lightning, but Linda had counted to twenty before the thunder clapped.

"It's miles away yet," Lavelle said, taking her hand. "But come on, let's hurry."

They set off at a brisk pace, but in the humid, almost windless heat, they soon slowed down to walk. Linda told Lavelle how that morning she had decided to confide in her uncle, and he had expressed no real surprise to hear the Pendowry inheritance was in dispute.

"In fact, she said, "He's spending the afternoon down at the creek organising the movement of equipment, so that they can move out first thing Monday morning. He's also looking forward to hearing about it all from you at dinner. I think there's a somebody he knows, who might advise you."

"That's swell."

She halted, staring ahead at the mill coming into view, the blackened walls towering against the darkening sky, and in that eerie light there was a metallic brightness about the windows, a glazed startled look, like the eyes of the aged. She shuddered and said, "Charlie was right. It does give you the creeps, doesn't it?"

The odour of decay reached them as they dropped down into the yard and walked across the cobblestones. Passing the outhouse, Lavelle spotted a door standing open. Last time it had been locked. He went to take a look inside. A wooden staircase led to the loft above; it looked like a carpenter's shop, a scatter of tools on the bench, fresh wood-dust in the teeth of the saw, some of it powdering the loose floorboards, many of which had been torn up.

"I guess somebody has been swiping the wood," he said, returning to Linda at the door.

Her smile was quizzical. "What a way to come for timber!"

They walked on towards the mill. Lightning flashed, reflecting from the windows and thunder grumbled among the surrounding hills. They were almost at the entrance when they felt the first spots of rain.

Linda would have rushed for shelter, but Lavelle pulled up short, catching her arm. He was staring at the drift of river sand, still stippled from the last visit with the pattern of their unmistakable Dunlop soles, but now there were clear impressions of other prints inter-crossing them.

"What's the matter?" Linda asked.

He shook his head without answering and stood, one hand on his hip, staring down at the footprints in the sand. They were the flat, low-heeled impressions of a man's shoes.

"I don't get it!" He said, "Ellis said he hadn't been up here, so what are his goddamn footprints doing all around the place?"

"How d'you know they belong to Ellis?" Linda asked.

He pointed out to the trail disappearing into the entrance of the mill. "Just see how the heel of the right shoe drags," he said, "The guy who left these footprints walks with a limp."

Her eyes widened. "You could be right," she said thoughtfully. "But why should he want to lie about it?"

Lavelle frowned. "I dunno, unless all that talk about the chest was just to fire my curiosity, a lure to get us up here looking for it, while he took a snoop around my yacht, looking for the evidence."

"Wait a minute!" said Linda. "He wouldn't need to drop you a hint, he knew we were coming here today."

"Knew we were coming?" Lavelle echoed.

"Yes, because I told him, the day he was asking me about you. I said we were all walking up to the watermill this Saturday afternoon for a picnic."

Lightning flashed again, the thunder nearer, rain was hitting the sand, but Lavelle was too gripped in thought to notice. If Ellis knew they were planning to visit the mill, maybe that was why he'd been here, to leave some deadly surprise lying around some place. He must have recognised Charlie the day he saw her at Pendowry and gone to quiz Linda to confirm his suspicions. And at this morning's confrontation maybe he just couldn't resist dropping the hint about the chest to double the incentive.

Linda was moving on into the mill out of the rain. He caught her arm. "Hold it, honey," he said, and waving her back advanced slowly inside. For a moment he stood, casting a wary glance in all directions, looking out for something untoward, small clues to the previous state of the place. Yet the same spars hung from the vaulted barn roof, the same heap of rubble to the left, the tract of river sand sweeping towards the inner door that led to the front of the building. But wait –the door was closed and he distinctly remembered leaving it open.

He crept towards it, lifting his glance to the stonework above; was there something loosened to fall the moment they passed beneath it? Not that he could see; the wall, draped with cobwebs, was undisturbed. Still, he tensed, held back by an inner caution, a premonitory sense of danger, as though the very walls around him were screaming down a warning, but both suspicion and curiosity urged his hand to the doorknob. He drew it back gently a fraction of an inch and felt a tension, a pull of weight holding it back.

"Jack, what's wrong?"

"I don't know," he said, bending to peer through the crack, but the gloom of the approaching storm had deepened the shadows. "There's something God awful the matter around here and I have to find out what it is. There's a gap in the wall at the side of the building. Come on, let's see if we can get a look at what's behind that door."

"Perhaps Ellis has had it shut up because of the danger," she suggested.

"You have to be kidding," he said wryly.

She looked at him curiously, sensing his concern, but he was already urging her out under the archway. They had barely taken a step when a jagged fork of lightning split open the blackness of the sky and a crack of thunder clapped its violent applause through the landscape. Then came the rain, torrential, vertical, bouncing off the ground in cascades of spray, turning the river sand to mud and pulling steam up from the cobblestones.

"Holy Moses!" cried Lavelle.

Linda drew back under the archway. "We can't go out in this."

"Look honey – I don't think it's safe." His tone was urgent. "You make a dash across to the outhouse and wait till I come."

"I'd rather be with you."

"Go on! Hurry! I'll be along!"

She looked back at him, reluctant to obey, but saw his jaw was set. Then she turned and ran splashing through the puddles. He waited until she reached the outhouse, then he ducked his head and dived out into the rain, feeling the wet smack of it across his shoulders. The light was diminishing under the leaden haze of the downpour, the blackened walls of the mill glittering with every flash of lightning, but he sloshed on towards the heap of streaming rubble at the other end of the building.

The stones were slippery as he climbed, the loose gravel giving way beneath him, but he clambered up, digging in with his toes and clawing with his hands until he could see through the gap over the wall. A blue green flash lit up the crumpled machinery, and momentarily he caught a glimpse of a line hanging that he had not seen before. He kept his eyes focused on the spot through the darkness left by the lightning, then as his eyes began to adjust, he could see there was a rope tied to the door handle. His gaze followed it almost to the buttress when another blinding flash illuminated the stonework, picking out some kind of structure. He waited again, peering hard into the gloom and saw the protruding spar, the prop beneath it, the plank with rope attached shifted sideways and he caught his breath.

Holy Christ! This was the deadly reception Ellis had prepared for them. To have pulled open that door another fraction of an inch would have brought the mill down in an avalanche of rubble and masonry, and a horrible bone-crushing death.

No wonder Ellis had been so willing to agree to their demands, for he was reckoning that by the end of the afternoon he would have nothing more to fear from any of them. They should all have died, buried under the tumbled debris of Tryun Mill. He'd been so keen for them to come up here to fall into the trap he'd set for them. Now it was going to put him behind bars. Maybe there were fingerprints, hard evidence of what he'd done here.

He slid back down the rubble into the streaming rain, and ran into the flashing, thundering storm towards the outhouse.

CHAPTER TWENTY NINE

The *Cape Columbo* was ghosting along, barely making way with the smooth, foam-marbled seas rising and falling all around her. The breeze was fitful, changing frequently in strength and direction, calling for short beats as they tried one heading after another, but Charlotte, at the helm, didn't care how many times they had to go about, just as long as she could be sailing.

Nick, glad to see her smiling again, wished they could have headed out round the Eddystone and back, but he didn't fancy the weather. The glass was astonishingly low, and the swell building up, suggested big seas farther out. He had already put a reef in the mainsail and set the small jib. Sudden squalls were common in these waters; sometimes severe enough to cause storm damage to the most seaworthy craft and the *Cape Columbo* had only just had a re-fit.

Out to the west the sky was a livid blue, with thunderheads banking up along the horizon. His glance shifted to the seas, rolling in steeper, crossing each other restlessly as the wind freshened again from yet another direction.

"We'd best head home, Charlie. The wind is backing sou'west now," he said, lifting his glance to the burgee ribbon tied to the forestay.

"Must we? We've got a reef in," she said, but she could see Nick had made up his mind.

She sighed. The thought of returning to port, to the reality of worrying about Matelot, depressed her. Last night, up at the creek, she thought she'd heard the dog whining, but Nick said the sound had come from another direction, down towards the river. They had searched in vain until dark.

The *Cape Columbo* heeled as they went about, the canvas rattling until the sheets were balanced, then the yacht was slurring forward, surfing, with the following seas building up astern. With the fluky wind there was a greater risk of jibing, and Charlotte had to concentrate hard to keep the yacht on course.

Nick stood, his hands on the coaming facing the bow, his wind-tanned face looked troubled as he stared shoreward. The distant coastline was blurring into blue and towards the estuary the sea was dotted with craft making for port. From the dark base of an anvil shaped cloud came a blue white stab of lightning. Nick didn't wait for the thunder. He leapt down into the cockpit to start the engine.

"You'd better bring the sails down, Charlie, we'll go in on full power. There'll be that high spring tide coming out against the wind."

"It doesn't turn until after five, you know."

"We'll be lucky to get back before. D'you want to take over while I get those sails down or can you manage?"

"I can manage," she said, confidently.

He shook his head, marvelling at her, always ready to tackle any job, especially at sea. It was in her blood. He watched her lower and furl the mainsail, tie it securely to the boom the way he had shown her. Soon she was lowering away at the jib halyard, gathering in the sail as it came, then quite suddenly she stopped, looking out beyond the shrouds. He turned his head to follow her gaze and saw away to starboard a white motor cruiser wallowing in a trough.

"Are they fishing?" Charlotte asked.

"Might be," he answered, frowning. He knew this craft. He watched her bow come up into the wind, slowly, hardly making any way as though her engines were only just turning over. There was somebody in the wheelhouse, a man in a cream sweater, bending over the controls. He appeared to see them suddenly and came out, waving. They waved back as was the custom at sea, but he then raised both arms and began shouting frantically, the words blowing away in the wind.

"I think he's in trouble," Charlotte said. "Perhaps there's something wrong with his engine."

They saw the man go back to the wheelhouse, saw him bend to cut the motor, heard the grinding of it cease, then he came to the side again, waving, this time with a rag in his hand.

Nick's eyes glinted and he met Charlotte's glance. "Do you see who it is?"

"Yes," she said disgustedly. "It's Richard Ellis."

Nick turned the wheel, altering course to bring them closer. "As much as I'd like to see him sink, I think we'd better find out what the trouble is," he said.

Slowly the gap closed between them. The lawyer looked hot and agitated. There was fear and urgency in his face as he leaned towards them gripping the gunwale of his boat.

"Ahoy there!" he shouted, "Can you people give me a hand?" There was a note of desperation in his voice.

Nick put the engine to dead slow and giving the wheel to Charlotte, came to the rail. "What's the trouble?" he called, holding on to the forestay.

"I've got a fuel leak," Ellis yelled back. "It's all gushing out. I've shut off the engine but I daren't start it again. My only chance to get back is a tow. Can you put me aboard?"

Nick hesitated, thinking of Lavelle's reaction to see his arch enemy coming ashore from the *Cape Columbo.* He cupped his hands to his mouth. "If you can hold on we'll get one of the boatmen to come out."

Ellis was staring at them in horror. "Hold on!" he cried, "I can't hold on! I'm in dire trouble!" Thunder deadened his words. As it rolled away they heard him shouting, "...don't like the look of the weather ... worried about all this fuel pouring out! One spark and we'll be up in flames."

Nick knew he was right. Petrol running free was a serious hazard and as the weather worsened he would soon be bobbing about like a cockleshell, perhaps enough friction to ignite it. Even if this didn't happen, his rolling boat could be swamped in the big seas when the storm broke. He thought quickly. He could hardly refuse the man assistance, not when all it needed was to take him off and put his boat in tow. The man looked frightened, his face was covered in sweat, and his voice was shaking as he pleaded.

"Please-please help me!" he cried. Then with a sudden desperate afterthought, went on. "Look! You're the people who have lost a dog, aren't you? I think I know where he is..."

Charlotte let go of the wheel, a flush lifting to her face. "Matelot!" she cried. "Have you seen Matelot?"

"I think I may have, a big dog, brown and white, isn't he? But look – this is no time to talk about a dog. I'm in danger here ... for God's sake help me!"

Nick gave him a hail. "You'll be alright. Put your fenders out and we'll try to get alongside. Be ready to throw me your line," he shouted and saw the lawyer turn quickly to put the cover back on the engine.

Charlotte. steering carefully, let the yacht carry on down wind until they were within fair distance of the stricken boat, then she brought the wheel round until the yacht was beam on to the seas and, with the engine barely ticking over, let her drift in towards Ellis's boat. As the gap closed, Nick hooked on the accommodation ladder and stood ready to take his line.

The wind had dropped away and the air hung hot and heavy, the restless, slopping seas lifting them closer and closer together. The turgid sky, sparking with distant lightning cast an eerie light over the swaying craft. The yacht was rolling heavily with the motor boat lifting beside her, only yards now between them.

Ellis was standing to windward, ready. Nick gave him a shout.

"Alright! Let's have your line!"

Ellis waited for the yacht lee rail to sink level with the gunwale of his boat, then he raised his arm and bowled the coil, sending it sailing over the skipper's head. Nick heard it drop behind him and made a dive for the loose line, snatching at it before it began to play out. Then he started to draw it in, slowly bringing the cabin cruiser up to the accommodation ladder, the boat hook ready to hold her off.

The smaller boat was now rising and falling alongside the yacht, Ellis hanging onto the wheelhouse grip with one hand, reaching out for the ladder with the other. Standing ready on the gunwale, he waited for it to come up. Then as it began sink down again he swung his foot onto the step and caught hold, clinging on with both hands. For a few moments he hung there, the cradle-roll of the yacht rocking him backwards and forwards like a see-saw, then gaining confidence he began to climb. Nick, leaning out to help him, caught a whiff of petrol as the man came aboard.

Ellis muttered his thanks but Nick was already busy fending off the boat.

"Helm down to port, Charlie," he shouted, as he leaned out with the boat hook to push the cabin cruiser clear of the hull.

Ellis had begun to think they weren't going to be taken in and might have even called his bluff by sending up a maroon for the lifeboat. But the experience had shaken his confidence. The yacht looked bigger than he had expected, the skipper fit, capable, no fool, and obviously a man with his wits about him. To outsmart him was not going to be an easy business. He watched the skipper taking the boat astern. The girl was at the wheel slowly bringing the yacht round to take the seas head on, so that the cabin cruiser would swing away behind them as Nick made her fast. Ellis moved along the rail, glancing uncertainly at the girl in the cockpit, only a slip of a thing. There should be no problem with her.

She was looking at him, her face flushed. "Where did you see Matelot?" she asked.

Ellis didn't answer. He mind was fully absorbed in the details of his plan and where to begin. Ideally. the time to act was now while the skipper was busily occupied securing the tow rope. To delay would only make the task all the harder. Ellis watched him warily. He had put down the boat hook and was playing out the line. The girl was repeating her question about the dog. It had to be now, Ellis decided, there might not be a better opportunity.

He took a step forward, leaning against the cockpit, his shoulders bent, his hand to his head. "Oh dear, I do feel groggy," he said weakly, trailing his voice like Penrose used to do. "Must be all the exertion, too much for me. My dear, I wonder if you would be so kind as to get me a glass of water."

He saw her hesitate, her eyes on the seas rolling towards them, but the yacht was riding more comfortably now, meeting the seas head on. "Let me hold the wheel steady while you go. I shall be quite alright if I sit down."

She glanced at him sharply, her expression hinting distrust.

He went on quickly, "Please, let me take her, and I'm quite sure your dog's safe, don't worry. Get me a drink and I'll tell you where I believe he is," he said, slumping down on the cockpit seat.

Charlotte looked at him curiously. He did look rather ill; his face white and drawn, his hand shaking, and since he was about to tell her about Matelot, she could hardly have him passing out.

"Alright," she said. "Just hold her steady. I won't be a minute."

He watched her as she went swinging her way amidships to the main hatch, but as soon as her head disappeared down the companionway, he was on his feet. The skipper was still up astern, now making fast the towrope, apparently unaware of the little scene in the cockpit and confident the girl was in charge.

The yacht was coasting slowly through slate blue seas, the line of land to starboard hazing under lowering clouds, deep as indigo and flickering with lightning, but Ellis hardly noticed. He was waiting for a flattening patch of seaway. When he found one, he let the wheel go and moved swiftly astern, crouching forward, balancing himself against the rail.

The skipper was leaning against the transom, his back to him, deeply occupied watching the cabin cruiser bobbing along on the tow, almost as though he was expecting it to burst into flames. Ellis saw a splash of rain hit the deck as he brought out his gun and for a moment he thought the skipper would turn and see him, but the lad remained oblivious, and with the slosh of the seas and the rumbling thunder, he did not hear Ellis coming up behind him.

Gripping the gun like a cosh, Ellis raised it to crack the skipper across the back of the head, but instead, as he struck, the yacht began to drift beam-on to the seas again, and as Nick lurched forwards and the blow caught him across the shoulder. Ellis too had been thrown off balance, but he grabbed hold of the backstay and hanging there, watched the skipper spin round, startled, then as the yacht rolled again he saw him stagger backwards towards the rail. As it came up he stood for a moment swaying, his arms wide, then the deck dropped behind him and when he stepped back it was no longer there.

Ellis gaped as he saw the man jack-knife in mid air, clawing out with his arms, and as he fell his hand reached out and grasped the rail, his fingers clamped hold, his body hanging over the sea.

Ellis winced, knowing what he had to do now. Fighting back his revulsion, he forced himself to lift the gun and bring it down mercilessly on the man's fingers.

He heard Nick cry out as he fell and heard the gulping splash as he hit the water. Ellis groped for the rail, clinging to it as the yacht rolled and was in time to see a huge wave topple over the man. He came up gasping, treading water, one arm crushed to his body, agony in his eyes, then he sank under another wave. Ellis waited the seconds ticking by for him to come up again, but the skipper's head did not appear. It didn't look as if he could swim. Ellis waited two agonising minutes, but all he could see was the man's white peaked cap floating on the surface.

Shaking with shock, Ellis dragged himself back along the rail, oblivious to heavy raindrops splashing the deck. Suddenly he heard the girl shout and looking round, saw her standing at the top of the companionway, holding an enamel mug in her hand looking at him indignantly.

"You shouldn't have left the wheel," she cried. "We're rolling again. What on earth is Nick doing? I thought I heard him shout."

Then as he came towards her she saw the gun in his hand. She took a step back down the companionway, her mouth opening in horror.

"Get back down there!" he said, thrusting the gun towards her.

"Nick- where's Nick?" she cried, in sudden alarm.

Ellis thought quickly. He would really have trouble if he were to tell her the truth. "I've shut him in the forepeak while I have my little talk with you. Now – get back down!" He saw a spark of defiance in her eyes, the self-same defiance he had often seen in Silas Trevelyan. "Do you hear me, Charlotte? Move!"

The girl stood her ground, glaring at him, her face full of fury. The yacht was rolling violently, crockery rattling in the galley below. He had been holding onto the hatchway with one hand, but now with the motion throwing them from side to side he needed two. It was then, as he reached out with his gun-hand to balance himself, that she lifted the enamel mug and threw the water into his face. While he spluttered she ducked under his arm and made a dive out of the hatch. He grabbed at her cotton shirt but the yacht lurched sending him sideways and he had to give way.

"The brat!" he cried, and, looking round for his gun, saw it bouncing away down the companionway.

He didn't bother to go after it. An unloaded gun would prove useless against this girl; it would take all his cunning to deal with her.

He struggled out of the hatchway only to be blinded by a blue white flash of lightning dead overhead and at the same time deafened by the bump of thunder. Down came the rain, roaring, clanging, holding him at bay. Through the shrouds, criss-crossed with grey skeins of water, he saw her, leaping, springing towards the foredeck. He made after her, ducking under the deluge, now all too uncomfortably aware that as the storm had broken he should be making his way back to port, not wasting his time with this girl. But he dare not leave her aboard the yacht. She would either have to go over the side or be shut up somewhere to go down with it.

He ran, crouching and staggering to the roll of the yacht, the spars and rigging rocking above him. He was drenched in moments, his breath coming short, but he hung on, grabbing at the stays for balance, steadying himself along the coaming. The bow dipped into a trough, the starboard gunwale awash, bringing aboard a slosh of seas round his feet. His legs went from under him and he slithered the rest of the way to the forepeak on his back. Shaken, breathless, he clambered backwards down the ladderway in time to meet her at the bottom, coming out of the cabin.

"Where is he?" she shrieked at him. "You said he was here!"

She was wet through, her hair hanging in streaks round her small tanned face, her eyes huge, the look in them threatening.

He opened his mouth to answer her, but she was not prepared to listen and tried to push herself past him, her hand reaching out for the ladder, but this time he was ready for her. He caught her arm just under the shoulder and held her in a metal-grip against the bulkhead.

"If you will kindly listen to me I will tell you where he is," he said. He had noticed a slatted door opposite the cabin. At a guess it was the poop locker, used either for storing sail or the anchor cable. He nodded his head towards it.

"He's in there. I'm afraid I had to bash him over the head to quieten him."

He heard her gasp as she struggled from him to hurl herself at the locker door. He waited for her to slide the bolt and swing it open, a second longer for her to bend, peering into the gloom within, then with the palms of his hands he gave her a violent push forward and as she stumbled inside, he slammed the door shut. Her scream came through the slats to him as he bolted the door and he saw her eyes glittering in a space between them. Relief spread through him like a drug.

"Now get out of there, if you can!"

"Let me out!" she shrieked, the door shuddering from feet and fists. "I have to find Nick."

"Tell me where you've hidden the draft of Silas Trevelyan's will and you shall both go free," he said quickly.

The door stopped shuddering and he heard her take in a sharp breath.

"So that's what you're after!"

"Don't waste my time. Where is it?"

"Please, I don't know."

"I believe you do!"

"You're mad! Let me out. Oh, Nick, Nick!"

Ellis could feel the floor of the forepeak plunging and reeling beneath him. He felt a dull thud as a wave hit the hull and the yacht heeled, shuddering, throwing him hard against the ladder, then came a shower down the hatch as they shipped a sea, a grim reminder that he had dallied long enough.

The girl started banging on the door again calling to him, but he ignored her and pulled himself up through the hatchway. The rain was easing slightly but the sky was dark, low cloud ragged over the sea, the swell becoming heavy, forming blue crinkled valleys sheltering under white tipped crests. He could hardly see the coast for a wet weather haze slanting down from black clouds coming in from the west. Another thud against the hull startled him and he glanced towards his own boat, afraid it had come adrift and hit them, but she was still riding astern on her tow line, cradle-rocking from side to side. His mind became suddenly full of little niggling worries; how much water she was shipping, would the engine start, the tricky business it was going to be scrambling back aboard her unaided, and would he reach port before the storm worsened and built up the seas? He was almost tempted to haul her in and start back there and then, but there was still something he had to do aboard the yacht. He had to be sure if that girl broke free from the poop, she would never reach port.

Gritting his teeth to the task, he made his way towards the main companionway, opening the hatches, the portholes below, smashing equipment and all navigational aids, taking with him the box of distress flares to throw overboard. After he had put the engine out of action he would have liked to have slashed the sails and cut the rigging, but the weather deterred him and from the seas already coming aboard, he didn't think it would be long before she foundered.

Weary now and bruised from the yacht's behaviour he finally managed to manoeuvre his boat alongside and as the seas crashed alarmingly against the yacht's hull, he timed his jump aboard from the ladder. The engine started first time and he put her head on into the waves.

Looking back astern from the wheelhouse he saw the *Cape Columbo* slumped in a trough, seas breaking over her bow and he could still hear the girl banging against the poop locker door.

CHAPTER THIRTY

Charlotte held on with both hands to the slatted door, the yacht rocking her sideways. She could feel the water rising cold up her legs and down again, fear held her dumb. She knew he meant them to founder the moment she heard the engine stop. There had been bumps and crashes as though he was breaking things and she had trembled to think what Frisco would have said. Then when all the bumping had stopped, she heard the spit and throb of his motor boat starting up. He was really going, leaving them to drown, leaving them for the sea to have ... like Uncle Silas' brothers. They too had died, trapped in a sinking vessel all those years ago in these very same waters, just as she was trapped here in the poop – helpless.

With every violent plunge a fresh deluge came slapping down the hatch as they took another sea. She could hear it washing across the floor of Nick's cabin opposite the slatted door, to come streaming back and into the locker around her knees. She thought of him lying helpless somewhere, bleeding, dying, gone – like Matelot! Everything she ever wanted, ever loved, was always being taken from her, every joy given snatched away; her father, Cornwall, Matelot, Nick... and now life itself.

She sank into the seawater, sobbing, giving way to her anguish. She didn't want to die. She was afraid. Oh God, please help her!

The water was slopping from side to side as she swung with the door, the seas they were shipping foaming up round her knees. Between the splash and gurgle of it running away, there were moments of silence, a desolate silence, full of foreboding, then to be broken by the creek of straining timbers, the thud of a sea against the hull and the rumbling thunder. She caught her breath sharply, aware that the roll of the yacht was slower, more sluggish, heavier with the water. It came to her then in a clutch of panic that they might be sinking and she screamed.

"Oh, Nick! Nick!"

It was then, as her voice trailed off in a lull between the slapping seas, she heard the cry. She stopped breathing to listen. Was it an echo of her own voice coming back to her through the yacht?

She waited, her ears straining to listen and then came a bump against the bulkhead, back behind the lumber of gear and chain stored in the fo'csle peak.

She staggered to her feet startled, staring into the darkness and the cry came again, dull, muffled, from the outside of the yacht.

"Char-lie!"

It was Nick's voice calling her! Her spirits soared. "Nick! Nick! Where are you?" she shouted.

"I'm here – hanging on to the bobstay! For God's sake come and help me!"

Charlotte felt a bolt of anger. She didn't need to guess how he came to be there. Richard Ellis must have thrown him overboard – left him to drown. But he'd survived, he was alive, and he needed her to help him. He didn't know she needed him to help her. He must be hurt or exhausted; otherwise he would have been back aboard, taking charge. A sob rose to her throat, first from rage, then frustration at the sheer helplessness of their plight.

A picture of him flashed across her mind, of him clinging like a crab to the bobstay, being plunged under every time the bowsprit buried itself in the sea, slowly drowning a little more every time.

Oh dear God! She would have to smash her way out of this place now; the very thought of him hanging there filled her with fresh determination.

"Nick! Nick hold on, I'm coming," she cried, and turned, hurling herself at the slatted door, throwing all her weight against it, again and again, but it merely jarred her joints, resistant to her efforts.

She drew back, her brain frenzied. Could she reach the latch if she pushed her fingers through the slats? Not long enough. Needed a stick to poke through. She fell to her knees, groping about under the water on the floor, desperation, excitement, driving her to hurry. Her fingers closed on smooth steel, rounded, hard, – a rod! She brought it up and recognised part of a winch handle, slim enough to go through the slats. But better still, she could use it as a crow bar to break one loose.

Lightning flashed and the spaces lit up blue as she inserted the rod. She levered it upwards and triumph soared as she heard the wood splinter. It was coming, the slat was breaking at the corner, going ... the wood came out, her hand went in, fingers fumbling for the bolt. Back it came and the door fell open. She was free!

A sea spilled down over her head as she climbed the ladder, a wet salt breeze came cool to her face and she saw the sky, low, hung with ragged lead-grey cloud. She pulled herself out onto the slanting deck and, slamming down the hatch behind her, gazed in horror at what she saw.

The *Cape Columbo* was lying a-hull, wallowing in a valley of crinkled sea that was leaping with curling white peaks. She was drifting sideways, carried by the wind as it thrummed through rigging, pulling her down until the gunwale was awash, and through the needles of rain Charlotte could see no farther than the heaving, bottle green hills lifting all around them. But the only thought in her mind at the moment was Nick, hurt and drowning, needing her help.

She reached the rail, and catching hold, felt the bow come up, then as it plunged her heart almost stopped to see the bowsprit go down, the bobstay buried beneath it in creaming seas. She waited horrified for it to lift out of the water. When it did she saw Nick hanging on, his arms over the chain, spluttering, gasping, gulping air.

He saw her suddenly and his mouth opened wide. "Get me a line! I'm hurt... hurry!" he managed to yell before he went down again.

For a moment she was overcome with a sickening sense of disaster and the enormity of the task before her; to reach him with a long ladder, to get him, hurt, up that leaping, plunging bow, and drag him aboard before they shipped a sea big enough to swamp them. But there was no time to dither, she had to act, find the strength.

The yacht reeling under her, she stumbled towards the slatted ladder they kept lashed under the bulkhead, her fingers tugging at the wet bowlines, her feet slipping from under her as she began to drag it along the heaving deck, rain and wind impeding her. She thought suddenly of Uncle Silas. He had survived when his brothers had died, survived because he found the will to hold on, to fight for survival, even though his leg was shattered, the ship was breaking up, the seas taking her, taking him, but he defied it all ... just as they would do.

With tears of fury and determination, she climbed down the swaying ladder with the line over her shoulder.

****

"I can't believe it," Linda said. "How could he have done such a thing? If you had opened that door we should have both been killed. It doesn't bear thinking about!"

"You can say that again!" Lavelle said, wiping the rain from his face.

They were sitting on the stairs in the out-building waiting for the rain to stop, but the downpour outside had become a deluge. They could hear it pelting the yard stones outside, and pinging off the windowsills.

Linda stared at the darkening pane, the glass bleary with running water. "Just listen to it!" she shouted above the noise.

Lavelle glanced towards the door, where, even as they talked a small pool was expanding inwards across the floor. He got up and pulled it open, only to be confronted by a curtain of rain, falling sheer, the force behind it sending it glancing up from the yard, lifting a shallow wave in over his shoes. Behind it, not fifty yards away, loomed the mill, blurred dark behind the rainfall. Lightning flickered against a window and he felt again the same uncanny sense of danger he had felt in the mill.

"This is awful," Linda said, coming up beside him.

Lavelle did not answer. He was listening to the roar of the rain. It sounded more like the roar of the sea, louder even than the thunder rumbling away though the hills. Then the rain was easing off, almost stopping, but the roar went on, becoming louder. It struck him then. It was the weir. His mind went back suddenly to the gloom of the mill, the contraption set up under the buttress, the line strung out to the door would be delicately set. It would only need the slightest nudge. and if the river was high, and rising, if it should flood in round that buttress....

The stark urgency of it gripped him, a chill to the root of his spine and he caught her hand.

"Linda! We have to get out of here!"

She hung back. "But it's still raining."

"Hell with that!" he cried, "All that water coming down the valley – if the river floods into the mill it could go!" He gripped her hand, dragging her forward. "Come on!"

They raced together across the yard, splashing through sheets of water, the rain hitting their faces; then as the gradient rose they were hopping over rivulets washing channels through the pebbles. The ditch over the stile was brimming with brown muddy water, the long grass matted, submerged, fed by a fast running stream coursing down the field path by which they had come.

"We can't go back that way!" Linda cried, looking ahead at the network of tributaries fanning out down the hillside.

Lavelle tugged her to the left towards a broken wall that was leaping with waterfalls. Immediately above it was a smooth rise of scrubland, ascending above the quarry that shelved down to the weir. He helped her over the stones and they began pulling themselves up, holding on to plumes of bracken and heather bents, to finally arrive, breathless at the summit.

Linda ran her hands down her dress, squeezing the rain from it. "I'm soaked to the skin!" she gasped.

He gripped her shoulder, "I have a sweater in the car you can put on."

They hurried on towards the quarry edge to look down at the terrain. The thunder clouds were moving away, lifting above the purple haze of hills and although it was still raining, the downpour was steadier now, a slanting, drenching Cornish rain the locals had been praying for, but the scene they saw below stopped them in their tracks.

They were no longer looking down on a valley, but a lake. The swamp had filled and the millpond was rolling over it, expanding towards the higher ground.

"It's doing just what I said it would do," Lavelle muttered.

His gaze moved along the course of the river, watching it creaming over the weir and surging on, filling the gully through which they had walked the day they came up from Trevada. Then it had been splashing prettily over the stones, now it was a raging torrent; Charlotte would have hailed it as the family curse come true.

Reminded of the kids he hoped they'd had the sense to make port before the storm broke. The wind had changed to sou'west and when the high spring tide turned against it could be tricky getting in over the harbour bar.

It was then as he turned that he heard it – the sound. Linda heard it, too, and glanced at him sharply. It began as a low rumble, not thunder and it came from below, immediately beneath them. They moved nearer to the quarry edge where they could look down on the mill and saw thin smoke lifting from under the eaves. Then suddenly the building began to quake, caving in towards the middle, bulging above, then breaking open like a jigsaw puzzle coming apart.

For a moment it lifted itself slowly, almost in revolt at yet another onslaught from the elements, all those years of being thrashed by the winds, the rains and the river had finally become too much, and now the whole edifice seemed to rise in protest, sending a thunder-clap of echoes through the valley.

Linda clutched Lavelle's arm and together they saw the mill fall, saw it hurl itself with a great whoomph of triumph, across the weir straight into the path of the raging torrent. For several seconds stone and water crashed in conflict; the crumbling, crunching debris heaping up their defences, the angry flow crashing against them like a sea to a harbour wall, showering spray, only to curl over and fall back in defeat. Dust rose then, billowing up over the river and trailing away over the valley like a banner.

Linda drew her hand up to her mouth. "Oh God!" she cried, "It's gone!"

Lavelle nodded, hardly able to speak. He was thinking of Richard Ellis, how the no good sonofabitch had scored again, because gone with the collapsed mill was the evidence that they could have used to expose him, to give credence to their claim. Now there was nothing left of the deadly trap he had set for them, nothing even to further their hopes of finding the will. They were back where they started.

He looked down on it bitterly, the tumbled stones clattering as they sank into the floodwater, the clouds of dust coming down and settling in a brown skin on the surface. He watched, waiting for the rubble to sink into the millpond, but it didn't. It was heaped up against the weir, higher even than the banked perimeter wall to which it reached, wedged there, cutting off the course of the river. He watched the onrush of water dashing up against it and the swirling, clay-coloured spume, finding no way down the valley, sheered off along the banking, sending a great tide across the water-logged marshes.

"Christ"! he muttered "It's going to damn up the river!"

Linda, looking at him, saw his face creased with alarm. "Surely the weight of water will break its way out somewhere," she said.

"Let's see if we can get a look behind the weir."

He started off and she followed him along the hillside, the wet bracken waist high drenching them afresh, the damp air upon their faces sweet with fragrances, given off from the thirsty plant life soaking up the rain. Soon they were able to look back on the weir below them. It glistened black, the rocks bare, the mill rubble towering above it, heaped into a solid embankment, stuck with rusted iron and splintered beams. It reached across to the perimeter wall – nearly as far as the steps they'd climbed the day they came up from Trevada. They could now see the overgrown gate, fountains spurting through the tight foliage like a sieve.

"That's where it'll break out!" Linda cried.

"Sure, but how much water is there going to be behind it before it does?"

They hurried back to for another look over the valley, and stood rooted in dismay at what they saw. The lake was expanding, rippling in the freshening wind like an inland sea, trees growing out of the water where it reached the woods, spray rising where it washed down to the high banked perimeter wall that was holding it back. But still it came, that surging brown torrent, roaring down from the hills, filling up the valley.

"We've got to do something!" cried Lavelle, "When that lot goes..." He glanced upwards at the high terraced hillside behind them, a jungle of bracken and brush, but there was a path leading round an outcrop of granite. "Come on! We have to warn somebody!"

They found the car but the plugs were damp and he had to swing the handle to start it. The engine spluttered at first but soon picked up once they were moving. The road was full of grit and stones, debris washed down from the banks, the swamped ditches matted with long grass, hedgerows flattened. The countryside was strangely deserted, just rain dissolving into the mist, but when they reached the turn-off for St Ruan there was an ex-army jeep drawn up against the banking and men in oilskins waving them down.

Lavelle braked and ran down the window as a Cornish brown face appeared under a dripping sou'wester.

"You'll have to go back," the man said. "The ferry's not running. The high tide has caused a flood at Trefoy. You might get round by Lanreath, but watch for the road fording. They've had a cloudburst up there."

"What about St Ruan?" Lavelle asked.

"You won't get that way. There's five cars stuck in the dip at Watergate, half submerged in floodwater. The police down there are trying to get them moved, but it might take hours..."

"You have to warn them," Lavelle broke in. "Tryun Mill has come down and damned the river. When it breaks lives could be lost!"

The man stared at him. "Oh, my good God!"

The others gathered round asking questions, but Lavelle cut in. "The town has to be warned. Where can we phone?"

"The lines are down here. You might try ..."

Lavelle didn't wait to hear, he was already putting the car into reverse, backing into an opening and grit and stones flew from under the tyres as he swung round onto the road. Then they were tearing back towards Lanreath, the water swishing up like a bow-wave from the wheels.

****

The Trefoy Hotel was crowded, everybody coming in early, dripping wet. The lounge was full of residents, lingering on from afternoon tea, waiters wanting to be rid of them. But more people were arriving, coming to stand at the tall windows, faces pressed against the glass, watching the storm. Excitement rose to see the high flood tide, heaving itself into the harbour, sending great green rollers spilling right over Whitehouse jetty, dashing the steps with spray.

"They must have stopped the ferry," somebody said.

"They do when it's rough," came an informed reply.

In reception it was near chaos; the girls behind the desk were having to deal with unexpected arrivals, many stranded from the waterlogged cars, all clamouring for rooms, and Rachel at the front, making her enquiries, found herself keeping back the crush with the points of her elbows.

"His name is Lavelle!" she was yelling at the flustered receptionist. "He must be booked in here. I've tried every other hotel in the town".

Judging by Rachel's rain streaked make-up and bedraggled appearance, the girl could quite believe her. She began running her finger down the register. "I don't think we-"

Voices drowned the rest of it.

"We left ours on the quay. When we got back the water was over the bonnet. My husband is out of his mind."

"We're on our way down to Falmouth. We're expected in at the Greenbank. We only came down here to look at the place."

"He's called Lavelle. He's sometimes known as Frisco."

"I don't think..."

"Have you a room for four – just for tonight?"

Another voice drowned the answer. "The Major tells me they have stopped the sailing. Isn't that the most frightful luck. The last race of the season!"

"No madam, we have nobody registered by the name of Lavelle."

"He's an American!" Rachel insisted.

The girl looked suddenly enlightened. "An American! You don't mean the owner of the *Cape Columbo* – the schooner from Marseilles"

"That's him!" cried Rachel.

"But he's not staying here, madam. He lives on board his yacht – with his daughter, Charlotte."

"*His daughter*!" Rachel's jaw dropped in astonishment.

"That's right," said the receptionist. "They've been here most of the summer. But the person to help you would be his fiancée, Linda Downing. She's staying here. They should both be in shortly. If you would care to sit in the lounge...."

Rachel was no longer listening. She was backing away into the crowd, allowing others to shoulder in before her, glad of the barrier of backs to hide her face as she slid anonymously away.

Of course, she thought. Charlotte had been in that boat bringing him ashore, the relationship rather more than casual, the first shadow of suspicion Rachel remembered trying to suppress, that Jack Lavelle had been deceiving her. He was not here to see Richard, to square it for her. He was down here with Charlotte, in league with her. It was his yacht she had been living aboard all summer. He even had another woman here, staying at the hotel.

Rachel wandered free of the crowd. She might have known he was behind it, being so close to Bill. He would be looking after the interests of his dead friend's daughter, not his dead friend's wife. Bill would have already poisoned his mind about her. Oh God! Would she ever be rid of the Trevelyan treachery?

She had always thought it too good to be true, her and Frisco. Now she knew he had never loved her, only used her. No wonder his letters had always been late, he must have sent them to someone in Marseilles to post. And the questions he'd asked about Richard, that made sense to her now, the good time he'd given her in London, the promises he'd made – all of it only to draw the truth from her about the will. And like an idiot she had told him everything!

The thought brought a rush of colour to her face. Good God! He's going to use the lot as evidence! Did Richard know? Most likely he did. That was why he'd had her down here to take Charlotte home. Hadn't he spoken of having everything under control, a plan to resolve the situation? Something vicious and underhand, she didn't doubt.

What a complete fool she had been to ever become involved in his hair-brained scheme! She must have been mad. Why did she ever leave Cornwall? Why did it not occur to her that once the war was over Trefoy would be teeming with wealthy holiday makers, perhaps somebody for her. She should have stayed on at Pendowry, made her peace with the old man, been fair to Charlotte. They might have even become friends, then she would have been sharing the money, not trying to steal it. Instead she had allowed herself to become involved with a man like Richard, his persuasive tongue promising her all she had ever wanted. Men were bloody.

Now the dreaming was over, no honeymoon in Corsica, no London house facing the park, the Joan Crawford image dead, out. Here she was back with Richard, not only committed, but also completely dependent on him, for who else was going to find a way out of this mess – for both of them.

She walked slowly on through the reception area, her head down, oblivious to the porter opening the door for her as she went dismally into the rain. The breeze was freshening from the sea, raw with salt as Bill used to like it. It buffeted her, carrying away her hat, the chiffon scarf sailing with it like a kite. She didn't even bother to go after it.

She began to walk down the Esplanade towards Richard's house.

CHAPTER THIRTY ONE

Nobody saw the dam break, but miles away people heard the roar of it bearing down on the valley. Nobody was there to see the overgrown gateway bulge and give way to the thousands of tons of water dammed up behind it. Nobody saw the mountainous clay-coloured wave, with its giant curled over crest, thick with mud and debris, begin that first thundering plunge into the narrow gorge towards Trevada.

Through the gully it roared. filling it up like a swamped ditch, breaking out through the woods at the bottom, demolishing Trevada Mill. It surged on, a great muddied torrent, swirling across the meadows, devouring all in its path: gateways, barns and hedges, down the long clough winding between the hills.

Amos Wilkes saw it from his hillside farm. He had been bringing in a frightened pony which had been bolting round her field, and he had stopped to look over the wall to see what had startled her. There was a watercourse of rapids chasing through Trigger Hollow. He watched it heading towards Watergate. It would never go under the bridge. It didn't; the giant wave curled over the top of it, sweeping into the queue of cars stuck in the dip, rolling them over into its mighty swell, engulfing their occupants.

And so it rolled on towards Pendowry, growing in strength, gathering speed but no mercy in it, charging through the narrow, snaking course of the river. It was a river, which normally trickled over green stones, was overhung with willows, thick with rushes, busy with wild life. Now rabbits, badgers and foxes, friend and foe, were on the run, and the birds, wood pigeons, herons, mallard rising noisily in flight. Travelling down towards Pendowry Water the bore was thirty feet high. The manor house grounds lay directly in its path, a rise of parkland sweeping down, the river crater curving round it. The edge of the wave took a short cut and went sailing over the grassy bank. The high wall of the old man's garden fell without protest and the flood hurried on towards the house, to smash its way in through the French windows, bringing down the conservatory with a shriek of splintering glass, the sound soon muffled under the deluge of water.

Ian MacDonald's company barge was moored up at the creekside jetty, three of the workmen on board. They had been loading the shed partitions and other equipment to move back to the station slip. The boss had suddenly decided to have everything sent down to another site at Salcombe and the men had been working all day. They were just about ready to leave when they heard the roar. Like one, they stood, heads cocked, listening, eyes turned towards the bridge. Then their jaws dropped in horror to see a billowing brown swell riding up over the top of it, but before they had time to shout it was upon them.

Ian MacDonald saw the wave, but he was lucky. If he had been on his way back to Trefoy by motor boat, as was his plan, it would have overtaken him. But he hadn't been able to get the engine started; the storm shower had swamped it. To have waited for the barge might have made him late for his dinner date, and as it wasn't raining quite so hard, he decided to walk up through the woods to St Ruan. He had almost reached the creekside path when he heard the boomph of crashing water, and, looking back, saw the curling lip of the bore leap the bridge into the creek. Down it came, hurling an avalanche of froth and spume over the jetty and half burying the cottages. He watched in horror as he saw the barge turn turtle and the three men vanish into the surging torrent.

Jed too was lucky because he'd left the boatyard promptly on six, knowing the dinner would be out of the oven, but the two boys who had been working with him were not; the wave claimed them because they stopped behind to bale their boat. Jed was climbing the veranda steps when he heard the torrent coming. He called to Joanna and the kids, who came rushing out to meet him. They all stared in utter disbelief at what they saw.

The Pendowry inlet was a raging turmoil of broken water, creaming up grey with the silt, and carrying with it a great variety of objects it had collected on its way down through the valley; drifts of wood, leafy branches, a barrel, a wagon wheel, a velvet chair, a dinghy or two. Jed suddenly recognised the upturned hull of the motor boat he had been working on that afternoon, closely followed by the corrugated roof of the boatyard tool shed. He leapt to the steps then, but his heart sank to see the yard under water, the stilts slipping, thrown up into the flow.

Joanna, gripping the veranda rail, was watching the flood, moving on into the Trefoy River, and she trembled for the craft it would meet in the crowded harbour. Already she could see the mastheads rocking about as if the devil had them, and her eyes were searching through the mist for boats she knew ... until, alerted by Jed's cry, she turned to see what the flood was doing to their own yard.

****

The white cabin cruiser pitched, bouncing, glancing, seas breaking over her bow, the spray pelting down on her, but Richard Ellis, wedged against the wheelhouse, stiff-jawed with concentration, held on. For nearly two hours, drenched with seawater, sick with fear, he had driven his boat into the steepening seas building up off the Trefoy estuary.

If he could have gone straight in he would have been back in half the time, but with the wind behind him, there was always the risk of a following sea slopping over the stern and swamping his open decked boat. The only safe course was to steer more to windward, keeping her heading into the waves, but to reach port that way meant constantly changing direction. At times it had been almost impossible to see through the windscreen for rain and spray, difficult to keep his balance as she bucked and rolled, the seas breaking against her hull with that nightmarish 'glump' that shuddered her timbers.

At last he was over the bar, sliding with the swell into the swollen harbour mouth, and it was only then as the immediate danger receded that Ellis began to reflect upon the what he had done. Until that moment he had been too concerned with his own survival to consider the consequences, but now the realisation came to him, seizing him until he shuddered cold with repulsion. Everywhere he looked he could see the foundering yacht, the seas spilling over her, swilling into the open hatches. He could still hear the girl's cries, the hammer of her hands against the slatted door, pleading with him. He saw the water rising above her head, her hands still reaching out.

He thrust such thoughts from his mind. These fears were understandable, born of fatigue and only to be expected after what he had been through. He must take hold of himself. What was done was done. Now he must prepare his alibi, get it straight in his mind; how his fishing trip had almost ended in disaster when he was caught in the storm. Engine trouble could have delayed him. He must be sure to mention this at dinner with Rachel and Ian MacDonald – unless of course, the news of the accident at Tryun Mill broke up the party before it began.

He was nearing Whitehouse quay, and amazed to see how the tide had come up! They said it would be a big one, but the sea was over the jetty! Crowds were lining the wall above, watching the breakers crash against the steps. He throttled down, looking for his moorings, and saw the dingy was half full of water. He would have to tie up at the iron stairway.

It was then that he saw Rachel walking along the Esplanade towards the house. She was all he needed. He was too exhausted, he wanted time to gather himself, but it was no use, she was making for the street gate, raising her hand to wave.

His boat bumped noisily. He had forgotten to put the fenders out. He cut the engine and looping the line round the rail, dragged his dripping self up the iron ladder. As he pushed through the gate he heard the street door close and looking up saw her coming down the steep steps to the patio, obviously surprised at the state of him.

Then he saw her halt halfway, her gaze suddenly frozen, but it was no longer directed at him, but lifted, staring out across the harbour. At the same moment he became aware of a noise like thunder, squeals coming up from along the wall above Whitehouse jetty. People were turning to run, others backing up the steps.

Then came Rachel's shriek. "Richard! Look out!"

He turned, feeling a cold clutch of alarm to see an enormous wave travelling towards him, rolling out from Pendowry Creek, heading straight for his foreshore, his house. There were yachts in St Ruan pool flinging their masts about, rearing their bows. He saw a keel go up, people in the water, black heads bobbing. Now it was coming for him!

Half way across the harbour it was twenty feet high, coming like a huge surf roller, thick with silt, stuck with debris, treetops, planking, clods of turf cradled beneath the curve of its snarling lip. There was something grotesque about it, almost evil. It looked like a monster, the crested head arching itself towards him.

He found himself mesmerised, held by the horror of it, able only to stare transfixed as it came. Above the moving wall of water, the misty sky was full of gulls wings, gulls cries, screaming above the roar. To him in his fright it seamed like vultures clamouring for carnage, dredged up in those wide open jaws of water.

It was almost upon him. Perhaps it would break against the sea wall, glance off in showers of spray but it was too high, too solid, He was suddenly possessed with a strange feeling that it was him it wanted. He shrank in horror, his back against the patio doors, arms wide as the towering sea crashed over the balustrade. Then he felt it, felt it slam into him, cold, taking his breath, lifting him up through the shattering glass doors and into the study, spread-eagling him against the wall. He tasted salt, felt gravel in his throat, his lungs giving up.

But there was no escape from that iron embrace, it held him suspended, pelting him with stones, while it seemed the sound of Silas Trevelyan's mocking laughter rang in his head, and in that blurred under-water moment he thought he saw the old man's eyes... or was it the girl looking up from the bottom of the sea?

There was no escape either from the watery tomb in which he was incarcerated or from the truth that came to him in that gurgling, suffocating moment of death, that he was of his father's blood, possessed of the same obsessive desire to cheat his way through life... whatever the cost. Only now did he fully realise that for all his cunning, all his foresight, it was all he had ever been able to inherit.

****

Rachel saw him go, saw the great swell sweep over the patio, engulfing him. She heard the crash of glass somewhere beyond the roar of it. She knew he didn't have a chance. In that fearful moment as she felt compassion for him, she was also conscious of a load being lifted from her mind. But the feeling was transient, instantly to be replaced by her own terror as the water swept up round her knees. She picked up her skirts and tried to make a dash back up to the street, but the sea plucked her off the steps, drawing her down into its embrace, the cold shock of it halting her breath.

She surfaced in a dirty sea, spluttering, thrashing out in panic. Swimming in the sea had always frightened her, even when it was calm. Now it was tossing, agitated, and almost at once she could feel the pull of the current. The water was pushing up her petticoats, lifting them around her like a flower, coming up against her arms, hampering her stroke. She didn't think she would have enough strength, enough breath to make the shore. It looked miles away and she had to swim strongly to avoid being carried into the mainstream.

She was not alone in her plight. She could hear screams, cries for help, others in the water, in trouble. She saw an empty rowing boat heading her way and she made for it, only to see it glide by out of reach. There were planks but they were being swept farther out. Her only chance was to struggle for the shore, put all her effort into it. She forced herself to breathe properly, tried to pretend she was doing a length at the baths. She could hardly see for her hair streaming like a wet veil over her face, but there was shouting above her, a blur of building rising out of the water.

She gulped air into her aching lungs and saw a humped shape coming up in front of her, the black turtle-turned hull of a boat. Exhausted, she reached for it, treading water and felt her fingers digging into soft rotting wood. She held on, heaving for breath, her strength going, then she gasped with shock to see a head bobbing up on the other side, a woollen cap shrunk to it, under the wizened face of an old man.

"Save me!" she shrieked at him.

His blue eyes were goggling at her under dripping white eyebrows, but only for a moment, for then she could feel a horny hand lifting up under her armpit, supporting her weight.

"Hold on, Missus Ives, I have 'ee, don't ee fear. My ole pulling boat 'twill keep us both afloat."

Rachel gasped for breath, coughing up water, and hung her arms over the hull. "W-we've ... got ... to get ... to the shore," she choked.

"Worry not, my good soul. Tez help coming. Sharkie Flint is on his way. Hold on, m' handsome. ..."

Rachel closed her eyes; her whole body was numb, slipping away. There were men's voices, men's hands strong beneath her, and looking up she could see the Pirate Inn rising out of the water, waves breaking over the steps where people were standing, people screaming with the gulls. All those years ago when she lived here, she never remembered seeing the tide come in so far.

****

Dusk came early that night on the Trefoy waterfront, the deepening shadows hiding the devastation left by the flooding river. The tide was on the ebb now, falling, a dirty swollen tide, going out against the wind, the slanting rain flattening the heaving swell. Occasionally the bluey glare of lightening leapt behind the mist, but the thunder rolled no more. The damage was everywhere. The quayside cafe had almost been demolished by the giant wave. The alleyway shops had their windows smashed, their cellars flooded. The teams of rescuers now searching with Tilley lamps for people still trapped.

It was already dark when Jack Lavelle turned the car down the winding hill to the harbour. Under the pale dashboard glow, his face was creased with anxiety. What had happened to the kids, his yacht? Linda huddled beside him, was concerned about her uncle.

It had been a difficult journey even from Lanreath; trees across the road, the foot of every hill a ford. Nearer Trefoy there had been traffic diversions, a fleet of ambulances with their headlights glaring, clear indications that the warnings they had given to the police had been too late to avert a disaster. Down the twisting main street people were standing on their doorsteps, their faces grim. At the bottom fire tenders blocked the alley to the waterfront, their crews pumping out the cellars at the Pirate Inn.

The town quay was a shambles. The front of the cafe looked as though a bulldozer had been through it, glass clinking under the boots of the men sweeping it up. The black iron jetty rail was bent inwards, seaweed and rubbish hanging from it. The quay was brimming over, waves sloshing into the place where Lavelle usually parked his car and scudding back, leaving ruffles of foam round the heaps of debris. Shocked locals stood in groups, their oilskins glossed with water, their faces greenish in the gaslight.

Lavelle looked out across the harbour, searching through the rain and mist for the *Cape Columbo*, but the moorings were dark, no sign of her riding lights. St Ruan pool was strangely deserted, all the craft seemed bunched up round the quays; no lights anywhere except for the steamy blur where the tugs were moored. Alarm plunged within him. They couldn't be back. They were still out there.

He turned, looking for a face he knew and saw the coastguard, Michael Coombe, glance up from his conversation with the lifeboat coxswain to give him a hail, but Linda was tugging his arm. She had seen her uncle hurrying towards them.

"Uncle Mac!"

Ian MacDonald looked slack jawed with relief. "Oh, thank God! Thank God you're safe," he gasped. "That mill-"

Linda began to blurt out the story, but Lavelle was turning to listen to the coastguard at his elbow.

"We saw your yacht go out this afternoon. Were you expecting her back?"

"Too damn right I was! And I'm worried," Lavelle told him.

"We've had no distress calls from her. She could have gone into another port for shelter before the storm started."

Jed Marney came to join them. "I don't see Nick going for shelter, Michael," he said to the coastguard.

"Me neither," said Lavelle. "They could be in trouble. Where do I get hold of a fast boat? ".

"Right here," said the coastguard. "We've already got the lifeboat standing by. If you're worried. We'll go out to look for them."

He turned to the coxswain, who overhearing, had come to join them. "Better get the full crew out. You want to come with us Jack."

"Sure."

"Then wait here and we'll get someone to bring down some oilskins."

He disappeared into the crowd and minutes later there came the sudden whoomph of the maroons going up, cracking across the sky, shaking down a shower of crimson stars that threw an eerie light over the river. For a moment there was silence, then a murmur ran electric through the crowd.

Lavelle felt Linda beside him, her uncle offering reassurances. "If anything should happen to those kids," he said, the anxiety showing in his face.

"They'd have been safer at sea than here when that bore came down on us," said Jed, "Took everything in its path! I don't know how many people have been drowned or how many boats sunk. Came straight through my yard, two of my men – gone!"

"Christ! But how about Luke? He okay?" Lavelle wanted to know.

"Damn lucky escape," said Jed. "His boat was smashed to pieces against the town quay."

They were all four talking at once, coming up with fresh disclosures. Then Linda, who had been listening to her uncle, turned suddenly to Lavelle.

"Jack!" she cried. "Listen to what Uncle Mac is saying! The lawyer – he's been killed!"

Lavelle stared at the property developer. "Ellis! Ellis dead? How for Godsakes?"

"The bore," MacDonald said grimly. "His house took the full force of it. A woman saw it happen. Apparently he'd been out in his boat and was just stepping onto his patio when the wave broke right over him. Slammed him straight through the French windows. They found him cut to pieces, heaped up behind a bookcase against his study wall. Somebody said he had a look on his face as though he'd seen the devil."

Lavelle gazed vacantly, struck by the irony of the lawyer's death. It was the mill. The mill had killed him. He set it up for them to be crushed to death, but when it fell he had been the one to die.

He shuddered, unable to deny an uncanny sense of something haunted, a force beyond ordinary human understanding. The premonition, the feeling he'd had when he'd moved to that inner door, a warning within him, as though the old place was screaming at him not to touch, to get away, to flee, and a sense of it again in the outhouse when he heard the warning roar of the river. It was as though some avenging spirit had lurked within those walls, maybe some Trevelyan ghost, conspiring with the elements to have Ellis' deadly plan rebound on him, stopping him in his tracks, seeing the guy pay with his life for his infringement of Cornish rights.

"You coming, sir?" A burly lifeboatman had arrived with dry jerseys and oilskins. "You can change aboard," he said.

Linda was at Lavelle's side. "Take care," she said.

He gripped her to him and kissed her. "You wait up at the hotel. Get into something warm and dry. I'll be over as soon as we get back. Okay?"

"Okay," she said, and watched him follow as the lifeboatman pushed through the crowd to the jettyside where the crew was assembled.

Minutes later the roar of the powerful engines filled the harbour as the lifeboat moved away into the mist. It returned just after midnight, but with no news of the missing yacht.

CHAPTER THIRTY TWO

The *Cape Columbo*, scarred but undaunted, battled bravely on into the misty darkness, her navigation lights casting a glow over her streaming foredeck. Charlotte was alone at the helm, the dark sails hanging above her, slatting back and forth as the schooner plunged into the steep seas, but she was rearing out of them now, tossing plumes of spray like a prancing pony. Nick was below, pumping out the bilges, hampered by his bruised shoulder and swollen hand, but Charlotte knew he was getting the job done, she could feel it in the wheel's kick. The yacht was coming up lively, the sluggishness gone, a lighter, thrumming tune in the swinging shrouds.

Peering under the dripping brim of her sou'wester she could see the glimmer of breaking waves, the hissing, rushing splash of them, lifting dark hills all around them; sometimes a gleam of green translucence against the bow. Her eyes were tired but she dare not close them. Out in the darkness there could be shoals of broken water, telling of reefs ahead. She tried to quell the aching anxiety, reminding herself of the drill, the action to take, nerving herself to face up to it, tense, ready.

She tried not to think of how cold and cramped she was, probably due to the strain of dragging Nick, weighted with seawater, back aboard. The thought of it still shuddered inside her, bringing him inch by inch up the side of that leaping bow, the wet line slipping, ripping at her hands. It was a miracle that she had managed to hold on. Where had she found the strength? But she would rather have died than let go. Then when all seemed lost a huge sea had lifted him, and a voice in her head so like her father's had said 'heave' and she'd felt the line coming, Nick with it, crashing down on top of her with tons of green seas onto the heaving deck.

For several moments they had rolled together, gasping, foam swilling over them, silky soft, so easy to have slipped away then. But the wind had been screaming in the rigging, pulling the poor old Cape over on her beam-ends, and with the green water pouring down through the hatches, there was no time to die, she had to be righted.

It was a miracle they managed to save her; they had no engine to help them. It wouldn't start, so they'd hoisted the sails to bring her up into the wind, so that the flooded cockpit would drain. In those conditions, rain lashing down, violent gusts carrying everything away, it wasn't easy, and Nick's face lit by lightning, had been distorted with pain. And he was still below, still pumping after all these hours. Poor Nick.

Now they were lost, not knowing where they were heading or what they would find. The storm had brought visibility down to less than fifty yards and it had been difficult to decide how far out or how close they were to the reef strewn coastline. In these conditions they needed sea room to survive, but with their position lost, the compass gone – and the patent log, Nick had to make a guess at the wind's direction to set a course that would take them away from the land. Once the storm had passed, the wind had dropped to fairly light, even though the seas remained steep, and with a reefed mainsail and the small jib set, he'd estimated they would be barely making more than three knots. Until the mist lifted there was little else they could do.

A square of light came from the main hatch and Nick appeared with two mugs, steam blowing off them.

"Hot cocoa," he said, "laced with Jack's rum."

Charlotte reached out for it, raising a grin. "You've got the stove going then?"

"Just about. Everything down there has been afloat; crockery crunching underfoot, but I've got us some corned beef in my pocket, no splits though. They were soggy. Want me to take her?"

"No, she's fine. Not half so heavy now."

"Shouldn't be," he said, slumping down in the cockpit, "all the hours I've been at the pumps."

"What time is it?"

"Long gone midnight. I think we'd best hove-to soon and wait for the dawn. If we'd been heading in shore, we'd have hit land by now. Here, have some corned beef. It'll keep the sea-sickness off."

"Thanks," she said, opening her mouth for the slice he was holding out to her. "How's your hand?"

"Not too bad, but my shoulder aches a bit. The sea was bashing me against the yacht. When I tried to cling on my hands just slipped down the hull. If I'd been on the lee of her, I would have been swept away. I was almost done for when I saw the bobstay coming up at me."

"He meant you to drown," Charlotte said bitterly.

"I know," Nick said. "That was why I dived under, where he couldn't take a shot at me."

"I think he would have shot me if he hadn't dropped his gun," she said.

Nick nodded. "I've put it carefully away in the saloon locker. There'll be his finger prints on it."

"It was the copy of the will he was after. Frisco must have kidded him it was on the yacht. That man must be mad! How did he expect to get away with it?"

"He almost did," Nick said heavily.

He dreaded to think what would have happened to her if she'd failed to get him back aboard. She wouldn't have had much chance righting the yacht on her own. Not that she wouldn't have tried, the guts she had. He remembered how he'd worried about leaving her at the helm while he manned the pumps, how he'd come up to see how she was faring. He needn't have troubled. There she had been, defying the danger, the spray coming over her head, her face pinched with determination, as she struggled to hold the yacht on course.

Charlotte gulped her cocoa, her teeth chattering against the mug. "Frisco will be worried about us," she said.

Nick heaved a sigh. "And what is he going to say about the yacht, the damage? Only yesterday he told me I had a job on her for life. Said when this business was over he would be quitting Marseilles, going back with Linda, and he was going to leave the *Cape Columbo* here with us, to come back for long vacations. Not going to trust us now, is he?"

"Oh, I don't know," said Charlotte, "He'll be glad we saved her-" she broke off. "Nick, I think wind's freshening, clearing the sky. I thought I saw a star then."

"Where?" he said, following her gaze beyond the bowsprit.

"See! There it is again! Oh, now it's gone..."

They peered ahead and saw through the thinning shrouds of mist the dark rim of the horizon, and upon it another blink of light. Then it disappeared.

Nick started forward. "That could be a lighthouse."

They waited for it to re-appear, their eyes focussed on the spot. There it was again, blink, blink.

"Two flashes!" said Charlotte.

Nick nodded. He was counting the seconds.

"Thirty!" he said. "Two flashes every thirty seconds. That's the Eddystone. Then we have been heading out to sea."

"Not bad reckoning with no compass."

"But we don't know for sure whether we are north or south of her. We'd best hove to now and wait for the dawn. If the mist clears we should be able to see the land. You go below and get some sleep in Jack's bunk. It's the only one that's dry."

She shook her head. "I'd rather stay with you," she said. "I always sleep better with my head on your shoulder."

He squeezed her to him. "How it'll always be when we're married."

"I know," she said softly.

Daylight brought a leaden sea, with a long heaving swell, and as the schooner lifted out of the hollows, they could see the lighthouse poking up above the wavecrests. The tide was taking them in closer, close enough to see the cormorants perched like vultures on the rocks, wet feathered behind the misting spray. They watched the lantern pale as the dawn came, watched the sky break in pearly streaks behind the grey granite pillar and soon to the north was the faint line of land along the horizon.

Nick was on his feet, but Charlotte was looking back out to sea.

"Look," she cried, "there's a ship – it's a sailing ship!"

He turned, scowling against the early light. "Tis an old one," he said, "Looks like a three masted barque. We could do with Jack's binoculars."

Charlotte went back into cockpit. "He usually keeps them stuffed down the seating – if Ellis hasn't had them."

Nick turned and saw her hand draw them out. "Proper job," he said as she passed them to him. He focussed on the ship, watched it come up sharp. It was a barque, and in full sail. "She's a beauty!" he cried, "But she's not coming this way, she's heading into Plymouth. Must be from out foreign – she's flying the yellow flag."

"She's weathered the storm all right."

"And so would we, but for that madman Ellis. Come on, let's get up some sail, and see if we can get her back to harbour."

****

Rachel too saw the dawn break, lying wide-awake in her hotel room. Sleepless, she reached for her robe, and pulling it round herself, wandered to the window seat to look out. The river was already awake – or had it ever slept? All night long there had been the mutter of motor boats, back and forth, voices raised above the cries of disturbed gulls.

She could see it all now, misted grey in the early light. The river looked strangely forlorn without the yachts swaying on their moorings, most of them jammed into the coal wharf at St Ruan, the gulls swooping and screaming above the mastheads, confused at the unfamiliar shift of their habitat. Midstream, salvage workers were still towing in wreckage and capsized dinghies, rescue teams dragging for bodies.

She shuddered, remembering. She too could have been such a casualty, dead – like Richard, but for the old man's boat and those who had helped her. There were those, she recalled with a twinge of guilt, whom she had chosen to alienate herself from once she had became involved with Richard Ellis.

Now he was gone she felt no grief for him, pity perhaps, but there was no void left by his passing, only relief that he was dead and no longer able to force his will upon her. For him the conspiracy was over, but not for her. She was left to face the outcome of their dilemma alone; answer for the fraud he had devised and she, in her blind infatuation for another man, had divulged. Now her betrayal would be used as evidence to contest her entitlement to Silas Trevelyan's will, with alarming consequences.

Why had she listened to Richard Ellis? She might have known Charlotte would have found her way back to Cornwall. There was too much of the sea in her blood, too much of Bill. Her eyes scanned the harbour, looking for the cream schooner. Perhaps they had moved down river to the docks to shelter from the storm. She was clear in her mind now what she would do. No more lies or deceit; she was done with the illusory image of herself that had been part of her downfall. At least she was now free to deal with the problem in her own way and this time justly and without prejudice. How else was she ever to find peace with herself?

Heaving a sigh, she lifted down her suitcase and began to pack for the journey back to London.

****

Lavelle stood before the lounge windows in the Trefoy hotel, his coffee gone cold on the table beside him; his eyes strained from searching the mist–blurred horizon for the *Cape Columbo*.

Earlier there had been a message from the coastguards about a report of a schooner off the Eddystone, hove to most of the night, but she had not called for assistance and had left at dawn. Now Jed and Fisherman Luke were working on the waterlogged *Flora Dora* so they could all three go out to meet her.

Lavelle had been watching for her from first light. The sea looked grey, still a ruffle of white round the points, weak sunlight putting a metallic shine on the water. Time and time again he thought he saw a speck in the distance, but always to dissolve into the blur of sea and sky.

Then suddenly a smudge, a shape coming clear; tall masts – this was a schooner, dark sails. He felt the emotion catch his throat. It was her, the rakish slant of her between the headlands. He watched her coming. She was under sail, dripping, storm bashed, her bowsprit lifting over the bar. And they were there, the two of them, up at the wheel – safe. Oh, thank God!

The vision blurred before him and he turned blindly across the room, oblivious to people, tables in his way, even the porter calling his name.

"A message from the coastguards, sir."

Linda 's voice. "Jack! It's them! You go. I'll find Uncle Mac."

He nodded, pushing on, catching from the crowd a whiff of tweed, summer silks, a glimpse of smiling faces, sharing his joy.

Then, as he burst into reception, there was Jed waiting for him at the desk, cap in hand, his forehead chalk–white without it.

Lavelle grasped him by the shoulder. "It's okay, I know! They're back!" he cried, assuming Jed was there to bring the news.

"Where?"

"Coming in now. Have you got the boat?"

"We've borrowed a harbour boat. Luke has her down at Whitehouse. We'd come to tell you...."

Lavelle wasn't waiting to hear. He was already pushing out through the glass doors, taking the steps two a time, almost colliding with a woman coming up, blind to all, but the schooner coming in.

It was only when they were speeding across the harbour that the real reason for Jed's arrival at the hotel finally came to light.

"We'd come to tell you," said Jed "that two of the harbour men up at Pendowry think they've found the dog."

CHAPTER THIRTY THREE

"The torrent!" Charlotte cried, when she saw the river, saw what the flood had done, how the giant wave had scooped up the silt and deposited it all along the Trefoy shore. Now at ebb tide it lay in grey mudflats for the gulls to sit, while the waters from where it came ran deep all the way to Pendowry, so deep that Fisherman Luke was able to run the borrowed harbour launch at full speed up the river creek.

"So the Trevelyan Curse came true!" Nick said, in utter dismay.

Lavelle, who normally would have been ready with a smart answer, nodded grimly. After all that had happened he was through making wisecracks about Cornish legends. Instead he could only sling an arm round each of them, glad to have them safely back.

Charlotte heaved a sigh. "I hope its Matelot they've found."

Lavelle squeezed her to him. "Don't build up too much hope, honey – 'til we know for sure."

They motored on, the kicker-kicker of the engine breaking the stillness. The creek had a battered, ragged look, the trees crowding to the waters edge, ripped sideways, trailing, the banks washed bare to the rock. The swollen river, brown as mud, still carried reminders of the bore; uprooted brambles, flower heads and smashed pieces of wood. In the shallows they saw a table drifting upside down, gulls using the legs for perches, and net curtains trailed from the brushwood.

Jed was giving an account of the damage. "Up near the old house the river changed course and brought down part of the west wing, must have scooped up the furniture like matchwood, the power behind it."

"Came upon us like a mountain," Luke recalled, reliving his own experience.

"What about Granny Bunt's cottage? And the creek house?"

"Washed out but still standing," replied Jed.

Round the next bend, the head of the creek opened out before them. It looked more like a crater with the bridge gone, now a heap of stones. Then they saw the harbour men on the slip, the dog with them on a length of rope.

Charlotte tensed, staring, at first uncertain. The shaggy coat was spiked out, wet, grey with silt. Then she saw his head go up, his tongue hanging, a muddied stick between his paws.

"It *is* Matelot!" she cried, and she leapt from the boat, splashing through the shallows, arms wide. Almost before she reached the shore he was upon her, his warm tongue washing over her face. She hugged him, feeling the heat of the wet fur against her neck.

"Where did you find him?" she asked the men.

"He was up in the old house, m' handsome. We'd gone in where the conservatory was down. We'd heard a whine, see, and he was at the top of the stairs, standing guard over a heap of rabbit bones..."

"The varmit!" cried Nick, "That's why he didn't come home when we whistled. He was living on those rabbits."

Matelot was leaping up at them in turn, yelping softly, and to demonstrate his delight even further, he dived into the grass for his muddied stick and staggered around with it, showing off, his whole rear end rolling with his wagging tail.

Charlotte watched him, laughing, then she stopped short as she recognised the stick. "That's the one from the house, the one with the clenched fist!" she cried.

The harbour men nodded. "It was floating in the flooded kitchen and he grabbed it as we took him through. Couldn't get it off him though, so we let him bring it along."

Nick bent, reaching out, "Here boy, give it to me."

But Matelot, ready for a game of tug of war, only waved it out of his reach. Nick, cursing, made a grab and caught hold of the clenched fist knob, but only to find himself flying backwards as it came away in his hand.

Charlotte caught her breath. "The top!" she cried, "It's come off!"

She threw herself upon the waddling dog, and holding him still, gently eased the stick from his jaws.

Lavelle took it from her and Nick handed him the top.

Lavelle saw that the underside of the clenched fist knob was shaped like a Morse tapered plug. It had been cleverly carved to fit into a recess at the crown end of the stick, but at that moment it was not the ingenuity and craftsmanship which interested him, but the cavity he could see half an inch in diameter hollowed down into the stem. But whatever there was inside was not dry but sodden with water.

He lifted a furtive glance, not prepared to share the disclosure with the harbour men, but they had already moved away to join Jed and Luke across at the jetty, where other boats were coming in. Turning back to the stick he began to poke with his finger into the recess. Charlotte hovered at his elbow, peering, impatient to look.

"It's hollow," she said, lifting her eyes to him.

Nick bent forward, squinting. "Something in there."

"Looks like padding," Lavelle muttered. He brought out his penknife and tried to loosen it, then turning the stick on end, banged it against the slipway wall. Two inches of soggy blue paper protruded from the stem. Beneath the sodden folds it felt hard like metal.

He tensed. Could this be a tubular container, its use to conceal a rolled document? Hope soared, perspiration pricking at his skin as he tried to draw it out. Then suddenly the soggy tissue collapsed under his fingers and there was a sudden scrunch, and out shot a shower of tiny silver coins, clinking and hopping from the pebbles on the beach.

"The threepenny pieces!" Charlotte cried, stooping to pick them up, "Granny's bus fare to Bodmin"

Lavelle, examining the coil of sodden tissue from which they had fallen, did not share her enthusiasm. Not for a moment did he believe this to be the copy of the will, and even if it was some letter of instruction to the probate officer at Bodmin, it was unreadable.

"Looks like the ink has run," Nick said. "The sea water soaking into it has washed out the writing."

"I guess so," Lavelle said bleakly.

He looked more closely at the sodden wedge in his hand and detected a faint image of neat handwriting beneath the blur of blue ink. Maybe there was a chance it could be deciphered, if he were to carefully peel apart the folded leaves of tissue and dry them out slowly. They would need something clean to wrap it in.

"There's another boat coming," said Charlotte. "It's Linda, with her uncle. She'll have something."

Lavelle looked up. "They're here to take us back to the hotel," he said. "Come on, let's go get you two some food."

Nick hesitated. "What about the Cape – haven't we some clearing up to do?"

Lavelle slung an arm round his shoulder. "Forget it. She's well insured. We'll worry about her tomorrow. Tonight I've booked us all in at the Trefoy Hotel. Okay? Bring that stick."

"I still don't understand how the top comes off," Nick said as they walked to the boat.

"The devious old guy made its top fit like a Morse taper plug," Lavelle explained, "Fitted in, its tight. Give it a crack and up comes the end, loose, easy to draw out."

"It was on tight that day at the house. I remember trying too pull it off."

"Yeah, but after being in a flood," Lavelle reminded him, "it could have got bashed against something. Then being afloat for hours the water seeped inside."

****

The unfolded sheet of thin writing paper looked more like a watercolour of Cornish blue skies than a letter. Only the heavier strokes of the pen had left the faintest impressions, and after hours of trying to decipher the words, even with a powerful magnifying glass, Lavelle's efforts had been futile.

The smaller of the two sheets which he had been able to unpeel and dry out was of a different texture to the notepaper, but all that one contained was a smudged number....7815334

Now four days after the flood, he sat in the galley of his battered yacht, staring down once again at the tray where the dried out papers were spread.

That afternoon Nick and Charlotte were making trips across to the town quay to pick up parcels of laundered bed linen, the mattresses for the bunks still airing on deck. Now the sound of their voices and the bump of fresh parcels coming aboard, stirred him from the task. He laid down the magnifier and rose stretching, his eyes tired as he went up on deck to give them a hand. They were already aboard, chattering by the starboard rail. He followed their gaze and saw there was a tall sailing ship, anchored not fifty yards away, her black shrouds silhouetted against the sky.

Charlotte turned to him excitedly. "We saw her when we were out at the Eddystone," she cried, "Full sail, making for Plymouth."

"She's a three masted barque," said Nick authoritatively. "This river used to be full of these old ships one time."

"When did she come in?" Lavelle asked.

"Over an hour ago. Wonder you didn't see her."

"We saw the Captain on the town quay," Charlotte told him. "He was asking about you. Said he'd follow us over."

Lavelle tensed, "Asked about *me*?" he echoed, anticipating some undesirable from the Med. about to pay him a visit.

His eyes rested on the ship, taking in the two oriental looking seamen in grimed singlets on the foredeck. This was a trader, the kind of set up you saw drifting in and out of the smaller ports down there; her flag a white crescent and star on red – a Turk. She also carried the red ensign and the Cornish flag. His glance dropped to the black hull, still wet with seaspray, where he could just make out the ornamental scrawl of the name...*The Ottoman. Istanbul.*

Tossing his cigarette overboard, he moved aft along the deck to watch the pram dinghy pulling towards them. As it swung round to come alongside, he relaxed. The man at the oars looked more like a Cornishman than a drifter. Nor he was wearing the traditional brass-buttoned suit of a captain, but was dressed more casually in a seaman's jersey over a neat white shirt; his leather bound peaked cap pushed back from greying hair.

He looked up at them, smiling, his eyes on Lavelle. "Mind if I come aboard?" he asked.

"Sure!" Lavelle answered, moving to the ladder to give him a hand. He must have been a man over fifty, but very fit, the way he swung over the gunwale to land on deck with a sailor's ease. He stood for moment, his glance resting on Charlotte, before turning to address Lavelle, who was now asking himself – where he had seen this face? He didn't have to wait long for the answer as the visitor offered his hand.

"My name is Tom Constantine, but my friends call me The Bo'sun," he said, "I understand you wanted to see me."

Lavelle's jaw dropped, and for seconds he could only stand speechless, unable to believe what he was hearing. "You can't mean it?" he gasped, as they faced each other, gripping hands.

Later in the saloon the revelations began. Arms on the table, coffee cups pushed aside, cognac in the glasses, they talked, the smoke haze of Turkish cigarettes hanging over their heads. Slowly, as each man's story began to evolve, the true picture was taking shape. With Charlotte and Nick gone to collect the rest of the laundry waiting on the town quay, there was nothing to disturb the verbal flow but the slap of the wake from passing craft and the cries of the gulls beyond the portholes.

"They thought you'd gone down with the Pandora," Lavelle told him.

"I don't drown easy," said the Bo'sun, "Too much salt in my blood."

He was a well-spoken man, his voice hinting just a lilt Cornish, and although he had the look of a traveller, tough and strong jawed, there was warmth in his brown eyes Lavelle believed he could trust.

"I reckon I've been shipwrecked enough times to know how to look after myself," he told Lavelle, "The truth is nobody saw me struggle ashore on the Brittany coast. And I decided to keep it that way."

"What happened?" Lavelle asked.

The Bo'sun heaved a sigh. "I never believed that hull was sound, despite the survey the owners showed me. They'd been working on it all summer, claimed to have years of boat building experience on the Solent. True, the yacht looked good, gleaming white paint and varnish, but there was a dank smell below that worried me. Parker, wouldn't have it, until we hit some heavy weather off the north Brittany coast."

"Amos said you were heading for St Malo."

"We were, but they first wanted to cruise east from the Cote du Leon, calling in at small ports, sightseeing. The August weather was good, so we set course for Brignogan Plage, the plan to anchor over night in the bay. The ketch sailed well in the fresh north-easterly breeze, dispelling my doubts – until dusk when the wind freshened. Soon she was thrashing into steepening seas and we had to reduce sail, which slowed us down, and it was long after dark before we could see the shore lights.

"By then I was noticing a sluggishness about the yacht, she was heavy, hard to steer. I left Mrs Parker at the helm and went below to find the bilges overflowing, water coming up over the floorboards. Parker was already manning the pump and assuring me it was just a leak he could soon repair. On deck I found a list astern, seas streaming into the cockpit, Mrs Parker pumping, then another sea struck and pooped us. I knew then we weren't going to make it. The yacht was being driven by wind and tide inshore, you could see shoals of white water crashing over the rocks."

"You were in trouble,"

"I yelled for Parker to help me get the life raft a-float, but he refused to leave the pumps. His wife went below to plead with him as I dragged at the lines. Then it was too late. We shipped a big sea that swamped us and as she heeled over my only chance then was to jump and swim for my life."

"They'd be trapped below."

"They were. The main hatchway door had gone and she'd filled up, the swell sweeping her shoreward. I hung about, hoping to see them surface, but...," he spread his hands.

"How far were you off shore?"

"Not too far, but I had a long way to swim to avoid the rocks," he replied, as Lavelle topped up his glass. "Then round the point, out of the wind, I could see an open beach and the tide took me in."

"You were damn lucky."

"I reckon I knew the drill. Warm clothes under light oilskins, a good life jacket, and the will to survive. I slept on the beach until dawn, dried out, discovered my wallet, money and papers safe in the waterproof holder sewn under my shirt."

Lavelle smiled. "Good thinking."

The Bo'sun sipped his brandy and went on. "I stayed a while looking for wreckage, but finding nothing climbed to the cliff path. Once on the road a lift south took me to Brest, where I picked up a ship and worked my passage to Lisbon. No one knew what really happened. But before I left France I did make a few telephone calls – to my publishers in London to keep my royalties coming and another to my bank in Plymouth. Both pledged not to breach the confidence."

"I guess you had your reasons," Lavelle said, curious, but wishing not to pry.

The Bo'sun's reply was non-committal. "You could say that," he said, "but then I had set out to go to sea, travel and write, and I meant to carry on. I worked my way on coasters and other vessels through to the Eastern Mediterranean and up to Istanbul. That was where I found the *Ottoman*. Her owners had gone broke during the war and dumped her. I got her for an old song."

Lavelle nodded. "Looks a good ship. Must have taken a lot of work."

"Too true, but fortunately labour over there was cheap and willing, and I had the time. Once the ship was seaworthy we began trading around the Greek Islands, carrying small cargo, spices and fruit, the idea to work our way back home. I knew Silas was getting old and I was becoming concerned about him, that he might need me. It wasn't until we docked in Plymouth that I heard about his death."

"I guess that was a shock," Lavelle said.

The Bo'sun nodded. "It was. Made me wish I'd come back sooner. I should have been at the funeral. We'd been close. I'd shared some of his passions, and I suppose his fears..."

"Like Bill, you too didn't trust the lawyer."

His eyes narrowed, the wrinkles at the corners creasing his leathery tan. "You're right. After years in the navy in control of men you get the feel about a wrong one. When Wilfred Penrose died, I was away in the navy, but on my first leave I begged Silas to get another lawyer, but he had a dread of strangers coming into his house. You couldn't reason with him. My concern was that Ellis would fleece him, fiddle the fees to line his own pockets, but Christ, I wouldn't have expected him to have forged the will."

"And the rest," said Lavelle, "He didn't care a damn what happened to Charlie, to Emma Bunt or anybody who got in his way. Would have seen us all dead, but it was his own evil that got him in the end."

The Bo'sun nodded, his eyes narrowed thoughtfully, "He should have known better than to tamper with Tryun Mill," he said quietly. "There was always something weird about that place. And I don't think it was ever safe; the river was getting into the foundations even when I lived there. I used to think it was haunted, the creaks in the night. You didn't sleep easy."

Lavelle dragged at his cigarette. "I bet you didn't," he said, "The moment I put my hand on that door, I was gripped with-with something, maybe a sense of danger, a force, I dunno..."

The Bo'sun nodded slowly, his eyes narrowed. "But *I* know," he said quietly.

They looked at each other, for a moment a silence between them, the thought shared but unspoken. Then The Bo'sun sighed. "I've always wanted to write a book about Tryun Mill. In fact, that was another reason I came home."

Lavelle drained his glass. "And you sure got a good story, Tom," he said, "You want some more cognac?"

Glasses topped up they went on to discuss Charlotte's inheritance and their search for evidence to prove her entitlement.

Finally, Lavelle rose to his feet and led the way into the galley where the sheets of blue stained note paper lay rough dried on the tray, the stick on the table beside them..

The Bo'sun smiled when he saw them, his eyes sparkling. "So you found the Brig Trevelyan walking cane," he said, lifting it from the table. "And, I see, the contents in the hollowed out stem."

"Yeah, but ruined," said Lavelle gloomily, "The stick was in the flood and the water got in. Washed out the ink. You can't read a goddamn word of it. I've been trying to decipher it for days."

"No need," said the Bo'sun, picking up the sheet with the smudged number. "You've got the important bit. You can just see the number on the docket. In fact, I have a better one. It's a safe deposit box number. The other sheet is the letter of explanation."

Lavelle was staring at him. "Are you saying the original copy of the will is in a safe deposit box?" he cried, a grin spreading over his face.

"That's right," said the Bo'sun. "This is the number I keep with the key I have in my own safe deposit box in Plymouth. With it is a letter Silas wrote authorising me to collect the contents of his box in the event of his death. That's in London and I have an appointment there on Thursday morning to do just that."

Lavelle covered his face with is hands. Sure. A safe deposit. His mind went back to those last hours on the storm lashed LST... Bill's words coming back to him. *'Didn't trust the lawyer... Silas had his copy of the will hidden away safe, where the lawyer will never find it, and only those close to him know where it is...* He looked at the Bo'sun. "A bank," he said. "that did cross my mind, but if that was so Ellis would have had access to it after his death and destroyed it. But I couldn't know that for certain."

"Pity Bill didn't give you the full story."

"There was a lot of talk that night, maybe he did, and I wasn't taking it all in. I was groggy at the time, we were hove to, the boat was rolling on her beam ends."

The Bo'sun nodded, understanding all too well, and went on, "Richard Ellis thought that copy was in Silas's desk," he said, "What he didn't know was that I had taken it to a secret safe deposit in London for Silas years ago. What was in the sealed envelope in the old man's desk was indeed the safe deposit box number and the key. Ellis was trying to get Silas to hand over the copy of his will on some pretext or other, and to put an end to the hassle he set fire to the desk, leading Ellis to believe it had been destroyed. Silas then decided to convert his stick into a hiding place and gave some cryptic instructions to Emma Bunt on how to open it."

Lavelle was frowning, "But we found no key," he said.

The Bo'sun lifted the stick, and taking a firm grip in the rubber cap at the tip, wrenched it off. Wedged inside was the key.

"We missed that," said Lavelle.

"You wouldn't have done, if you had been able to read the letter hidden in the stem" he told Lavelle. "There were two other identical copies of the safe deposit number, each with an identical key and a letter of authorisation. Mine I kept safe in my own bank, and Bill kept his in the lining of his wallet. That could have gone missing on Omaha beach."

Lavelle agreed. "Too right. So with Bill gone and you away in the navy, he guessed that putting Emma wise was his only chance of the that copy being found."

The Bo'sun nodded, his eyes thoughtful. "For all his dreams and fantasies Silas was no fool. He must have suspected what Ellis had in mind. Gossip would have reached him about Rachel seeing the lawyer or Ellis in his fancy for her might have given himself away. At the time I thought the old man's idea about the duplicate keys was going too far, but if it was what he wanted I was easy. Silas had set his mind on Charlotte becoming his heir, and he wanted to make sure in his own way that she would."

"Poor old guy," Lavelle said angrily, "He must have been really spooked when Ellis moved Emma away."

"But he still had me, once I was back from the war.."

"Sure. Lucy Gribble talked of you having 'tea on the bridge with the Captain.'"

A glimmer of amusement came into the Bo'sun's eyes. "Those clandestine visits," he recalled, "It was the only way Silas would have it. I was never allowed to leave my car in the drive. He insisted I parked behind the bottom watermill at Pont, and walked along the river path to the house. He was always afraid Ellis would arrive unexpectedly and meet me face to face. Silas once told me that if Ellis was ever to find me there, the lawyer would see to it that I never came again

"He sure was wise to Ellis," said Lavelle ruefully.

"Too true. At the time I put it down to his vivid imagination, only to be expected when he spent so much time alone. When the *Pandora* went down, I telephoned him the moment I reached Brest. He was relieved to hear I had survived, but he made me promise to keep quiet about it. If Ellis were to believe I was dead, I would be safe with his secret forever more. I went along with it to humour him. I thought he was obsessed."

Lavelle nodded, understanding now why the Bo'sun had been careful not to make known his escape. "And you kept in touch, I guess."

"He wrote occasionally and I sent him cards with pictures of ships and ports I visited on my travels. He told me he gave them to Lucy Gribble to paste into her scrapbook, so that Ellis wouldn't find them. Not that it would have mattered. The messages were cryptic and unsigned. I knew that would please him."

Lavelle sat back in his chair, slowly shaking his head. He was thinking about Lucy's scrapbook and the postcards from the sailors. Now he knew who the sailors were.

The Bo'sun stubbed out his cigarette. "The last card I sent him was just after Christmas when I gave him the news I was coming home. He would have died knowing that I was on my way." He sat, reflecting, his eyes sad, then he drew in a sigh, and looked mindfully at Lavelle. "But we still have Rachel to contend with, I suppose."

"She'll be no problem," Lavelle assured him.. "Charlie's had a letter from her, begging forgiveness and renouncing any claim to the inheritance. She says no papers were signed and from the sound of it, she's on her knees scared sick of being implicated."

"And how does Charlie feel?"

"She's a good kid, she won't see Rachel go short. And what the hell! Ellis was the monster and he's dead. And now, thanks to you, it's all legal." He glanced at his watch. "Say, Tom, how about you coming up to the hotel and having dinner with us tonight, meet Linda."

The Bo'sun was shaking his head. "Let's do that when I return from London. Now I need to leave on the tide, get *The Ottoman* back to Plymouth and be fresh for the early train to London tomorrow," he said, as they went up on deck. "But I'm home to stay, and perhaps find anchorage here in this port, a quiet place to write my books. I hope you will all come aboard sometimes and drink some of *my* brandy."

"We'd sure like that," said Lavelle.

They stood, looking out across the harbour. The tide was high, the rollers coming smoothly over the bar, and up in the hills beyond Pendowry Water, the river rippled languidly through the creek to meet it.

The *Dipper*, loaded with the last of the laundry was halfway across the harbour, Charlotte at the tiller, waving when she saw them.

The Bo'sun's rugged face crinkled with smiles. "I knew who she was as soon as I saw her on the quay," he said, "A lot of Bill in her."

"The Cornish spirit," said Lavelle. "The bum lawyer never really had a chance against it."

"Not a chance," said the Bo'sun. "That old mill was on our side."

THE END

Printed in the United Kingdom
by Lightning Source UK Ltd.
104249UKS00001B/88-189

9 780755 205028